The Pleasuring of Rory Malone

Charles Panati

ST. MARTIN'S PRESS
NEW YORK

For John and Chris

Copyright © 1982 by Charles Panati
For information, write: St. Martin's Press,
175 Fifth Avenue, New York, N.Y. 10010
Manufactured in the United States of America

Library of Congress Cataloging in Publication Data

Panati, Charles, 1943-
     The pleasuring of Rory Malone.

     I. Title.
PS3566.A558P5   813'.54   81-16715
ISBN 0-312-61731-3   AACR2

Design by Manuela Paul
10 9 8 7 6 5 4 3 2 1
First Edition

PRINTED IN THE UNITED STATES OF AMERICA

Author's Note:

Because, in many instances, I have described actual laboratory experiments conducted by real scientists (some of whom I have met), I wish to state that none of the characters in this book in any way resembles these researchers.

Also, to appreciate the attitudes of today's teenagers to the proliferation of easily accessible pornographic magazines and films (a rarity in my own youth), I have interviewed several young men. While I found their views immensely helpful, none of the characters drawn here in any way resembles a real-life person. For their views, I especially thank Glenn, Kenny, and Rick.

I lose my respect for the man who can make the mystery of sex the subject of a coarse jest, yet, when you speak earnestly and seriously on the subject, is silent.

—Henry David Thoreau

I love the idea of there being two sexes, don't you?

—James Thurber

Birth, and copulation, and death.
That's all the facts when you come to brass tacks.

—T.S. Eliot

Id That part of the psyche which is regarded as the reservoir of the instinctual drives and the source of psychic energy; it is dominated by the pleasure principle and irrational wishing.

—Webster's Dictionary

The snake's muscles tensed; coiled for attack, its red tongue flickered feverishly. An enemy invaded its terrarium, yet the snake's vigilant eyes, blinking, its head darting to and fro, saw no intruder. Nor did the camera filming the event record any image but that of a noticeably perplexed black snake poised to strike an invisible presence.

Concentrate, Rory. You can do it. You're in there. Intensify your presence.

Her voice encouraged him, begged him to perform.

The snake felt the knot of magnetic tension in the far corner of the terrarium, the warping of space; it sensed the slight depletion of oxygen in the air. It was infinitely more sensitive to these environmental changes than was the inquisitive, dark-haired woman observing the event.

He knows you're there, Rory. Move closer. Threaten him. You can do it. You must.

Now she was ordering him to act.

Brighten your Tinkerbell, Rory.

"Don't use that sissy name," he wanted to shout, but that would shatter his concentration entirely.

The dumbfounded snake glimpsed the faint ball of light hovering inches away, pulsating as if it were a luminous breath. Squinting, the woman surveyed the terrarium for the light but saw no sign of it. Yet she firmly believed the light existed.

Intensify, Rory.

I can't. No more, please.

You can. You must. Do it for me, Rory. I'll be so proud of you.

He was tempted; her approval meant everything to him.

Suddenly the snake hurtled its sleek body across the terrarium, mouth open, fangs threateningly bared. The hard teeth struck the glass with a brittle ping and, dazed if not thoroughly confused, the snake slid down the wall, coming to rest listlessly on the pebble-and-sand floor.

You did it, Rory! My God, you did it! I love you. I'm so proud of you. Rory, did you feel anything? . . . Rory?

Rolling down the glass like liquid pearls, two beads of venom stretched into white, translucent streams. On reaching the sand, they disappeared.

Relax, I'm coming in, Rory. You'll be all right.

She glanced at the snake: it lay unconscious. Smiling, she hurried into the Red Room to check on the boy.

Friday
Day 1

1

If she had not been feeling ill she would have spotted him following her. She might have recognized his face: fair-skinned, handsome, a boy her own age, from her high school.

Oh God, the cramps were returning! Knives jabbing, twisting in her abdomen. The pain!

At the corner of Fifty-first Street and Lexington Avenue she slowly descended the steps to the subway station, supporting herself on the railing. The rush-hour crowd was pushing her . . . *Please stop!* . . . she tightened her grip on the banister, unaware that Rory Malone walked five steps away, that he had slowed his pace, debating whether to approach her.

I must appear healthy, normal. Walk erect. Oh, the pain!

Although the shade of the station offered merciful relief from the searing July heat, it seemed to concentrate the oppressive New York humidity. Stifling air masked her face, making breathing difficult. Thank God she had dressed lightly: her sheer white cotton skirt, beige blouse, and no bra.

As she stepped away from the token booth, he was in her line of sight; his eyes eager for any sign of recognition from her, any excuse to introduce himself. But now, even if she stared directly at his love-struck face, she wouldn't recognize him, for she saw no one very clearly. The pounding in her head had blurred her vision.

Passing through the turnstile, she pushed the steel spokes with her hand so as to not soil her skirt. The skirt had come out of the dryer wrinkled, but she'd put it on anyway; then her mother had entered the bedroom. "You can't go to the doctor's looking like you slept in your clothes. Take that off. You have time to iron it."

She had felt so listless and nauseated that her mother had had to press the skirt.

On the subway platform she glanced only casually at the travelers. Normally she would single out those men her mother referred to as white-collar gropers—neatly dressed, clean-shaven businessmen who in a crowded train press up against any attractive woman. She knew the kind. Many times a hand had crept between her legs and touched her private parts. Or a hard bulge had rubbed against her thigh. Today, though, she didn't want to think about it. Her head throbbed incessantly; her body ached. Let them steal their cheap thrills; she was too sick to care.

She knew she must not stand too close to the edge of the platform, but why?

Her dizziness, of course. Yet there was another reason. Oh, yes, the pushings. Her uncle, a city policeman, had warned the family:

"Another loony's on the loose. Grabs a purse as the train comes in, then pushes his victim onto the tracks. In the confusion he escapes. Be careful."

Yes, she was being as careful as she could today. Instinctively her arm tightened against her shoulder bag.

Dancing pain paraded throughout her body; into her nipples, stiffening them. How her nipples ached where they pressed against her blouse.

Where's the train?

She was growing weaker every minute. Perspiration trickled from her hairline, pasting her tight blond curls to her damp cheeks.

Every month the same pains; lost schooldays, canceled dates; the embarrassment and humiliation of it all. Her girl friends never suffered these problems.

The crowd grew quickly in size. To catch this train, to be on time for her doctor's appointment, she would have to fight her way forward. Yet that was impossible. She was too weak and unsteady to push and shove.

The far end of the platform appeared less crowded, so she began walking slowly, carefully, in that direction. It required great effort to steady her trembling legs, to hold herself upright. Clenching her teeth, she pressed a hand against her abdomen. The pain was going to make her vomit.

Fight it back. Appear normal. You've done it so many times before.

2

He had recognized her immediately: Kathy Sue Bauer, a recent graduate of Forest Hills High; the prettiest, most popular girl in school.

He had spotted her passing the magazine stand at the Citicorp building. Embarrassed by the copy of *Chic* in his hands, its erotic pictures reflected in his eyes, he had sheepishly dropped the magazine back into the rows of glossy pornography. Reaching into his pocket and arranging himself vertically to conceal the evidence, he had then timidly waved to Kathy Bauer. But his limp gesture had not caught her attention; she had stared unswervingly forward as if she saw no one. He was too shy to shout her name.

And if he had called her, would Kathy Bauer had even recognized Rory Malone?

He loved her—every boy in Forest Hills High did. With a regularity that cut deep into his afternoon gardening job and several times almost lost him clients, he had watched her during fall cheerleading practice, his fingers curled through the school's rusted hurricane fence. When the cool air chilled her bare legs, turning them a splotchy pink and white, he had wished he could rub his own warmth into them. Warm her all over, cuddle close to her, kiss her. If only she had acknowledged him—just once.

On the street he had followed her, hoping to muster the courage to finally introduce himself. But his fear of rejection once again had won out, so now he was settling for the next best thing: fantasizing about her. He had changed, matured, in the two months since he had last seen Kathy Bauer. Gerhardt, his psychotherapist, had convinced him that his fantasies about women were natural and innocent.

"Rory, it's healthy to indulge in fantasy. In fact, I encourage it; consider it part of your treatment."

She was walking to the far end of the platform. All the better; fewer people. He could focus on her more clearly.

Focusing was everything, Dr. Hartman had told him. Focusing and concentrating.

Intensify your concentration, Rory. Pump all your energy into the target. Focus sharply on it. Pinpoint your power. Think of nothing but the task at hand.

Kathy looked troubled, or sick. In school she had often been mysteriously ill, missing classes and cheerleading practice. When she returned, he had always wanted to express his sympathy over whatever chronic illness she suffered. But he never did. He was sure that a girl as popular as Kathy Bauer had no time for a loner like himself.

Eyes closed, she rested her head against the tiled pillar.

He could advance closer.

He imagined that he was introducing himself to Kathy, delighting in the touch of her hand, the warmth of her smile. Unlike many of the boys in his class who thought primarily of sex, he was fundamentally a romantic who preferred conjuring gentle fantasies. And yet as innocent, misty, and romantic as he constructed loving scenarios, they invariably transformed themselves into sordid thoughts. He had noticed lately that the transition from softcore to hardcore sex was accelerating. Alarmingly so. Was this a sign of male maturity? An obsession with lust instead of love, concupiscence over caring? God, he hoped not.

Standing so he caught Kathy's profile, he clearly discerned

the large, dark brown nipples pressing against her blouse. Was it his steamy imagination, or did Kathy Bauer actually resemble the girl in *Chic*? Both were blonds, about the same age, built like mature women. The girl in the magazine was kneeling naked, doggy-style, buttocks bared to the camera. The image returned and charged his blood.

Damn magazine stands; porn at every corner, blatantly displayed. It always screwed up his day, shattered his best intentions to be good, and, worst of all, launched his fantasy into dizzying orbit.

"A healthy, normal fantasy," Gerhardt had assured him. *"Every man fantasizes about undressing a woman he sees on the street. Making love to her. That's innocent enough."*

Recently he had begun to wonder if Gerhardt was right. After all, he, Rory Malone, was different. Gerhardt and Dr. Hartman knew that better than anyone.

Lately something was happening to his body that he didn't understand. The overload of sensations in his nerve endings, tingling, rippling, and pounding for release, was frightening. Often he longed to cry out in protest, in pain. At times like this all he knew was that his special power—his talent, they called it—held him in a tenacious grip.

In the racing blur of images it was becoming impossible to separate Kathy Bauer from the girl in *Chic*.

They fused.

Focus . . . Concentrate . . .

Damn! Two women, their platinum hair sprayed stiff, walked into his line of sight.

"It's a buy, I tell you," whined the woman in bright aquamarine slacks. "I saw the same thing at Bloomingdale's for twice the price."

"Maybe so," said the woman in turquoise slacks, "but it's still unattractive. I wouldn't have it in my apartment." The top of a black and orange gooseneck lamp jutted from her Conran's shopping bag.

They had stopped in front of him, obstructing his view of Kathy. He needed a clear view, at least to begin.

Moving down the platform, he now stood about twelve

feet from Kathy. Positioning himself against the tile wall, he squinted at his lover, softly centering her in his field of view.

"Mentally frame the target, Rory. Box it in. Exclude everything extraneous. We're educating your talent."

His talent! He was beginning to wonder if it wasn't really a curse. He'd had a recent foreboding presentiment that . . . Quickly he ditched that troubling, intrusive thought.

The distant rumble of the train. Damn!

Focus . . . Concentrate . . .

Once he held Kathy's image firmly in mind, he unbuttoned her blouse, tossing it onto the train tracks.

"I'm sorry to rush, I truly am. I want to caress your breasts, linger over your body, stimulate you to starry new heights, but we haven't time."

Her breasts were more beautiful than the girl's in the magazine. Fuller, the skin silkier. Nipples larger; dark, dark brown. Already spongy firm.

Her skirt unzipped easily, falling in a faint swoosh onto the platform. Clinging tightly to her flat stomach, her panties puffed out at the crotch, moist and transparent. Easing his thumbs into the elastic band, he gently maneuvered the nylon panties down her legs then kneeled at her crotch. He inhaled its piquant scent, nuzzling into the curly blond hair until it brushed against his eyelids.

He would have to leave this area or he would come immediately, and he wanted to linger over Kathy, this girl he had waited so long to pleasure, until the last second before she boarded the train.

Running his tongue up her abdomen, out along one breast, he attempted to swallow it whole.

All this time he felt as if he were physically in contact with her. Lately this was the case with all his fantasies of women. It both amazed and delighted him. At first he had been able only to mentally strip a woman of her clothes. Gradually, though, he'd developed the ability to feel her flesh; later to taste and smell every inch of her body. He had learned to pump so much of his abundant sexual energy (or was it his psychic energy?) into a fantasy that it became real to him, an innocent but real fantasy. He experienced every erotic sensation. He came! That was the ultimate beauty of it: Orgasm with any woman he desired simply by fantasizing about her. She, his lover, felt . . .

Nothing! *Absolutely nothing!* Please, God, let that be true.

"Purge every extraneous thought from your mind, Rory. Hold only the target image."

The roar of the train increased. Soon people would block his view of Kathy, sweep her away from him.

Focus . . . Hurry . . .

The magnificent hills of her breasts, the delicious slope of her mound. Quickly running his hand down her belly, he cupped her crotch, panting, "I've loved you for so long. I hate that we have to go this fast, that we can't be more loving."

It was a protean fantasy that his power had conjured and sculpted, then turned to flesh; a fantasy that demanded resolution, and that made that objective so easy, so irresistible, that he didn't even have to touch himself.

"All men fantasize, Rory. Don't worry about it. Enjoy your fantasies."

But he wondered if other men experienced their fantasies as potently, as realistically, as he did.

The platinum-haired woman in the aquamarine slacks again turned to study the handsome young boy leaning against the wall.

What a crying shame, she thought. His glassy stare, watery eyes, listless body; his trembling lips, mumbling . . . what? A plea for more drugs. He's definitely high on drugs. Heroin, probably; it was all over the city. And such a clean-cut, all-American boy, dressed neatly, not in torn, faded jeans and T-shirt but pressed khakis, white webb belt, pale blue short-sleeve shirt. She followed his stare to the girl, who was partially hidden by the pillar. Young man, she wanted to admonish, any decent girl will have nothing to do with a drug addict. Don't you approach her, you hear?

Above the din of the station she strained but failed to decipher his jumbled utterances. He appeared so wholesome and endearing she had an irresistible urge to lecture him against drugs. Someone should save a boy like that—if it's not already too late.

His fingers entered Kathy first, gently guiding his way into her warm secret place. Lips pressed against her ear, he whispered, "Oh God, I love, love, love you." Then in a paroxysm of pleasure he slid into her, experiencing every sensation of warmth, pressure, wetness.

Kathy's signs of excitement commingled with the roar of the approaching train.

No! Her screams of protest. Damn! She was resisting his advances, rejecting his love.

But then he had had to love her so quickly of course she resisted. With time to gradually arouse her, though, to tenderly caress and worship every curve of her body as he preferred to do with his lovers, she would be accepting him now.

Above the cacophony on the platform he heard the beating of his power in his brain, heart, muscles—all surging to his groin. Somehow he felt certain that it was not blood that swelled him hard but psychic power, and he shot not come but concentrated psychic energy.

Suddenly the light of the train shone directly into his eyes, bleaching out Kathy's image, momentarily blinding him. That didn't matter now; he was delirious, into sexual free-fall. He suppressed the urge to scream out in pleasure, and yet—he heard screams.

He came.

Still dazed, his eyes only partially open, he began to realize that the screams came from people along the platform.

"Stop the train!"

"Holy Jesus, that girl!"

Opening his eyes fully, shaking his head to regain alertness, he spotted the terrified faces of the two platinum-haired women. Then people waving frantically at the approaching train.

He had to escape. Running along the platform, he shoved people aside.

"God, she'll be killed!"

"Someone save her!"

The shrill screeching of train wheels against tracks echoed in the tunnel.

I didn't mean to hurt you. More than anything I wanted to love you, to have you love me. I'm sorry.

He was through the turnstile, heading for the stairs, when he heard the first shouts directed at him.

"Stop that boy!"

"Grab him!"

"He pushed a girl onto the tracks."

Racing up the stairs, he was aware that the train had stopped.   Despite the chorus of pleas to apprehend him, no one attempted to as he pushed through the throng of people descending the stairs and emerged into the harsh sunlight.

A woman screamed, "Arrest that boy, officer! Grab him!" causing him to glance toward the street. Stuck in bumper-to-bumper traffic idled a blue and white police car. Its two cops stared at him, simultaneously flung open their doors, and darted through the traffic.

3

Rory raced down Lexington Avenue, west on Forty-ninth Street past St. Bartholomew's Cathedral; he darted through the dense Park Avenue traffic, the policeman half a block behind.

God, let Kathy live!

"You're getting stronger, Rory. Each session is proof of that. I'm proud of you. So is Gerhardt."

Three cars screeched to a halt. A taxi swerved, missing him by a hair.

"Get the fuck outa the street!" blasted the red-faced hack,

obviously torn between a desire to speed on or to jump from his cab and beat the kid to a pulp. "I shoulda hit ya, ya shit! I'm fuckin' sorry I didn't kill ya!"

They had turned him into a monster. A freak, his father said.

"Stop or I'll shoot."

The cop won't shoot in this crowd, thought Rory; he's trying to scare me. He could easily outdistance this fat cop if the crowd only parted for him as it did for the policeman.

"Grab that kid! Somebody stop him!"

No one did.

"Your testosterone production is abnormally high, Rory. That's usual in such cases, though."

That incontestably meant he was sexually abnormal. God, how he hated his slavishness to all things sexual: silky fabrics, sweet flowery scents, sheer stockings, women on subways and buses standing or sitting in seductive poses. Most of all, after orgasm, he hated himself.

"Jesus, somebody, anybody—grab that kid!"

The cop's voice sounded labored, breathless; he was tiring fast, yet he remained undaunted in his pursuit.

I can outrun him. I must.

Passing the show windows of Saks Fifth Avenue, he glimpsed the summer display of mannequins in flimsy, pastel-color negligees. He reached Rockefeller Plaza exhausted; in the ninety-degree heat he had to force himself to continue running. Sweat dripped from every pore, rapidly dehydrating his body. The sticky front of his jockey shorts clung to his abdomen, a link to the crime, a heinous reminder of what had happened.

Signs of impending disaster had tormented him for almost two weeks. That woman in the bookstore had flushed, wiped a handkerchief across her brow, turned to him with a fearful, enigmatic stare, then hurried out the door. In McDonald's the blond seated a table away from him became faint and clutched her breasts. Staggering to her feet, aided by her boyfriend, who demanded to know why they were leaving half their meal uneaten, she'd darted furtive, frightened glances his way.

Those women; others; the experiments with Dr. Hartman;

his phenomenal success in the Black Room; all led to a single, inescapable conclusion. And yet he had ignored the evidence, hoping it was specious. Still he prayed his suspicions were wrong.

Please, God, let it all be a figment of my imagination.

Approaching the canopied entrance of the RCA Building, he knew the first thing he had to do was ditch his shorts. They provided a tangible link to Kathy Bauer, an incessant, intolerable reminder of his perversion. What would the police think of his wet, stained shorts? If Kathy had felt him, if she talked . . . if the police learned about the experiments with Dr. Hartman, they'd make the connection.

First, lose the cop among the maze of corridors in the sprawling basement of the building. Then he knew where to go to rid himself of the evidence.

Al DeCosta realized he couldn't run much longer. His lungs burned, his parched throat ached with each short irregular breath, and the dagger-sharp pain in his heart intensified with every bounce of his beleaguered body. With twenty-odd years on the kid and more than sixty pounds, he'd been a fool to undertake the chase. O'Hare should have pursued the kid; he was in better condition.

Asshole, that's just why you ran: to prove to yourself, and ultimately to Webb, that you're fit, despite your disgusting flab and defective ticker.

He'd refused Webb's offer of decreased patrol hours to enable him to enroll in the Police Exercise Program, because first you had to submit to a physical, and they'd sure as hell find out about his heart. He'd be pulled off patrol, off the street, and trapped behind a desk. He'd rather be dead.

Shit! Where *are* the cops when you need them, he thought. Midtown at peak rush hour, and I'm the only goddamn fucking cop in sight. Thank God the kid had run into the RCA Building; a security guard was bound to be stationed at the door; he'd help.

4

"The boy pushed her, officer," exclaimed the platinum-haired woman in turquoise slacks. "That girl was waving her arms, trying to fight him off, and then he just pushed her." Her fleshy fingers, each adorned with an ornate gold ring, fidgeted with the wire mesh In basket on Captain Thomas Webb's desk at the Seventeenth Precinct.

"Well, I was closer," chimed her darkly tanned look-alike companion in aquamarine slacks. "The boy wasn't anywhere near that poor girl. He didn't touch her. She fell."

"Ladies, please!" barked Webb, interrupting their bickering for the umpteenth time. "I'll take each of your statements separately. Now won't you please wait over there with the other witnesses?"

These twin quidnuncs would drive him batty before the evening was over, he thought. Since arriving at the station they had been at odds over the events on the subway platform, each unequivocal and unrelenting in her testimony. How two witnesses can view the same happening and interpret it in utterly opposite ways never ceased to amaze him.

Reluctantly the two women crossed the room.

Carrie Wilson, Webb's assistant, was clearing her desk when he approached her. Carrie, now twenty-six, had been hired by Webb two years ago after she'd completed her master's degree in criminology. She had sought practical experience at a precinct, and more than her degree and straight-A grades, her green eyes, strawberry-blond hair, and perfect legs had landed her the job. He had been doubly pleased when he first glimpsed the exquisitely analytical mind behind that extraordinary exterior; but he'd soon found himself intimidated by her frank interest in him. No woman had ever pursued Thomas Webb, and at forty-nine he didn't know how to respond to such an open and honest declaration of feelings. Besides, he had been married then, which had only compounded his awkwardness in fending off Carrie's advances.

"Luv, how about some grub and coffee before you go?"

Carrie smiled. "The usual unnutritious, filling junk?"

"Yeah, and lots of coffee. It's going to be a long night."

"Chief, you should change your diet. It's really gross."

"Don't lecture me, luv. It'd be easier for me to change assistants."

Conciliatory, Carrie leaned across his desk. "I'm not leaving for the Hamptons till tomorrow. I could come back after the rally if you need an extra pair of hands. Or legs."

"Just get the grub," he said. God only knew why that heavenly creature pursued him; he was old enough to be her father. Still, since his divorce from Julie, he had been tempted to ask Carrie out.

"You're sure?" she crooned, peering straight into his eyes.

"You enjoy the rally and the weekend," he answered.

He would have to devote his full attention to this new subway pushing, which differed significantly from the previous three this summer and provided the first real lead they'd had.

He scanned the names of the witnesses. Twelve people had seen the boy run from the subway station and come voluntarily to the precinct. Amazing. A dozen New Yorkers, late on a Friday afternoon, delaying their feverish exodus to the Hamptons, Fire Island, or just air conditioned apartments, volunteering to bear witness. It clearly attested to public concern and fear over the new wave of subway crimes. He'd have to interview them himself, since Sergeant Bauer wasn't due in till eight and Rookie O'Hare was still at New York Hospital, where the girl had been taken.

She had been unconscious when O'Hare reached her, the train's wheel having severed her right leg above the knee. Fortunately the rookie had had the sense to call for ice, which was provided in buckets by a nearby deli. While medics attended to the girl, O'Hare had packed the amputated leg in ice in a plastic bag. The doctors were reattaching her leg right now. Webb wondered about the girl's identity.

Carrie placed the plastic-wrapped pastries and coffee on Webb's desk.

"The rally is only at Bryant Park," she said. "I could sneak away after my talk and be back here by eight. Like to reconsider my offer?"

"Nope. I wouldn't deprive you of a minute's joy in the park. You've worked hard on that talk. Before you run off, though, call the hospital and see when O'Hare plans to return. I need info on the girl. By now the *News* and the *Post* probably know more about her than we do."

Crossing the room, he invited one of the platinum-haired women into his office for questioning; might as well get rid of these dolls first.

"Luv," he called, "check on DeCosta, too. He should have been back by now."

He would have to lecture DeCosta and O'Hare. The fools. They'd been stuck in traffic when the boy had emerged from the subway station. Young O'Hare had assumed the more difficult task of attending to the girl, while portly veteran DeCosta, who got winded climbing the precinct steps, had run after the kid.

DeCosta hadn't returned yet. Was it just possible that flabby DeCosta had actually overtaken and apprehended the boy?

5

Rory had lost the cop. It had been much easier to do in the RCA Building than on the street. Still, he didn't feel safe.

Hundreds of people had seen him running—on the subway platform, along the streets, in the building—all could identify him.

Entering the men's room, he proceeded directly to the last stall, which was unoccupied. The old wooden door, etched with graffiti, closed with an unexpectedly loud bang that startled him. His nerves were really threadbare.

His luck took a nose dive when he saw the door, missing a lock, come to rest about ten degrees ajar, leaving an opening of several inches that might indicate to a prospective occupant that this john was empty. The other johns were in use, and he had to ditch the evidence which pressed annoyingly against his abdomen.

With one hand holding the door tightly shut, he used the other to unfasten and remove his khakis. Stepping out of his shorts, he tossed them into the john and flushed. With a fistful of toilet paper he cleaned his abdomen. The fluid's bleachlike odor filled him with self-loathing.

"Rory, together we've taken a wild, random force and tamed it into a willful talent."

I'll never use the talent again. Not for Dr. Hartman. Certainly not for my own pleasure. She'll never coax me into the Black Room again.

The shorts resisted the downward pull of the whirlpool and bobbed up to the surface. Again and again he flushed, and each time the shorts surfaced as if to taunt him.

Wondering if the man in the adjacent stall was staring curiously at the pair of calves bare from sweat socks up, he moved against the opposite wall, which extended down to the floor. As the man left the stall, Rory wondered if he might tell a policeman in the building, "There's a real weirdo in the men's room, last stall. Better check it out."

Despite his concern for his own safety, Kathy Bauer's life weighed heavily on his mind.

Damn! What was wrong with him? He had desired only to pleasure Kathy, to make her confess her craving for him, and instead he may have hurt her.

"Rory, everything in your past—your mother, the nuns and priests at school, your church—has taught you to regard women as pure, asexual creatures, yet you dream of turning them into sex-loving creatures like yourself."

"I do, but why?" he had asked Gerhardt.

"If you get the woman in your fantasy to admit she enjoys forbidden sexual pleasures, your own anxiety and guilt are appeased."

Abandoning his efforts to flush away his shorts—they just wouldn't go down—he struggled into his khakis, then leaned his back against the door in order to fasten his fly and belt.

Jesus! Even in this public place in the RCA Building sex was everywhere: lurid drawings either scratched into the wall or drawn in pencil or marker; girls' names, phone numbers, and descriptions of what services they rendered best; offers for blow jobs, clandestine rendezvous. Apparently other people existed, and in sizable numbers, who were as obsessed with sex as he was.

"Rory," Dr. Hartman had said the day she showed him the results of his testosterone test and attempted to assure him he was not abnormally oversexed, "we live in a society that is antisex to its core but is also sex obsessed." She had rummaged through the basket beside her desk and come up with the Book Review section of the *New York Times*. "Look here," she'd said, pointing to the bestseller list. "Three books on sex all at the top." He'd looked, spotted them, and memorized the titles. On the way home from the laboratory session, though he was flushed with embarrassment, he bought *The Joy of Sex*, since it sounded the hottest of the lot.

He knew he should wash up at the sink and restyle his hair, perhaps comb it straight back. That might alter his appearance enough for the time being.

Opening the stall door, he froze. Leaning over one sink, splashing water on his face, was a cop—the one who had chased him. Gently closing the door, he pressed his body weight against it, certain the cop had followed him into the men's room and knew he hid in the last stall. The cop was playing cat-and-mouse with him, delaying the kill.

Through the crack between the door and the wall he had a

clear view in the wall mirror of the cop as he reached into his shirt pocket, withdrew something from a small white container and popped it into his mouth, then gulped down water. The cop did not look well. In fact, under the bright fluorescent lights the cop's face appeared deathly gray, and his eyelids were almost completely closed. Suddenly the cop turned and darted across the room toward the last stall.

Rory threw all his 138 pounds against the door, his heart thumping wildly. He would be caught, pulled into the precinct, asked for explanations. "Why did you run from the subway station?" "What is your relationship with Kathy Bauer?" "Why, young man, did you dispose of your underpants in the toilet?"

The force of the cop's hand slamming against the door momentarily jarred Rory and the door forward. But immediately he responded by offering an equal and opposite force. The door banged shut.

He girded himself for another attack, but none came. Instead the cop raced into the adjacent stall.

Rory was trembling so violently that the door rattled against its frame. The cop was going to crawl under the partition and grab him around the ankles. Trapped, unable to bear the tension any longer, he considered opening the door and surrendering. Then from the adjacent stall he heard the unmistakable sounds of a man gagging, retching. The putrid odor wafting under the partition confirmed that the cop was vomiting.

Suppose the cop didn't know his suspect was in the next stall? Suppose the cop, feeling sick, had wandered into the men's room? Suppose he was so ill he had already abandoned the search for his suspect?

If he escaped, thought Rory, he would locate Kathy Bauer. He must know what she had experienced on the subway platform, what she would tell the police.

6

"I simply can't expect them to wait a minute longer," said Dr. Elizabeth Hartman, pacing the hall outside her physics laboratory at Columbia University. "Clearly Rory's not coming."

"The ungrateful snot," snapped her husband, Gerhardt Kiner. "He knows what this means to you. To us. And not even a phone call. Didn't I warn you he'd turn out to be unreliable?"

"Calm down. And please keep your voice down; they'll hear you. Perhaps he's frightened of performing for an audience. He's a shy boy. And he was terribly upset last week when he heard we were inviting guests." She should have devoted more personal time to him at the last session. Even before she had mentioned the visitors, he'd been visibly troubled about something, and it had diminished his performance. Instead she had hurried him into the Black Room, eager for more verifiable data.

"Gerhardt, if you'll set up the projector, I'll make the necessary apologies." Her voice sounded remarkably composed considering her inner frustration. She enjoyed being told she resembled a young Elizabeth Taylor, though tonight she felt thoroughly, hopelessly unattractive. A week of nerves, tension, inhuman heat in her unair-conditioned laboratory; so much riding on Rory's performance, and now heart-wrenching disappointment, total humiliation.

Rory, dear boy, why are you doing this to me!

Returning to the laboratory, she explained the dilemma to the two visitors from the Department of Defense.

"We've traveled from Washington specifically to witness the subject perform," said James Gregory, DOD's assistant budget director for university funding. "You promised Mr. Malone would be present. This is most unprofessional."

Short, stocky, possessing squinting eyes and a perpetually constipated tightness around his mouth, Gray had immediately repulsed Liz Hartman. Her intolerance for unattractive people was a personality shortcoming, but not one she had any intention of modifying. Gray's bleating, singsong voice and his repeated innuendoes that many people at DOD disbelieved her claims of success with Rory Malone did not win him any compensating points. Nonetheless, she needed his approval on her proposal, and she'd do whatever she had to do to charm him.

"I too am greatly disappointed," said Liz. "The subject has progressed considerably since my last report to you. However, we'll watch a film of Mr. Malone from footage I've assembled. At least it'll give you a good indication of how I—we—have educated his talent."

Liz lowered the window shades while Gerhardt set up the projector.

Dr. Cheryl Roland, a DOD electrical engineer, who had come to inspect the technical aspects of the Malone research, was more compassionate. "Mr. Malone may arrive while we're viewing the film." Her voice was thin and melodic, canarylike, thought Liz. "Afterward, Dr. Hartman, I'd like to spend some time studying the Black Room. As an engineer I'm quite impressed with the specs you sent us."

Petite, blond, twenty-six years old, with bland features and a slight body, Cheryl Roland contrasted sharply with Liz's dark voluptuousness. Women scientists were still a relatively rare breed, thought Liz; maybe this was what had forged the immediate bond between them.

For the last few months Liz had been filing biweekly reports to the grant office of the National Institutes of Health. Apparently some high-placed honcho had been suitably impressed to notify the Defense Department. Now a hundred-thousand-dollar research grant to locate other gifted subjects like Rory Malone rested on winning the DOD's approval.

On the screen covering the front-wall blackboard appeared a closeup of a handsome, boyish face. His square chin was dynamically sculptured and clenched in a fiercely determined bite; long, curling lashes framed blue eyes that, in the piercing intensity of their gaze, were troubling. Those eyes are attempting to move mountains, melt leviathan icebergs, thought Cheryl Roland. And strangely enough, she felt they could do it. The face on the screen imbued her with a sense of awe and trepidation she had not felt on reading Liz Hartman's reports.

Pulling back, the camera revealed the boy lying in a leather recliner, his wavy brown hair parted where seven silver electrodes jutted from his scalp. His bare, hairless chest, leanly muscular and suntanned, was wired in the vicinity of his heart.

"He certainly is attractive," said Roland.

"He is that," answered Kiner.

"This is our star subject, Rory Malone," began Liz. Composed, gentle, yet exactingly precise, her voice rode above her shaky emotions. Resolved now to showing the film, her anger toward Rory was quickly subsiding, and being replaced by concern for his well-being. Something was wrong, terribly wrong. She should have questioned him last week.

7

"How close were you to the girl?" Webb asked the woman in turquoise slacks sitting opposite him. He wished he at least knew the girl's name so he could refer to her more concretely.

"Six feet. Maybe closer," said the woman. "And unlike my sister, I don't wear glasses. Which she wasn't wearing."

"Were you looking at the girl when she fell?"

"Yes. Normally I'd mind my own business, but this girl was acting strange, like she was sick or on drugs."

"Your sister claims it was the boy who acted drugged."

The two of them probably had been so busy chatting that neither had paid much attention to the boy or the girl until the moment of the incident. Still, he would have the hospital check the girl's blood.

This time he would get the break in the case he'd been hoping for. So far two deaths, one critical injury, numerous wild leads, and no suspect. In the past there had been no eyewitnesses. The other incidents had occurred late at night on nearly deserted platforms: two in the Bronx, one on the Upper West Side. Sergeant Bauer, who headed the investigation, suspected that a different kid was involved in each incident.

"It's some kind of sick summer thrill," Bauer had said. "Soon all the niggers and spics will be doing it. Last year they were snatchin' gold chains." Hothead Bauer. His incendiary temper had gotten him temporarily suspended from the force twice in the last five years.

Webb, on the other hand, suspected the assailant was one kid. And this time the bastard had been seen, spotted up close by at least a dozen witnesses.

Pressing the intercom to Carrie's desk, he asked, "Anything on O'Hare or DeCosta yet?"

"Granted I'm fast, Chief, but I'm not Wonder Woman."

"Let me know the minute O'Hare arrives. And for Christ's sake have somebody find DeCosta." He turned back to the platinum-haired woman, who hadn't taken her eyes off him.

Actually he enjoyed interviewing witnesses. In high school he had read every detective novel he could get his hands on, and the books had played a major role in his decision to become a policeman. But later on the daily drudgery of police work had almost convinced him to quit the force. Julie had saved his career by suggesting he enroll in a night course at Fordham; in six years he had a B.S. in psychology. Studying the psychology of criminals, suspects, and witnesses added an exciting dimension to police work.

Two years ago he'd written a prizewinning article for *The*

American Journal of Criminology: "Women and Crime: The Role of Premenstrual Tension in the Female Crime Rate." For the past year he'd been deep into research on the connection between violent, aggressive pornography and sexual crimes. Carrie, a member of the national group called Women Against Pornography, had first interested him in the subject and handled all the library research.

Focusing on the witness, he asked, "Why do you believe this girl was sick or on drugs?"

"The way she leaned on the pole with her eyes closed, rubbing her stomach. I thought she might fall."

"Did you approach her, ask if she was sick?"

"I was going to. But she started to act very peculiar. She kept touching her body all over. Then her hands suddenly flew into the air." The woman's eyes widened. "Come to think of it, I'll bet that girl was having an epileptic fit."

There came a knock on the door.

Carrie leaned in. "O'Hare just arrived, and he says it's urgent he speak with you. Would it be okay if I left?"

"Okay? I've been trying to get rid of you." He excused himself to the witness and in the outer room glanced automatically at Carrie's lithe legs strolling toward the door—he'd ask her out soon, very soon—then he joined O'Hare in the adjacent office.

"How is she?" he asked, closing the door behind him. O'Hare seemed unnerved.

"Massive internal injuries and hemorrhaging," said O'Hare. "The docs aren't sure they can save the leg."

"Goddamn bastard. We'll get his ass this time. He's pushed his last victim."

"I'm afraid that's not the worst of it, Chief." O'Hare overturned a brown leather purse, and a wallet fell onto the desk.

Webb opened the wallet and froze. Kathy Sue Bauer, 170-52 Baker Road, Forest Hills. "Jesus," he whispered. "Holy shit! Bauer's niece." He had met Kathy only once—she couldn't have been more than thirteen then—but at this instant his memory of her was strikingly vivid. So sweet and delicately beautiful, with a terrific personality.

He had to think fast. Bauer was due in at eight o'clock. Webb debated whether to first call Kathy's parents or Sergeant Bauer. Or had Bauer heard already? The incident must be on the evening news. Those portable minicameras catapulted every crime into an instant media event. And the stations won't let a juicy one like this get away. They'll go with graphic on-the-scene pictures of the amputated leg, of Kathy Bauer on the stretcher. They'd play up this incident big and come down hard on the police for not yet uncovering the identity of the Subway Pusher.

Should Bauer be pulled off the case? He would probably sooner resign than miss out on tracking down the slime that had pushed his own niece. Webb knew Bauer's temper all too well.

Bauer's last suspension had been for clubbing a black kid who had run a red light. He'd testified that when he had started to write the ticket, the kid had pulled a knife. But the bludgeoning he'd dished out, almost killing the kid, had been "in conscious disregard for the value of human life," according to the judge, who had suspended him for six months without pay.

Webb straightened up. "Get the art boys down here, pronto! I want a composite of this kid in an hour. I'll call Bauer, then interrogate these witnesses thoroughly. We'll know if this kid is guilty before the night's over. Move, O'Hare!"

8

Rory did not have to wait long for the cop to leave the men's room, though he didn't emerge from the stall for what seemed like an eternity.

At the sink he splashed cold water on his face, then with a paper towel dried his face, neck, and chest. Soaking his hair, he combed it severely back, flattening its natural waves about his ears and along the top of his head. He had no idea if it would remain tamed when it dried. In the mirror he looked only marginally different, and the extreme hairdo only accentuated his already large and expressive eyes—eyes that blazed with his guilt, fears, and suspicions. His heart still raced.

Kathy had seen him, he was absolutely certain of that. A second before she fell, she'd turned and stared directly at him. And recognized him, too. From the terror on her face, he suspected she somehow knew, or actually felt, his every action.

He must know. It meant everything for his future.

He would have to somehow question her, preferably before the police did.

Leaving the RCA Building, he headed west on Fiftieth Street until he reached Broadway. The area was thronged with commuters on their way home and with tourists carrying cameras, returning to their hotels after a day of sightseeing.

He positioned himself near the open front of a pizza stand so he could easily hear the radio that played music from beneath the counter. Whatever the station, it had to broadcast the day's news eventually.

"Do you want something?" asked a fat, middle-aged man, shoveling a pizza slice into the oven.

"No, thanks." Food now would nauseate him.

"Well, then, kid, move on. You're blocking my store."

He started down the stretch of Broadway that was his bane. With peep shows, porn parlors, and hardcore movie houses cluttering every block, this part of the city normally excited him. Just passing the storefronts set his pulse racing, charging his power, forcing him to locate a lover in order to release him from the clutch of sexual passion. Last week, wanting desperately *not* to locate a lover—already frightened by intimations of disaster—he had defused his sexual energies in the Metropole.

Now he found himself recalling that visit.

* * *

"Live sex show one flight up. Two of the prettiest ladies you've ever seen. Watch them love each other as you would."

Admission was a dollar. Not much, considering they were usually great-looking girls; young, too. He had been up there many times before. It was a small room with a low, makeshift stage at one end and a bruiser the size of his father to protect the girls if a man in the audience, carried away with excitement, climbed onto the stage.

But the audience arena was never dark enough for him. He had never been able to masturbate in his seat like the other men did. Turning his head, he would invariably find some older guy ogling *him* instead of the naked girls intertwined on stage.

Five P.M. An hour before his session with Dr. Hartman. He had plenty of time.

There was a crowd tonight. Men in business suits carrying attaché cases milled around the books and films; several ventured upstairs. Clearly these were normal men: husbands, fathers. They visited here before returning home to their wives, girl friends, children. Whenever he criticized himself for being an oversexed degenerate, he'd recall these ordinary men and temporarily feel normal himself.

At the front counter he exchanged a dollar for four quarters, proceeded to the long row of private booths, and studied the advertisements for each film. Bestiality left him cold, but out of curiosity he scrutinized several pictures that depicted women engaged in sex with dogs and horses. That *was* degenerate and filled him with disgust; another reassuring sign that he was sexually normal.

But was he? Other films depicted violence, and he had viewed them. Simulated violence, of course. Nonetheless, some of it had turned him on. Not the bloody beatings, the gory stuff; but strangely enough, the women held down, forced into sex. That he liked. Especially *Football Orgy*, in which an entire team ravaged two cheerleaders in the locker room.

"That need not worry you, Rory," Gerhardt had responded on hearing about the films.

"You don't seem to understand; I'm beginning to like this stuff. Sick stuff. It's like I've become another person. And he's not a very nice guy." Once, not very long ago, the thought of forcing himself on a woman was enough to render him soft instantly. Now, depending on his mood and degree of horniness, aggressive fantasies turned him rock hard.

"It doesn't mean you're sick. Many men view those same films. Otherwise that place—and all the others—wouldn't offer them."

"Yeah, I guess so. And those men aren't sick?"

"Rory, the sickness develops when a man acts out his aggressive fantasies against his partner's wishes—and with disregard for her well-being."

He couldn't tell Gerhardt that he had intimations that his sexual fantasies somehow *were* being enacted through his power. The evidence was too weak, too insubstantial, to jeopardize Dr. Hartman's research.

"But some of the stuff turns me on, drives me crazy. I don't like what it does to me."

"Then I recommend you not view sexually aggressive films."

He hadn't since that conversation.

He chose *Lesbian Lovers*, a gentle, erotic picture he'd viewed before. Entering the narrow cubicle, he deposited his first quarter.

By masturbating he hoped to slake his horniness, though sex in any form would definitlely weaken his performance at Dr. Hartman's laboratory. He had learned that just recently. The hornier he was, the stronger his talent.

With his pants open in front, he watched the film, holding himself firmly in one hand, the other hand clutching a tissue. He felt embarrassed to shoot onto the floor, as most of the men did. He knew this, for as soon as a man vacated a booth, a hunched attendant ran a wet mop over the floor.

He left the Metropole and dropped the used tissue in a public waste basket on Broadway. Feeling relaxed, confident he would be able to concentrate on his session with Dr. Hartman, he boarded the uptown subway to Columbia University. He would still perform for her, enter the Black Room and make her proud of him.

*　　*　　*

That had been last week. Now, walking down Broadway, he passed the Metropole, watching men exit with sheepish expressions and stealthy gaits. Tonight the place held no allure. Rather it exuded seediness, as did this entire part of town and the subhumans who inhabited it.

I'll never return to the Metropole. Never watch another porn movie, thumb through a dirty book. I'll burn my porn collection.

Not likely. He had made these promises scores of times before. How easy to swear off sex just after you came. When he got horny, though, once the juices skirted from his groin to his brain, they siphoned off his best intentions.

Heading down Broadway, he listened for a radio broadcast of Kathy Bauer's condition and to learn if the police were searching for him. For blocks he heard only music, and he continually ignored the steady gaze of an effeminate boy about his age who strutted a few feet away. Dressed in a stretch midriff top that revealed small breasts, the boy either was wearing falsies or on female hormones.

Rory shuddered; not at the boy's blatant interest in him but at thoughts stirred up by the boy's breasts. Gerhardt had advocated female-hormone therapy to destroy his power; only Dr. Hartman's merciful protests had saved him from that horrible fate.

Dr. Hartman! He'd forgotten about the session. Checking his watch, he found he was an hour late. She would be demolished if he didn't show tonight of all nights. The government investigators would be present; she was counting on him to impress them with his talent and secure her grant. Dr. Hartman had helped him in countless ways; he couldn't disappoint her now. And yet in his anxious, agitated state he couldn't tolerate the pressure of the session, certainly not in front of spectators.

Nor could he return home yet without arousing his father's suspicions. So he settled on a movie. The Rivoli featured *The Pink Panther,* starring Peter Sellers.

The theater was dark and chillingly air conditioned. He

would try to relax, to devise a cogent alibi for Dr. Hartman, for the police, and to figure a way to talk with Kathy Bauer.

9

As the film rolled Liz attempted to conceal from her guests her growing concern for Rory.

"The subject turned seventeen last month and will be a high school senior in September. His background is Irish-Italian, Roman Catholic; a very religious, rigid rearing. His mother, the emotional pillar of the family, died in a street accident not quite two years ago. He lives with his father, Michael Malone, a cabinetmaker, in Queens."

To miss a session, an important one, was thoroughly unlike Rory, Liz thought. Still more uncharacteristic was the lack of a phone call. He must be experiencing problems again with his father; a serious conflict. She'd interceded before in Rory's behalf and would do it again, despite Mike Malone's contempt for her.

The image on the screen shifted abruptly to the Malone family living room: poorer quality photography, dimmer lighting, older footage. Roving throughout the room, the camera cataloged a scene of destruction. Ashtrays, glasses, bric-a-brac, most of it shattered, lay strewn across the golden-wheat carpet. Books from a shelf above the stereo system were scattered on the floor, as were record albums that seemed to have been jerked with random force from their cabinet. A broken plaster madonna, its head a foot from the torso, rested by a leg of the television set; a brown Formica coffee table lay overturned, one leg precariously close to the television screen. Everything but the largest items in the room—a tufted burgundy sofa and two brown corduroy armchairs—looked as if it had been in the path of a typhoon.

Liz explained.

"Rory Malone was sixteen when he caused this destruction, the third and worst incident in his parents' home. It occurred shortly before his father sought professional help. As you read in my first report, the subject represents a classic case of the poltergeist phenomenon: pent-up anger and frustration, usually with an underlying sexual component, that suddenly is unleashed in a torrent of destruction. Psychoanalyst Nandor Fodor has described the poltergeist as a 'bundle of projected repressions released like a reflex reaction.'

"While the destruction has often been attributed to ghosts, every case that has been carefully investigated reveals two indisputable facts: an unhappy adolescent between the ages of twelve and twenty resides in the household; and he or she is always present when the so-called poltergeist strikes.

"Why some children store psychic energy like a dynamo and unwittingly release it like a bolt of lightning remains a mystery. Sex hormones—in fact, the entire endocrine system— are believed to play a role. Nevertheless, when my husband and I took over the case a year ago, we decided to attempt a revolutionary treatment of the poltergeist child."

With the amateurishness of a home movie the film showed a large, balding, fair-skinned man, Rory's father, stiffly lifting each felled item, dutifully offering it for the camera's scrutiny.

Silly, needless footage, Liz thought, embarrassed now that she had included it in her film. To counterbalance the footage her voice assumed an ultarprofessional air.

"As you know, a poltergeist child receives psychiatric counseling; in extreme cases, hormone therapy. As his personal dilemmas are resolved or his endocrine system is balanced, his psychic energy vanishes. This has been well documented."

Did James Gray and Cheryl Roland really believe Rory had caused this destruction, Liz wondered. Or did they think the film was a hoax? She wished she could see the expressions on their faces.

Oh, Rory, my love, why aren't you here to show them what you can do!

"My husband and I modified that approach. Of course the subject visits a psychotherapist weekly; in fact, my husband. It would be cruel not to attempt to delve to the root of his traumas. But we did not attempt hormone therapy. You've seen his endocrine tests: exceedingly high testosterone levels.

"While his psychic energy still exists—for it will probably vanish before adulthood—we have proved that that energy can be, as I like to say, *educated*—channeled into consciously controlled actions. And we've been immensely successful."

Liz, old girl, that sounded awfully smug. No more self-praise.

The film cut to an image of Gerhardt, broad-boned, six feet three inches tall, wearing a white lab smock that, combined with his pale complexion and white-blond hair, almost bleached him out of the overexposed footage. Rory, his forehead creased by lines of concentration, sat at a table on which rested a cylinder, a ball, a suspended glass pendulum, and a compass. From the rear of the room Gerhardt's sonorous voice assumed the narration.

"After three months of effort we were finally able to teach Mr. Malone to move lightweight objects mentally. Of course, he had lifted much heavier objects at home, but through spontaneous bursts of psychic energy. In the lab it was a question of convincing him that with sufficient will power he could consciously exert this energy as a useful physical force. My wife receives the credit for this accomplishment; she has the gift of infinite patience."

In truth, Gerhardt knew he had failed miserably with Rory. Poor personal chemistry, rivalry for his wife's attention, his severe authoritarian manner—all had prevented him from winning Rory's confidence and love. Then, too, he had almost scared the boy to death with his early insistence on female-hormone therapy to destroy the power; Liz had been wise in opposing that treatment.

Once Liz had joined the project full-time (in effect, took over), she had immediately forged a bond with Rory. Gerhardt suspected that his wife, with her warm, naturally affectionate manner—toward people she liked—had become a surrogate for Rory's recently deceased mother. Whatever the reasons, Gerhardt privately resented Rory and his wife's unqualified success with the boy, and he realized that Rory sensed this, for he performed significantly better with Liz at the computer controls.

On the screen Rory squinted at the glass pendulum, his concentration palpable. Smoothly it began to sway.

"Do you have more recent footage?" asked James Gray in his supercilious whine. "Not that this is uninteresting, mind you, but the research with the animals—a snake and a cat, if I recall correctly—impressed me as more dynamic evidence of Mr. Malone's talent. Of course, I'm not a scientist; I'm speaking strictly as a lay person."

I question if you're even a person, thought Liz, but she calmly answered, "You'll see that research shortly."

Deeply worried, she no longer watched the film. The last time Rory had fought with his father and missed a session, he had called from a pay phone in his neighborhood. He had apologized repeatedly, profusely, for the inconvenience he'd caused her. Conscientious, considerate; that was the Rory Malone she loved, for his problems and talent, the boy she had so painstakingly molded into a scientific marvel. She had taken an immediate shine to him, and the more she'd learned of his unhappy home life with his father, the more her sympathy and affection had grown.

"Freak! That's what you are, a goddamn freak," his father had often shouted. "You didn't inherit that power from me. It's not in my genes or your mother's. Thank God she's not here to see this."

Gerhardt continued the narration through the footage that chronicled Rory's progress, from moving light objects to heavier ones, first with the objects nearby, then gradually more distant; until finally the film revealed an empty room in which a cylinder rolled mysteriously across the floor; a large wooden block floated unsteadily in the air, teetering, vibrating, then struck the floor with a thud as though the invisible beam of energy that suspended it had been abruptly shut off.

The film returned to the initial scene of Rory in the recliner. In a voice in which pride and underlying jealousy mixed, Gerhardt announced: "Gentlemen, from here my wife takes full command. The Black Room is her baby. She conceived the brilliant concept, and it remains the crowning glory of her work to date with Mr. Malone."

Liz found herself studying Rory's face, attempting once again to identify that peculiar expression in his eyes—those beautiful yet strangely menacing eyes—that had recently disturbed her. You're withholding a secret from me, Rory—a terrible secret that continually torments you and diminishes your laboratory performance; it demands that you hold back your power.

Liz wondered if she were too emotionally involved with Rory, if she had already lost all scientific objectivity. Perhaps. Forty and childless, her maternal interest in Rory seemed as perfectly natural as it was inevitable, and she found it immensely fulfilling. She loved this handsome, uniquely talented boy more than she had ever thought she could love a child. Important as Rory was for her research and her career, she realized she'd abandon it all for his well-being and happiness.

When she was finished with the visitors, she would phone Rory's home. The potential for violence and serious harm occurring between Rory and Mike Malone was real.

Steeling herself to go on with the narration, she straightened her shoulders and lifted her chin. If anything would win the visitors' approval and secure the grant, it was the Black Room experiments, for they pushed Rory to extraordinary levels. After all, this was the research that had piqued the interest of the Defense Department and compelled it to assume responsibility for the grant.

The film shifted to the Black Room.

Liz was about to speak when suddenly a cold rush crossed her shoulder blades and rippled up her neck—a fleeting sensation, a foreboding that seemed clearly to presage that Rory was in trouble and needed her help. So strong and eerily chilling was the presentiment that it temporarily froze her vocal cords, rendering her speechless.

My God, what's happened to my baby?

She should terminate the session, dismiss the visitors, immediately find Rory and console him, learn his secret. And yet the scientist in her spoke of the need for objectivity, the importance of the grant, the desire to impress the visitors with her talented child, who in many ways was now more a creation of hers than of his mother's.

Saturday
Day 2

10

Returning home at precisely ten P.M., the time he normally arrived from his session with Dr. Hartman (he hadn't phoned her; he couldn't yet), Rory had hoped to catch the eleven o'clock news, but his father was deep into a movie, then the Johnny Carson show, so he had gone to bed depressed.

But he had found sleep impossible.

Every time he closed his eyes, Kathy's terrified face haunted him. And in his ears droned the chant he had heard at the rally in Bryant Park.

"Two, four, six, eight—pornography is woman-hate."

Quietly he climbed out of bed and on tiptoes so as not to awaken his father, he crossed the creaky floor and gently closed and locked his bedroom door, then turned on the desk lamp.

Three A.M. He'd lain awake four hours, thinking. At least he now knew the first step toward his salvation; the beautiful girl at the rally had made that clear enough.

Don't wait till morning. Begin now!

From between volumes of the encylcopedia set his Grandmother Malone had left him, he began extracting his secreted pornography: damaged hardcore photographs purchased at the Metropole for half-price with his lawn-mowing money; slender issues of *Danish Erotica*, which couched the sexual exploits of its heroines in stories of escalating eroticism and violence; selected centerfolds carefully removed from *Penthouse, Chic, Playboy*, the staple holes patched with clear tape.

Look analytically, not sexually, at the pictures! Do not get aroused!

He had all night to scrutinize the pictures and sort them

according to the wisdom he had heard in the park.

Unable to enjoy the movie at the Rivoli, he had left the theater, wandered along Broadway, then east on Forty-second Street until he had spotted the crowd in Bryant Park. Just his dumb luck to happen upon a feminist rally against pornography.

But he had not realized the nature of the rally when he entered the park and, anxious to catch news of Kathy Bauer's condition, sat on a bench beside a boy holding a portable radio.

Rock music blaring from the radio swamped the woman's voice coming over the loudspeaker and muffled the frequent cheers and boos from the large audience—an audience he later realized was composed of an incongruous mixture of well-dressed women, a handful of businessmen, and many derelicts.

The periodic chant from the group of young women in the front row finally caught his attention and piqued his curiosity. Moving toward the podium, he couldn't take his eyes off the woman with streaked blond hair and oversize sunglasses who was leaning over a microphone. Her voice boomed:

"Pornography is to women what Klan literature is to blacks or Nazi propaganda is to Jews."

Like cold water flung in his face, her words opened his eyes, and quickly he became aware of the multitude of homemade placards bobbing and swaying above women's heads—hundreds of heads, brown, red, black, blond—all glistening in the fast-ebbing daylight.

> WOMEN UNITE, TAKE BACK THE NIGHT.
> AGAINST OUR WILL!
> PORNOGRAPHY IS NOT PROTECTED
> BY THE FIRST AMENDMENT.

Edging closer to the elevated platform and women speakers, he noticed the neatly printed banner advertising names that were unfamiliar to him: Abzug, Steinem, Brownmiller.

Next to him a middle-aged man attired in an expensive-looking suit shouted to the speaker. "Women who want the government to ban sexist material are the new McCarthyites. It's the same old censorship in radical garb."

On the dais and in the audience women suddenly stared in his direction. Not at him, but he felt as if they were. Intensely uncomfortable in the moment of silence that followed, he fought the urge to run. There was something to be learned here. As the speaker regained composure and resumed her talk, a reddish-blond-haired girl in her mid-twenties who was standing in front of him turned.

"You're confusing pornography, which is marked by cruelty and violence, with erotica," she said. "Erotica is rooted in the idea of free will and love."

"Bullshit!" said the man.

Rory was between them. The girl was lovely, and her words struck him as revelatory and relevant. For a moment he swore she had addressed him, and, blushing, he avoided her bright green eyes.

"Pornography," she said with deliberate equanimity and patience, "is about brutality, degradation, humiliation. It's about power and domination over women. It has nothing to do with sex. Erotica is about sex."

"You're full of it," bullied the man. "Obviously some guy's done a job on you. I buy what I like."

"And so too can this young boy, a minor, at any of the sex shops along this street. That's wrong and dangerous."

His impulse to run was overpowered by a stronger impulse to stare at this lovely, sexy creature, this angel who seemed wise beyond her years, who apparently possessed answers to his many perplexing questions. Never, for instance, had he heard of—or imagined—the distinction between pornography and erotica as she expressed it.

A group of women who had been listening to the conversation began booing the man, who in turn flicked them the finger and began pushing his way through the crowd. Rory thought the women were going to assault the man physically.

Glancing back, his eyes locked with the girl's and he thought he would burst with the desire to touch her, to become acquainted with her, to share her wisdom. A few words from her would be worth thousands from Gerhardt.

"You understand," she said, smiling at him, lips glistening pink against her tanned, slightly freckled face, "we're not against erotica. That's fine. And healthy."

Talk, you idiot, say something, this is your in, your big chance. But his dominant thought was to kiss those delicious lips.

"Aggressive pornography is responsbile for the increase in crimes of wife beating and rape. You should listen to the whole rally. By the way, how old are you?"

". . . *my pleasure to introduce our next speaker, Carrie Wilson.*"

"Excuse me," she said, touching his arm and squeezing past him, her hair brushing against his face. "They're calling me. It's my turn."

Roses. Her hair smelled of tea roses, and he imbibed the fragrance.

"Here's some of our literature. Read it; pass it on to your buddies."

Even when she had moved through the crowd to ascend the steps to the platform, he found himself involuntarily inhaling, attempting to recapture the fading scent of her hair. Where she had touched him, his arm tingled, the sensation suffusing his entire body. The next thing he remembered was hearing her amplified voice.

"*I used to think of rapists as old or decrepit men hiding in alleys. But they're our uncles, fathers, boyfriends.*"

He squirmed.

"*I've seen them from all walks of life . . . from doctors and lawyers, to the unemployed.*"

How did she see so much?

"*It's difficult to find a commonality, except that in their minds sex and aggression are inextricably paired.*"

His heart stopped. Perspiration poured down his back. She knew him. Her talk had been written for his benefit, tailored to his behavior. He pleasured women with his thoughts, against their will, and now he suspected they felt his advances. If . . . if it was true, he was a rapist. Never before had he categorized himself with that ignoble breed of men, and the startling association shot a pain through his groin. He'd raped Kathy Bauer. All the others. *Pleasuring* was a euphemism for *rape;* his lovers were victims; his lovemaking was a travesty of loving.

Certain Carrie Wilson could read the terrible secret of his eyes, he had hurried from Bryant Park and wandered the streets of Manhattan until it was time to return home to Queens.

Seated at his desk, attempting to distinguish pornography from erotica turned out to be far more difficult than he had imagined; Carrie Wilson's guidance would have been invaluable. Did a woman laughing render an aggressive scene harmless? Did a man shooting sperm over a woman's face constitute an act of "humiliation and degradation"? Carrie had used those words. He would certainly find the act humiliating and degrading if someone did it to him. In numerous pictures a woman was forced to accept an erection into her mouth, the man's hands, holding her head firmly in place, the only evidence of force—did this qualify as violence?

Painstakingly scrutinizing each picture, separating the material into two piles—one to be burned, the other saved—he found it impossible not to get excited over the glossy images: the young girl in a bathtub, her legs draped over the tub's sides, the water from the faucet pleasuring her, the water an infinitely long penis perpetually penetrating her. The tanned, naked brunet in the swimming pool ecstaticly nuzzling her crotch over the inflated nose of a lifesize rubber dolphin. Before he had finished sorting the material his erection poked through the fly of his pajamas, and he realized that he'd been involuntarily rubbing its head against the underside of his desk top.

Reaching down, he began to stroke himself, confining his eyes solely to an erotic, not pornographic, picture. And yet spontaneously, uncontrollably, Carrie's face, her radiant green eyes and golden strawberry hair, crept into the inchoate fantasy. Carrie was the woman in the tub, and he opened the faucet to drive into her thicker and harder. Leaning closer to the picture, he actually smelled her rose-scented hair.

No, not Carrie; I want to think of her only in romantic, sexless ways.

And his greatest fear, the one he dared not articulate, was that wherever Carrie was, she might feel his lips on her breasts, his fingers slipping between her legs.

He selected other pictures, other women, but they all became Carrie. No, he mustn't sully her, subject her to a sordid fantasy. He never did it to Melissa and wouldn't to Carrie. Yet the pulsating energy that fueled his power had already forged the infrangible link between his mind and his groin. He recognized the sensations—the pounding in his head, the electricity sparking nerve endings throughout his body, the urgent contracting of his scrotum—and he knew events were beyond his control. He was held hostage.

Not Carrie; please don't let me take her.

Might he be able to spare Carrie by fantasizing a lover he had pleasured before, one who had provided an exceptionally strong, satisfying experience?

As the image of a lover flashed to mind, he heard his father in the hall: footsteps approaching his bedroom door. Holding his breath—he hadn't realized how loud he was panting—his jerking hand stopped, tightly squeezing his erection as if strangling it silent, dead. The footsteps passed his door, scuffed down the hall, and entered the bathroom. Although his door was locked, he could not risk his father investigating and finding out about his pornography. All hell would break loose. Quickly he slipped the material under the mattress, turned out the desk light, and jumped into bed.

11

Webb hadn't slept much. Now, at sunrise, he sat at the kitchen table attempting to concentrate on his paper for the

American Journal of Criminology. But his thoughts remained scattered.

First the shattering disappointment that he didn't have a strong suspect in the subway pushings. Having laboriously interviewed the twelve witnesses, the case against the boy who'd fled from the subway station was dishearteningly weak. One witness swore the kid pushed Kathy Bauer; one was equally certain he never touched her; ten only saw the boy fleeing. Fleeing for what reason, though? There must be an explanation for the boy's peculiar behavior.

He'd also lain awake mulling over Sergeant Bauer's reaction. Bauer's determination to catch the assailant had transformed a prefunctory police duty to an obsessive, maniacal quest. That augured danger, especially with Bauer. It could lead to a hasty false arrest; an innocent kid condemned for life, all to assuage a sergeant's thirst for revenge.

"Release the goddamn composite," Bauer had insisted on arriving at the station and finding the artist's sketch completed. "What the hell are we waiting for?"

Webb had offered logic. "Lou, I interviewed the witnesses myself. Only one woman claims she saw the kid push your niece. And I must admit her story is riddled with inconsistencies."

"Then why the fuck was he running?"

"I don't know. Maybe he is a criminal. Maybe he planned to steal a wallet or purse. Perhaps he intended to push someone off the platform, and when he saw Kathy fall, he panicked and hightailed it out of there."

"With the sketch in the *News*, the *Post*, and on TV, we'd get him fast. We always do."

"So we'd have a suspect. A kid's name, face, family history, what he eats and when he shits are splashed in the media. All while we try to construct a case against him— something I doubt we can do. If he's innocent, we've ruined his life. No, it's not my way. We need more concrete evidence first." Of course, when—and if—Kathy Bauer regained consciousness, he'd question her.

Bauer had fumed.

"Look, Lou, that's my irrevocable decision. If DeCosta had brought the kid in immediately after the incident, we could have questioned him then and let him go if we thought he was innocent. But if we bring him in through a manhunt, the media will massacre the boy."

By ten o'clock there was nothing more to detain him at the station. He had dismissed Bauer to spend the night at the hospital with Kathy's parents, and he'd long abandoned the wild hope that Carrie just might return after the rally. Though if she had, he wondered if he would have spent the night at her apartment; consummated their strange relationship. Unlikely. Though it was becoming harder to deny his longing for her and his suspicion that if he didn't act fast he'd lose her. He had decided then that if the subway case was solved by late August, he would accept the offer to vacation at her summer place.

On the horizon the sun flared a brilliant orange. You didn't have to be a detective to know a scorcher was in the making.

Tossing a stale, half-eaten Twinkie into the trash bag beside the refrigerator, he returned to the kitchen table to commence work. The tabletop was concealed under neat piles of notes, journal articles, newspaper clippings, and criminal statistics books—all material for his paper, "Pornography and Crime." He hadn't touched the stuff since Carrie had stopped by a few nights ago—"just to deliver more research; no ulterior motives, I swear"—and organized his scattered notes.

He had been drinking and felt nervous being alone with her for the first time. Had it been so long since he was with a woman that he was afraid of failure? After two drinks and some stiff precinct talk, they'd argued.

"You realize you have less than a month to complete the paper to qualify for this year's award. The deadline's Labor Day."

"Luv, I'm well aware of that. Don't lecture me. I not only intend to beat the deadline but win that goddamn prize again. I don't know why it means so much to me."

"Because you have to prove you're more than just a New York City policeman; that you're a psychologist first."

"Did you come here to belittle me?"

"There you go. I belittle you by calling you a cop. See what I mean, thickhead? Jesus, why do I bother with you?"

"Then don't. I didn't invite you here. The research could have waited till tomorrow."

She had stormed out the door, and he had spent the rest of the night regretting his words—and inaction.

He glanced at the stacks of dirty dishes that filled the sink, spilling onto the counter; at the day-old Pepsi perched precariously on top of the pile of books on the kitchen table. The place had never looked this disheveled under Julie's fastidious hands. Carrie had offered to clean up, but he'd refused.

He must clear his thoughts of Carrie and focus on his paper. With three hours remaining before reporting to work, he should at least be able to write the opening paragraphs. His thesis, though it was controversial, was quickly gaining acceptance: In males—though not in females—exposure to aggressive pornography causes increased aggressive behavior. This in turn can—and does—lead to violent sexual crimes.

"A man's sexuality," Carrie had answered smugly when he had asked her to account for the sex difference, "displays a greater capacity for objectification, is performance oriented, and thus responds actively and aggressively to visual stimuli. We women internalize and romanticize sexual stimuli; thus we render them passive."

"I'll bet there's nothing passive about you," he'd joked, and she had challenged him to research that hypothesis personally.

How to begin? Perusing the index cards, he selected one and studied it. He needed a sensational opening sentence but was having difficulty concentrating. Bauer was still on his mind, specifically the words they'd exchanged on parting.

"Lou, by any chance is your niece prone to epileptic seizures?"

"Shit, no! Why?"

"One witness claims Kathy was spastic before the accident, that she seemed sick."

"She's no epileptic. Occasionally she . . ."

"She what?"

"Gets headaches, migraines. It's nothing, really; runs in the family."

Bauer might be concealing something. At the top of the page, above the title "Pornography and Crime," he typed:

check into kathy bauer's medical history

He picked up Carrie's notes on that summer's National Conference on Violence Against Women; she had attended the four-day meeting in Montreal and had been impressed by the lecture of psychologist Gerhardt Kiner. Using college students, Kiner had conducted a landmark experiment that offered the strongest proof yet that violent pornography was responsible for increased aggression toward women. Kiner was at Columbia University, Webb recalled; he'd pay the psychologist a visit this coming week. On the third page, midway down, he spotted Carrie's notes on Kiner's lecture and a gripping statistic to open his paper with. He typed:

"One out of every four girls born in the United States will be raped or molested by the time she is eighteen years old—by a father, brother, uncle, or stranger."

For him the beginning was always the toughest part; now the rest of the paper should flow easily. He might polish it up at Carrie's summer place if he indeed went; she'd be a big help.

Carrie. He wondered how her presentation had been received at the rally. Successfully, he hoped. She had sweated over the speech, extracting statistics from the research she'd completed for him. Blockhead! You should have been there to cheer her on. You could have spared the time. He would phone her. Too early to now; but later in the day.

12

Rory anxiously waited for his father to finish with that morning's *Daily News*. An article on Kathy Bauer's condition and the police's suspicions concerning the accident must be in the paper. Suppose it were accompanied by a drawing of him and the headline BOY WANTED FOR QUESTIONING. Would his father, his classmates—especially Melissa—recognize him?

His father sat at the kitchen table, a bowl of soggy Grape Nuts protruding from beneath the open paper.

The morning sunlight, already intense, sprawled across the kitchen counter, stopping short of where Rory stood, eating from a box of chocolate-covered doughnuts. He hadn't had any appetite for the orange juice, eggs, and cereal he had by routine prepared for his father. But with three gardening jobs scheduled today, he realized the need to get something into himself.

"Any more coffee?" Mike Malone asked from behind the paper.

Orders or criticism were his father's two occasions for conversation, and these comments invariably wafted from behind a newspaper, or over the rim of a beer can, or ricocheted off the television screen.

From a plastic container in the refrigerator he poured cold coffee into a pan. He'd learned to save considerable time by preparing large quantities of coffee and food once or twice a week and reheating it as needed. Some of his warmed-over dishes appeared decidedly unpalatable (he didn't eat them), but the taste of food was his father's least concern; he only griped if a meal was not on the table at the expected time.

"This fuckin' city's sick," said Mike Malone as Rory placed the coffee on the table.

His father had spotted the article on Kathy Bauer!

"Thirteen fuckin' bank robberies yesterday. Ten the day before. If the damn niggers and spics want money let them work for it. Nobody wants to put in an honest day's work."

Rory retreated to the sink and began washing dishes.

"It's even spread to that fancy Upper East Side. Two town houses burglarized, and some pervert killed an old lady for her diamonds. They don't print the prick's name because he's a minor. Jesus! They should write it in the sky and electrocute him in Times Square. I'd sure as hell be there. And you can bet I wouldn't be the only spectator."

A picture of Kathy. A drawing of him. They had to be there.

"I should have listened to your mother and gotten her out of this city years ago. She'd be alive today."

Rory wanted to shout, "Shut up! Her death was an accident that could have happened anywhere." Returning home from shopping one afternoon, Grace Malone had walked alongside a building to get out of the rain. A brick fell from the facade, killing her instantly. The police report read "accidental death," but Mike Malone didn't buy that. "They'll never convince me it wasn't thrown by kids after sick thrills," he'd insisted.

For weeks after the accident his father had remained despondent, taciturn, so consumed by his own grief that he had never even inquired about Rory's pain. When his father resumed living it was to take up a different life—in fact, he became a different man. While prior to Grace Malone's death, Mike had spent only one night out, Wednesday (and this was a continual source of friction between his parents, though Rory didn't then understand why), with Grace gone, Mike ventured out almost nightly, returning home, usually drunk, at all hours or sometimes the next afternoon.

If Rory had not assumed all the household chores he might not have learned of his father's whereabouts. One morning, emptying pants pockets for the wash, he had found a ticket stub for Xtascy, a midtown massage parlor he'd frequently seen advertised in *Screw*. Shocked, but now alerted to this aspect of his father's personality, Rory began taking extra care emptying all shirt and pants pockets, and within a month's time he had accumulated stubs to more than a dozen parlors, many with names unfamiliar to him.

He guessed the nature of his father's previous Wednesday nights out, the reason for the friction between his parents, for his mother's hysterical tears; and the aphorism whispered to him by his father when he was intoxicated—"Boy, there are two kinds of women: one you marry, one you fuck"—assumed a disturbing new light. At this time the poltergeist events mysteriously began around the house. ("Triggered by grief over the loss of his mother, rage and hatred at his father's cheating," Gerhardt Kiner had said on first analyzing the case.) Three months later Mike Malone discovered Rory secreting the stubs in a shoe box beneath his bed and thrashed his son mercilessly. That evening marked the first poltergeist attack, in which objects suddenly flew in all directions at Mike Malone. ("Understandable," Liz Hartman had commented.)

His father laid down the paper, stood, and was about to leave for work in the garage, which he had converted into a carpentry shop, when Rory tentatively approached him.

"If it'd be okay, I'd like to borrow the car tomorrow night."

For the first time that morning Mike Malone stared at his son. "Christ! what did you do to your hair?"

"It was too hot, long. I cut it."

"You mean you scalped yourself."

Rory shrugged.

"Boy, why'd you do a thing like that?"

"I didn't have money for a haircut."

"I thought you were pulling it in hand over fist from your lawn jobs."

"I'm saving that for college."

"Well, you should have asked. I'd have given you the money. Jesus! You look like a fuckin' freak."

Instantly Mike Malone regretted what he'd said. *Freak* was a dangerous word between them. When Mike had first realized that Rory was responsible for ashtrays, glasses, and silverware sailing through the house, striking him, drawing blood, he'd begun calling Rory that. After a particularly violent incident in which a letter opener gashed his cheek dangerously close to the eye, Dr. Hartman had cautioned: "Mr. Malone, if you want these attacks on the house and on you to stop, I suggest the first thing you do is stop referring to your son as a freak." And he had.

Now he monitored Rory's reaction to the incendiary word.

"You don't have to worry, Pop. The power is gone. It is. You believe me, don't you? Nothing's happened for a year."

His statement was partially true. The random, uncontrolled power was gone. He could never let his father know about his work with Dr. Hartman. She was supposed to have destroyed the power, not refined it.

"I hope so, boy. I really hope it's gone for good."

But Mike Malone wasn't really convinced. The power had suddenly come out of the blue, and surely it could return just as unexpectedly. A week before the first freaky events began, Mike recalled, Rory had experienced sleepless nights. Well, the boy had been awake last night all night; Mike had heard him up and about, quietly locking his door, pussyfootin' around the room. Was the freaky power building up strength, getting ready to erupt? Burly Mike Malone didn't like living in fear of his son one fuckin' bit; in fact, he wouldn't tolerate it again.

"Pop," Rory said, "I'd like to borrow the car tomorrow night."

"For that drive-in again?"

"Yes."

"What's wrong with a real theater? Too respectable for you?"

"They're more money." He knew his father's real concern: Melissa. Her black hair, dark brown eyes, and creamy skin reminded Mike of his wife Grace when they'd first met. From pictures in the family album of Grace Bellini as a teenager, Rory could see the resemblance.

"I never took your mother to a drive-in. A guy goes there for one thing."

"Pop, I've never touched Melissa. She's not like that." That was the truth.

Standing at the kitchen door, his father scowled: "Well, see that you don't. She's a damn decent kid. If you want to fool around, there are girls aplenty for that kind of thing."

Finally Mike Malone was gone.

Leaning over the newspaper, Rory scrutinized each page. A shooting. Knifing. Bank robberies. Coke bust. Disco fire. It *had* to be there. He started again, more carefully this time. On page 5 he spotted a short article and sank into the chair. "Doctors Reattach Girl's Leg." It had been played down, labeled an accident, not a crime. That was why his father had missed it.

Nausea overtook him. Oh, God, poor Kathy!

The phone rang, startling him. He couldn't answer it now. He raced through the article . . . "fell under a train . . . taken to New York Hospital . . . a four-hour operation . . . still unconscious (then they haven't been able to question her yet) . . . critical but expected to pull through."

She'd live; he'd be able to speak with her.

The phone stopped.

No mention of a boy running from the scene. That astonished him. Perhaps he wasn't a suspect after all. The people on the platform must have told the police he had never touched Kathy Bauer. If so, the police wouldn't be after him. That must be why there was no mention of a boy, no police sketch. How foolish he felt. He had been needlessly sweating the police.

Then he remembered Kathy Bauer. When she regained consciousness, the police would surely question her. He had to know what she would tell them. Now he knew where to find her.

13

Again Liz phoned the Malone number. Rory or his father had to be home; it was Saturday. She wanted desperately to speak with Rory, but so urgent was the nature of her call that now she'd even settle for Mike Malone, distasteful as that would be. Not only was she terribly worried about still not hearing from Rory, but she had a request that needed an immediate reply: Cheryl Roland had entered the Black Room and been so astonished with the room—and her performance in it—that she'd convinced James Gray to spend the weekend in the city and return to Columbia on Monday to witness Rory perform—if Liz could guarantee he would show up.

Oh, Rory, please be home. Answer the phone. Please promise me you'll come on Monday. This time she would let it ring an hour if necessary.

"Is it really the blackest place on earth?" Cheryl inquired.

"Absolutely," answered Gerhardt. "Blacker than black. We took extraordinary measures to ensure that it was theoretically devoid of all light—even single photons."

"It has an ambient dark current of less than one billionth of an ampere," said Liz, correcting Gerhardt's slight exaggeration: A few photons sneaked in. "You can't enter the room wearing certain types of clothing—nylon, for instance—because its electrostatic discharge registers as light."

"My blouse is cotton," said Cherly Roland, accompanying Liz, Gerhardt, and James Gray down the hall to the Black Room.

"It's dyed yellow," said Liz, "and the fluorescence of

certain dyes is also detected by the photomultiplier tubes. They're liquid-nitrogen cooled and extremely sensitive to even a few photons. I'm afraid you'll have to remove not only your blouse but strip entirely." Amused at the aghast look on Cheryl Roland's face, Liz immediately added, "Don't worry, I'll give you a neutral fabric cloth to wrap around your waist. But you will have to remain bare from the waist up. Human biocurrents are very weak."

Gerhardt, turning to James Gray, offered, "If you'd like to enter the room, I'll loan you a pair of special cotton briefs. Of course, the less you wear, the better the chance of measuring your biocurrents. My wife and I enter in the buff. So did Mr. Malone initially, but that's no longer necessary with him."

"No, thank you; I'll watch."

Timidly Cheryl Roland slid behind the screen to undress while Liz draped the neutral fabric over the top.

"We even had to avoid using certain construction materials and paints," said Liz, "because they emit too much radiation. It required three months of testing before we hit on all the right materials."

"This light you claim to measure," whined James Gray, "is a human electric field, an aura—something we all possess?"

"Some of us possess it to a greater degree than others," Liz intoned. Then immediately regretting the dig, she added quite technically, "The human body is wrapped in a finely spun electromagnetic cocoon. The currents are invisible to the naked eye, but of course we measure heart biocurrents in an EKG and brain biocurrents in an EEG. Our detection equipment in the Black Room measures the entire human field, or glow, if you like. For Rory Malone, his Tinkerbell." She had given the traveling light that name because it reminded her of the fairy in *Peter Pan*.

"I'm ready," came Cheryl Roland's voice from behind the screen.

Gerhardt and James Gray turned their backs while Liz escorted Cheryl Roland (blushing so much that Liz wondered if that would increase her biocurrents) into the Black Room and positioned her in front of the array of photomultiplier tubes that resembled the greatly enlarged eye of a fly.

"Stand as still as you can and breath rhythmically. When I leave the room and lock the door, the light will automatically go off. You'll be in utter blackness."

"You'll come back for me?"

"Of course. There's nothing to be afraid of. You're in a sealed vault, shielded from every earthly stimuli. By the way, what part of your cycle are you in?"

"My what?"

"Your menstrual cycle. What time of month?"

"Is that relevant?"

"Very much so. Harold Burr at Yale found that a woman's biocurrents take a huge voltage increase at the time of ovulation, and that high persists until menstrual flow begins."

"If I'm on time, my period should start early next week. I'm pretty regular."

"Perfect," answered Liz. "Enjoy the solitude. You'll probably never be so alone again."

Cheryl Roland had glowed with a respectable dark current of 0.5 microamps. Liz had then explained that the week prior to her own period she usually registered a dark current of 1.9; while Gerhardt, depending on his mood, health, or degree of exhaustion, ranged from 0.002 to 0.4.

"Of course, Rory Malone makes us all pale," Liz had added. "A supernova to our meager sparks. Not only can he drive the equipment offscale on good days, but he doesn't even have to be in the room bodily to do it."

"Hello."

Mike Malone's voice. She hated to speak with him.

"It's Dr. Hartman, Mr. Malone. I hope I'm not disturbing you."

"You brought me in from the shop." The fuckin' ringing was driving him crazy; he had no choice but to answer the phone. Now he wondered why she was calling. He hadn't heard from her in a year.

"May I speak with Rory?" asked Liz, aware that Mike

Malone apparently still hadn't forgiven her for prying into Rory's home life.

"He's out mowing lawns. I don't expect him back till late in the day."

She didn't wish to get Rory in trouble, but her curiosity and concern for the boy surfaced.

"Mr. Malone, I realize we haven't spoken for quite some time. There really hasn't been any need to. Rory tells me everything has been fine at home. Well, lately Rory's been a little distant at our weekly meetings, as though something was troubling him. I don't mean to interfere in your personal affairs, but this is important. You realize that, I'm sure. Has there been any friction between you and Rory?"

Mike frowned. Jesus! It *was* happening again. She too detected a change in him. The power was returning.

"There's been no friction here," he assured her.

"None?"

"That's what I said."

Mike Malone suddenly was uncomfortably aware of the moisture between his palm and the phone receiver. "Tell me the truth, doctor; is his power returning? Level with me."

The unconcealed fear in his voice surprised Liz, but it shouldn't have. She recalled that when she and Gerhardt had first met Mike Malone, terror had shone in his eyes. Mike Malone, a bully, she was sure, suddenly was frightened of his young son. The stitches in his cheeks had been a source of intense embarrassment, and when she'd inquired if he'd been struck during any other poltergeist bursts, he had reluctantly unbuttoned his shirt to reveal a whopping bruise covering his right lower ribs. "A marble ashtray," was all he'd proffered.

"Mr. Malone, I can assure you there will be no more poltergeist outbursts at home. None." That was true enough. She wondered how he would react if he knew that instead of wasting Rory's talent, she'd nurtured it into a genuine scientific marvel. Not very well. Not well at all.

"How was he last night?" Mike asked.

The question startled her. Wherever Rory had gone, it was also a secret to his father.

"Rory was a little quiet last night. But as long as you assure me there's no trouble at home, I assure you we have nothing to worry about. Nothing at all. I'd like to speak with Rory when he gets home. Would you have him phone me? It's important. I'll be at the laboratory until six o'clock, then he can reach me at home . . . Mr. Malone?"

"Yes, yes, I'll tell him . . . You don't think . . ."

"Think what?"

"Nothing. Forget it."

14

Mike Malone hung up the phone and wiped his sweating palms on his overalls. Even if the power was returning, Rory had no cause to use it against him. Sure, they'd never been pals, but for the last several months at least there'd been no arguments between them. They'd gone their separate ways, conversing only when one of them required something from the other.

Relax; you're no chicken-shit. You can protect yourself from a scrawny kid if you have to.

But then he wouldn't have to. The power wasn't returning. The doctor had assured him of that. He was just being paranoid. She was getting rid of the freaky thing, had already destroyed it. "Don't tell me how you're gonna do it, just do it," he'd once told her, and he still didn't want the details.

Twelve thirty. He should have lunch—phone Lil. She was probably just opening McGregor's. He'd better call before the afternoon crowd descended on the bar.

"It's Mike. Just checkin' what time you're comin' over."

"Hi, Mike! We might be real busy tonight. I might have to stay extra."

"So you come afterward. Whatever time, it doesn't make much difference."

"Well, Mike, I don't know."

"Ya don't know what?"

"If I'm coming over."

"What the hell do ya mean, you don't know? Every Saturday for two months you've come. Ya had to work last week, now this week. What's up?"

"Nothing. Nothing, really."

"Lil, what the hell's troubling you?"

"Mike, is Rory going to be home tonight?"

"What the shit difference does that make?"

"Will he?"

"If he is, he'll stay in his room."

"Mike, Rory doesn't like me. I don't think he approves of us. And he doesn't respect me because I work in a bar."

"Has that bastard ever said anything to you? I'll break his fuckin' head if he has."

"Oh, no, Mike, he's never said a word. Your kid's always decent enough with me. It's not his words that bother me."

"What then?"

"I don't know. I can't put my finger on it. The way he looks at me sometimes. It's creepy. I feel he hates me. That he wants to hurt me. Break us up."

"Lil, it's all in your mind. You're crazy."

"No, Mike, something's wrong with *him*. I'm glad we're finally having this out. I've seen it in his eyes. Something real strange. I can't look directly at him. Neither can you, I've noticed."

"Cut that shit out! Ya hear! Never another word about him! You get your ass over here tonight or else we're finished. He won't be home. I'll make sure of that."

He slammed down the receiver and dropped into the kitchen chair. For a long while his mind was a complete blank, his fingers idly shredding the edge of the newspaper that lay open in front of him. Then he thought what he had been avoiding thinking throughout the conversation: Lil feels it, too: the power, the threat of violence. Rory *was* turning into a freak again.

He had never really been cured.

15

With his Sony radio swinging from the handle of the lawn mower, all morning Rory had kept current with news reports on Kathy Bauer: Her general health had improved, but she remained unconscious.

However, by noon the announcer was reporting that Kathy Bauer was now believed to be the latest victim of the Subway Pusher: A witness claimed she had seen the girl being pushed by a young white boy. Rory knew the woman was lying but wondered if she'd told her fabrication to the police and if they had believed her. If so, he thought, the police would definitely question Kathy. The temptation to abandon the day's lawn jobs and head directly to New York Hospital was overwhelming; but suppose Kathy didn't regain consciousness for several hours? Loitering around the hospital could only increase his appearance of guilt. No, he would wait and go at the right moment.

At least gardening in the hot sun had helped divert his thoughts from Dr. Hartman and sex.

Mowing the Bronsons' three acres, weeding Mrs. Bronson's vegetable garden, and trimming the hedges that lined the property had taken him two and a half hours. Now he was weeding around the shrubbery in the area of the swimming pool. He had purposely avoided this section for as long as possible because irresistible temptations lurked here.

Diving, swimming, sunning themselves, and acting sophisticated (for his benefit, he was certain), Christina Bronson and four girl friends, probably college classmates, provided stimulation he could do without. Clad in a brightly colored bikini, each girl was disturbingly attractive. Periodically glancing up from the shrubbery, he wondered if all the women at Christina's college had such knockout shapes. Wet, the bikinis clung to the contours of their suntanned bodies; the white suit on the blond on the raft in the pool was practically transparent.

As he moved from bush to bush, the girls joked, sipped drinks, lounged either on red rafts in the pool or on white-and-green recliners. For a while they seemed to be deliberately ignoring his presence: Older girls often acted blind to a kid his age. But when he began weeding between the small, T-shape evergreens in full view of them, they appeared to flaunt their bodies in his direction. He was certain of that.

Christina Bronson stood more erect, her chest out; the redhead in the green bikini definitely strutted in a smooth, sexy gait when she passed by; and the blond on the raft frequently propped herself up on her elbows and adjusted the top of her suit. It wasn't just his imagination, either. Perhaps girls did this instinctively, in innate female response to a male presence. Only the two girls on recliners, their eyes closed, were not teasing him.

Shirtless, wearing loose-fitting cutoffs and a red terry cloth headband to keep the sweat from his eyes, he finished amid the bushes and began weeding around the begonias, closer to the girls.

"Can you believe the summer's almost over?" said Christina, pouring cranberry juice and vodka from a frosted pitcher, offering the glass to Blythe Smith, who was not quite finished applying suntan lotion to her legs. "It's positively diabolical how fast summers go. Do you think it's a plot to make us miserable?"

"I've always believed parents control the seasons," mused Blythe, "lengthening the dreary months, shortening the sweetest ones. My summer in Europe, which was costing my parents oodles and oodles, passed with suspicious speed."

"How perceptive of you, Blythe, dear," called Danielle Critchett, floating on a red raft in the pool. "And what a smashingly original hypothesis. Do parents also control the lengths of our love affairs? They must. I always get bored just when he becomes most devoted to me."

Flipping off the raft, she swam in long, clean strokes to the edge of the pool and hoisted herself out of the water onto the artificial grass that surrounded the pool. Squeezing water from her long golden hair, she whispered, "Christina, who is that sexy cherub?"

"A little young for you, dear, don't you think?"

"If he can make me bleed he's old enough."

"How gross!" exclaimed Blythe. "Must you always attempt to shock us with your crass expressions?"

"To say nothing of her even crasser behavior," called Sissy Germain, sitting up on one of the recliners and for the first time spotting the young gardener. "Holy Toledo! Danielle, you could practically be his grandmother."

Sexy cherub. Then it wasn't his imagination. At least the one in the pool had been eyeing him. The sexiest of the bunch, too.

Be good. You must.

Collecting the pulled weeds and shaking the soil from their roots, he emptied them into the wheelbarrow and moved on to the last flower bed. This brought him still closer to the girls, but he swore he wouldn't look up at them, regardless of what they said about him.

And he didn't.

But he must have, for how else did he know that the blond had removed her top and now lay stretched out on a towel on the grass? He'd uprooted two begonias before he realized he was staring at her.

Don't get excited. You mustn't let her get to you. You've been good all day.

A Siamese cat darted from beneath an evergreen, ran across the grass, and rubbed affectionately against Christina Bronson's leg.

"Go play, Biffy. Catch a butterfly. Scat."

The cat meandered across the lawn and sat on the towel next to the blond. The brush of fur against bare flesh startled her upright and her tanned breasts bounced, then came to rest, dangling slightly downward.

No, don't do it to her. Think of Jeepy. Remember, you killed Jeepy!

That might act as a deterrent.

Jeepy.

Dr. Hartman had obtained a stray kitten from the Humane Society and surprised him with it. For a month he exclusively was to raise the kitten, establish a friendship—"a dependency," she'd said. "Cats are supposed to be the most psychic of all animals. If that snake in the terrarium detected your Tinkerbell—I'm sorry, Rory, your presence—a pet kitten, totally dependent on you, should be an even more sensitive detector."

And Jeepy had been.

At the end of the month he had brought Jeepy back to the laboratory, and Gerhardt had placed the cat in a small room in which the floor had been scored in a large checkerboard pattern, each square numbered. Alone, the kitten cried and wandered randomly about the room, seeking an exit. Concentrating in an adjacent room, he eventually succeeded in projecting his energy—his consciousness, Gerhardt called it—into the room with Jeepy. Immediately Jeepy ceased crying. Psychically he moved from square to square, as Gerhardt called out various numbers over the intercom. And amazingly, Jeepy followed his invisible presence, sitting herself on a particular square, purring contently, then suddenly shifting to another square as he changed locations.

The experiment had been running smoothly until Gerhardt had suddenly conceived a brainstorm idea.

"I want you to pick up the pussy, Rory. You can do it. You've lifted objects ten times heavier."

He would have to concentrate his energy considerably to perform that physical task, and instinctively he worried that Jeepy might be frightened by the strong force field. Until now he'd lifted only inanimate objects, never a living creature.

"I better not do it."

"What do you mean, Rory? Of course you can do it. Concentrate on the pussy. Wrap your arms around her. Pick her up."

"No, Dr. Kiner. She'll be afraid."

"Go after the pussy, Rory. Get her. Come on."

"No, please. I may hurt her."

"Nonsense, Rory. I order you to pet the pussy, hug her, lift her. Now!"

The blond on the grass stood. She lifted the Siamese cat into her arms, and it nuzzled its head against her bare breasts.

"Oh, Biffy, you tickle! Stop that."

Automatically his eyes locked onto her swaying breasts. The flesh glistened with a beaded layer of perspiration on top of tanning lotion; her nipples were hard, brushing against the cat's furry coat.

He imagined what it must feel like to be in Biffy's place, under those pendulous breasts, smelling sweat commingling with suntan lotion, licking it off.

As the blond petted the cat, he imagined her stroking his hair, clutching it between her fingers, tugging at it, directing his parted lips to her nipple, him taking the nipple gently between his teeth.

"Wow, easy, Biffy! Don't use your claws."

Don't do this to her. Stop yourself. Now!

"Hug the pussy, Rory. Caress her. She's your pussy. You won't hurt her. Lift her. Now!"

Please, God, let me spare this girl. Please!

But the infrangible link was forged. The power pressed achingly against his cutoffs, throbbing, attempting to break free.

Run! Run away from here, before it's too late.

That was his only hope. Standing, covering his crotch with his hands, he turned and began racing across the lawn.

"Get the pussy, Rory. Hug the pussy. Lift her in your arms."

But it was too late. He felt the power pulsating in his scrotum, squeezing its way through his abdomen, a hot, surging fluid sinuously routing itself to an exit. But he was not going to let the power escape this time.

Control it. You can do it.

"The pussy, Rory. Hug the pussy. NOW!"

He was beyond the main hedge that lined the property, vaulting the low stone-and-mortar wall, when he heard a girl's shrill screams. Landing on the pavement, not stopping to glance back, he knew only one thing: The power was already subsiding, and he had not come. He had controlled himself, averted an orgasm midstream. That was a first in itself, an auspicious sign.

Was it the blond who was still screaming? Maybe she had felt his power, even briefly, and been terrified by it. But at least he had not pleasured her.

Two blocks from the Bronsons' he slowed to a walk, confident that the crisis had passed. He was safe, and so was the tempting blond.

Hysterically Danielle Critchitt stared uncomprehendingly at her bloody arms, at the blood rolling down her legs, dripping onto the towel. At Biffy, who lay cradled in her arms, arms paralyzed by fear. A crushed Biffy, blood oozing out of the cat's eyes, ears, mouth. As though the cat had been squeezed in a vise. But her arms had not tightened around the cat; she hadn't the strength to do this.

"Bitch! Bitch!" cried Christina Bronson. "You've killed Biffy. Why? To get even because we teased you? You bitch! You fucking bitch!"

16

Mowing the Rhomleys' lawn, Rory was still elated that he, the greatest sex maniac of all times, hadn't come. Rory Malone had actually averted an orgasm midstream.

For once your cock didn't rule your brain. Good boy. You must do this more often. Maybe there is hope for you after all.

Guiding the mower exactingly along the delicate white trestled fence surrounding the roses, he noted for future reference the clever stratagem he'd used to break the sex link. That Siamese cat had been the major factor, providing a vivid recollection of Jeepy, bringing images to his mind of a crushed Jeepy, Jeepy lying on the checkerboard floor, Jeepy's blood filling square after square, his own tears and hysterical shouts. He had finally complied with Gerhardt's order, and engulfed Jeepy in a potent force field, and as the terrified kitten began to cry, his love for it poured into the room in the form of still more psychic energy. Hugging Jeepy to console her, before he knew what was happening, his incredible strength had crushed the tiny kitten. That flood of recollections had revulsed him, thwarted the swelling power.

Luck, in the form of the cat, had been with him at the Bronsons'. But . . . would you have been able to spare that blond, disperse your power, if that cat had not reminded you of the past?

Truthfully, he didn't know.

Raking up cut grass, the sun intense on his shoulders, perspiration dripping off the tip of his nose and chin, he pondered what had happened to all the psychic energy that had been coursing through his body on the verge of erupting. Was he like a reservoir that had been emptied?

He didn't feel empty. In fact, darkening the proud, self-congratulatory feelings hung a pall woven from doubt (why had that blond screamed?), an augury of disaster (would he be forced to locate a lover before the day was over?), and lingering sexual excitement. He hadn't come; he was still slightly aroused. His semierection rubbed annoyingly against his cut-offs as he stooped repeatedly to gather up grass. He never wore undershorts on gardening jobs to minimize the amount of clothes he had to wash each week, but perhaps that was a mistake that heightened his sexual sensitivity. Though he was loath to admit it, he had to acknowledge that the power seemed to be idling at low somewhere in his body.

Granted, the mile walk from the Bronsons' to the Rhomleys' hadn't helped calm him any.

He was astonished that even in affluent, residential Forest Hills pornography had taken root and was flourishing. Every one of the magazine stands along Continental Avenue openly featured some kind of high-quality porn. Just last week, with lawn money recently earned, he had purchased from one of the stands the magazine *High Society* and *Mates* a newspaper devoted exclusively to personal sex advertisements: Men and women voluntarily mailed in pictures of themselves (usually nude), their names (pseudonyms?), post-office-box numbers, and sometimes telephone numbers. Incredible! To an attractive young woman's advertisement for "Private Swedish Massages," he'd composed a reply but never mailed it. Two porn bookstores had opened in the area this very summer, despite vehement protests from local residents.

Was it his imagination or was sex spreading like brushfire through all neighborhoods, through society, into every home. Three evenings a week (if his father was out) he watched softcore porn on cable television's channel J: "The Dirty George Show," in which a guy luridly filmed and exploited nude women, and "Interludes," in which couples, interviewed in the nude, fondled each other and the host. And the thought of owning his own VTR and film collection was more than a fleeting temptation.

Squatting on the lawn, wiping the mower blades clean of slimy green grass pulp, he grew acutely aware of his fleshy semierection edging its way out of the leg of his cutoffs. He tucked it back in. He'd have to be on his best behavior until he got home and masturbated. Avoid Continental Avenue with its magazine stands, bookstores, and women shopping. Take a back route home.

Wheeling the mower into the Rhomleys' garage, he checked his watch. It had taken him only one hour to cut, trim, and clean up two acres. Out of sexual frustration he must have worked at breakneck pace—and still done an excellent job. That was important, since the Rhomleys were brand-new clients.

Ascending the flagstone steps to the porch, he realized he had left his radio at the Bronsons' and wondered if Kathy Bauer had regained consciousness yet. He would watch the television news as soon as he got home. After several minutes of patiently rapping the brass knocker, the front door finally opened.

"My, that was fast!" smiled Evelyn Rhomley, glancing beyond him to survey the lawn.

"I did everything your husband asked," he said defensively.

"It appears that you did," she commented. "The O'Neills, who recommended you, claim they wouldn't permit anyone else to manicure their property."

Cold air rushed out of the hallway, comfortably cooling his perspiring body. With the back of his hand he wiped sweat from his chin.

"Come inside; it's cooler. I'll get your money. That is if I can recall where Stewart said he left it. Well, it's here to be sure."

He'd glimpsed the interiors of several of his clients' homes, and all of them in Forest Hills were magnificent. But by far the Rhomleys' home ranked the most spectacular.

A gigantic central foyer (bigger than his living room) led to a seemingly endless hallway, off which sprouted numerous rooms. To the immediate right was an immense living room decorated in white and beige, then an only slightly smaller music room in shades of beige and gold, to which Mrs. Rhomley escorted him.

"Surely you'd like a cool drink. Soda? Iced tea?"

"No, thank you," he said shyly.

"Young man, I suggest you have something." She laughed. "It may take me a little time to locate the money." Now where had Stewart said he was leaving the envelope? In his study? She had been only half-awake when he left to play golf and had not paid attention to his instructions. She had fallen back asleep and finally awakened to the buzzing of the lawn mower beneath her window. It had at first startled her. Then she remembered: The new boy was manicuring the grounds. She had gotten up and was just finished bathing when he rang the doorbell.

"Well," she said, smiling at him, "what will it be?"

"Seven-Up if you have it." Struggling not to stare at her, he estimated that she was about forty years old, around Dr. Hartman's age. Though she was not as pretty as Dr. Hartman, she had an exceptionally shapely body. Why at two P.M. was she wearing a negligee?

He watched her waltz from the room. The negligee of white silk, trimmed at the top and bottom in fine lace, was covered by a barely visible cape. Her attire reminded him of that month's feature spread in *Penthouse*. Her buttocks wiggled under the silk, and immediately he imagined that her breasts were bouncing wildly.

Stop! You're torturing yourself. She's not leading you on.

Then why is she dressed so seductively?

He must find a distraction. On a shiny black grand piano rested a picture in a gold frame. He recognized Mrs. Rhomley and assumed the man was her husband, whom he had only spoken to over the phone. "The mower and all the equipment you could possibly need are in the garage," he had said. "I'll leave it unlocked. Just return everything to its proper place when you finish." He had. "My wife will have your money."

Hearing a door open, he turned. Mrs. Rhomley, carrying a tall glass of soda, crossed the dining room, coming toward him. He wanted to avert his eyes, but instead they automatically fixed on the glass she held at the height of her breasts. Why there, dear God, where I can't avoid them. They loomed bigger and bounced even more lusciously than he'd imagined.

She's not teasing you, you idiot. Where else is she going to carry the glass, on her head?

Why a negligee unless she were deliberating trying to seduce him? She knew he was coming to the house to collect money. Why hadn't she dressed properly? Decently?

You're just hypersensitive, horny. You'd misinterpret anything she did.

Maybe. Yes, of course. But hadn't his friend Ken Greenberg been seduced by housewives twice? He'd bragged about it. They had invited him into their bedrooms after he'd worked in their yards. To get money. They'd given him more than cash. "Sexually frustrated housewives," Ken had said. "They don't get it from their husbands."

"Here we go," she chimed, handing him the glass. "Dear, you look terribly exhausted. I imagine it's blisteringly hot out there. Now you sit here and relax."

She was touching his shoulder, easing him into the chair. Why did she smell so flowery, so enticingly sweet?

She's not leading you on, you pervert. Do you expect a woman like that to smell sweaty and rank like you?

"Dear, are you all right? You don't look well. Perhaps you overdid it. This is the worst time of day to work outdoors."

"I'm fine. Really."

See, she's a kind woman, concerned about you, you shit. She probably has a son your age. Leave her alone.

"I'll be right back. I believe Stewart said the money was on his desk."

Again he watched her dance, waltz, float from the room.

No, she's not dancing. Your sick mind is seeing romance, sex in everything she does. Lay off her.

From the chair he had a clear view of Mrs. Rhomley searching through the clutter of papers on her husband's desk. A quality of fantasy suffused the room. Sunlight tinted amber by the orange diaphanous draperies streamed through the bowed window behind the desk, showering the study with a hazy glow. The glow, this heavenly light, softened every harsh angle, muted every vivid color like the image of an unfocused photograph . . .

No, please. Oh, please no.

She stood in profile, leaning over the desk, her negligee made maddeningly translucent by the light. The pointed silhouette of her breasts swayed over the papers, then over the typewriter, then brushing the top of the desk lamp . . .

Oh God, I don't want to. I really don't. Help me, please.

Turning, she sorted through a stack of papers, mail and scattered books, her back now facing the living room. Through the silk negligee shined the dreamy outline of perfect legs, the lambent image of thighs meeting in a dark shadowy place, for an inviting rendezvous . . .

It's happening and I can't help it.

But I must!

All day he had fought to be good and won. Now with every passing second he was losing the battle. He couldn't take his eyes off her, off the silky negligee bathed in golden light, off the rich mahogany walls stacked with leather-bound books. The *Penthouse* picture! That's what the scene reminded him of. And Mrs. Rhomley did resemble the Penthouse Pet.

The power rose, swelled, stiffened. Taking control.

His mind turned the page. The picture of the Pet, negligee on the ground around her feet, body covered only by the sheer cape. On the opposite page, reclining in the large, stuffed leather chair, one golden-tanned leg draped over each of its oversize arms. The leather-bound book in her hand cast an elongated shadow over her crotch, the darkness broken only by a pinpoint of light that pierced her vagina, ran up inside its warm, glistening wetness.

"It's got to be here. Stewart wouldn't have gone without leaving the money. He never forgets a thing. Nothing. I hope you don't mind waiting. It is so much cooler in here." She spoke softly, without glancing up.

Leave now, without the money. She'll mail it to you. Run! Run!

But so gripping was the power, so total its control, it left him paralyzed. Never had the power rendered him so completely helpless. Was this because it had been seething, percolating all afternoon?

Then a thought struck him. If he must pleasure Mrs. Rhomley—and he knew there was no retreating now—make it count. Use it to learn if he actually possessed the ability to stimulate a woman at a distance, to make her feel his hands, tongue, cock. Here was the perfect opportunity. Maybe Kathy Bauer had never felt his advances. There was no subway platform here. He couldn't hurt Mrs. Rhomley. In fact, he would be gentle, kind, do as little as possible to discover the truth . . . to reach that demanding, liberating orgasm.

Squinting, he framed Evelyn Rhomley into a tight image,

and instantly the connection between hard cock and soft brain clicked into high gear.

In dreamy slow motion the negligee slid softly from her shoulders, drifting to the carpet. He maneuvered her back, back into the leather chair, copying the picture he had recalled moments earlier.

Gentle. Be gentle.

Intensifying his concentration, he projected himself through the music room and into the study, next to her naked body. Her skin radiated in the amber glow. He cupped her pendulous breasts, the skin soft, creamy, warm under his fingers; her flesh smelled sweetly of soap and flowers.

Do as little as possible. Be gentle.

His tongue washed over her breasts, licking, twitching. He fought the urge to bite down firmly on her nipples, to slide his trembling fingers, eager erection, between her legs. Opening his mouth until its corners felt as if they'd split, he accommodated the breast's rounded fullness.

He came.

Gradually the room zoomed into focus. He blinked. Stared. It had all happened so fast; faster than he'd planned. He had been supercharged and shot almost immediately, prematurely.

Walking toward him, Mrs. Rhomley was opening an envelope, counting bills.

His pants clung to his flesh, hot and wet. Thrusting one hand into his pocket, he stood, pressing the all-too-slowly-subsiding evidence against his abdomen.

"My husband will call you in a week or two. However long it takes grass to regrow."

She was offering him the envelope, but he stared transfixed at her face for a sign.

"Young man, are you sure you're all right?"

He nodded.

"Here, take your pay. You did an excellent job." She was leading him to the door. "I'm sure Stewart will approve of your work and call you again. The grounds look quite beautiful," she said, holding the door open.

Hot, humid air assaulted his face and chest, dulling his

already uncomprehending senses. He was still staring at her, attempting to fathom what had happened, if anything, and apparently making her self-conscious of her attire for the first time.

"Excuse the way I'm dressed. You caught me as I was getting out of the bath. You know, you should go directly home. You don't look at all well. Even a boy your age can suffer heat stroke. My son did during baseball season last year. Good-bye, dear, and take care of yourself. Oh, and thanks again for a lovely job."

The door closed.

Negotiating the porch steps methodically as though he were stepping onto an escalator, he wondered whether he had done anything to Mrs. Rhomley. Apparently not. She'd smiled at him, wished him a cordial good-bye. Obviously she hadn't felt so much as a lick or a nibble, hadn't even guessed what he was fantasizing.

So the fantasies *did* take place entirely in his head. His pleasuring of women was not a physical manifestation of his power after all, merely a figment of an overactive, oversexed mind.

Leaving the Rhomleys' property, he felt jubilant. Kathy Bauer had fallen, and he had played no part in it. The woman in the bookstore, the one in McDonald's, the others who appeared terrified and ran—all were delirious projections of his guilt for having involved innocent, respectable women in his debauched escapades. Amazing the tricks a fertile, sex-crazed mind can play.

Desperately he wanted to believe this. And yet deep inside a voice whispered:

You're wrong, Rory. You are responsible. It's just that some women react to your power and others don't.

Was that the voice of guilt, attempting to shame him for entertaining dirty thoughts in the first place?

"In the eyes of Our Lord, a deliberate dirty thought equals a dirty action, Rory. Both are sins."

Under the onus of his power, Father Francis Bianchi's words suddenly adopted new significance. God, Holy Mother

Church, the nuns and priests at St. Vincent's—they all equated a dirty thought with a dirty action. Ironically he, Rory Malone, might possess an ability that imbued that centuries-old equation for sin with a perverse new dimension. For him a sinful thought just might materialize into a sinful action.

But if he did possess this power to transform sexual fantasies into actual escapades, then why hadn't Mrs. Rhomley felt a damn thing? Had he been too gentle with her? Had he come so fast she didn't know what hit her? Or was it true that some women simply were immune to his power while others fell easy prey?

Whatever the reason, the experiment had backfired, for he realized that now he was more confused than ever.

17

The phone rang, startling Webb. "Hello."

"Kathy's regained consciousness," said Lou Bauer. "I'm at the hospital now."

"Wonderful, Lou. That's just great."

"Well, it doesn't mean she's better by a long shot. The docs say her condition's guarded and that's she's gonna have a rough fight all the way. *If* she makes it."

"She'll make it," said Webb, crossing the kitchen with the receiver, flicking off the power of his electric typewriter. "Pornography and Crime" was turning out to be a bitch of a paper to compose. "I'm so glad for you and Kathy's parents."

"The docs say we should be able to question her shortly. You wait and see—she'll finger that kid. Give you all the damn concrete evidence your heart desires."

Webb wanted to say, I doubt it, Lou. You see, several facts

surfaced this afternoon that seem to exonerate the kid from all wrongdoing—and equally indicate that you deliberately withheld relevant medical information on your niece's health.

But preferring to drop his bombs on Lou Bauer in person, Webb merely said, "I'm leaving my place now. I'll be there in a half-hour." Kathy's testimony should clinch the kid's innocence.

Traffic approaching the entrance ramp to the Lincoln Tunnel seemed unusually mild for a Saturday night. But of course, you perceptive dick! Most sane people are already at the shore—where you and Julie used to go, long ago, before sowing those seeds that sprouted into "irreconcilable differences." Julie. Thoughts of her still hurt. Although the divorce had been short and clean, it had also proved amply painful (for him at least) to quench his thirst for women, sex, and marriage for quite some time. Their big scenes, played out banally in the kitchen or bedroom, hadn't even had the dignity of originality but smacked of melodramatic dialogue befitting an afternoon soap.

"You're married to that job, and I can't take it, won't take it any longer. We have no life together. You spend all day being a cop and nights and weekends playing psychologist. Where do I fit in? When do I get time?"

Julie, much to his continuing pain, found a place to fit in fast; she had remarried within a year.

Carrie, though; she understood him, shared similar interests; maybe he would fit better with her.

Carrie.

He'd finally called at three that afternoon, awakened her, and had to wait a few minutes before her conversation became coherent.

"So how'd the rally go, luv?"

"Super."

"And your talk?"

"Even better, if I say so myself. Mostly wild cheers; just a few boos from a handful of disgruntled men. Listen, though— during my talk I think I saw a way to structure your paper. (Thank God, he had thought, for the paragraphs he'd written so far read as if they had been strung together at the toss of a coin.) It hinges on using Kiner's research as a focal point. I made some notes last night that I'll show you Monday. I'm still too zonked out now to go into it. Anyway, you're going to have to interview Kiner. Or I'll do it, if you like. And the sooner the better. You don't have much time."

"I'm one step ahead of you, luv. I've already planned on one of us seeing Kiner."

She had perfunctorily inquired about the subway case investigation, but because of the tiredness in her voice, he'd spared her the latest details and instead asked why she was sleeping at midday.

"I was biting everyone's head off around here this morning, so they told me to take a nap. I had a bad night."

"A wild party, luv? An orgy?"

"We women have a quite respectable house. In fact, I went to bed early. And, I might add, alone. It's just that I didn't get much shut-eye."

"Lay off the late-night coffee."

"It wasn't coffee, Chief."

"Luv, I thought there were no drugs in your house."

"We're five young women, two fresh out of college. Of course there's a little grass. Joanie brought out some new home-grown stuff. God, was it potent! And did I ever hallucinate!" Probably because she had had no dinner, for it hadn't affected the others that way. "Anyway, don't ask me to go into details; they'd stand your hair on end. Dynamite grass!"

"Luv, that stuff's illegal. I could come out there and pull you in."

"That's why I'm telling you, dummy."

He had told her to resume her nap and to lay off the pot. Maybe he was old-fashioned, but he didn't approve of that stuff.

Leaving the Lincoln Tunnel, he drove up Eleventh Avenue, then east on Sixty-fifth Street through Central Park.

He mulled over the information he had withheld from Carrie out of kindness and from Lou Bauer with calculated intent. In all likelihood Kathy Bauer had not been pushed.

Shortly after noon he had received a call from the Twenty-fourth Precinct. A purse had been snatched from a thirty-five-year-old woman, and she'd been pushed onto the subway tracks at the Ninety-sixth Street Station of the Broadway line. Fortunately the conductor had been able to stop the train just inches in front of her.

He had instantly fit the new piece into the puzzle. Four "pushings." Three on the Upper Westside. All involved purse snatching, and from older women who presumably would be carrying more money than a young girl. One "pushing" on the East Side, of a seventeen-year-old girl. No attempted robbery. That piece didn't fit. The crimes weren't related. He'd stake his reputation on it.

He didn't have to. An hour later his belief received further confirmation. The Twenty-fourth Precinct apprehended a black teenager carrying a broken watch from the fourth victim's purse as well as her credit cards. What's more, he confessed to the Ninety-sixth Street incident and to two others. Not to the East Side event. The kid swore he hadn't even heard of it.

New York Hospital, a mammoth complex of buildings with virtually every window lit, beaconed at the end of East Sixty-eighty Street. He had last been there with the peacekeeping force when the shah of Iran had occupied a suite in the main building.

No parking spaces on Sixty-eighth Street, nor on York Avenue. The hospital lot, too, was full. Hell, he'd park in the semicircular driveway of the main entrance. After all, this was police business.

He had phoned Catherine and Frank Bauer after receiving news of the arrest from the Twenty-fourth Precinct. Catherine Bauer was at the hospital; he should have guessed that. Frank Bauer was at home. Under other circumstances he would have sent O'Hare, DeCosta, anyone else to conduct the interview; but he had gone himself.

Despite their four-year age difference, Frank Bauer bore a close resemblance to his older brother—broad-shouldered, stocky, with a veined nose and acne-pitted cheeks—but he had a kinder, gentler voice, a less frenetic manner.

"She was on her way to the doctor, a gynecologist at Mount Sinai. Top-notch guy in his field. My wife had made the appointment because I insisted on it."

Frank Bauer explained that since the age of thirteen his daughter had suffered from premenstrual tension—severe physical and mental discomfort a week before her period. A year ago the discomfort intensified to the point that each month she was incapacitated for several days, missing school.

"I couldn't bear to see her suffer anymore," Frank said. "The migraines and dizziness were only part of it—the smallest part. Her joints ached, she had unbearable cramps, and sometimes her breasts got so sore she couldn't wear a bra."

"Was she on the pill?" Webb asked.

"I don't think so. I never discussed that with my wife."

Webb knew that the pill raised the level of progesterone hormone in women suffering from premenstrual tension; this could greatly exacerbate their symptoms, as could certain foods like herring, chocolate, cheese, and wine.

"My wife," said Frank Bauer, "was convinced Kathy's problems were psychological. She still is. But that just didn't set right with me. She's such a happy, well-adjusted girl. I insisted she see a doctor in the city. Now this." He cried.

Frank Bauer had listed his daughter's physical symptoms, but Webb guessed the behavioral ones: anger, aggression, irritability, muddled thinking. He'd covered the entire PMT spectrum in his paper "Women and Crime" and recalled his astonishment in learning the extent to which premenstrual tension so miserably incapacitated many women, radically altering their behavior. Statistically, he'd found, four out of five crimes committed by women occur during the week of PMT.

He had been downright flabbergasted by the cogent evidence in recent years linking PMT with an increase in the female crime rate, and with the legal ramifications. Courts in France and England had already ruled PMT to be a valid defense against crimes of violence. "In terms of law," a Harvard Law School professor had argued in a *New York Times* editorial, "severe PMT, with its significant hormonal changes, should be analogous to a plea of temporary insanity."

He had left the Bauer home that afternoon convinced that Kathy Bauer had fallen, but he was still totally confused as to where the fleeing boy fit into the picture.

Now, entering the hospital's rotating door, he recalled the quote he'd used in his paper from Dr. Katherine Dalton of England's Royal Society for the Prevention of Accidents: "Women should take into account that they are two and one half times more likely to have an accident during the paramenstruum." More ammunition he would use to make Bauer see reason.

In the hospital's central lobby, an immense, dome-shaped rotunda, he spotted Bauer by the information booth, talking with three kids. Catching the sergeant's attention, he signaled him toward the bank of elevators.

"How's she doing?" he asked when they were alone.

"A slight improvement since I called you. Her mother's with her. It may be an hour or so before they let us question her."

Directness was his approach. "Lou, why did you withhold medical information about your niece?"

Bauer didn't flinch. The facts were bound to emerge sooner or later. "Because you'd been so gung-ho on that damn project of yours last year. One hint of Kathy's condition and you'd have immediately lumped her into your statistics and concluded she got dizzy and fell. You might not have ordered a sketch on the kid."

Maybe so, thought Webb. He had been enthusiastic over his paper and findings. You had to be to do quality work. His project also had been the brunt of jokes by the men in the department. Especially Bauer. Every time a woman suspect had been brought into the station, regardless of the charges, Bauer had cracked, "Probably on the rag. Release her."

"Kathy was pushed," emphasized Bauer, "and we've got to catch the fuckin' bastard that did it." Sensing disagreement in Webb's sober countenance, Bauer quickly added, "I want you to talk with some of her classmates. They'll tell you what a careful kid she was. I had warned her about standing too near the edge of a subway platform just last week. In fact, she passed the warning onto her friends. Come on. Listen to these kids."

Appease him for the moment, thought Webb, let him present his full case, then hit him with the black boy's arrest and confession. Soon the doctors will permit us to question Kathy Bauer and settle the issue once and for all. He followed Bauer across the lobby to where three kids were being interviewed by Nancy Parker, a popular reporter with "Eyewitness News."

18

Rory entered the hospital from Seventy-first Street. He'd heard on the evening news that Kathy Bauer had regained consciousness, and he'd wasted no time getting to the hospital. The police car parked by the main entrance had sent him scurrying around the corner in search of an alternate entrance. The police must be there to question Kathy, were probably with her now.

Wandering through the labyrinth of halls, past blue-and-white signs—Radiology, Urology, Emergency Clinic, Cafeteria One Flight Down—up ahead he spotted it: Lobby. The arrow pointed to the right.

He would locate the information station, present himself as a concerned fellow student from Forest Hills High—which he was—and learn Kathy's room number.

Walking in the direction of the lobby, he concocted the fictitious name he'd use: Tony Mora.

He felt exhausted. Every muscle ached, and his headache had only been aggravated by the subway's clanking ride and screeching stops at the dozen stations between his home and the hospital. The day had been an emotional roller coaster, and the ups and downs seemed to sensitize him to harsh sounds, bright lights, and the sweltering heat.

He had started the morning frightfully anxious, desperate to get his hands on the *Daily News*. Learning that Kathy Bauer's leg had been severed by the train had devastated him. Then the bewildering ups and downs with Christina Bronson's friend and Mrs. Rhomley. Finally, the news that Kathy had regained consciousness. He had felt instant relief for her, but dread for himself, for now she would surely talk to the police.

Passing through the swinging doors, he spotted two signs: Visitors' Elevators. Lobby. Both straight ahead.

The bustling of doctors and nurses, of attendants pushing wheelchairs and carts stacked with medical supplies, and of visitors in street clothes swelled the corridors, making him feel less conspicuous. But now he wondered if other students, hearing the news about Kathy, had rushed to the hospital? Or would his sole and sudden presence arouse suspicion?

He must risk that chance, for lingering uncertainty about the imaginary or actual manifestations of his power were disrupting every aspect of his life; particularly his four-month-old relationship with Melissa Adams.

Despite a desire to be alone after leaving the Rhomleys', he had felt compelled to stop at the Nicholas Dance Studio, where Melissa took summer ballet classes. Preoccupied with his own problems, he's been avoiding her lately and realized it hurt her. Yet there was no way he could disclose the truth.

For twenty minutes he had sat in the hot studio opposite the wall of mirrors, watching Melissa and six other girls dance to taped Chopin waltzes. In the sunlight that poured through the floor-to-ceiling windows facing west and Pine Street, Melissa executed every movement with grace and precision. She was serious about a career in ballet, and though he didn't care for the two ballets she'd coaxed him to see at Lincoln Center, he loved to watch her dance. With her light, slender frame, her straight brown hair falling to midback and opening into a delicate fan when she spun on point, Melissa seemed identical to the ballerina onstage.

"We worked on speed today," she said, zippering up her dance bag and swinging it over her shoulder. "You can't imagine how hard it is to keep perfect form when your feet are moving a mile a minute." She realized his thoughts were elsewhere. "A busy day?"

"Two big jobs—three and a half acres and two acres—and the works on both."

"Your shoulders look burned. You should wear a shirt in this sun." She was staring at his hair.

"I think I like it," she said with a smile, running her hand across its uneven, prickly surface. "It's very extreme, though, don't you think? I can't decide if it looks more punk, new wave, or marine."

"It's cooler."

"I bet. Sometimes I wish I could cut mine short, real short. But ballerinas should have long hair—the longer the better."

Descending the steep and narrow stairway to the street, its walls plastered with posters of music recitals and dance programs, she took his hand; her palm felt silky smooth against his callouses and the fresh nicks that had yet to scab.

"You're awfully quiet," she said as they reached the street, reminding herself not to push him too far. Lately he'd been so moody and sullen, irritated by the most innocent statements.

"Sorry. I'm just bushed. It was a hell of a day. I bet I smell."

"A little, but I don't mind."

"I should have at least hosed down."

"Don't be silly. I'm just as sweaty." She laughed. "Do I smell?"

"A little, but I don't mind."

Carefully phrasing her words, she asked, "Should I make plans with Monica and Linda, or do you think we might go out tonight? If you're not too tired." This time she at least gave him an out.

He had to be free when Kathy Bauer regained consciousness.

"You better call Monica. I have three jobs tomorrow, so I should make it an early night." Aware of her disappointment, he added, "Besides, we're going to the drive-in tomorrow. Pop gave me the car."

"I'll be coming from Linda's place, so meet me at the corner of Continental and Seventy-third." Then she sighed. "I hate to deceive them, but it's for their own benefit. They're so old-fashioned, really; they'd never understand."

At sixteen she was old enough to make her own decisions, but her parents had forbade her to go on a car date, particularly to a drive-in. Well, maybe they didn't trust her, but she trusted herself.

And Rory—to a degree; though occasionally she had to keep him in line. Too narrow a line, she wondered? Although she hated to lie to her parents, it was necessary in this case in order to maintain Rory's interest. He had been so distant with her lately; he'd not phoned last night, but she would ignore that. Her questions the previous week as to why he hadn't phoned for three days had soured his mood and spoiled their one and only evening together that week. Perhaps he was seeing another girl. The thought sent a chill through her overworked body, and she felt her leg muscles might cramp. "Easy," she cautioned, and took several long, deep breaths.

"You're sure the drive-in's okay?" he asked. Walking from the Rhomleys' to the dance studio, he had begun to question the sagacity of attending a drive-in with Melissa after all that had recently happened. In fantasy he had so far successfully dispelled all spontaneous images of her, but in the privacy of a car, in the flesh, under her gentle touch, gazing into her large, almond-shape, brown eyes—might the power somehow manifest itself in her presence? Even now, holding her hand, emotionally drained as he was, he had to refrain from squeezing her in his arms, covering her eyes and cheeks and lips with kisses, running his tongue around her ear, blowing warm hot breath into it.

Perhaps it would be wisest, safest, to avoid seeing Melissa altogether until he discovered the truth about himself, about the power.

Was there any excuse that would not hurt her terribly, crush her? None.

"Yes, the drive-in's fine, really. Don't be silly. If I recognize anyone I'll just slide down in the seat," she joked. She knew how much he enjoyed the privacy of the car; it was the only place they could really be alone. "You believe I want to go, don't you?"

"I do."

With the lawn money from Mrs. Rhomley, he treated Melissa to lunch at McDonald's on Queens Boulevard, and while they sat eating, he had once again pondered their relationship: Why had he permitted himself to fall in love with the purest, strictest Catholic girl in the neighborhood? Other guys dated sexually free girls, all on the pill. Melissa didn't need a pill, diaphragm, anything like that; with her, sex was never even an issue open to discussion. How could he love her so much, if she continually provided tormenting frustration? Had his mother been alive, though, she'd have approved of Melissa. Two hundred percent.

The hospital corridor opened onto a huge, domed-ceiling lobby, teeming with people—and two television cameras. He recognized Nancy Parker, the Channel 7 reporter whose live coverage had first brought him news of Kathy's improvement. The television crew was too close to the information booth for him to approach it. He didn't want to be accidentally photographed or, worse, interviewed.

"Are you here to see Kathy Bauer? What's your name? Your relationship with her? Why did you come so soon? Do you believe she was a victim of the Subway Pusher?"

By now the media were sure to be bent on establishing that Kathy Bauer was the fourth victim of the Subway Pusher. Besides knocking the city police force, it sold more papers.

After learning Kathy's room number, he might have to wait hours for the police and her parents to leave before she was alone. Should he hide out in the stairwell until after visiting hours? He still had no definite plan for how to get into her room, but he would cross that bridge soon enough.

At the Coke machine against the far wall, depositing coins, stood . . . Thomas. Thomas what? Yes, Emma Thomas, that was her name—a former classmate of Kathy's. He edged back behind the large, square column, confident he'd not been recognized. Most likely Emma was there with several friends. So Rory Malone was not the only Forest Hills student who had rushed to visit Kathy. He would not arouse suspicion after all.

His heart skipped a beat when he saw a short, stocky, ruddy-faced policeman approach the Coke machine. The cop waited until Emma Thomas had removed a can of soda from the dispensing lip, then got himself one. They spoke briefly; he wished he could hear their exchange, but it was probably nothing he couldn't guess.

"Are you here to see Kathy Bauer? A classmate of hers?"

"Yes. We were both cheerleaders. We graduated in June. She was the most popular girl in school. This is so tragic."

"Don't you worry, miss. We'll catch the bastard who pushed her."

He stayed near the elevator bank, hidden from view by the column, until he spotted a nurse who looked friendly. When he was certain she was alone, he approached her.

"Excuse me. I'm from Forest Hills High."

She greeted him with a cordial smile. "You kids are wonderful. So thoughtful! You must be the twentieth classmate who's come by the hospital today. Kathy Bauer must be a very sweet, popular girl."

"She is," he answered. This nurse was making it easier than he'd expected.

"If you brought a card, I'd be glad to take it to her room."

Damn! He should have brought a card; he would have something to deliver. They might even admit him to her room.

"What's your name?"

"Tony Mora," he said. He had selected the name of one of his father's friends rather than that of another student. Good thing, with so many students arriving.

"Is there a place in the hospital where I can buy a card?"

"The gift shop. It's just around the corner."

He hesitated. "What room number should I put on it?"

"Room 210. Of course you can't go up there; not yet. It'll be a few more days before Kathy can have visitors. But I'm sure she'll be delighted to receive your card. Just leave it at the information booth when you finish."

"Are you a classmate of Kathy Bauer's?"

Abruptly he turned. Nancy Parker held an Eyewitness News microphone inches from his chin. The lens of a mini-camera stared in his face. He was speechless. An hour seemed to pass before he heard the nurse answer for him. "Yes, he's a classmate. Another of her concerned friends. I was just telling him where he could buy Kathy a card."

"Do you know Kathy well?" asked Nancy Parker, immediately discerning the boy's shyness. It was amazing how people clammed up the moment they felt the camera on them. She often had to put words in their mouths. "You probably were in Kathy's graduating class. You must know that she had planned to start at Barnard College in the fall?"

Weakly he smiled, shook his head and in a barely audible whisper said, "I'm gonna get a card."

In a flash he was down the hall, around the corner, and past the gift shop. It took him awhile to regain his composure. Only then did he remember why he was at the hospital.

Kathy Bauer was conscious and in room 210.

19

"Who was that boy you were talking with?" asked Webb of the nurse who was about to step into the staff elevator.

The elevator door closed. Heck, thought Nurse Graybar, that thing comes once in a blue moon. Now I'll have to wait another eternity or walk up five flights. Her feet were already killing her.

"One of Kathy Bauer's classmates. And they say kids today are heartless and self-centered. I've never seen so much concern and compassion for a young girl."

"Did he want to see her?" Webb was puzzled. The kid looked strangely familiar.

"They all want to see her. I told him that was not possible yet. He was going to get her a card. I sent him to the hospital gift shop."

Two of the kids Webb had been speaking with approached. Emma Thomas, the plain blond girl wearing tortoise-framed glasses, asked, "Officer, do you want to ask us any more questions or can we go?"

They had provided him with no new leads. However, they had confirmed his belief that Kathy Bauer had fallen. The two girls had verified, in front of Sergeant Bauer, just how severe her cramps could be and how she often had to be excused from class, dizzy and doubled over. Bauer hadn't appreciated that information.

"You girls can go. Thank you for your help." Turning to the nurse, he asked, "What was that boy's name?"

"Tony Mora. As Sergeant Bauer requested, I've taken down the name of everyone who's come to see his niece."

"Oh, no, that's not his name," said Emma Thomas. She faced Webb, her small, twinkling eyes delighting in uncovering this curious lie.

"Well, Tony Mora's what he told me," said Nurse Graybar defensively.

"But that's not his name. He'll be a senior this year. Rory Malone's his name. A transfer from St. Vincent's." Then she turned to her girl friend, Sally Barrett. "I think he was much more handsome with longer hair. I just don't go for guys with crew cuts. Too severe. He looks—well, I don't know."

Sally Barrett suggested, "Punk. You mean he looks punk."

In seconds Webb was racing through the gift shop, checking each aisle. Why hadn't he brought along the artist's sketch. But never mind—now he was certain that was where he'd seen the boy's face.

Nothing. At the register he asked the clerk, "Was a young

man with very short brown hair in here a few minutes ago? About seventeen years old."

"No, sir. At least not since I came on at six."

He quickly searched the hallway beyond the gift shop. So many small rooms, labs, offices, most of them empty at this hour. All places to hide. But wait. Why would the kid hide? He didn't know his lie had been uncovered.

He had told *two* lies. His real name was Rory Malone. And apparently he didn't want to buy a card. What did he want? Her room number? Had that nurse provided it? And why the sudden severe haircut unless he wanted to pass unrecognized?

The hall branched off to the Whitney Pavilion, another wing of the hospital. Webb passed through the swinging doors into the smaller, darker corridor.

Thoughts cascaded through his brain. The kid might have had something to do with her fall after all. Had Rory Malone dated Kathy Bauer? Had she recently thrown him over? Perhaps they had fought on the street and he'd followed her onto the subway platform; they'd argued, jostled, she'd fallen, and he'd panicked. The witness who swore she saw him push the girl just might be nearer the truth. Or—is this boy also a Subway Pusher? Is Bauer correct that there's more than one? If the kid's afraid Kathy Bauer will finger him, he may be here to silence her. Kill her. His police brain churned at top speed, in suspicious gear, hemorrhaging with possibilities. Think the worst, plan for the most extreme contingency.

20

Rory felt safer in the Whitney Pavilion, away from the telvision cameras and the police.

In a niche between a huge pillar and an angle in the brick

wall, he rested, assured he was well hidden.

So he knew Kathy's room number. Where did that get him? Her parents were probably with her. The police might be questioning her at this moment. He was powerless to stop that. But he reminded himself that he was here for a personal reason: to ascertain whether he could—and did—rape her. If he possessed that power. If he was responsible for her amputated leg.

Somehow the image of an amputated leg reminded him of Melissa. How as a dancer she prized her legs, protected them from abuse, chill, from overexertion when they went to a disco.

Suppose he couldn't get to Kathy Bauer? That now seemed a real possibility.

Confused, depressed, he was almost tempted to abandon his efforts and leave the hospital, but he was afraid of running into the police, or the television cameras. He wondered if he had already been photographed. With a shudder he recalled his father's reaction to the broadcast that Kathy Bauer had regained consciousness, and his suspicion concerning her accident.

After escorting Melissa to within a block of her home—because her parents disapproved of their dating—he had returned home. From the refrigerator he took a pan of beef stew, placed it on the stove over a low flame, and with a spoon broke the waxy yellow layer of fat and scooped it off.

It was five thirty. His father would finish in the shop promptly at six and expect dinner on the table. He mulled over the idea of burning his violent pornography in the backyard along with some dried tree branches and hedge clippings he'd raked into a pile, but his father was wary of fires in the yard and insisted on supervising them. No, the stuff could only be burned while his father was away on a job or an errand.

Passing through the living room, he flicked on the television news, turned up the volume, then went to his bedroom to undress to take a shower. On his desk was a note. "Dr. Hartman. Call her at home."

He panicked. He should have phoned her first. He had meant to. Had she told his father that he had missed the last session? It had been a year since his father had hit him in anger—not since the last poltergeist outburst—but lies sent his father into blind rage. Deliberately he had remained silent, letting his father assume he'd seen Dr. Hartman as usual.

And how had his father reacted to Dr. Hartman? Not well, for sure. For a year he had never mentioned her name, never inquired about the weekly trips to Columbia University. As long as the "freaky stuff" ceased around the house, that was all he cared about.

Emptying his pockets of keys, change, and wallet, he tossed his red headband on the bed and proceeded to the bathroom. He locked the door, stepped out of his cutoffs, glancing at the incriminating stain on the inside, and dropped them into the hamper. He could do that without fear of embarrassment now that he did the wash.

As he showered, he grew increasingly apprehensive and almost wished he'd made plans with Melissa. At least he'd be away from his father's accusatory stares—and from that woman. How could his father date Lil Rust? Her bleached hair, revealing an inch of brown roots, harshly capped the coarse appearance of her tight, frilly clothes; and in her attempt to hide fifty-plus years behind heavy makeup, she reminded him of women he'd viewed in porn movies and occasionally onstage at the Metropole. That she addressed him in effusively warm and motherly tones, which rang falsely, only increased his repulsion. Lil was the antithesis of his mother.

Drying off in the bathroom, he heard the familiar voice of Nancy Parker. The television volume had been turned down; his father was in the house.

"Young Kathy Bauer has regained consciousness. The atmosphere at New York Hospital is one of optimism. The police so far refuse to comment on rumors that the girl was pushed from the subway platform. Earlier I spoke with Mrs. Bauer. Here's that interview."

Draping the towel around his waist, he entered the living room, eyes fixed on the screen. Mrs. Bauer looked familiar; he must have seen her at school. She spoke between sobs about how fortunate her daughter was to be alive, to have had her leg successfully reattached.

He moved behind the chair in which his father sat nursing a beer.

"Jesus, boy! I told you never to sneak up on me like that. You wanna give me a heart attack?"

"I'm sorry. I didn't mean to scare you, Pop."

"You startled me, boy, you don't scare me. Not anymore."

"Of course, Pop."

"You're damn right. I won't tolerate that stuff starting up again."

"It's not. I swear, it's not."

"Did you phone that Hartman woman?"

"Not yet, Pop."

"Well, you better. She called twice, damn near frantic."

He waited for his father to probe, but instead Mike Malone glanced back at the screen.

"You can bet that girl was pushed. Kids don't just lose their balance and fall in front of trains."

"Eyewitness News," said Nancy Parker, "has learned that Kathy Bauer will be questioned soon—possibly within the next few hours—to determine if the teenage boy who many witnesses saw running from the subway platform is indeed the East Side Subway Pusher. I'll be at the hospital all evening to keep you posted. Now back to you, Jerry."

"Don't stand behind me like that."

"Sorry, Pop."

"They'll get the fucker who pushed her; he should be strung up by his balls. Boy, get dressed. This ain't no locker room. How many times have I told you about parading around here indecent?"

After washing the dinner dishes he had headed straight for New York Hospital. Now he seemed trapped there—and unable to get to Kathy Bauer. Suddenly he happened upon an idea. In Dr. Hartman's earlier experiments he had projected his consciousness—his body? He wasn't exactly sure—into the Black Room and recognized objects in total darkness. Encouraged by this success, Dr. Hartman had placed a tape recording of various popular songs in the soundproof room. With practice he had learned to identify the music. Perhaps he could see and hear with these special senses into room 210. See if Kathy Bauer was alone or being questioned by police. Even hear her answers. It was worth a try; it could spare him the danger of attempting to sneak into her room. Why hadn't he thought of remote sensory projection earlier?

He knew. He had been trying to put as much distance as possible between his laboratory work with Dr. Hartman and real-life events. Especially recent events.

He closed his eyes. What to focus on? What target? The numerals *210*. He etched them into his mind.

Relax . . . Drift . . . Mentally, physically . . . See the door . . . Beyond it into the room . . .

Nothing.

He didn't know the room's location, the wing of the building—important factors in zeroing in. Having never seen the actual door, he found it impossible to conjure the perfect image he needed to serve as a target.

Kathy!

Of course—her face. He would never forget that face. Her expression of recognition, of terror.

It was painful to recall her features in the extreme detail required for remote projection, but he struggled to reconstruct her face in his mind.

21

Thomas Webb spotted Rory Malone purely by accident.

Ready to abandon his search of the Whitney Pavilion, he had walked to the far side of the cordoned-off foyer that was under repair and stared out the window into the courtyard, the only place he hadn't checked. It was small and well lit; the kid wasn't there. But as he turned around, he glimpsed Rory

Malone standing behind a pillar, its paint mostly scraped off, the blue chips littering the marble floor.

Now he wondered: What the hell is the kid doing there?

The quiet of the foyer was continually shattered by the paging of hospital staff over the public-address system.

Webb positioned himself on the opposite side of the deserted foyer behind a torn-out public phone booth, where he had a direct view of the boy and could, if necessary, conceal himself quickly.

He was thoroughly perplexed. The kid's eyes were closed, his head tilted backward, resting against the freshly patched concrete wall. Was the boy sick? He certainly didn't look well. His lips moved slightly. His features wrinkled. In pain or concentration? Over his chest lay his folded hands.

What the hell! He must be praying! That had to be it. Rory Malone was praying for Kathy Bauer's recovery. Certainly no criminal who intended to kill a witness would behave in this manner. For Webb this private, touching act of contrition reaffirmed his belief that Rory Malone had fought with Kathy Bauer and caused her to fall, perhaps struck her in a moment of rage.

Suddenly over the loudspeaker he heard his name.

"Captain Thomas Webb. Emergency. Report to the central information booth. Repeat, emergency."

Although he regretted having to leave before questioning Rory Malone, he had all the information to thoroughly probe into the boy's background and his relationship with Kathy Bauer; quietly, without Sergeant Bauer's knowledge. And he would question Rory in the privacy of the boy's home.

Hurrying down the hall, he thought that private snooping would definitely be the best approach in this case. No sense tarnishing the boy's reputation without sufficient cause. And certainly he was not going to let the press latch onto this presumably innocent boy and use him as a scapegoat to vent public fear of the Subway Pusher and their own vituperation at the police's "ineffectual efforts" in the case.

He took a wrong turn, found himself in an unfamiliar corridor, and just as he was about to ask a nurse for instructions to the information center, his name again sounded over the PA system:

"Captain Thomas Webb go directly to room two-ten. Emergency and correction. Repeat. Go directly to room two-ten. Two-one-zero."

The nurse directed him to the closest elevator, and he took off down the hall, praying that Kathy Bauer had not taken a sudden turn for the worse or died.

22

Mention of that room number had immediately shattered Rory's concentration; the foggy, inchoate image that had been crystallizing in his mind—of Kathy Bauer, of three people at her bedside, one in a police uniform—had abruptly vanished.

He rushed from the Whitney Pavilion to stand, stunned, outside in the small park, flanked on one side by the main entrance of the hospital and on the other by the staff parking lot.

What emergency in room 210?

He fought to recall the fuzzy, flickering image he had discerned: Kathy lying flat on white sheets; yes, her eyes were open. She was holding a woman's hand, presumably her mother's, and a policeman was leaning over the bed . . . no, over Kathy's face, close to her ear, whispering . . .

How he'd strained to hear the policeman's voice, any sounds in the room. But the images played like a silent movie in slow motion.

What emergency?

Standing in shadows in the small garden, the night air still and muggy and hot, he was beginning to recall something else, something strange. At one point Kathy had seemed startled.

Her eyes became wide, glassy, fearful; her mouth opened in what appeared to be shouts. But of course he had heard no sound. Had the cop said something that frightened her? Or, he thought, had she somehow sensed his presence in her room, slight as it was, hovering near her bed?

He must attempt again to see into the room, more clearly this time, and to hear, too, for he had to learn if the emergency involved him.

Concentrate . . . Focus . . . You can do it . . .

"Vinny, that boy's watching."

"Who?"

"The boy, by the tree."

"Like hell he is. Put on your glasses, babe. He's staring off into space. But now if he was watching, the kid could pick up a few in-val-u-ble pointers from the pro."

"Well, the pro is wrinkling his girl's uniform."

"Jesus, Carol, you'll go back into that operating room and in a few minutes be covered with blood, and now you're worried about a few damn wrinkles. Hold still and kiss the pro."

In shadow, in the parking lot adjacent to the small garden, Carol Murray leaned pinned against a '77 Monte Carlo coupe by the suavely gyrating body of her current boyfriend, Vinny Fiorello. Her nurse's uniform, unbuttoned to the waist to fully reveal her white bra and pearly white belly, stretched open under Vinny's caresses.

Hell, she hated to return to duty, to that damn OR. In fact, she was fed up with four straight weeks of night shift, with its emergency life-and-death surgery; fed up with the frustrating reality that sex between her and Vinny, who worked days in a Brooklyn fabric warehouse, no longer existed—unless you counted the hanky-panky in his car on her hour break. Which she didn't.

She hungered to be naked in Vinny's huge bed, his soft black curly chest hair tickling her breasts, cheeks. Most nights they got each other off in the car, taking turns, but God Almighty! That was kid's stuff. Tonight, though, they couldn't even do that: She had back-to-back surgery stints—a car-accident victim and a cabbie shot in a robbery—with only a fifteen-minute break while orderlies cleaned up the OR.

Now Vinny had unbuttoned the uniform to her crotch; only two buttons kept it from falling completely open. Funny, though, she had to admit there was something thrilling, even nostalgic, about being half-naked on a balmy summer night in a parking lot; it resurrected memories of her first sexual encounters, when a car in a deserted lot was the only source of privacy. God, was she hot; if they only had time to slip into the car.

Rory did not know how long he had been staring in their direction. Until this very moment he'd been unaware of their presence. Yet the crackling electricity in the air, a charged arch between himself and the nurse in the open uniform, had suddenly distracted his concentration, robbed him of the nascent imagery of room 210.

Never before had he felt the ambient air so replete with static current, almost popping with sparks. Somehow the potent energy he had generated to peer, to fly, into Kathy's room, had been diverted toward that nurse.

Strange, though, since he had been unaware of her presence. Even now he was not particularly aroused by the scene at the edge of the parking lot twenty feet away. And yet a bridge of sizzling electric current seemed to stretch from his body to the nurse's, forming a spontaneous, unintentional link that enabled him to sense her body heat, her arousal, her sexual electricity. Yes, almost as though *she* were siphoning off his energy.

In no mood for this new and disturbing development, he turned to leave the garden before arousal enslaved him.

"Vinny, really, this time I've got to go. I should be scrubbing now." She pulled away and began buttoning her uniform.

"Shit!"

"I'm just as desperate as you, but it's only another week of night shift. Then we can—"

He grabbed her again, pressing his groin against her white nylon panties.

"Now *no!* Jesus, I'm just as horny as you, but I'll be fired if I miss scrub-in. You know Shiller's a bitch. She takes no excuses. Please go, and don't be mad at me. Promise?"

He smacked her ass, shook his head in utter disbelief— Vinny Fiorello, pro, can't even get it off with his foxy lady—and hopped into the Monte Carlo.

Leaning in the window, she kissed him and said, "Don't go picking up some other chick. You hear!"

He pulled away, burning rubber, and she buttoned up her uniform, straightened her seams, smoothed her hair into place. Shiller hated slovenliness.

The air felt so peculiar, she thought. The night had been perfectly still, but now a breeze sailed through the parking lot, tossing her long hair. Her uniform rippled, fluttering along the hem. Then, charged with crackling static electricity, it began to ride up her legs. With each step she took, it shimmied higher.

Ouch! God, the sparking between her uniform and stockings actually stung her legs. Each time she pushed down the uniform, it immediately sprang back up, up above her knees, her thighs. On dry days static electricity was an annoying problem with these new uniforms—all the nurses complained—but it had never been this bad. This is ridiculous, and painful, she thought as the skirt shot up to her hips and she fought vainly to lower it. And the wind, which had picked up to a small gale, did not help.

Ouch! Jesus, I'm afraid to walk for fear of being electrocuted.

Now sparks flashed up and down her uniform like speeding galaxies of stars. Suddenly her hair stood on end, as if she'd touched an electric generator.

Leaving the garden, Rory hurried across the hospital's main driveway, past the parked police car, past visitors leaving through the revolving doors, racing against the magnetic attraction that sucked him backward.

A war raged in his mind: One part of him definitely wanted the nurse (she would be so easy to have); another part didn't even want to think about sex. Again images of the naked nurse flashed to mind, and while he was fighting them off he sensed psychic energy leaking, then gushing out of his entire body, filling the air. It was a new and frightening feeling.

All around him the air swirled, crackled, flickered with light, and he wondered if this was the result of his thwarted sexual arousal: Was the power somehow releasing *itself* on the surroundings? Praying that these events were merely hallucinations, he raced against the wind, afraid to glance back.

"Christ! What a wind," exclaimed a man to his wife, and she answered, "It's going to pour. Hurry, dear. Remember, we're parked three blocks away."

Behind this couple Rory spotted two policemen emerging from the revolving door. Panic exploded throughout his body and propelled him down the driveway, racing along the building in shadow, terrified that the cop car might pass him before he reached the street and disappeared into the crowd.

"Holy shit!" said Bauer. "Isn't it a little early for hurricane season?"

A cloud of dry dirt from the garden assaulted his face. The cap blew off his head, and he chased it down the driveway, where it rolled like a Frisbee on edge.

Webb gripped the arm of an elderly woman who was on the verge of being blown backward. Bending forward, battered by the wind, he pushed her into the safety of the revolving door.

Leaves dry from a rainless summer ripped off trees, littering the air like confetti, swirling in tight vortices, stingingly painful as they whipped the cheeks and eyes of visitors who now fought fiercely to maintain their balance as they scurried for cover.

Holding down her tattered uniform with little success, Carol Murray ran across the garden, more frightened now than embarrassed by her exposed legs, for this freak storm obviously packed a tumultuous, terrifying intensity.

Apparently the rush of static electricity that had nearly fried her and had finally ripped her uniform had been a harbinger of the storm. Now she raced for cover, thinking: Shiller's never going to believe a freak storm did this to me.

Sunday
Day 3

23

Susan Stiner awakened groggy, sexually aroused, her nipples hard and creased like the shell of a walnut. It must have been a wild dream, though she couldn't recall the details.

Reaching over for Carl, she remembered he was still away on business. Damn that Mexican deal! It had kept them apart for three weeks. She missed him, desperately needed him to make love to her now.

Pushing the sheet off her naked body, she reached down between her legs. Oh God, was she ever ready! If Carl touched her now, she'd explode, flood the bed.

The streetlight outside her apartment window flashed off; it must be daybreak. What irony! He's the one who's hot and rock hard every morning; she peaked at night. Boy, would he be proud of her now.

Drawing up her feet, her legs fell apart until they came down flush with the mattress. Carl had helped her shed many of her sexual hangups, but masturbation wasn't one of them. She never did it in front of him, though he begged her to, claiming that his earliest and most potent fantasy was of women pleasuring themselves. She even was embarrassed to masturbate in private.

Fantasy! What a wonderful invention! Her three fingers became transformed into Carl's lips and tongue, massaging her clitoris, alternately squeezing, rubbing it. The fingers of her other hand edged gently into her vagina, an inch, then a spasm convulsed, sucking them deeply inside her.

Her juice, hot and silky, trickled along her fingers into her palm. In a steady flow it saturated the flesh between her legs, accumulating on her rectum, falling into . . . Carl's mouth, every sweet drop caught by his warm tongue.

"Oh yes, now, please! *Now!*"

Suddenly the room brightened. The streetlight must have come back on. Strange. But quickly she lost that train of thought. Her back arched as Carl jerked her buttocks off the bed, her blood rushing, pulsating to her head.

Her eyes were closed as the ball of light in the far corner of the room intensified, then moved nearer to the bed. It approached her tentatively at first, then urgently. Her body bucked in spasms as Carl plunged into her, more forceful than he had ever been. But she didn't mind one bit. She loved it, moaned, "Further in, harder, faster!"

She had to tell him that oh yes yes this was the way she always wanted him to be but was too embarrassed to ask. Please, always take me this forcefully. Always, always . . .

24

5:30 A.M. The Manhattan apartment of Liz Hartman and Gerhardt Kiner

"I shouldn't have been so insistent," said Gerhardt, fluffing the pillow and adjusting it beneath his head. "It's just that we've been so busy lately, preoccupied with the Malone work, that we haven't had much of a sex life. Zilch." He kissed her. "You can't blame a guy for occasionally wanting his wife."

Liz rolled next to him, pulling the blanket over her body,

while the air conditioner buzzed at its coldest setting. Gerhardt preferred sleeping with blankets even in summer.

"Of course I didn't mind," said Liz, wondering if she'd be able to fall back to sleep. "In fact, I enjoyed it."

"Well, you fooled me. I thought you were a million miles away. Did you come?"

"Sort of."

That answer always amused him. With him there was no halfway about it.

"You're just very concerned that everything run smoothly tomorrow."

"Smoothly? Gerhardt, what an understatement. We don't even know if Rory will show." That fear had caused her insomnia on getting to bed, and now that it had surfaced again, she was probably up for the day. If she didn't call Cheryl Roland and James Gray by six that evening, they would take the eight o'clock shuttle flight to Washington. What a damn shame that would be, with Cheryl so highly impressed with the Black Room and the respectable magnitude of her biocurrents and so eager to watch Rory overload the photomultiplier tubes without even being in the room.

"I'll bet Mike Malone is lying," she said, sitting up, leaning against the headboard.

"About what?"

"Trouble between him and Rory. It's the only explanation for Rory not having called by now. I've left three messages, and I stressed the urgency of speaking with him. Gerhardt, listen a minute," she said, seeing that he'd rolled on his side, his back to her. "I don't think Rory ever got those messages; his father never told him I called."

He faced her. "Honey, you're being a trifle melodramatic. If anything, they fought, and Mike Malone threatened Rory not to go blabbing about it to you. For all we know, Rory might have a black eye or a cut lip and he's afraid to get us involved again, knowing his father's temper and past behavior."

He was just dozing off when she touched his cheek. "Something *was* bothering me earlier, Gerhardt."

His eyes opened.

"I know it sounds silly, but I had the strangest and strongest feeling that Rory was in the room, watching us having sex."

"Oh, come on, Liz, you've got that kid on your brain."

"I admit I do. Nonetheless, his presence seemed real, as though he were spying on us." How ridiculous that sounded. But was it, considering what Rory did in the laboratory?

"Gerhardt, please pay attention." Excited, she drew the blanket up to her shoulders. "We know Rory can see through walls—or some part of him, his astral body, whatever that is, sees—and it actually travels from the Red Room to the Black Room. I mean, we've detected his Tinkerbell there. Well, if steel and concrete walls mean nothing to him, why should distance be sacrosanct?"

Now Gerhardt was listening; again Liz was onto something he should have thought of first. On the one hand, he hated to be upstaged by her; but a shining display of her analytical prowess also made him proud to be married to this brilliant, beautiful woman.

"Of course distance is meaningless," said Liz. "Ten feet, ten miles, a hundred miles—I'll wager it's all the same for Rory. Though we'll have to prove it, of course." She instantly conceived the experimental protocol. "I'll bet it's as easy for Rory to travel from his home in Queens to our Manhattan apartment as it is for him to project himself from room to room in the lab. Rory discovered it himself."

Jesus, thought Gerhardt; her excitement was contagious. Why hadn't they—he—anticipated this? Because, of course, to them, to everyone else, distance is an immutable reality. Ten miles was very different from ten feet. But not for someone with Rory's talent. If Rory had been in their bedroom, thought Gerhardt, *wow!* The peeping-Tom possibilities for a boy of seventeen, for anyone . . .

Suddenly he was remembering himself at seventeen, the times he had stared out of the darkness of his bedroom window, searching apartments across the court, spotting couples who had forgotten or simply never bothered to draw the shades. It had been a nightly ritual.

He recalled the couple he'd watched regularly. He'd learned their nights for sex: Monday, Wednesday, Saturday. Like clockwork, week after week. Another apartment: silhouettes of lovemaking cast on the drawn shade. The many drawn shades that he wished he could project himself behind. Watching. It was his obsession as a teenager, his biggest turn-on.

Gerhardt, voyeur.

Rory Malone, voyeur?

"I know what you're thinking," said Liz. "It's written all over that lecherous smile. Rory wouldn't use his talent to spy. And my God, certainly not on people having sex."

"Why not? You claim you sensed his presence."

"Well, I thought I did. I could be wrong." She wished she were. "Rory just wouldn't spy on people having sex."

"You tell me why."

"For one thing, he's too good, too clean-cut, clean living. For another, you had to convince Rory that it was normal to fantasize about sex, to masturbate. The boy had some terrible inhibitions regarding sex. Are you forgetting that they were one factor that contributed to the eruption of the poltergeist events?"

"For all we know, I've done a superb job of sexually liberating Rory. Perhaps the boy's making up for lost time and missed experiences. I can understand that."

God, could he.

Since turning forty, five years ago, he had regularly experienced pangs of regret at the sexual opportunities he'd missed out of shyness, lack of savoir faire; out of dedication first to school, then career; and most lamentable of all, all those healthy, normal, beautiful young women he had never bedded because when he was a teenager, healthy, normal, beautiful young women didn't engage in premarital sex. This personal jeremiad worsened with age, and at times he selfishly longed for halcyon days of strict morality—if Gerhardt Kiner couldn't have all those tender young things, no guy deserved them.

"If anything," said Liz testily, "you've helped Rory to be sexually *normal*." She abhorred this sudden new image of a sexually eager Rory Malone. Besides, he viewed her as a mother-figure, so why in the world would he enter her bedroom?

"Honey, you underestimate the sexual drive and curiosity of a normal young man. Every one of those guys in my study was quote normal, and look at the way they shocked the women."

His study last year on aggressive-erotic pornography and its effects on behavior had already been hailed as a definitive, classic, landmark work, and when he had presented the paper at the annual meeting of the American Psychology Association in Montreal earlier that summer, he'd received a standing ovation, behavior itself that was quite uncommon at a staid scientific session.

In the experiment 150 male college students were intentionally angered by shouts, commands or shoves from either male or female graduate psychology students—the "tormentors." They then were shown either a neutral, erotic, or aggressive-erotic film. A few minutes later each male subject was given the opportunity to deliver electric shocks to the fingertips of the original male or female tormentors.

Of course, the subjects were intentionally misdirected to the nature of the research and unaware that the films were even part of it. In short, they were duped.

Gerhardt discovered that those subjects who were exposed to aggressive-erotic films administered significantly more shocks to their tormentors; *especially when the tormentor was female*. When he repeated the experiment using 150 female subjects, there was no correlation between the kind of film they watched and how often they shocked their tormentors. Furthermore, male and female tormentors received shocks with essentially equal frequency.

"Men experience an undeniable love-hate polarization toward women," Gerhardt had written. "But traditionally, at least, the converse aparently is not true."

"The point," he now said, "is that the sexually liberated Rory Malone may be a person we really don't know that well at all." On sexual matters Rory was painfully shy.

"I doubt that," said Liz forcefully. "We've been seeing him at least once a week for a year. If he'd changed significantly, we'd have spotted it." She was angry at Gerhardt's suggestions. The thought of Rory sexually snooping on *her!* "He's still a kid; he sees me as his mother."

"Liz, get it through your pretty head that Rory's a young man and you are not his mother."

Hurt, she said somewhat pointlessly, "well, if I had Rory's talent, I certainly wouldn't spy on people having sex."

"Liz, honey, from all we know about the psychology of the sexes, voyeurism, exhibitionism, aggressive sexual behavior, hardcore pornography—it's all far more thrilling and stimulating to men than to women. If Rory can fly into people's bedrooms—and I suspect he can—then we must discuss this with him immediately."

"Not tomorrow, please. Oh, please, Gerhardt. I don't want anything to upset him. The session must run perfectly."

"If, of course, you get through to him."

A determined look crossed her face. "If Rory doesn't call by noon, I'm going to his home. Nothing—absolutely nothing—is going to screw up tomorrow's session. Rory will be there if I have to drag him myself."

She slipped down into bed. Gerhardt kissed the top of her head and they moved apart, claiming their territories on the queen-size mattress.

After several minutes Liz asked quietly, "Gerhardt, if you had Rory's talent, would you spy on people having sex?"

Following a silence, he answered softly, "I might." Then a few seconds later he said, "Yes, I would. You're damn right I would."

Pushing the covers off his bare shoulders, he lay staring at the ceiling. It was six o'clock. The early rays of sunlight filtered through the blinds. If Rory can spy on distant locations, he thought, that's one talent that will sure as hell clinch the grant from the Defense Department.

Suddenly he felt vulnerable. Instinctively his eyes searched the room for an asymmetric bright spot—one squeezed tightly in a remote corner, peeking from behind the television set, lurking over the top of the lampshade. Any stealthy sign.

Abruptly his head turned as he caught sight of a flicker of yellow light darting across the ceiling and vanishing into the wall. He hadn't imagined it; the light was real. Jesus! Rory had still been in the room. Maybe he'd heard their conversation.

A second later a fuzzy ball of white light followed the same trajectory across the ceiling, disappearing at the wall. Then a red light, and another yellow one. Then Gerhardt realized these were the reflections of sunlight off the roofs of cars passing beneath their window on West End Avenue.

Still, he felt decidedly uneasy. For even if Rory were still in the room, watching this very minute, his Tinkerbell would be invisible in the ambient daylight.

Gerhardt drew the blanket up over Liz's shoulders.

25

7:30 A.M. The Malone home

"Yeah, boy, what do you want?" asked Mike Malone in response to the timid knock at the bedroom door.

"Do you and Mrs. Rust want breakfast, Pop?" In the past half-hour Rory had ventured several times from the kitchen to the hall, listening for signs that his father and Lil Rust were awake. Melissa had already arrived to accompany him on the day's gardening jobs, and they had to leave soon.

Lil, her arm draped over Mike Malone's portly reddish-haired belly, whispered, "Tell him no. I don't want your kid feeling he has to fix me breakfast every time I spend the night. He already hates me."

Leaning up on his arms, which from shoulder to mid-bicep were as ghostly white as his belly, then turned darkly tanned and freckled, Mike shouted, "No, boy. You go do your lawns."

"Oh, not so tough," whispered Lil. Then, raising her naked body from the bed and smiling as if Rory could see the wide grin, she said sweetly, "No, thank you, lovie. I'll take care of your pop here." She patted Mike's belly. "You go out and play." Hearing Rory's footsteps leave the hall, she sat up and tossed off the sheet. "God, Mike, this room's like an oven. You should invest in air conditioning."

"Too expensive."

"Well, things wouldn't be too expensive if we split them."

"Don't start that again." She had uncovered his naked body, and Mike pulled the sheet over himself. Lil enjoyed parading around naked—and he liked to watch her—but nakedness was not his style. Even when his body had been lean and muscular, he'd kept it clothed. It was a question of modesty; as was having sex with the lights on, something Lil requested and he forbade. Immodesty in women was enticing, he thought; in men, repulsive and degrading. "Besides, just last night you said you couldn't live in the same house with my boy."

"We could send Rory away to school, Mike. Oh, those schools upstate are supposed to be so nice. You know, the ones you always see advertised in the back of newspapers. He'd probably love it. And we'd have the place to ourselves." She ran her fingers through her hair, fluffing out its long, dry curls. Lil Rust would land Mike Malone if it killed her.

They had met shortly after Grace Malone's death, when Mike had become a regular customer at McGregor's Grill, where Lil tended bar. For the last five months they'd been dating, and she had been pushing for a ring half that time. But Mike's boy was a thorny obstacle. He clearly resented her taking his mother's place; because, she supposed, she was so very different from everything she'd heard of Grace Malone.

Grace Malone had been petite, soft-spoken, and delicately beautiful. Lil Rust was the opposite in every way. Long ago Lil had decided to rectify her protuberant, pointed chin with a high, fluffy hairdo; to dramatize her thin lips by drawing on a voluptuous lip outline and coloring it in China red; to doll up her narrow, expressionless eyes with palm-size lashes, thick strokes of black liner, and swatches of lavender, green, and blue shadow. It gave her a "look" that "mature" men liked.

Once, apologetically, she'd said to Mike, "I'm a good woman; it's just that I'm not very genteel. Even as a teenager I looked hard, like I was an easy lay. But guys soon enough found I wasn't."

"You are now," Mike had chortled.

"Smart-ass, you're only the second fellow since my Joe died four years ago. And that's because I got special feelings for you."

"Lil, what if I said yes, I'll marry you, but the boy stays home?"

He was testing her, not on marriage but on Rory. Initially she had liked the boy, or so he'd thought, but she claimed that when Rory didn't respond in kind, she'd grown to feel uncomfortable in his presence and took every opportunity to avoid him. Naturally he had revealed nothing of Rory's past. Then one evening she'd said, "Mike, your kid acts so freaky sometimes."

"Don't ever call my boy a freak, you hear?" he had said.

"I'm sorry, really sorry, Mike. It's no reflection on you, but Rory's behavior is kinda strange. He's so quiet and secretive, and he always looks so depressed, like if you say *boo* he'd cry."

Since that exchange he'd noticed Lil chose her words carefully when they were discussing Rory.

"Much as I'd want to say yes to any proposal you make, Mike, I'd have to say let's wait till your boy goes to college."

"Why?"

"You know why—because Rory and me just don't get along." She had to say it: "And it's not my fault, Mike. God knows I've tried. Tried everything to win him over. Like when he got home last night. Tired as I was, I forced myself to be cheerful and pleasant. So what does he do: sulks, pretends I'm not here. I swear, he doesn't talk unless you force him, and he never looks you in the eye. To tell the truth, I'm afraid that something I say or do will make him go berserk, like a psychopath."

"It's your imagination. The boy's fine, just quiet. A loner. He's always been."

Well, she *would* tell him what she'd heard, smelled. He had to stop thinking she was the strange one, realize the boy was downright bizarre. And probably dangerous.

"Well, it wasn't my imagination that I heard Rory up all night, doing strange things in his room." Good, let Mike know the truth about his son.

He sat up. "What'd you hear?"

"Well, first I smelled smoke. I was going to wake you, 'cause I thought the place was on fire."

"He was probably sneaking a cigarette."

"No, Mike, this wasn't cigarette smoke, 'cause then I heard Rory tearing up papers. Well, it sounded like papers. Your boy was burning something in his room. All night long. I didn't get much sleep."

"Shut up!"

"No, I won't." He never permitted her to talk about Rory, but that had to stop. It would. Now.

"I've been quiet too long, Mike. Rory's ruining our relationship. You've got to see that I don't blindly hate your kid. I love kids. I regret Joe and I couldn't have any. It's just that Rory's not a normal boy. He's weird, freaky."

He struck her across the face; her head bounced off the tufted headboard. He didn't want to hear any more of her hysterical, paranoid nonsense. Rory would never burn anything in the house; he knew that was absolutely forbidden. Even fires in the backyard had to be supervised.

"Let's get up. I got a busy day."

"You get up," she said quietly, holding her stinging cheek. "I'm going to wait till he leaves."

Lil strained to hear the sounds coming from the kitchen. The boy was washing dishes, probably from last night's dinner that she had fixed for Mike. Huh! To make her look bad. The bastard! She'd get even with him. He wasn't going to destroy what she had going with Mike Malone. For too long she had walked on eggshells in the boy's presence, curbed her tongue and sugar-coated her words. Now she was declaring war. All's fair in love and war, she thought, and I'm going to have your dad whether you like it or not.

As Mike Malone dressed with his back to her, she listened to the kitchen sounds. Rory was talking, but she heard no other voices. Jesus, now he's talking to himself, she thought. That boy needs a psychiatrist. He's loony. But let someone else tell that to Mike Malone.

26

8:00 A.M. Kitchen of the Malone home

"Come on, we've got to go," said Rory, slipping the red terry-cloth band around his forehead.

"I haven't finished drying," whispered Melissa, gently placing a stoneware plate in the plastic yellow rack.

Rory had assured her that his father and Mrs. Rust were awake, but she knew how her parents demanded absolute silence until they had their coffee. She would never understand why something so vile tasting was essential to start the day. Rory had left a fresh pot of coffee on the stove for his father.

"I have only the glasses," she said, wrapping the first one in the dish towel. She enjoyed helping Rory whenever he would let her, enjoyed sharing anything with him; it was a chance to be near him, even if he remained mostly silent.

"They'll dry themselves."

The sun poured over the counter, reflecting off the immaculately clean glasses.

"But I want to finish, Rory."

"We don't have time." He checked his pocket to make certain he had Mr. Coe's instructions on how the hedge was to be reshaped from square-topped to pointed and which plants were to be relocated to the new patio area.

"The glasses will only take a minute," insisted Melissa.

"I said I'm late. The Coes like me to get the mowing done while they're at church." The sound of the mower gave Virginia Coe a migraine, she claimed.

"Okay," she said good-naturedly, putting her arms around his waist. "I'm ready."

Contrite, he kissed her sweet-scented hair, forehead, cheek, the tip of her nose, then her lips. "Thanks for offering to help. With everything."

"Any time. You don't even have to ask."

She was touched by his gentle show of affection, because he had been exceptionally quiet and sullen since she'd arrived at seven-thirty. His bloodshot eyes seemed to indicate that he'd been up late last night or had gone out, which clearly contradicted what he'd told her yesterday: You go ahead and make plans with Linda and Monica; I'm staying in and going to bed early. Though she trusted him, she couldn't help but wonder if he'd had a date. Anyway, she had him all day to herself—and all night, since he had promised to take her to the drive-in.

Hand in hand they went out the screen door and circled around the house to the front lawn.

"I wish my parents would decorate their yard like this," she said, admiring the profusion of flowers that lined the house, driveway, and flagstone path to the front door. "Dad has all those horrible pebbles over the ground. 'Because,'" she said, imitating her father's voice and manner, "'you don't have to mow stones or water them.' Really, our yard's so tacky. In a way, I'm sort of glad you don't come over. You'd hate our place. Inside, too. I've tried to get—"

They were halfway down the block when Rory realized he had forgotten it. "Wait," he said abruptly, interrupting her. "I'll be right back." Then he tore off down the pavement.

The sun was already intensely hot, and Melissa stood in

the shade of a sycamore tree, wondering what Rory had forgotten. Somehow she would test him today to learn if there was another girl; for if Melissa Adams had competition she wanted to know about it—and plan how to win Rory back.

In a moment he appeared, running toward her, carrying a brown paper bag.

"Lunch?" she asked when he took her hand.

"No."

"What then? Something for the lawn? Fertilizer?" she guessed, leaning over, sniffing the bag.

He pulled it away.

"Rory, what's in the bag?" she teased. "A surprise for me?"

"It's nothing," he said, and she felt his hand tense.

She hated when he was secretive but had learned that that mood was best handled by not prying. Let him have his secret, play his game. She would know the contents of the bag soon enough. Maybe not, though. Suppose the bag contained something his date last night had forgotten and he was returning. No, Rory would never do that in front of her.

Three blocks from the house she was surprised when he tossed the bag into a public trash basket.

Later that afternoon, after she had helped him on three lawn jobs, after he'd treated her to lunch at McDonald's, then walked her to within a block of her home, she returned to the trash basket to retrieve the bag.

A day's accumulation of newspapers, coffee containers, and sundry garbage from the deli two doors away filled the can. Digging deep despite the ketchup and greasy scraps of food that stained her arms, she couldn't locate the bag. For a while she wondered if the basket had already been emptied once that day. But, embarrassed as she was in front of the passersby, who suspiciously glanced her way, she persevered. Eventually, spotting a plain brown bag, she pulled it to the surface, knocking debris to the pavement.

For the longest while she stared at the fine powdery, black ashes, wondering what the big secret had been. What had Rory burned? But, of course, there was no big secret. Rory Malone had just been in one of his touchy moods and hadn't felt like answering questions, regardless of how trivial they were.

Or else, Melissa thought, this wasn't Rory's bag. Of course, it's not. There was no point in taking a silly bag of ashes from your house to a public trash basket blocks away. Searching awhile longer and finding no other brown bag, she gave up, concluding that Rory's bag, whatever it contained, had been picked up earlier in the day. She would never know its contents after all.

27

8:10 A.M. Webb's home, Montclair, New Jersey

"No, don't wake her," said Webb. Shit! He shouldn't have called so early.

"She says she's awake. Anyway, she's coming down the steps." Debra Logan covered the receiver with the palm of her hand. "It's your boss," she said to Carrie. "I thought you'd want to be called."

"What time is it, anyway?" asked Carrie, rubbing gritty particles of sleep from her eyes.

"About eight. Joanie and Karen just left to play tennis. I didn't think you wanted to be awakened for that."

"Thanks," Carrie said, taking the phone, clearing her throat. "Hi there!"

"Hi, luv! A frog in your throat? I hope I'm not calling too early."

"A call from you could never come at the wrong time. What can I do you for? Or are you just calling to inquire about my health?"

"Sleep better last night?"

"Yes. But now that you ask, I do recall being awakened by some pretty strange dreams." Damn! Now she'd forgotten the details, and last night she had specifically instructed herself to remember in the morning. Why? What had been so God-almighty important about that dream? Well, now she knew that memory technique didn't work.

"Smoke again?"

"No, I didn't smoke again, Chief." God, she'd give anything if he were less a concerned father and more a passionate lover. "Joanie says Bill treated the grass with some chemical he got from his lab—you know, he's the biochemist—and the chemical, profluoro-something-or-other, stays in your system twenty-four to forty-eight hours. Maybe longer."

"I hope not. Tomorrow's a work day, have you forgotten?"

"Why did you call? Certainly not to chat."

"Maybe I did." He did miss her on weekends—the realization had only recently penetrated his thick skull. "But don't count on it. I actually called about business."

"Oh, really?" Funny, she knew he was lying. Well, maybe she was making progress with him after all.

"Luv, where the hell did you hide that damn paper from Kiner. The copy of it you brought back from Montreal? I've searched everywhere."

"Well, I'm delighted to see you've been working hard. But have you forgotten? You asked me to extract the essence from Kiner's paper and type it up for you. It's done, on my desk at home. Now, see, if you had taken the key I'd offered to my apartment, you could go get it."

"No matter; it can wait till Monday. Just bring it in with you."

He sounded disappointed; he must really be devoting the entire weekend to his paper. "Listen, Chief, if it'll help, I can catch a nine o'clock train to the city and be at my apartment by eleven. You could meet me there, pick up the paper, and I'll show you the notes I've made on organization. We could spend the rest of the day working. I wouldn't mind one bit. I've had enough sun. My skin's starting to feel like cowhide."

Her offer was tempting, but he declined. Why? Because

work would lead to dinner and then bed; he wasn't ready for that yet. Soon, but not tonight.

"Catch some rays for me," he said. "I've got to get back to work."

She could tell he was eager to get off the phone. "How's Bauer's niece doing? I heard on the news last night that she regained consciousness. Have you spoken with her yet?"

"I have."

"Well, Sherlock, what did you learn?"

"Not much. She was delirious from a high fever. She screamed and was hallucinating badly. Bauer and I couldn't make much sense out of it."

"Oh, really?" She was feigning interest to keep him on the phone.

"Yes, really. Look, you get out to the beach. It's a beautiful day. Be thankful you're not in the city."

"I could be. Just say the word."

"I've got to get back to work, luv."

"What about the boy? The one who was seen running from the subway station. Do you know who he is or what he was up to?"

"Yes, to the first; no to the second. Bye, luv."

"Do you think he's the East Side Subway Pusher? The papers are making a big thing about that black kid's confession to only the West Side incidents."

"No, and bye, luv. I mean it this time."

"What's his name? I didn't see the artist's sketch in yesterday's paper. I looked. You did have one drawn up, didn't you? I recall hearing O'Hare order it just before I left Friday."

"I'm hanging up now, luv."

"Just say the word, coward." Goddamn! He'd hung up. Well, he was a coward.

28

"Why am I not making sense?" demanded Cheryl Roland, irritated that Gray was paying more attention to the Hilton breakfast pastries than to her exciting new speculation. Her fellow DOD scientists would certainly be riveted by her idea— if, of course, someone else hadn't already thought of it. They must have; that was why her department was so interested in Rory Malone.

"Pass the jam, please," said Gray, scooping up a shell-shaped patty of butter.

"Jim, if Rory Malone can travel from one lab to another, why then shouldn't he be able to travel miles? Across the Atlantic Ocean? Across Europe to the USSR?" She'd have to ask Liz Hartman about this idea that had struck her as she was bathing an hour ago.

"Because you're forgetting that we have only their word that the boy can project himself *anywhere*, or see and hear at a distance. The film's no proof. I'll believe it when I see it." He chortled. "Which may be never. Do you want more coffee?"

"No, thanks."

Of course, Jim was right. So far all they'd seen was a poor-quality film and the interior of the Black Room. So she'd shone in the Black Room. All that meant was that Liz Hartman had succeeded in designing an exquisitely sensitive detector that measured the body's electromagnetic currents—an impressive achievement, certainly, but not what they'd traveled to New York to witness. Now if Rory Malone could actually *project* his consciousness (for that was how she preferred to interpret the light, his Tinkerbell) into the Black Room, then . . . But Liz Hartman had phoned the hotel six times yesterday, heartfully apologetic, to say she had been unable to contact the boy, beseeching them to remain in New York another day. She'd had a job of it convincing Jim Gray to stay.

"They're stalling," Jim said last night during intermission of the play *Sugar Babies* at the Mark Hellinger Theater. "The boy's afraid to show up because he's a phony, an actor they've conned into their game. Like that Israeli psychic a few years ago. What was his name?"

"Uri Geller," she'd volunteered.

"Yes. That was before you joined the agency. But you wouldn't believe the number of scientists filing for grants to work with Geller. Then he's proven to be a magician, and they're left with egg all over their faces. Serves them right, the gullible fools."

She had been unable to enjoy the second half of the play.

No, Liz Hartman was an honest person, a highly skilled scientist, and sincere in her efforts to contact Rory Malone. Yet if she couldn't guarantee the boy's presence at the laboratory tomorrow, they'd have no choice but to take the last shuttle that night to Washington.

"You think I'm crazy for believing the Malone stuff, don't you?" Cheryl asked Gray, who was pouring his third cup of coffee.

"Not just the Malone hokum but all that poltergeist bullshit."

"At first I was skeptical, too."

"Come on, that's the standard prelude to occult talk."

"Well, the least you could do is read my department report."

She had initially doubted the genuineness of the poltergeist phenomenon, but, unlike Gray, she had consulted Liz Hartman's bibliography in her first NIH report. As she investigated Liz's sources documenting recent poltergeist cases, Cheryl became a believer.

She phoned the Long Island home of Mr. and Mrs. Robin Tompkins, where sixty-eight mischievous events had occurred, from objects sailing across the room to bottles spontaneously exploding. They had a son, thirteen.

She contacted the Wilson family in Indianapolis; the parents had suffered eighteen mysterious arm and leg punctures that resembled bat bites; some invisible energy pricked their skin like needles. The Wilsons had a fifteen-year-old daughter.

The home of Mrs. Fay Rayout in Clayton, North Carolina, was illuminated nightly by sudden flashes of energy. Glowing flares exploded like flashbulbs without warning. The Rayout's seventeen-year-old son had always been at the scene.

Parapsychological literature was replete with poltergeist incidents involving adolescents, and often the activities showed a measure of intelligence or purpose, with objects aimed at particular persons.

In connection with the Malone case, she was impressed with the research conducted on sixteen-year-old Tony Solari, an employee in an Atlantic City warehouse. He'd been present on numerous occasions when scores of items had crashed to the floor. Suspecting that Tony possessed a "poltergeist personality," scientists had subjected him to a battery of tests. In addition to evidence of "anger, frustration at not being part of a social group, and feelings of being unloved and unwanted," endocrine tests indicated high testosterone levels and overactive adrenal glands. After six months of psychiatric counseling, however, Tony Solari was completely normal.

"Jim, if you'd read my report you'd realize that the Malone case is not all that different from many others. Except, of course, instead of palliating his poltergeist power, Liz Hartman has *educated* it."

"*Educated*, is it? She and Kiner have really sucked you in. Look, I had an emotionally traumatic adolescence, full of sexual frustration and ill feelings for an alcoholic and abusive father. Many a time I wanted to belt the old man or tear up the house, yet there was no damn poltergeist ghost in me."

"No one knows why some children—"

"Hey, Hartman and Kiner will remain shysters in my eyes until they produce that Malone kid and until I see him perform. Now, how do you want to spend the day?" he asked, calculating the tip for the American Express form: eggs, bacon toast, coffee, and pastries for two came to an outrageous $27.45. On the line labled tip he wrote $1.00; no sense being extravagant, even with the department's money. "The museums are closed. How about a movie?"

"You go if you like. I want to head up to Columbia University."

"What in God's name for?"

"To go into the Black Room again. Dr. Kiner claims that with practice I can increase my aura. I'm sorry," she said at his grinning expression, "I mean my *biocurrents*. Is that better?"

"Not really. You scientists are so gullible, ready to believe anything that smacks of novelty, mystery, challenge. Well, go ahead. I'm sure Drs. Kiner and Hartman will be delighted that you want to increase your glow." He chuckled. "And I'll make you a bet."

"What?"

"They'll measure higher biocurrents from you this time. Just to string you along. They know a sucker when they see one. I think I'll take in some science fiction myself. We might as well both be engaged in the same thing."

As they stood up from the table, Jim Gray said, "The next thing you'll tell me is that you want to be part of their experiment. That you believe your astral body can fly."

Just loud enough for him to hear she said, "Jim, take a flying you-know-what."

29

10:00 P.M. Clearview Drive-In, Brooklyn

*   *   *

Melissa sat in the car, terribly worried. Since the movie had started Rory hadn't once kissed her or even touched her. He had hardly uttered a word. Whatever troubled him apparently was serious and persistent, for he'd been taciturn and jumpy all day; now, although Rory stared unswervingly at the giant screen, his thoughts clearly were not on the movie, which she found funny and touching. Tonight, Melissa, she thought, you must make the first move.

Fortunately the drive-in was not crowded, so the chance of being recognized was slight. Still, they'd parked in the front row.

She edged next to Rory, resting her head lightly on his shoulder, stroking the golden-white hair that lay like peach fuzz along his bronzed forearm. His skin radiated heat; cuts and scabs from the day's gardening coarsened the back of his hand.

"I knew his fingers were going to get stuck in the bowling ball," she said, then laughed as the film character hid the ball under his T-shirt, unwittingly appearing pregnant. However, throughout that hilarious scene and the ensuing side-splitting fracas in the college cafeteria, Rory's face remained expressionless. Dare she ask him the problem?

Several times that day she had been tempted to. Not long ago he'd been thrilled at the prospect of attending college and majoring in horticulture; today, though, he'd surprised her with the succinct statement: "If I go, it'll be for psychology, then maybe to med school to become a pyschiatrist."

"Why the change?" she had asked above the din of the mower, but when he'd pretended not to hear, she had let the issue drop.

Later his sullenness had turned to sharp irritability, and on the Luce estate he'd yelled at her for the first time ever, bringing her to the verge of tears. All because of a harmless mistake.

At his request to turn on water for the garden hose, she had inadvertently activated the sprinkler system. She'd rocked with hysterical laughter as he darted across the lawn, dodging the fine geysers as though they were dangerous mines. Her accident had provided the one humorous high in an otherwise low and dreary day, and she was gleeful at her innocent mistake. Before Rory could shut the sprinklers off, they had both gotten soaked to the skin. Wet, her white cotton carpenter's pants and T-shirt molded to her body with shocking transparency, and though she was embarrassed, she'd roared with laughter. Instead of laughing with her, however, Rory had stared furiously and yelled, "You idiot! I told you the green faucet, didn't I? Sometimes I think you don't have a brain in your head."

She still didn't comprehend his anger. Certainly the water didn't hurt the grass, and in the intense sun their clothes had dried quickly, though like a sponge, the padding in her bra had tenaciously held moisture, uncomfortably refusing to dry, annoyingly refusing to release its grip on her T-shirt. He had brought her near tears a second time when he'd abruptly broken his self-imposed silence to say, "I shouldn't have brought you along. I work faster when I'm alone." After all the work she had done.

Rory's hand rested on the steering wheel and she took it in hers, intertwining their fingers. Calloused in several patches, his palm felt like the paw of a wild animal that foraged night and day over rocky terrain; she loved the sensation. But his fingers tightened only weakly, disinterestedly around hers. Pressing her lips gently against his neck, she became aware of the large pulsating vein above his clavicle. Well, at least he's alive, she mused half-heartedly.

Was his father the problem? Perhaps. But she had learned early in their relationship that mere mention of his father could send him into withdrawal for hours. Something had seriously disrupted Rory's home life when he was a freshman or sophomore, resulting in missing school for weeks, months; she wasn't certain about the time or the events. Rory flatly refused to discuss it. But Rory Malone was not the juvenile delinquent her parents insisted he was. There had to be some logical reason for his long absenteeism, his sudden, midterm transfer from St. Vincent's to Forest Hills High, and the fact that, as she had overheard her parents say, Rory Malone sees a psychiatrist.

It hurt that she could not confide to her mother that she

dated Rory, loved him, that one day they'd marry. She couldn't even invite him to her house.

With a half-dozen gentle pecks she kissed his neck, blew softly into his ear, then ran her tongue in the grooves. He smelled of soap and aftershave, and she resisted the urge to bite his neck. How his prickley crew cut tickled her nose. Amazing, she thought, even that severe, ridiculous haircut did not detract one bit from his handsomeness.

Mrs. Rust! Was she the source of Rory's recent moodiness? He disliked Lillian Rust, and when she had inquired, "Is your father going to marry that woman?" he'd shuddered, saying bitterly, "She's never going to be my mother." She understood his feelings.

No, his father and Mrs. Rust were possibilities, but she had to face the truth: Rory had become disinterested in her. Why else did he remain unresponsive to her every touch?

There *was* another girl.

The brown bag *had* contained something from his date the previous night, when he was supposed to be home. Flowers he had given her? Or clothing dirty and stained from their lovemaking, something his father should not find?

And the mysterious call he had made from a public phone booth on their way to the drive-in had been to this new girl friend. "Who'd you call?" she'd asked a second time after he'd resumed driving, and testily he'd answered, "Why must you know everything I do?" Because I love you; but she hadn't voiced that.

Suddenly everything zoomed into focus: Tonight he intends to break off with me; a boy is always irritable and moody when he has to end a relationship. She imagined the phone call to his new girl friend. "Yes, Melissa's waiting in the car now. Look, I do want to see you, but the least I can do is take her on this last date, break it to her as easy as possible. But I'll be over at your place after I drop her off."

Glancing at the beautiful coeds on the screen, she recalled how she had been so afraid of losing him next year when he went away to college; now he had been stolen right from under her nose. She knew what the couple in the next car were doing and felt certain that Rory had lost interest in her because she wouldn't do those things. But if that's what it took to rekindle his interest, to win him back, she'd try. She must win him back.

Lifting his hand from the wheel, she placed it on her leg just above the knee, flattening his palm against her pink jeans. Even through the fabric she felt his heat. As Rory curiously turned toward her, she raised her face from his shoulder and met his lips. First her tongue brushed his lips, parched from excessive sun, moistening them. Then she kissed him warmly.

How much she loved him! More than any boy she'd dated.

Smoothing one hand over his head, delighting in the bristly sensation of the crew cut, she slid her tongue between his lips, teeth, touched his tongue. Rory was returning the kiss not passionately but perfunctorily. Had he already fallen in love with this other girl? Had she waited too long to give him what he wanted, needed, what the new girl undoubtedly offered?

Raising her hand from his, she maneuvered the bottom of her T-shirt from the constricted waist of her jeans, deliberately fluffing the shirt in front. When Rory still didn't respond, she gripped his hand and guided it under the shirt, across her stomach, toward her bra. Strange, she thought, a minute ago his hand was hot, radiating heat like a furnace. Now his fingers were icy cold; she pressed them tightly against her flesh to warm them.

"That's okay," she whispered, "I want you to undo it. Go ahead, take it off."

When he didn't, she unlatched the bra, slipped it off, and laid it on the car seat.

"No, baby."

"It's all right." She lifted his hand to her chest.

This was the first time she'd ever let Rory—let any boy—touch her bare breasts, and her face flushed with embarrassment. Suddenly conscious of the other cars, other lovers, the possibility that someone might be watching, she placed a hand behind Rory's neck and gently tugged him forward, lowering her body until she rested flat against the seat of the car.

"Mel, you're going to miss the movie." Why was she doing this to him?

"I don't care."

"But I thought you were enjoying it."

He began to sit up, and she pulled him down. "What's the matter?" she pleaded.

"I'm just sort of out of it tonight." Of all times for her to decide to come onto him.

"It's me, isn't it? You've lost interest." Her voice was trembling.

"Not at all."

She *had* to say it: "There's another girl, isn't there?"

He sprung up, but she still clung to him. "There's not!"

"Don't lie, Rory; I've suspected it for a while."

"Maybe I've ignored you lately, but I swear there's no other girl."

"There has to be. I don't turn you on anymore."

"You do." How could he explain?

Convince me, her eyes pleaded, and she began passionately kissing him. Soon he lay against her on the seat, and she could tell that he was not totally disinterested, for while his kiss remained passionless, another part of his body gave undeniable evidence of his arousal. She felt relieved. Maybe it wasn't too late to win him back. If this was what she had to do to keep him, she would. Of course, she would draw the line at some point. There were limits. But just how far she'd go—have to go—was presently unclear.

Elated when he began kissing her neck and eyes, caressing her hair and whispering sincerely, "Baby, I love you, forgive me if I've been a bastard," her embarrassment returned when he lifted her shirt and began kissing her breasts. She felt so naked, so shamelessly exposed, that she eased his face away.

"Wait a minute, Rory."

"You don't want me to do that?" *She'd* taken the bra off.

Recognizing the confusion in his eyes, she compelled herself to draw his lips toward her breasts, fighting her natural timidity, softly saying, "Yes, I do want you to do it. Go ahead."

As his tongue flicked over her nipples, his breath hot and moist on her skin, the tips grew rock hard. When he took one breast fully into his mouth, she instinctively moaned and sighed, but she quickly realized he had interpreted those sexual sounds as permission, willingness to explore her body further.

One hand had moved up her thigh and now rested snugly where no boy had ever before touched her.

He's so aroused, she thought, so hard. Why did boys go from cold to hot so fast? Is there nothing in between? But she left his motionless hand on her crotch and whispered, "I love you Rory. I love you so very very much."

For a long while he kissed her lips and breasts while he kneaded her crotch with his hand, and though she would have gladly settled for less intimacy, she did revel in the fact that Rory still loved her, wanted her; and measuredly she moaned and responded with as many body motions as she could permit herself. Even when he climbed on top of her, pressing his groin against hers, his hands clutching her breasts, she sighed to please him.

But now she was seriously beginning to wonder where she would draw the line. Just when would it be safe to say, "No, Rory, no more"? And would he be furious with her?

30

"Another minute, Melissa. Just a minute longer, please."

Why was she pushing him off, he wondered, quickening his motions. So close, so very close he couldn't stop now if he tried. Just let me finish.

"Rory, no more, please." Pinned by his body, she felt suffocated, trapped under his gyrations. Again pulling her lips away, she said urgently, "Please, Rory, stop that." He was humping rhythmically, and the thought of what he was simulating frightened and repulsed her. It was so base, so animalistic.

"You said okay," he breathed.

"Not to this."

"Our pants are on." *So close now.*

"I don't like it."

"A second longer, please."

"Stop! Let me breathe. I can't breathe. Please stop!"

When he didn't, she panicked and began to fight; stiffening her arms against his chest, she squirmed out from under his body, sat up, and pulled her shirt down.

"Didn't you want me to?"

"No, not to do that. Why didn't you stop when I asked you to?"

"I'm sorry," he said, glancing at the screen, vaguely aware of the bicycle race in progress. "I just thought . . ." His voice trailed off.

She grabbed her bra, tucked it into her pants, and opened the car door. She saw he was still aroused.

"I'm going for a soda," she said, confused and angry. "Do . . . do you want popcorn or anything?" When he didn't answer, she left the car and headed toward the food concession at the rear of the lot.

Excitement commingled with frustration and anger. Blood pounded in his ears. Energy surged throughout his body. Stretching his legs, he unzipped his pants to relieve the aching tension. Another minute, that's all, and he'd have come harmlessly, naturally. Everything would be fine now. They'd kept their jeans on.

His fingers gripped the steering wheel. How could he not be enraged with Melissa, his beloved Melissa, who had encouraged his advances, aroused him, then shut him off, leaving him to feel dirty, guilty about the very desires she had gone to such pains to provoke?

Why did Melissa—why did women—do this to men?

Well, maybe Melissa, maybe women, can go only so far and stop, but not men. Not him; especially not Rory Malone.

Suddenly he recalled jock Mitch Gerson's fury over girls who teased, titillated, drove a guy wild, then, satisfied by his desire, his visibly stiff rod, feigned disinterest. "I want to smash every last one of them cockteasers in the chops," Mitch had fumed, and the other guys in the locker room had cheered.

And his rage was not just the result of a horny, prejudiced

male imagination, for he recalled the words he had underlined in red in *Men In Love: By variously offering and denying sex women control men, incite male rage, hatred. And when sex comes it is usually with strings attached.* That was written by a woman.

But Melissa was no cockteaser. Had she done this to control him?

Anger fueled his power, which was thumping, aching for release. So close, so very very close there was no turning back now. Masturbate, do it fast, he thought, fighting off the image of Melissa's breasts.

Suddenly the air crackled with electricity, a sensation he had felt only once before, with that nurse. Sparks and current seemed to soar through the car window, transported over an invisible bridge. Then, inhaling deeply, automatically, he smelled sex, imbibed the unmistakable scent of an aroused woman. The fragrance wafted over the same infrangible bridge, lusty, pungent, and provocative.

Turning, he spotted a couple necking in the adjacent car. A young woman's face—eyes closed, lips parted, breathy—rested on her lover's shoulder ten or fifteen feet away. Invisible as the bridge was, one foot stood clearly planted in that car.

The woman's sighs and moans rode the electricity, accumulating charge, and on reaching his ears exploded like firecrackers. The sparks in his brain ignited the power to a searing new high. Then a new sound accompanied the scent and sighs; the sound of rhythmic plunging, the sloshy sound of suction forged and broken. Straining, squinting, Rory stared at her lover's arm rocking back and forth. And somehow through the car doors he saw (or did he imagine?) the location of the lover's hand, of his fingers slipping in and out between the woman's legs.

Never before had his senses been so astonishingly acute nor the power so all-controlling. Already ineluctably linked with that woman, their blood beating in unison, he realized he had only two choices: Drive away now, fast, leaving Melissa (if it were already not too late); or drift over the bridge to possess that woman.

He couldn't hurt her, as he had Kathy Bauer, but would she feel his pleasuring? He'd run from the nurse in the parking lot, from Christina Bronson's blond girl friend, but he had fantasized about Mrs. Rhomley; he had come and she had felt nothing. Certainly that hadn't been rape but mere harmless fantasy. And it had appeased his power.

If you don't appease the power fast, it may do something horrible to Melissa, something you'll deeply regret. Forever.

Squinting, concentrating on the woman's face illuminated by moonlight, by flickering blues, reds, greens from the movie screen . . .

Drift . . .

Float toward her . . .

"No, Jerry, don't. Just keep up what you're doing. That's enough for me."

"But not for me, baby. Think of me. Lay back."

"No! Please. Just your fingers. That's all."

"I said lay back. Jesus! Think of me for a change."

Hanging on the window of their car, the portable speaker that had been broadcasting the film began to fill with static. First the voices of the actors became scratchy, then garbled, and finally inaudible under the random noise. The speaker, in direct line of the electric bridge, was being gradually shorted by overload.

"That's better baby. Good girl. Back flat on the seat. That's more like it."

"No, Jerry, stop pushing."

"Slip those pants off."

"Don't force me like that."

"I'm not forcing you."

"Oh Jesus! You tore my pants."

"I didn't touch your pants, I swear. Ah! that's it, open them legs. Wider. Wider. Come on."

Out of the speaker's ribbed front shot sparks: first faint, scattered sparks; then the emissions grew, escalated until the box poured forth a fusillade of white-orange stars, popping, cracking, showering the back of the young man's sweaty shirt. The speaker rattled against the window as some invisible current overheated its wires, overcharged its circuitry. Flames danced at the point where the black cord connected to the speaker, and though it was invisible, the metal pole that held the speaker when it wasn't in use became electrified.

Rory was oblivious to these things; his power had a single focus . . .

"Stop, Jerry! Get off me. Get up!"

"Oh, I'm up all right. Up and hard."

"You're hurting me. Ouch!"

"Quiet, baby, I'm not even in you yet."

"Take it out!"

"Easy, you crazy chick, I'm not even in yet. But I won't hurt. Promise."

Lost in fantasy, Rory rode hard, the woman's shouts ringing in his ears, her pelvis bucking, trying to throw him off. Oblivious to the fact that the car containing the lovers, his Tinkerbell, rocked, bounced . . .

Another second.

Tightly squeezing, attempting to force him out, her thighs pressed against his sides in a vain effort to hold him off. But he forced her legs apart, entered deeper, rode harder.

Another instant.

Her hands tore at his neck, fingernails lacerating the flesh, groping for hair to yank back his head.

Like a splitting torch, the speaker hurled a tongue of flame into the car, then died, silently emitting plumes of velvety black smoke into the night sky. The overload had been more than its circuits could handle.

Rory exploded inside her.

Suddenly her lover felt the fire on his back and sat up with a start. Jesus! Holy shit! His shirt was on fire. Rapidly he pressed his back against the vinyl upholstery, suffocating the flames.

Rory rested against the car door. After such an experience he had always been dazed, but it usually passed quickly. Now he was having to fight to shake the grogginess, to gaze through the dense fog that filled the air between the two cars, as though the air, like himself, depleted of electricity, became misty, coated with milky opacity.

This new effect alarmed him. Shaking his head didn't help. Nor did rubbing his eyes with his fists. Only time seemed to ameliorate the effect, for gradually he began to discern the images of the lovers. The girl was sitting up, zippering her pants; the young man stood outside the car, holding the door open.

They were shouting, fighting about something. Then he realized he was deaf. He knew they were fighting only from their actions, the movement of their lips, but he heard nothing except a faint internal ringing, like what he had experienced for hours after leaving an ear-shatteringly loud disco.

When the lovers drove away, he turned up the volume of the speaker that hung on his window and placed his ear against it: a murmur, nothing more. The power had engaged his senses of sight, hearing, and smell with new-found acuity; did this mean that it held onto these senses with greater tenacity? It must, for he realized that he did not smell that bleachlike odor that always filled him with self-loathing. Whatever had happened in that other car seemed unimportant in the light of these sensory deprivations. What was happening to him?

Through the rear window he spotted Melissa heading toward the car. Quickly zipping up his pants, he wondered if on this hot, humid night Melissa would smell the odor of sex that eluded his nose. Still he heard no clear sound from the speaker. How long would he have to mask his deafness by pretending to be too angry to converse with her? As Melissa approached the car, her image remained cloudy, unreal.

Monday
Day 4

31

Again Susan Stiner awakened from a dream, its imagery blurred beyond recognition. Yet the sexual sensations lingered. Carl had been riding her from behind, slapping her buttocks.

How vivid the dream had been! Her flesh still tingled. Definitely a dream, though. Carl would never fathom her need to be handled roughly. After a year of seeing a therapist she barely comprehended the sickness herself. Something to do with low self-esteem, a deep-rooted belief that wanting sex, enjoying it, was wicked and mandated punishment. She had been making wonderful progress until lately; now she seemed to be slipping back into her old, self-destructive fantasies.

The bedside clock read 4:30 A.M. Only six more days and she would be with Carl. He had phoned from Mexico. Another week of business; he suggested she then fly down and they'd have two glorious weeks of vacation.

She was still aroused, wet. She would never get back to sleep unless . . .

From the drawer of the night table she reached for the vibrator Carl had bought her—pink, ribbed, thick; as thick as Carl. Rolling onto her stomach and pulling her knees up, her buttocks raised above the bed. So wet. She inserted the vibrator into her vagina to lubricate it, then withdrew the long shaft. Her cheeks still burned.

Dipping her fingers into her vagina and moistening them, she rubbed the slippery juice around her sphincter, stretching it open, wetting its inner wall.

Carl was kneeling behind her, entering her outstretched

cheeks. The penetration burned and her sphincter throbbed in spasms. The pain was delirious pleasure. His hands dug into her hips, pulling her towards him, preventing her escape.

The streetlight seeping through the blinds seemed unusually bright. Briefly she glanced toward the wall to see if the night light was on. It wasn't.

At the head of the bed, on the wall, was the elongated shadow of her arched back, of her buttocks, of the vibra . . . of Carl riding her. She rubbed her clitoris in rhythm with his forceful thrusts. Warm juice flooded her hand, rained down her thighs, soaking the sheets. He drove her to a height of arousal she had never before experienced.

When he pulled out of her, quickly, she screamed in pain and pleasure, collapsing onto the bed, immediately falling into a deep sleep.

32

Webb was finally going to question Rory Malone and the boy's father; he had purposely waited till dinnertime to increase the likelihood of finding them both at home.

The Malone house ought to be close by. Waiting for the traffic light on Queens Boulevard and Seventy-third Avenue, he consulted the address Forest Hills High Principal Langdon Dawson had given him that afternoon: 145 Chestnut Street. At most the place was a quarter-mile away.

At six P.M. the day was still a scorcher, and Webb wished he had reserved one of the new air-conditioned cars. But four of them sat useless in the repair shop, and by the time he'd finished precinct business, packed Carrie off to interview Kiner at Columbia, and was ready to head out to Forest Hills, the two functioning cars were in use.

From Principal Dawson he had learned that a year ago Rory Malone had transferred to Forest Hills High from St. Vincent's High, a Catholic school much nearer the boy's home. "We didn't want to take the boy," Langdon Dawson had emphasized in his haughtily precise voice. "Of course, we knew he was a problem child and that there had been conflicts at home. I'm not at all surprised he's in trouble now."

Webb had explained to the portly, balding, nattily dressed principal only that he sought background information on Rory Malone, but Dawson, a supercilious windbag, as Webb had immediately labeled him, had eagerly jumped to his own conclusions. He had initially assumed Webb had come to discuss Kathy Bauer. "That poor, sweet girl. A straight-A student. Sickly, though; she missed school fairly often. Still, she maintained excellent grades and participated in all school activities." Etc., etc.—and had launched into the routine he'd probably performed for the press.

He had seemed disappointed when Webb announced the true purpose of his visit, but once the windbag got to discussing Rory Malone, his verbose manner carried him like a flood tide.

"We had to accept him, though. We're a public school, and he does live within our district. I'm always wary of transfers. There has to be a substantial reason why a boy would suddenly be pulled out of one school and placed in another one more distant from his home—and not a religious school."

To Webb's surprise, Principal Dawson appeared honestly to possess no information on the specifics of Rory Malone's "emotional problems," though he readily acknowledged that they had resulted in the boy missing a considerable amount of school at St. Vincent's and receiving a spate of low grades.

When Webb asked if Rory Malone had been a problem student at Forest Hills, Dawson had reluctantly answered, "Well, not that I'm aware of. He's quiet. Sticks to himself. A real loner. The kind of kid who usually ends up in trouble." Dawson had been noticeably frustrated by Webb's refusal to explain why he sought information on Malone and transparently disappointed when Webb emphasized that the boy was not in trouble with the police.

He turned onto Chestnut Street, the four-hundred block. The Malone house was just three blocks down the street. The contrast from the extreme wealth of Forest Hills Gardens to this lower-middle-class environment within such a short distance was dramatic. The grand Tudor-style mansions, lushly land-scaped, shaded by century-old sycamore, spruce, and maple trees, had abruptly given way to modest-to-shabby clapboard houses where any landscaping seemed to be left to the capricious, eclectic style of nature.

It was amazing that Carrie had actually seen Rory Malone and spoken to him no more than an hour after Kathy Bauer's accident. And while damn slowpoke DeCosta was searching all of midtown for the boy. What a freak coincidence. But then that's how most police cases got solved; not through painstakingly analytical sleuthing but some out-of-the-blue coincidence.

Carrie had sat in his office that morning, her crystal-green eyes, strawberry-blond hair and pearl-white teeth all vividly heightened by her sinfully golden tan, her beautiful bare legs crossed, her rose-scented hair tumbling over her shoulder, presenting organizational suggestions she had worked up over the weekend for his paper.

He had had to marshal all his powers of concentration to follow her. The clever state-by-state juxtaposition of dollar figures on the magnitude of the proliferating pornography business, with demographics on the increase of violent crimes against women; the sagacious lumping of statistics on rape into a single paragraph—"Everyone knows that only one out of ten rapes is reported, that only thirteen percent of the men arrested are convicted," she had said. "Instead, play up the seventy-percent recidivism rate for men imprisoned and not treated versus half that for rapists who receive psychological help. Then hit the psychology angle, and that will lead you right into Kiner's seminal study." Finally she'd employed Kiner's study of college students exposed to aggressive-erotic pornography to strike a crucial, though unanswerable point. "Kiner measured significant aggression toward women from normal, healthy men. Imagine the effect of aggressive-erotic pornography on men who are mentally disturbed or just plain sadistic! God, the correlation must spike right off the graph."

When she finished, he found that he was also marveling at her mind. Carrie Wilson had hit on a method of organizing reams of research that had eluded him.

"Now these questions on experimental protocol and the follow-up work on women college students—which is sketchy in his paper—will have to be answered by Kiner himself," she'd concluded.

"I've already scheduled an interview, luv. Tonight at five." When Webb had contacted Kiner by phone, the psychologist had at first claimed he was too busy for an interview, but on hearing that it was for the New York City police department, he'd squeezed it in.

"I hope you don't mind some business after hours," said Webb.

"I thought you'd never ask."

"Luv, your mind can switch tracks faster than a quark. You'll have to go alone. I'll be in Forest Hills interviewing that boy in the Kathy Bauer case. And, luv, please have your questions ready for Kiner, because he's only alotted us an hour of his precious time. You're to meet him at five promptly, room 730 of William James Hall, and the interview will last until precisely 5:55, says the doctor. I hope he's as exacting in his work as he is in scheduling his affairs."

Standing up, she spotted the artist's sketch on the table behind his desk.

"That's Rory Malone," Webb said. "It seems he's a loner, with some serious family problems, which I'll know about shortly. But I doubt that he intentionally pushed Bauer's niece."

Even accidentally, he thought, for over the weekend he had formulated a new scenario. Kathy Bauer's father had admitted that his daughter had left the house feeling nauseas and dizzy (and he'd been furious to learn that her mother had not accompanied her). At New York Hospital Kathy's classmates had particularly stressed her chronic dizziness and loss of equilibrium, the one PMT symptom she couldn't conceal at cheerleading parctice or in gym classes. Suppose that Kathy Bauer and Rory Malone had fought and that the heat of the emotional argument had exacerbated all her symptoms that day, particularly the dizziness. She could have fallen, clear and simple. Rory Malone felt responsible, and he had fled out of guilt and fear that his involvement might be misinterpreted. On the other hand, if the argument had been sufficiently violent he might have inadvertently shoved her; then she might have lost her balance and fallen onto the tracks. Well, whatever the truth, he would soon get Rory Malone's side of the story.

"Luv, I admit the boy's a looker, but you don't have to drool over him. He is only seventeen." Her eyes had been riveted to the sketch since she had lifted it from the table. That dull tugging in his heart certainly couldn't be jealousy.

She continued scrutinizing the picture quizzically.

"When I spotted him at the hospital he had a crew cut," Webb said. "From the looks of it he must have taken a scissors to himself sometime in the twenty-four hours between Kathy Bauer's accident and his appearance at the hospital." He'd sworn her to secrecy about the boy's identity.

"That's him! Oh my God, that's the boy I spoke to at the rally. I even handed him some of our literature. I thought he looked familiar."

"Are you sure?"

"Absolutely."

"What was Rory Malone doing at a Women Against Pornography rally when he was supposed to be running from DeCosta?"

"I don't know, Chief. Maybe he was hiding in the crowd. We did draw a large audience. I recall he stared at me. In fact, he couldn't take his eyes off me, as if he'd seen a vision."

"I've always admired your modesty."

"No, seriously, the entire time I presented my talk, his eyes were glued to me. I remember thinking how wonderful that a kid his age was so interested in such a vital issue. Then suddenly I glanced up and he was gone. Vanished. And before I'd finished my talk."

"Maybe he got bored, luv."

"Oh, you've got it in for me today. Just because I organized your paper?"

After signing some department requisitions and initialing the men's overtime reports, he'd turned to find Carrie still staring at the sketch, pensively this time.

"What's up, luv?"

He had apparently startled her mid-thought, for she responded with an abrupt and lackadaisical, "Oh, nothing," returning the sketch to the table. Then: "I'm just amazed at the coincidence myself."

Yet there had to be more to her pensive expression. He had gone directly to the parking lot, found the two air-conditioned cars missing, and returned to bitch to Sergeant Mifflin, as well as to order that one car always be kept on reserve for him. Passing the door to the bullpen office, he'd automatically glanced in, checking up on his men, and spotted Carrie at the Xerox machine, duplicating the sketch of Rory Malone. If she wanted a copy, why hadn't she asked? And why the hell did Carrie Wilson want her own picture of Rory Malone?

The Malone house was a simple two-story structure of faded red bricks up to the bottom of the first-floor windows, weathered aluminum siding extending to the dark green shingled roof, and peeling white shutters: small, slightly shabby, in need of minor repairs.

In contrast the grounds were immaculate. Obviously someone loved flowers. Yellow daisies, multicolored zinnias, and giant orange marigolds fronted the brick; along the driveway bushy abelieas, their white honeysuckle flowers just blossoming, alternated with pink live-forevers. The evergreens tapered into perfect triangles, and the recently cut lawn was cleanly delineated from the cracked pavement by a sharply drawn narrow trench.

Receiving no answer at the front door, Webb called into an open window. "Anyone home?" Dawson had said that Grace Malone was dead and that Mike Malone, a carpenter, worked out of his home.

"Round back," sounded the gruff voice. "In the garage."

Clearly not a welcoming voice, thought Webb. But then Principal Dawson had warned him that Mike Malone was not a very friendly fellow. Well, at least the father's home, and with luck the boy will be here, too.

Through the garage window Mike Malone spotted the police car parked at the end of his driveway and immediately broke into a sweat. Then he realized that he had nothing to hide. The sweating was a conditioned reflex, acquired seven years ago when the police arrived at his home on an anonymous report of child abuse. He watched the cop walk slowly down the driveway, scrutinizing the house, the garden, Mike's '72 Chevy; his probing, insinuating look irritated Mike; he felt guilty when he had no cause to be. The cop's superior demeanor reminded Mike of the two policemen who had arrived that night. Early that morning he had taken his wife, Grace, to the Parkview Hospital for the removal of two breast tumors, and later in the day he had dropped Rory, then age ten, at a neighbor's, two blocks from their home.

"You stay with Mrs. Fedinick, you hear? Your mother will be fine."

"Where'd mommy go?" asked Rory. He didn't want to stay with Mrs. Fedinick. His parents might never come back for him.

"She needed a vacation," explained Betty Fedinick, "a little rest."

Rory pulled away from Mrs. Fedinick and grabbed his father's shirt sleeve. "Will mommy come back?" He fought to keep his voice from quavering, aware of his father's contempt for any show of weakness.

"Of course she will."

"When will mommy get me?" They weren't going to return for him. He was being given away because he made mommy cry. He didn't know why, but lately she seemed to break into tears over the slightest things.

"Don't be a baby. And no tears! You hear? Now stop that crying."

"I want to stay with you," sobbed Rory.

"Don't be ignorant with Mrs. Fedinick. She's been nice enough to offer to watch you."

"You'll be here only a week, Rory," said Betty Fedinick, running her hand over his hair. "It'll be a vacation for you, too. You can play with Rob and Bruce. Even sleep in their room."

"If he's any trouble just call."

"Oh, he'll be fine once he starts playing with my boys."

That night, alone and restless, Mike drove to McGregor's Bar for a few beers and met a woman named Gloria. At least he thought that's how the slightly plump, pleasantly attractive woman seated alone at a table introduced herself. Once they were home and in bed, lustily intertwined, boisterous in their grunts and groans, Mike knew he could never ask her her name—in fact he preferred it that way. To think of her concretely, as Mr. So-and-so's daughter, as Billy Somebody's mother, or as a secretary or a computer specialist (which he vaguely recalled her mentioning) would greatly diminish his sexual fire.

The house was dark, except for the light from a street lamp post that dimly illuminated the bedroom and fell on the naked bodies rubbing together heatedly.

"I heard a noise, Mike, in the hall. Maybe it's your kid."

"It's nothing. The boy's with the neighbors."

"Perhaps he came home."

"He wouldn't dare."

"But he—"

"Forget it!"

"But . . . ooooh, Mike!"

He hadn't liked her damn comments, just when he was peaking, so he'd attempted to sidetrack her by going down on her. It worked, and soon they were again intertwined, Mike breathing heavily, peaking.

"Mike, I swear, there's someone in the hall."

"Jesus fuckin' Christ!"

"There is." She jerked away from him and pulled the sheet over her body.

Angrily he strode to the door and glanced down the hall.

He glimpsed a small silhouette darting into Rory's bedroom, and then he heard the door close.

"You stay here. I'll teach that bastard not to spy on me."

Rory's room was dark. Mike flicked the wall switch and found Rory crouched on the floor of the closet. Grabbing him by the shirt, he lifted the boy into the air.

"You came home to spy. So you could report to your mother." The alcohol in his veins intensified his feelings of rage and embarrassment and he struck Rory across the face.

"No, Pop. I was lonely. I wanted to be home."

He tossed Rory on the bed. "What'd you see?"

Rory's face burned and tears streamed down his cheeks. "Nothing."

"Don't lie to me." He struck Rory more forcefully and blood gushed from a gash above his lip. "How long were you there?"

"I didn't see anything. I didn't."

"Bullshit! How long were you watching?" His fist landed against Rory's eye and the reddened flesh instantly began to swell.

"Mike!" shouted Gloria from the doorway, "don't hit him. Leave the boy alone. He—"

Mike shoved Gloria into the hall—"Stay the fuck out of this"—then he slammed the door and locked it.

"Mike, the kid did no harm. Don't hurt him." Through the door she heard the slaps and punches, and Rory's muted moans; then his breathless sobbing.

"You won't tell your mother, you hear?" raged Mike's voice. "Not a word to her."

The boy was so small, so thin, thought Gloria, a brittle twig to Mike's towering timber. She pounded on the door, frantically shook the knob, and then raced to the living room and called the police. Swiftly she reported the nature of the emergency, gave the name of the street, but had to run to the front door to get the house number. She thought of leaving immediately after she hung up but was afraid Mike might kill his son before the police arrived.

Standing in the hall she shouted, "I called the police, Mike.

They're coming. You better leave the boy alone." Then, not trusting Mike's temper, she raced out the door.

When the police arrived Mike was calm on the exterior but trembling inside, afraid that Rory might reveal the truth. Even though he had hurriedly washed the boy's face and combed his hair, his appearance was shocking. Rory's right eye was by now swollen shut, and the flesh around it was a brownish purple. In addition to the cut above his lip (which required twelve stitches to stop the bleeding), there was a smaller gash above his eye, and another on his cheek. But under his father's watchful gaze, Rory nodded in agreement as Mike Malone explained how the boy had fallen down the stairs. Hours later, when the police brought Rory back from the hospital, Mike knew from the boy's expression that he had stuck to the lie—that he would never breath a word of the incident to his mother.

Mike turned off the powersaw and went to the garage door to meet the cop. The cop's visit, thought Mike, has to be connected with the return of Rory's power. The fuckin' freak must have hurt someone. That was all the proof he needed that the power had never really vanished. That it probably never would.

33

Rory had arrived at the lab at precisely six P.M. The session was progressing smoothly—a 0.65 millivolt readout indicated his Tinkerbell was already in the Black Room, though weak—but Liz Hartman still felt nervous. It was an uncharacteristic feeling for her. Needlessly fidgeting with the vernier photomultiplier pots and adjusting the paper on the ink recorder, she reminded herself of a freshman under the watchful eyes of her professor.

Why the jitters, old girl? Cheryl Roland and even James Gary are certainly giving their undivided attention to the experiment.

Yet a strange feeling nagged her. The fear of failure? That Rory would not perform tonight and she would never land the grant?

Gerhardt stood by the picture window of the soundproof Red Room, his portable movie camera aimed through the glass at Rory. He had begun filming the session with Liz attaching electrodes to Rory's scalp and chest. "We should have a film of our recent work," she'd suggested over the weekend. "One of better quality, that displays his Tinkerbell." Gerhardt had agreed immediately; then tonight he had arrived last-minute. How inconsiderate of him to have scheduled that interview with the police criminologist just before the lab session. She had had to test-run the delicate equipment singlehandedly, setting up the EEG and EKG recorders, positioning the secret targets in the Black Room, even loading film into his camera, goddamn it!

Relax, old girl; calm down. You're going to need all your energy and wits to pull off the night.

From her position behind the computer control console, she glanced at the singular subject of Gerhardt's camera: Rory's face, bathed in the restful red glow of the Red Room. Although his eyes were closed and his facial muscles tensed with concentration, she nonetheless could read his discontent. Whatever has been troubling him these last few weeks persists, she thought; after the session, in the glow of their joint success, they would have a long overdue heart-to-heart.

The needle measuring his presence in the Black Room edged slightly higher, and she found herself cheering him on. Good boy; you can intensify your energy. You must be strong tonight. Don't let me down.

Yet he would disappoint her. Instinctively she sensed failure.

She hadn't for one second believed his excuse for missing the last session. "I had to meet with a new client about a lawn job. They couldn't make it any other time." His voice had been utterly unconvincing, and his excuse for not returning her calls—"I meant to but was busy"—was shamefully lame for a boy of his manners and thoughtfulness. And when he had finally phoned late last night, in the nick of time for her to stop Roland and Gray from checking out of the Hilton, it was not from his home but from a public telephone booth; she had heard the street traffic. On top of that was the fact that Mike Malone clearly believed Rory had attended Friday's session. She'd wanted to ask, now I know there's trouble between you and your father—what's up? You know you can trust me, but that definitely would have unsettled him and jeopardized the evening's work. Well, she would inquire after the session.

Staring through the picture window, she realized that another thing bothered her: his hair. That absurdly short, choppy cut. "Long hair's too hot for summer. It was bugging me." Yes, maybe so, but deep down he's a vain boy, always meticulous about his appearance. Why then would he mar those good looks?

A pinpoint of light formed in the upper-right corner of the television screen on top of the control console. Rory's Tinker-bell current was strong enough to trigger the camera circuitry. Liz checked her watch: 8 minutes 33 seconds into the session. Great; he was solidly in the Black Room. He definitely had the power to perform tonight. Thank God he wasn't going to fail her after all.

"Gerhardt," she called, gesturing toward the screen. Rory could hear her only when she activated the intercom to his room.

As Gerhardt approached the screen, his camera filming all the while, James Gray, who had been sitting silently beside Liz, spoke up.

"This light, I assume, is Mr. Malone's energy projection, a manifestation at a distance of his consciousness." Despite Cheryl's weekend lecturing, he still found it hard to believe that any kind of body energy could be concentrated into a ball and, in effect, thrown yards or miles away.

"We're not exactly certain what part of the subject's biocurrents it represents," Liz answered patiently. "Personally, I feel we're dealing with a form of psychic energy that is only indirectly related to electromagnetic biocurrents. Nevertheless, the light is physical evidence that the subject is in the Black Room and undergoing a physiological transformation. Look here." While the EEG revealed alpha brainwaves characteristic of a meditative state, the EKG's smooth and spaced spikes indicated that Rory's heartbeat had slowed roughly fifteen percent. A pneumatic monitor on his chest recorded a corresponding drop in number of breaths per minute.

"The physiological changes correlate perfectly with the detection of the light," said Liz, "and with Mr. Malone's subjective report that he feels he's in the Black Room."

"It's as though his physical body idles in place while his astral body is out traveling around," suggested Cheryl Roland. During her visit to the lab yesterday she had inquired just how far Rory Malone could project his energy—"For miles, do you suppose?"—and Liz had confided that that was an issue she hoped to address if the grant was approved. For the second time Cheryl had entered the Black Room, and her biocurrents were significantly higher.

"Undoubtedly because you're still in that period between ovulation and menstruation," Liz had explained. "The endocrine system is working at full tilt, gearing up for possible pregnancy, and naturally your biocurrents reflect the increased activity." Later Jim had proffered a smug "I told you so. Now they've really got you hooked."

All morning she had experienced the tension, backaches, and headache that characteristically presaged the onset of her period by almost exactly twenty-four hours. Maybe she would ask to enter the room after the session; she felt certain her biocurrents were at a peak.

The light on the television monitor shimmered, and Cheryl thought, Amazing! He doesn't even have to enter the room bodily to trigger the photomultipliers. Then a brainstorm hit her: Liz's proposal involved a search and screening for other talented subjects who might be able to perform—or be taught to perform—energy projections like Rory Malone's. Well, given the fact that a woman's biocurrents peak on a monthly basis, might certain talented females be naturally more accomplished than males? Of course, with his poltergeist history, Rory Malone was a special case. But still. . . . Oh, she'd have to discuss this with Liz.

The dot of light on the screen resembled a distant star, thought Cheryl; small and bright. But it differed in two significant ways: This dot grew bigger by the minute; and it pulsated, or as Gerhardt had forewarned them: "You'll see that it breathes as it grows." In unison with Rory Malone's own diminished breaths, she wondered, immediately glancing at the pneumatic readout, smiling when her suspicion was confirmed.

For Liz and Gerhardt, existence of the light had been a serendipitous discovery that blossomed into a source of friction and jealousy between them.

After Rory had mastered lifting objects in an adjacent room, one day Gerhardt, pleased and dumbfounded, had asked, "How do you think you do it?"

Rory puzzled for a moment, then answered, "I go there. Really. I feel that part of me travels from this room to the next."

"What part of you?" Liz had asked.

After considerable deliberation he had answered, "My thoughts sort of become a tight ball of light. It's the ball that travels wherever I direct it. The ball lifts the targets."

That night, in bed, Gerhardt had conceived the idea of using animals to detect Rory's alleged light. "If the boy projects an energy field, an animal may be able to sense it, and we could search for changes in the animal's behavior." He had designed the experiment employing a snake in a terrarium, then the kitten on the checkerboard floor. When both yielded positive results, Liz had immediately jumped at the chance to obtain concrete physical evidence that part of Rory left his body and traveled to target locations. In light of the hard physicality of the Black Room measurements, Gerhardt's weaker, subjective, capricious animal work paled. In effect, Gerhardt had sighted a UFO, while Liz had captured one.

Now, in quick, slow breaths the ball of light expanded from the diameter of a dime to that of a golf ball: 29 millivolts.

"He's strong tonight," said Liz proudly. But no sooner had she uttered the praise when the ball suddenly shrank to a dot. She glanced at Gerhardt, who was filming the television screen.

For a while the light waxed and waned, unable to maintain a fixed size. Correspondingly the charting of brain waves and heart rate also fluctuated.

Rory's having trouble concentrating, thought Liz. Something other than the experiment is on his mind. She threw the intercom switch for the first time.

"Rory, I know you're in the Black Room. Now intensify your presence. You can do it. Concentrate on your single goal."

Gradually the ball grew larger, but then it again shrank.

"Please, Rory. I know you're strong tonight. You can perform. Make me proud of you."

Slowly the dot grew to the size of a softball and appeared to stabilize.

"Excellent," said Liz. "You're doing wonderfully. Now proceed to one of the targets and identify it."

Drifting, the light traced a streak of white across the screen, a ghostly veil. Identification of a target was only the initial task in the evening's work, and to make it more amusing Liz had asked Roland and Gray to bring with them any object to place in the room. Cheryl Roland had brought the Nikon camera and zoom lens she'd purchased on Saturday. Having made no purchases and packed nothing but his clothes, James Gray had smuggled out of his hotel room a twelve-inch-high vase and a porcelain figurine of a clown holding an I Love New York banner.

"You can do it," said Liz, knowing how crucial her encouragement was.

Cheryl Roland's eyes widened in astonishment as the light illuminated what appeared to be a large, elongated, patterned object. Then she recognized it.

"It's a vase," said Rory. "Blue and white. With birds on it."

"Excellent, Rory," said Liz. Positive feedback was also crucial to his performance. "His visual and auditory senses have grown very acute these last few weeks," she said to her guests, then depressed the intercom. "Lift it, Rory. You can do that easily." He could; with his light intensity—87 millivolts— he definitely had the power to lift the vase effortlessly.

Suddenly, with a shiver, the ball of light dissipated to dot size.

"Concentrate, Rory," begged Liz. "You must maintain a single thought. The target. The task at hand. Empty your mind of all extraneous thoughts." Hell, he was incredibly strong tonight. What was distracting him?

When it became apparent that Rory could not—or would not—lift the vase, Liz asked him to proceed to another target. He soon located a tall grandfather clock, but after much encouragement failed to swing its pendulum.

"I don't know what's wrong with him tonight," said Liz apologetically. "He musters the required strength but for some reason can't sustain it."

"Perhaps he's just nervous," said Gerhardt. "He's never performed before for anyone but us."

"That's not it," snapped Liz. "He's just not concentrating."

"Well," said Gerhardt, "I think we've demonstrated that he can project his energy into a sealed vault and identify objects there. That's no mean accomplishment, as our guests will readily agree. Perhaps we should be satisfied with that and call it a night."

"Definitely not," said Liz. "He possesses the strength, and he will perform."

Gerhardt had suggested terminating the session because he had been aware of Liz's extreme nervousness all evening. Now he realized he'd misjudged her determination. He also knew that she had not yet forgiven him for granting that interview to the criminologist an hour before the session. But the woman, Carrie Wilson, had been so knowledgeable about his own research, so flattering in her praise of his experimental protocol. His ego needed an occasional boost, too. And after all, the interview was for the benefit of the New York City police department.

Her comment at the end of the interview had reminded him of Liz. "Your experiment is of course open to criticism on two counts: the artificiality of the laboratory setting and the fact that you measured aggression only immediately after exposure to violent pornography." She smiled warmly and added, "There clearly exists the need to assess the effects of aggressive-erotic pornography *outside* the laboratory context and over a period of days or weeks. Don't you agree?"

He explained that he had already designed such an experiment and hoped to undertake it as soon as he and his wife finished collaborating on their present research. Walking to Liz's lab, he had wondered if he didn't possess a weakness for beautiful women who criticized him.

Liz was staring at him.

"Gerhardt, would you please activate the scale," Liz said, then depressed the intercom, determined to score one physical success.

"Rory, dear, locate the scale. When you do, apply force to the pan. As much as you possibly can."

The scale represented the latest refinement in the experiment and measured how much force Rory's Tinkerbell could exert.

In the flickering light the image of the upper pan of the electronic scale appeared on the screen. The ball came to rest on the pan. But from the readout on the control console, Rory weighed no more than a feather.

"Push," said Liz. "Exert all your strength."

The dial remained motionless.

Liz turned to Cheryl Roland. "We've measured up to one hundred and sixty-seven pounds. Twenty-five pounds more than the subject's own body weight. And I believe that with practice he'll be able to exert even greater force at a distance."

The lab was stifling hot, thought Liz, making breathing difficult.

"I'm impressed indeed," said Cheryl Roland, excited by the demonstrations she had already witnessed and eager to see more. If only she felt better; those irritating premenstrual symptoms were dampening some of the enjoyment of the evening.

"Rory," said Liz, patiently, "exert more force on the scale. Push down. Please."

Nothing.

What in the name of God is distracting his concentration? Or is he deliberately holding back, refusing to demonstrate how powerful he is? But why would he do that?

At the desk where Cheryl Roland sat the metal container holding paper clips teetered and fell to the floor, breaking the tense silence in the laboratory. "I'm sorry," said Cheryl, "I must have knocked it off." As she bent and reached for the box, a tiny spark jumped from the metal to the tip of her index finger. Momentarily her hand withdrew, then she slapped the box forcefully to mask any further static shock and picked it up. The box was surprisingly warm; it must have been sitting in direct sunlight.

"You will do it, Rory. Push! Harder!"

Over the intercom for the first time came Rory's voice. "I can't."

"You most definitely can," said Liz forcefully. Calm down, old girl. You'll kill yourself in this heat. Her heart raced; the air seemed tight, depleted of oxygen.

"Not tonight, Dr. Hartman. Please don't ask me to do it tonight."

"You must do it, Rory. Show me how strong you are. Make me proud of you." Appeal to his vanity, his need to please you. She wiped perspiration from her brow and opened the top two buttons of her blouse. Her breathing was labored.

The silver necklace with the teardrop pendant that hung around Cheryl Roland's neck grew warm. Then a flush of heat rushed along her body. The heat flashes have started, thought Cheryl, realizing that she'd be grumpy and irritable on the flight home tonight and for the next few days at the agency.

"That's it, Rory! Push harder. Make me proud of you." The scale readout crept up gradually, notch after notch, kilogram after kilogram. "Good boy, Rory. Keep it going." He wouldn't let her down; he realized what the grant meant to her.

Cheryl Roland pushed the nylon dress down over her knees. Static electricity caused it to pleat like folds in draperies. She had worn her cotton dress on the first two visits to the lab and couldn't wear it again, so she'd put on the only other dress she'd taken with her. They had planned to remain in the city one night, not three, or else she'd have packed a variety of clothes. The dress rode up, and again she tugged it down, never before recalling a static problem with this dress.

"No, I won't do it," Rory's voice boomed over the intercom.

"What do you mean you won't," said Liz, furious, agitated. How dare he hold back; she suspected that was what he had been doing all evening. "Press on the pan, Rory. I'm not going to let you out of the Red Room until you show me how strong you are. You can sit there all night."

"Please don't force me, Dr. Hartman. Please! I just can't perform tonight."

"You certainly can. You must!" She felt strangely dizzy. The heat, her inflamed annoyance at Rory were sapping her energy, enervating her body.

"Do it, Rory! Exert your power!"

"No! No! I won't."

Suddenly the ultrasensitive dial of the electroencephalograph that had been charting Rory's brain waves shot off the paper. By thrashing his head, he'd thrown loose the ear electrode; another slipped from his chest, which was covered with perspiration, driving the electrocardiograph wild.

"Maybe we should call it a night," suggested Gerhardt, as Liz approached the picture window.

"No," she answered tersely. "He's definitely got the power, and I'm determined to persuade him to use it. I'm going in to reattach the electrode." She would talk with Rory, soothe away whatever was troubling him, temporarily, at least. It would be a relief to escape the hot laboratory for the air conditioned Red Room.

Once inside, though, she found breathing no easier. In

fact, she felt dizzier, as if even less oxygen was in this room. Was the ventilation system broken?

Picking the electrode up from the floor, she gently applied clear paste to Rory's right ear. His scalp and chest were covered with perspiration; she had better reattach all the head and chest electrodes.

She began in a soft, soothing voice. "Rory, you can do it, you know. You'd make me so happy if you'd perform just one physical feat. It doesn't have to be the scale. Make it anything you choose. Anything at all."

34

How could he tell Dr. Hartman that it was impossible to concentrate on the targets, that something nearby was tugging on his energy, distracting his thoughts, filling his body with erotic sensations? That a bridge of current had gone up unexpectedly—and along with it uncontrollable sexual arousal? But this time he could not sense who stood at the other foot of the bridge.

Was it Carrie Wilson? Oh God, he hoped not, but throughout the session her image had periodically flashed to mind.

Why did he have to spot her in the quadrangle today of all days? He had recognized her hair first, from the opposite side of the quadrangle, and his heart had nearly stopped. Though he'd positioned himself directly in her path, praying she would recognize him, Carrie had passed not more than two feet away with her head down, extracting a tape from her Sony recorder. She must be a Columbia student.

Strange, though, he had not been thinking of Carrie Wilson when suddenly the bridge sprang up full force.

Did Dr. Hartman stand at the other end? All dolled up tonight for those guests. Makeup, perfume, snug-fitting street clothes, not her usual lab smock. Sure, it wasn't meant for his sake, but the effect had not passed him unnoticed. He was only human.

And tonight, ultrasensitive.

To be extra strong—for Dr. Hartman's sake, because the grant meant so much to her—he had refrained all day from masturbating. Even the wake-up erection that confronted him every morning, every day before his eyes fully opened to sunlight, had gone unappeased. Now he was supercharged.

He did not want to think of Dr. Hartman in sexual terms, but she was driving him crazy; her fingers rubbing his ear, her breasts only inches from his face; cleavage exposed at the top of her opened blouse. Sweet lilac perfume suffused his nostrils.

She only aggravated matters when she began reattaching the electrodes to his scalp. Bending closer, her arms encircling his head, she drew him nearer to her cleavage. The warmth of her flesh radiated to his cheeks. Didn't she realize she was driving him insane? She wouldn't stand so close, so exposed, if an older guy were in the chair. Did she think he was so young that he wasn't turned on by the very things that drove grown men wild? Well, he was. Why didn't women realize that a young boy is every bit as horny as an older guy. More so. Especially him; particularly in his present state.

He placed his hands over his crotch to conceal himself.

Closing his eyes to shut out the image of her breasts, his power immediately conjured a fantasy. But on opening his eyes to disrupt the fantasy, her breasts were even closer. He watched diamond beads of sweat tumble down her cleavage, disappearing into the warm, dark, sweetly scented place.

Yes, she mothered him continually, but he did not see her as a mother figure. He never had, not even at the beginning. She was too young, too sexy. She had always turned him on, and he had always successfully fought it. Until now; he was failing.

If Dr. Hartman had not been at the foot of the bridge before, she was planting herself squarely in the middle of it, and he had to do something to save her.

Removing the four body electrodes, she placed them on his lap and with her handkerchief wiped the sweat from his bare chest. His nipples stood up hard, and when she brushed over them again, they broadcast hot signals to his groin. He grew harder.

Gently rubbing on patches of paste, she proceeded to attach the four electrodes one at a time; each time dipping into his lap, inches from his erection. She bent forward while working and her blouse hung free from her bra, revealing her full breasts and, through the stretched-thin beige fabric, huge brown nipples.

Although her lips moved, the buzz in his ears now overrode her words.

"You can do it, Rory. If only you concentrate. First relax, though. Empty your mind."

Massaging the tense muscles of his neck and shoulders, she whispered, "My God, my boy's a bundle of knots. Relax now. Take it easy."

The air conditioning's not working, she thought. The air's so stale, so depleted of oxygen that every breath is labored, painful, as if a ton weight pressed against her chest.

Dizzy, she glanced up at the window. Was that Gerhardt filming her? Was that other hazy image Cheryl Roland peering through the glass? Gerhardt and Cheryl seemed to be floating in a tank of rippling water, blurry and bloated.

She had to get out of that room or she'd keel over any second. The space around her felt knotted and warped and galvanized; her legs weakened as a peculiar sensation rippled along her body; no, within her body. What was that infernal crackling in her ears? Closing her eyes, she immediately hallucinated Rory's face, an image as vividly real as the one in her bedroom.

Then suddenly she realized what was happening. Rory *was* concentrating—*on her*.

I'm his target! He's wrapped me in his force field!

A cold sweat erupted on her body. Sensing his force tightening, choking, her hands dropped from his shoulders. Pulling away required the greatest effort, and she was rapidly weakening. Glancing at his face, she realized that he was concentrating harder.

What's he trying to do to me?

For the first time she was frightened of his awesome power and understood the sense of helplessness that Mike Malone must have felt during those poltergeist incidents. Victim of an unknown, unlimited power. A power from the deepest reaches of the human mind.

Air! I can't breathe. He's trying to suffocate me. Why, Rory? What have I done to anger you? Have I hurt you?

She could not break free; he was actually pulling her toward him. The force felt like a giant hand, no, hundreds of hands that groped and pawed her body. Stiffening her arms, she braced herself against his shoulders, but Rory's strength was incredible. Never had she thought that he could use his force on people. How foolishly naive, how utterly stupid to have overlooked the full extent of so formidable a power as his.

"Holy cow!" shouted James Gray, glancing at the television monitor. "Holy cow in heaven!"

The screen flashed in a burst of blinding light, then glowed. The grandfather clock leaped off the floor and sailed through the air, smashing into the wall—or was it through the wall of the Black Room? The vase struck the ceiling, its pieces continually swirling in a circle like the blades of a blender. The camera bounced from wall to wall like a rubber ball. Every object in the room was airborne, a lethal projectile.

As the screen flashed, Cheryl Roland, who had been at the window watching Liz, was knocked to the floor, dazed. Then her body jerked in spasms as if struck by a tidal wave; it swept her up in its roaring head, repeatedly battering her against the ground.

Then the screen went blank.

Cheryl lay motionless, not comprehending what had hit her.

Gerhardt ran to the controls and threw the switch that lighted the Black Room.

Destruction. Total devastation of every target in the room, of the Black Room itself. The rectangular array of metal photomultiplier tubes that had once resembled an unlit stadium scoreboard had melted from overload and now looked like a surrealistic sculpture, an oozing, viscous fluid frozen in time. Escaping from fractured pipes, the liquid nitrogen coolant that at minus 196 degrees centigrade had given the photomultiplier tubes their extreme sensitivity had vaporized in plumes of thick white smoke. The pan of the scale that Liz had insisted Rory press upon now curved backward, folded around the sides of the scale, which itself was crushed to half its original height as if an elephant balanced on one foot had stood on the scale's pan.

Trembling, terrified, Liz retreated from Rory.

He attempted to kill me!

Backing out of the room, she avoided his stare, which seemed to be part quizzical, part apologetic.

You know what you did, she thought. You deliberately focused your energy on me. You tried to suffocate me, to crush my body with your power. You wanted to kill me! Why, Rory? She was not surprised that he didn't attempt to speak to her; no words could justify his behavior. And at the moment she didn't care to speak to him; all she wanted to do was escape his staring eyes.

No, don't leave, thought Rory. Please, Dr. Hartman, help me. But this time the power had stolen his voice. Her expression was one of stark horror, and he wondered what she had experienced.

He wanted to explain. I didn't do it purposely. You begged me to perform, then got me hot and the power took over. But I fought it for your sake, diverted it to the targets. Don't run away.

Still groggy, he leaned forward, offering her his hand. Please hold it—I'm frightened, too. I don't know what's happening to me. But his gesture only hastened her exit from the room. The door slammed closed. I'm sorry. Oh God am I sorry.

Clutching the camera, Gerhardt raced down the hall to the Black Room to film the devastation. Tight on his heels ran James Gray, his belly bouncing as he strained to keep pace with Gerhardt.

In the lab Liz passed Cheryl Roland, who leaned against the wall by the window, clearly dumbfounded. When Cheryl attempted to speak, Liz turned away and hurried from the room into the hall.

She must be alone to collect her thoughts, her composure. Already she was doubting her initial judgment: Rory wouldn't attempt to kill me. There must be some logical explanation for what transpired in that room. And exactly what did Gerhardt and Cheryl witness? Certainly they couldn't see what I felt; Rory's force field is invisible. How then did they interpret my peculiar behavior?

Hurrying down the hall, her mind raced. If Rory's assault was accidental—it had to be—then her talented child was more dangerous than she had ever imagined, or he himself had realized; she'd have to protect him until these new manifestations of his power could be controlled.

As she passed the elevator the door opened and out stepped a policeman. Not a campus cop; this one wore a New York City uniform. Averting her head to avoid conversation, she hurried on, but he pursued her.

"Excuse me," he said just as she was about to enter the science library. "I'm looking for Dr. Elizabeth Hartman. The guard said I'd find her laboratory on this floor."

He must want Gerhardt, she thought, something to do with that interview. More questions. Why this intrusion now!

"I'm Dr. Hartman."

"Captain Webb, Thomas Webb, Dr. Hartman. Pleased to meet you. If you can spare a few minutes, I'd like to ask you some questions. About a boy. Rory Malone."

She stiffened. Glancing down the hall, she saw that she had left the door to the laboratory open.

"Why? Who sent you?"

"Mike Malone, the boy's father. Seems I just missed Rory at home, and his father said I'd find him here."

Flashing a calm, and what she hoped was a friendly smile, Liz said, "Captain, today's not your day. You just missed Mr. Malone here, too. He left about ten minutes ago."

"Perhaps it's better that I speak with you first. Can we use the library? Or your office?"

In her peripheral vision Liz spotted Cheryl Roland exit the laboratory, cross the hall, and enter the lady's room. "The cafeteria on the first floor will be better," she said, leading him back to the elevator and praying that Rory did not emerge from the lab.

Oh God, Rory, what have you done?

"The cafeteria is fine with me," he said, following her brisk steps, wondering if Carrie's interview had run overtime, if he might catch her. They could have dinner together, exchange their respective findings. The conversation with Mike Malone had left him with some very pointed questions for the lovely Dr. Hartman.

Glancing at her in the elevator, he thought, Jesus, they didn't make professors like this when I went to school. Or else I'd have gone on for a doctorate.

35

Gently Rory turned the key in the lock. The house lights were out, his father asleep. It was well after midnight; he should have been home hours ago.

After regaining equilibrium he had left the Red Room and found the laboratory empty. Had he frightened them all away, he wondered? At the end of the hall he'd spotted James Gray and Gerhardt filming the havoc in the Black Room. Fortunately they had been too preoccupied to notice him. While he'd succeeded in diverting his energy from Dr. Hartman to the targets, he still wondered how much she had felt: obviously enough to terrify her.

It was probably best that he'd been unable to locate Dr. Hartman, for he could not have apologized anyway: His voice returned sometime on the subway heading downtown.

He had left the campus perplexed and hating himself. The electric bridge that had sprung up out of nowhere remained a mystery. Carrie Wilson seemed the only quasi-logial explanation. And the inability to suppress his sexual desire for Dr. Hartman, for the woman who treated him like a son, attested to his innate turpitude and loathsome nature. She must have sensed that he was being swept away by sexual thoughts and assumed that this was not the first time he'd desired her. If she never wanted to see him again, he would understand and abide by her wish.

You're scum. And dangerous scum at that.

As he passed the sofa, the telephone rang and he leaped for it, lifting the receiver midway through the first ring. Had the sound awakened his father? Realizing that the only person who would phone at this hour must be Dr. Hartman ready to confront him, he was tempted to hang up. But she would only call back. He had to face her sooner or later.

"Hello," he whispered.

"Rory?"

"Melissa! It's after midnight. Are you crazy?"

"You said you'd call and you didn't. I waited . . . all day, Rory. I have to speak with you."

"Not now, baby. Can't it wait till morning?"

"No, please. I've felt miserable since the drive-in. I can't eat or sleep. You hate me, I know you do."

"I don't." But he had, briefly. She had encouraged him, gotten him intensely aroused, responded to his every sexual advance, then at the last minute, when he'd ached beyond control, she'd cut him off. He had despised her for that until after he came, when he'd despised himself even more for having experienced such rage toward the girl he loved.

"You do hate me. You ignored me in the car; then you don't call. I only did it to win you back."

"What?"

"I know there's another girl. Who is she, Rory?

"Baby, there's no other girl. Now please, let's talk tomorrow." He glanced toward the hall, straining to hear if that sound came from his father's room.

"Rory, you don't realize how much I love you, how hard it is when you don't call."

Mike Malone's voice stormed from the bedroom. "Who the hell's calling at this hour?"

"I've been thinking," said Melissa. "I could be more—well, you know—more open."

"Melissa, please, hang up."

"That's what you want, though. Don't you? You want me to be like other girls."

"No, I want you to hang up. Pop's awake."

"You do, Rory. I realize why I'm losing you. And I'm going to try to change. I promise I'll try."

His father's bedroom slippers scuffed through the hall.

"I gotta go," said Rory, "Pop's up."

"See me tomorrow, please? Promise? We'll go to the drive-in if you like. Okay?"

"Yes, okay. Now baby, please hang up." He placed the receiver gently into the cradle just as his father entered the darkened room.

"Who the hell was that?"

"Melissa," he answered softly. "I'm sorry she woke you."
Please, go back to bed, Pop. Don't start on me.

Mike Malone's black silhouette moved to the end of the sofa, his arm reaching toward the table lamp.

"Never again, you hear! Tell her never to call this late."

The room lit.

His father's eyes did not appear groggy, as if he'd been sleeping. Had he been lying awake, waiting to issue a reprimand for coming home late?

"Where have you been, boy?"

"After Dr. Hartman's I went to a movie. In the city."

"Don't lie to me."

"I'm not, Pop. I swear."

Reading the fury in his father's eyes, he instinctively stepped back, expecting a flying fist.

But none came.

"You had a visitor tonight, boy. You wanna know who? A cop. A cop to see a kid of mine! He wanted to know all about your 'emotional problems.'"

Oh Jesus! The police were onto him. Had Kathy Bauer talked? Had witnesses identified him?

"What did you tell him?" he asked hesitantly.

"Tell him? Nothing! Fuckin' nothing! I sent him to your goddamn Dr. Hartman. Let her do the blabbin'."

He'd not seen such anger in his father's eyes for some time. His father inched closer.

"That cop wanted to know something else, boy. About your funny haircut."

They *had* fingered him.

"I told him you did it to be cooler. Ya know what he asked, boy, right away? 'But when did Rory cut it?' *When?* He wanted to know the exact day."

They had seen him since the accident. How else would they know about his hair? Suppose they've been trailing him? Even to the hospital?

"I said I didn't remember. Sometime last week. But that was one persistent cop. He even wanted to know the exact time of day. As though it was real important. Then he said he wanted to question you. About your relationship with Kathy Bauer."

Had the cop gone to Dr. Hartman's? Is that why he'd been unable to locate her?

His father drew closer.

"I didn't do anything wrong, Pop. I swear."

"Don't lie to me! Cops don't come to your house asking all those questions because you're innocent. What'd you do?"

His father's hands clenched into fists.

Stay away, Pop. Don't come any closer, please.

"Not till that cop left did I remember when you cut your hair. You know what refreshed my memory, boy?"

Don't hit me. I warn you.

"You were on television tonight. Seven thirty news. I almost missed you. I was about to go back to the shop when I heard they were doing a special report on that Kathy Bauer girl. They showed interviews with her family and friends. Then suddenly you. Shy, you were. Real shy. Like the cat got your tongue. Wouldn't even give your name. They showed you practically running away from the camera. Then you know what that nurse said?"

I'm strong tonight, Pop. Stronger than I've ever been. And I've learned . . . learned how to direct the power.

"Real sweet like, bubblin' over, she said, He's another classmate. Tony Mora.' Tony Mora! What the hell are you up to? What'd you do to that young girl? And using my pal's name."

His father grabbed him by the shirt. He pulled free.

Don't touch me again. I can direct it any way I want.

"It's returning, ain't it? That freaky stuff? That's why the cops wanted you. You pushed that girl."

"No, Pop, swear to God, I didn't."

"I thought it was gone. That it'd never come back once you started seeing those doctors. But it has. Even Lil's detected it and won't be around you. It's a curse you can't get rid of."

His father grabbed him by the shoulders, shaking him violently.

"You fuckin' pushed that poor girl. Why? Because she'd have nothing to do with a freak like you?"

He was being pushed back into a corner of the room. He'd be beaten as he had in the past.

"I didn't touch her."

Back, Pop. Get back. I'm so strong I don't know if I can control it.

"You fuckin' liar! Freak! I'll kill you. That's the only way to get rid of that curse."

His father's fist came flying toward his face.

But it never connected.

In an instant the fist froze midair as if restrained by an

invisible rope. Then like a missile Mike Malone soared into the air and rocketed against the sofa, which toppled over, taking with it the floor lamp, which struck Mike across the face. Scrambling to his feet, stunned, blood trickling from the gash above his right eye, Mike approached Rory again, fists up.

"Go back, Pop, I warn you."

But Mike Malone lunged forward, shouting, "I'll kill you!"

Again he jerked into the air, sailed across the room, crashed into the wall, and slid to the ground.

Rory did not have to direct the power—indeed, he was only peripherally aware of events around him. Once it was unleashed, the power flowed from and was driven by anger and fear, possessing a life and purpose of its own. There was no electrified air, no flying sparks or crackling sounds, no bridge with Mike Malone at one end, for this power derived not from the groin but the heart and stood rooted in an appetite far more primitive than sexual satisfaction: self-preservation. Aside from dulled sensory awareness, all Rory experienced was a rainbow of colors scintillating on his retinas as if he had stared into a blindingly bright light, then pressed his fists against his eyeballs. This was the rudimentary, unrefined, uncultivated, uneducated power that had spontaneously surfaced a year and a half ago, with one major difference: Now it lashed at Mike Malone with hell-bent vengeance.

Books became projectiles, flying off shelves, rocketing into Mike Malone's body, knocking him to the ground every time he attempted to stagger to his feet. Records leaped out of their jackets in choreographed progression and swirled like razor-sharp flying saucers, first skirting, then slicing at Mike Malone's head, neck, shoulders, legs and shredding his clothes. When he finally struggled to his feet, arms shielding his head and face, a vase from the top of the television bulleted into his stomach, smashing and causing him to double up in pain.

"Freak!" Mike shouted, blood issuing from his mouth. "Fuckin' freak!"

Suddenly the television screen exploded. Glass fragments, piercingly sharp, lodged in Mike Malone's cheeks. A large, triangular piece drove into his neck.

Running down the hall toward the kitchen, Mike shouted, "Get out, freak! Out of my house!"

Suddenly there came an ear-shattering explosion.

All Rory remembered later was hearing plates, glasses, pots, and pans crash to the kitchen floor. Then the loud popping of windows; first on the ground floor, then upstairs.

That night he left the house—what remained of it—forever.

Tuesday
Day 5

36

Webb sank into the cushioned wingback chair in Dr. Gerhardt Kiner's office, which actually was one room of the West Side apartment he shared with his wife, who was at her Columbia laboratory. He'd been amazed to learn that Liz Hartman's husband was the psychologist Carrie had interviewed, and that Kiner had been treating Rory Malone for emotional problems for more than a year.

In Kiner, though, Webb had finally found someone who would talk candidly about the boy, for lately he had been getting the runaround.

Langdon Dawson, the principal at Forest Hills High, claimed that only Rory's father could disclose the problems that had necessitated the school transfer. But Mike Malone had proved to be equally closed-mouthed as well as aggravated, if not strangely unsettled, by Webb's visit, and had dispatched him to Liz Hartman with a gruff, "She's supposed to have cured him of his problem. Let her tell you about it."

Liz Hartman had played cat and mouse with him as she tried to extract more information than she would reveal. He'd told her the bare minimum—that Rory Malone might have witnessed the recent subway accident of Kathy Bauer and consequently was wanted for questioning—and he'd gotten even less in return. Rory Malone was the subject of her current research, but she staunchly refused to discuss that work until he first spoke with the boy's therapist, concluding: "It's only ethical that his doctor, if not his father, reveal the nature of Rory's problem. Although I must add that neither do I now, nor have I ever, viewed Rory Malone's talent as a problem."

From Kiner, at least, now he knew the nature of Rory Malone's talent, but considering the violent poltergeist outbursts that had occurred more than a year ago in the Malone home, he viewed the boy's ability decidedly as a problem and wondered how the lovely Dr. Hartman rationalized it to be a talent.

"I find it all very hard to believe," said Webb with an enigmatic grin, "but I've read about the poltergeist phenomenon. I just always assumed it was a hoax."

"I assure you that this case is legitimate," said Gerhardt.

"Do you know why the mother's death triggered the phenomenon?"

"I believe so. At age five Rory witnessed his parents engaged in intercourse. He interpreted his father's aggressive assaults—and his mother's abhorrence of the act—as a brutal battle, sort of an attempt by the father to kill the mother. For years he harbored this belief. And when his mother died, the belief became reality, even though by then he was knowledgeable about sex and the innocent events surrounding her death."

"So hatred toward his father peaked," said Webb, enjoying as he always did an excursion into psychology, a discussion with another student of the mind. "What kind of man is Mike Malone? I found him quite secretive."

"A sexual hypocrite."

Webb frowned, confused.

"One side of Mike Malone prizes virginity in a woman; the other lusts after whores. He harbors that destructive dichotomy that there are two kinds of women: One you marry, one you fuck. Excuse my French. He's instilled this belief in Rory, and we've been working to overcome it."

Gerhardt added: "If this were not enough for the poor boy, his sexual problems were greatly compounded by the nuns and priests at St. Vincent's High."

"Through Catholic teachings?"

"One in particular. They preached strenuously against masturbation, and after Rory had confessed masturbating several times to a Father Francis Bianchi, do you know what that sick man told him? 'The next time you're tempted, remember your mother's in heaven watching you; she'll see you perform that vile act.' That of course stopped him cold for six months. And during that time the poltergeist events reached their peak intensity."

"A combination of hatred for his father, a high adolescent sexual chemistry, and intense sexual frustrations," said Webb, more than a little pleased at his concise summary.

"Exactly."

"Have you been able to help him?" asked Webb.

"As part of Rory's therapy I recommended he transfer to a public school and that he masturbate whenever he wanted—ten times a day if he desired. And that he enjoy sexual fantasies, which he then regarded as sins."

"Even fantasies?"

"By strict Catholic teaching, a deliberate sexual thought that leads to arousal—not even orgasm—is equivalent to committing the action itself."

"Did your suggestions help?"

"He had trouble masturbating at first. The image of his mother was a potent inhibitor. To obliterate that image I encouraged his use of pornography. In fact, Captain, he was so afraid to buy even mildly pornographic magazines that at first I provided them for him. To further assuage his guilt over fantasizing, I loaned him Nancy Friday's book *Men In Love*. It assured him of the universal nature of fantasies, their importance in sexual development and marriage." Gerhardt laughed. "He was amazed to learn the book was a national bestseller and that people were reading it openly on subways and buses."

"Is he a virgin?"

"Yes, though he finds this a source of great embarrassment."

"Doctor, if Rory Malone was angry enough at someone, might his poltergeist energy be sufficient to knock that person over?"

"That would require considerable strength," said Gerhardt cautiously. Liz had warned him not to reveal too much of their research. "If you'll excuse me, I have a patient waiting."

"Just one more question. If you have been sexually liberating Rory Malone, what has your wife, a radiation physicist—I checked her background—what's she doing for him?"

Liz had pleaded with him not to reveal her work. If it became necessary she would do it herself, but first she wanted to speak to Rory. "Delay him until I can get to Rory, please, Gerhardt," she had said. "I've got to find out if he had anything to do with that girl's accident."

Gerhardt stood. "Now that we've spoken, my wife will gladly fill you in on her research. She's tied up today. Perhaps you would like to see her tomorrow?"

Webb followed Kiner into the hall, which, with two straightback chairs, a magazine rack, and a floor lamp, served as a waiting area. In one chair, reading an issue of *Vogue*, sat a striking brunet; in her early thirties, Webb guessed. She greeted his stare with such honesty that he smiled, and she warmly returned the gesture.

He liked her immediately. He lingered. "Does the Malone boy pay for his appointments?" he asked, diverting his eyes only for a moment from the brunet.

"No."

"He sure charges me an arm and a leg," joked the woman, standing. "Well, Doctor, no money from me for two weeks."

"Is something wrong, Susan?"

"Wrong? No, everything is wonderful. Carl called from Mexico. I'm joining him for two glorious weeks of vacation. I leave at noon."

"Lucky you," said Webb; then to Kiner, "I may have more questions in a few days." Before passing out the front door, he shot a beaming farewell smile to the charming brunet.

"Let's begin," said Gerhardt. "I wouldn't want you to miss your plane." Then he thought: Liz asked me to phone her when Webb left; she's probably dying to know how things went. "Susan, if you would rather cancel this appointment, if you're pressed for time, I'd understand. There would be no charge."

"Well, I am cutting it close." Boy, could she use the time!

She hadn't finished packing. Then traffic might be heavy to JFK, and she didn't have her boarding pass, which meant waiting in line. The temptation to accept Dr. Kiner's kind offer was strong. Should she, though? The hallucinations were probably nothing serious, nothing that couldn't wait two weeks. But they had been troubling, confusing. Why should a boy, a very young one at that—a boy she'd seen a few times at Dr. Kiner's office; they'd only exchanged hellos—why had he entered her sexual fantasies? God knows she didn't lust after him. He was a baby. Granted, she had some bizarre sexual obsessions, but not chicken. Sue Stiner wasn't into robbing the cradle.

Yet more than once during her fantasizing, his image had replaced Carl's. They'd switched places. A superimposition. And that boy, that child, did things to her—marvelous things—that Carl would never do. Perhaps that was why she had substituted someone for Carl. But why a child? She must be sicker than she thought. She had better tell Dr. Kiner. He would have an answer.

"Thanks but no thanks," she said. "I'd better keep my appointment. There's something I must tell you."

37

Bauer stormed out of the intensive-care unit. His poor baby was gonna die. Lying there delirious, rambling incoherently under a high fever. If she died, her fuckin' assailant would be up for murder; the punishment was too easy for the fuckin' animal.

He headed downstairs to the hospital cafeteria. He'd had nothing to eat since his sister-in-law phoned at three in the morning with the news that Kathy had taken a turn for the worse.

The reattached limb hadn't taken. Circulation had broken down; nerve endings had died. Shriveled. Kathy had come out of surgery shortly after ten A.M., her condition listed as grave. A lung infection had at first made the doctors reluctant to operate, for her health was too weak to sustain the shock of reamputation. But then they'd had no choice: Gangrene began to fester in the dying, dead limb.

With a container of coffee and a buttered roll, Bauer returned to the main floor. Still no sign of Webb. Where the fuck was he? He'd promised to be there as soon as possible. That was four fuckin' hours ago.

If Kathy died, Webb better launch an all-out effort to find her killer. Drag in every suspect, regardless how circumstantial the evidence. They should have done that already.

Avoiding the lobby, he headed toward the doctors' private lounge.

Fuckin' reporters. TV cameras. They'd swarmed into the lobby at nine like sharks on the scent of blood. They smelled Kathy's death. Wanted to photograph her last breath, her mother's tearful sobs. Didn't they respect anyone's privacy?

Least of all his. Since being identified as the girl's uncle, his phone hadn't stopped ringing. Requests for fuckin' interviews from *Time* and *Newsweek*. Would he write an editorial on crime in the city for the Sunday *Times*? A column on the case for the *News*? Pose by his niece's bed for a picture for the *Post*? Disgusting. The biggest money offers for his "exclusive" story came from the *Enquirer*, with the *Star* trailing by a mere three hundred bucks. Fuckin' media. Desperate for news.

Well, at least the media believed that Kathy was a victim of a subway pusher and were putting pressure on Webb. "They always suspect the worst," Webb had said after reading several newspaper versions of the incident. "It makes better copy."

Bauer recalled how the media had attacked him for beatin' on that fuckin' nigger. They just couldn't see he was doing society a favor, by teaching a lesson to a good-for-nothing who by now was probably a mugger or a murderer. Well, for all its faults, at least the media were right this time in suspecting the worst.

Locked.

The fuckin' lounge was off limits to anyone without an M.D. The first time he'd entered the lounge, strolling in behind a doctor and taking a seat, several doctors had viewed him with disdain. But they'd been smart enough not to say a word.

He rattled the door again.

Knocked.

Voices inside. But no one opened the door.

Fuck 'em.

Returning to Kathy's room, he sat on the empty bed.

He'd been there only a few minutes when Nurse Graybar entered.

"Sorry, Sergeant Bauer, but I've got to put fresh sheets on that bed."

His eyes widened. "She's being moved back here?" he asked. That must mean she's out of danger. At least less critical.

"Another patient's been assigned to this room."

Then Kathy *was* gonna die. They were so certain of it they were taking away her room.

Grudgingly he got off the bed.

"Today's the day we had thought she would be well enough to have visitors. So many of her classmates were going to come back." She stripped the bed, put the used sheets into a plastic bag, and began applying new ones. "Those who don't read the morning papers or listen to the news won't know. They'll probably come thinking they can see her."

Nurse Graybar suddenly remembered something she had wanted to ask Captain Webb. But he hadn't been around for a few days. Sergeant Bauer was staring out the window.

"Sergeant, did you ever find out why that one classmate lied about his name?"

Bauer turned. "Who lied?"

"I forgot the name he gave me. Oh, wait. More . . . Mora. Yes. Tony Mora. That's it. But then two of his classmates told us his name was really Rory Malone. A nice boy. He was buying her a card." She paused. "Funny, I don't recall opening a card with either name on it."

Bauer was next to her. "When did this happen?"

"A few days ago. It would be recorded on my daily list of visitors."

"Why didn't you tell me? Then! I said I wanted all the names."

She was taken aback by his burst of anger. He'd always been gruff and sharp-tongued with her, with everyone, but he'd never attacked her so pointedly.

"Well, Captain Webb was there. He heard it. I just assumed—" Bauer's stare stopped her short. Clearly Captain Webb had not told Sergeant Bauer about that boy's lie.

"Look at this," he said, pulling the artist's sketch from his pocket. To hell with Webb's orders not to circulate, even show, the drawing. "Does this resemble that kid?"

She studied the picture carefully. Obviously there was more to that boy's lie than she'd assumed. "Slightly," she answered. "Some of the features are the same. But that boy had very short hair." Then her hand shot to her mouth. She remembered.

"Two girls, his classmates," she said. "They commented that he'd cut his hair. Very short. Yes, I recall they preferred it longer. They said he was handsomer with longer hair. Thought the short hair was too punk. Sergeant, that's the same boy. I'd swear to it. What has he done?"

Bauer was out the door before she had finished the question.

Rory Malone. Forest Hills High. The bastard! Hell with Webb's pussyfootin'. Get the kid, now.

Rory Malone, I'm comin' for you. You'll be in the station house within the hour.

38

That night Rory left home forever.

Returning to the city, he slept on the grass in Central Park. The number of young people bedding down with sleeping bags and backpacks astonished him: foreigners, tourists, all concealing themselves under bushes from the dozen or so park police who patrolled the grounds.

A German couple offered him a blanket, but he declined, for the night air was warm, the grass cool and comfortable. Besides, his senses of hearing and speech had only partially recovered from the enormous unleashing of psychic energy. At that time, too, the events that had transpired at home still had not come into clear focus. In fact, they did not until early the next morning, and he wasn't certain whether this temporary deterioration of memory represented still another side effect of the power or if it was a purely psychological matter in which guilt and remorse combined to cloud the facts. Whatever, he slept fitfully; though among the camping tourists he felt less a runaway or a homeless degenerate.

Now it was late morning, and he felt ravenously hungry. Leaving the park at Fifty-ninth Street, he walked two blocks down the Avenue of the Americas to the coffee shop adjacent to Carnegie Hall. Eighty-six dollars from lawn jobs lay folded in his wallet; about three hundred more remained at home hidden in his bedroom. During a breakfast of pancakes, bacon, and a chocolate shake, he debated whether to get the money but decided that would be too risky. The cash on him would last for weeks.

Weeks. He wouldn't be free that long with the police on his

trail. By now they were probably familiar with Dr. Hartman's experiments and the havoc at home; they had undoubtedly spoken to Gerhardt, too.

Should he phone Dr. Hartman, seek advice? More than anyone else, she cared about him. Yet he was too embarrassed to face her. If the power had pawed her body, then she was shockingly aware of his true sexual desire for her. He wondered if all friendships, all relationships between people would collapse if each person could somehow know the full sexual designs and predilections that another person had?

For instance, throughout the night he had dreamed wild, passionate fantasies of Carrie Wilson. How would that heavenly angel regard Rory Malone if she knew the parts of her body his lips had kissed, the crevices his tongue had explored and tasted, the orifices violated by his fingers and cock? Over and over, again and again? Lust was never meant to be transparent, and yet his power might make it just that.

Should he phone Gerhardt? He had never felt close to him. He was thankful Gerhardt made him realize that all men fantasize, that masturbation is normal, grateful for the sexual liberation—and yet . . . wasn't it this very liberation that lay at the root of his present torment?

Staring at the customers eating breakfast, he realized that he'd never felt so absolutely alone, and he attempted to make eye contact, to at least have his presence acknowledged by someone, anyone. Yet his glances were either overlooked or ignored. He'd smiled warmly at the waitress when she had taken his order and again when she had returned with the food, but she too didn't seem to notice him. He felt invisible, a nonentity, as he'd often felt around his father.

Paying the check, he made one final attempt to break through the waitress's invincibility with a cheerful "Thank you." Even though she didn't respond, he secured a dollar tip under his water glass.

Wandering through stores, he worked his way down Broadway, past souvenir shops, discount drugstores, art galleries that featured paintings on black velour and framed psychedelic posters. After an hour he bought a bag of hot cashew nuts and an Orange Julius.

He was thoroughly confused. Suppose the police found him—and he was certain they would. What case could they construct against him? So he had poltergeist energy. In the laboratory he lifted heavy objects; in anger he tossed a human being, destroyed a home. There could be no question in anyone's mind that the energy still percolated in Rory Malone. That it was more directional, controllable . . . Thank you, Dr. Hartman.

But then you didn't want the female-hormone therapy. The side effects had terrified you. You consented eagerly, gratefully to Dr. Hartman's plan to educate your talent.

Yet all that wasn't proof that he was responsible for Kathy Bauer's accident. The only proof could come from Kathy herself, and what could she say? "Rory Malone violated me, raped me. His hands and tongue raced all over my body. He penetrated me and it hurt terribly. But he never came near me. I just can't explain it any better."

Would the police believe that?

In fact, just because Rory Malone could mentally lift objects did not imply he could pleasure women with his thoughts. Indeed, he himself remained uncertain that the ability was genuine and puzzled how it had developed in the first place.

His fantasies about women were normal, he thought, until the first time he came without touching himself. It happened during a romantic daydream at a school basketball game. From the bleachers he was admiring the untouchable Chrissy Skelton, a perky blond with a reputation for dating only jocks, who was substituting as head cheerleader because Kathy Bauer was ill. Each time she leaped into the air, arms and legs spread, chest arched, breasts bouncing, her short skirt flapping to reveal panties in the school colors, he caught her.

Once he carried her off under the bleachers, and on the polished floor they kissed, fondled, rolled over each other, and she confessed he'd been her secret love all year. "Oh, sure, you're quiet and shy, but that's why I like you—you're refreshing. I'd hoped you'd get up the nerve." Though he was highly aroused, the sudden spasm in his groin, followed by the squirt of fluid against his abdomen, caught him by surprise. Embarrassed, he'd glanced from the bleachers at Chrissy, who for an uncharacteristic moment was standing still, and she returned a warm, inviting smile.

Washing off in the men's room, he had reassessed the smile and concluded it had been wishful thinking, an extension of his daydream. Chrissy Skelton wouldn't give Rory Malone the time of day.

The next day, however, she had approached him in study hall. "Terrific game, wasn't it? We sure walloped 'em. I—uh—have you heard when Kathy's returning? Me neither. Spotted you in the bleachers. Say, see ya around." Had he asked her out, he was certain she'd have accepted.

Two days later it occurred again: in the Laundromat where he did the weekly wash. An attractive brunet, about twenty-three, was bouncing a baby on her lap, kissing and cuddling the child. Its face repeatedly brushed against the woman's breasts, as did its tiny, groping hands. After transferring his clothes to the dryer, Rory took a seat opposite the woman and stared, imagining himself in the child's place, smothered in the woman's loving embrace.

He didn't instruct himself to concentrate, to drift, to float, as he did in the laboratory, but later he realized that that was precisely what had happened. At the moment all he knew was that the tingle of the woman's blouse on his cheek, her lips on his forehead, her arms snuggling his body, were astonishingly real.

Several times she had glanced at him curiously. "It's just because I'm staring," he assured himself; and when she smiled, then beckoned with a friendly nod, he knew it must be his imagination playing tricks. When she stood, the baby's hand yanked on her blouse, exposing a bare breast, and he came. Shamed by the incident, he'd spent the rest of the time in the back of the store by the dryers.

Stuffing clothes into the laundry bag, he had sensed the woman behind him.

"If you fold them now, they won't need ironing."

She placed the baby in the stroller and, helping him fold clothes, chatted in an exceptionally warm and familiar manner.

The embarrassing wetness in his pants had made him even shyer than he normally was.

182 . . .

Certain now that the fantasies were uncommonly real to him, he began to wonder if his imaginary lovers could somehow read his thoughts, and Janette Wojno had almost convinced him of this.

Janette Wojno was his twenty-five-year-old French teacher, and though he had a desperate crush on her and trumped-up endless excuses for private counseling after school, he could never rouse her from her cold, detached professionalism. One afternoon she gave him a list of verbs to conjugate while she washed the blackboard. As her hand, holding a wet sponge, swept the board in swift circles, her ass, rocking in unison motion, became the focus of a potent fantasy.

Tenderly he made love to Miss Wojno, and for the remainder of the session she was unusually friendly; she even called him Rory instead of Mr. Malone. Always a stickler for correct pronunciation, escorting him to the door, she had said, "Don't worry about pronunciation; stick to the grammar. And Rory, ask for help any time. After all, that's why I'm here." From that day on a special rapport had existed between them, and he fantasized about her frequently.

All this led him to formulate a theory: A man becomes irresistible to a woman by implanting in her mind his own romantic fantasies of her. This magical exchange, however, accomplished, is the basis for "sex appeal," that elusive chemistry that transforms certain men into high-scoring Romeos. He thought he'd found the ingredient that accounted for some men's extraordinary ability to woo women, while others of seemingly equal attributes seldom got to first base. With practice, he considered, could this fantasizing become automatic, unconscious? Then a guy wouldn't even realize he was turning a woman on with his thoughts.

Such theorizing was not the kind of thing he'd reveal to Gerhardt, though.

Whatever the cause, his sex life had changed. Encouraged by the unexpected friendliness of several previously disinterested women—and the prospect (though not the guarantee) of spontaneous orgasm—he began romantically fantasizing about every girl in school, every woman on the street, who turned him on. In a short time he was reaching orgasms frequently enough to make the practice of fantasizing an addiction. Soon, though, hugging, kissing, and feeling up his fully-dressed lovers was not enough.

As with any addiction, each experience had to be more dynamic than the last, so he began undressing his lovers. Quickly, naked body contact yielded to copulation, then to cunnilingus, and finally to every sexual practice he learned about from magazines and films.

Somewhere in this progression from romantic daydream to hardcore sex, he realized that he had changed. An unknown force seemed to have taken control of his body. His sexual appetite greedily demanded more frequent feedings, and when he spotted a potential lover his libido shouted out for instant gratification. While he didn't understand what was happening to him, he did know that some part of his mind was obsessed with achieving sexual satisfaction—and worse, that insatiable part of him appeared to be blindly amoral, selfishly demanding whatever it wanted with total disregard for the other person's rights and wishes.

He strongly suspected that Dr. Hartman's experiments were instrumental in teaching him how to transform fantasy into reality. Without proof, though, he couldn't reveal his suspicions and destroy her research. He had to be certain he could mentally pleasure women, and the most recent evidence was decidedly contradictory: He'd fantasized about Laurette Delgado and she had laughed. Patty Bunnell ran. Heather Rollefson introduced herself. Gloria Lohse ignored him. Kathy Bauer fell. Evelyn Rhomley smiled. Susan Stiner moaned. Alice Tobias chuckled. Kitty Brennan screamed. Liz Hartman backed away.

Such varied reactions didn't make sense. But then, he thought, you have always been too dazed, too sexually involved in the fantasy, to really study a woman's full reaction. The one experiment with Mrs. Rhomley thankfully had produced negative results. Perhaps another experiment, more carefully planned and executed, would confirm that the pleasurings are all figments of your imagination. Yes, you must do it. You must know the truth.

*   *   *

A block from the Metropole he conceived the plan that would ultimately test his power to stimulate women at a distance. If his worst suspicions were confirmed, then he would know the power was genuine and . . . What? Submit to the humiliation of hormone therapy? Or run away, hide in seclusion until his power faded with his adolescence?

It was 12:30 P.M. when he entered the Metropole.

He had never been there at this hour, and the first thing that struck him was the size of the crowd. Scores of businessmen in suits and ties, on lunch hour. Of course, he thought, this way they can get their rocks off and still be home on time at night, their wives none the wiser.

He checked the wall poster for the show times.

He would have to wait till one o'clock to test his power. In the meantime he would charge himself up. Get really hot and horny.

39

Bauer had found twelve Malones in the Queens directory, spread all the hell over the borough. It was too vast an area to attempt a door-to-door search, so he'd gone straight from the hospital to Forest Hills High School.

Principal Langdon Dawson's welcome had been none too friendly. Bauer had come asking only for the address of Rory Malone, but Dawson had launched into a fuckin' sermon, ending with:

"As I told the other officer, I can reveal nothing about the boy's emotional problems or why he was transferred here. It would be unethical. You'll have to speak with his father."

Secretive bastard, Webb.

Driving to 145 Chestnut Street, Bauer pondered why Webb had revealed nothing about his own investigation. It was an extensive one, probably, knowing the captain. He'd had a few days head start. He'd spoken with Dawson and undoubtedly the kid's father, Mike Malone. Maybe the kid himself. God knows who else. And he'd kept it all quiet.

Bauer fumed. He spoke to himself in the air conditioned police car. "You've never forgiven me for beatin' on that nigger. Six-month suspension wasn't enough for you. You wanted me dropped. Out. Fuckin' ignorant, righteous bastard. You think I'll beat the shit out of this Malone kid. Bring him in bloody. Why not? He'd be getting off easy with black eyes and a few busted teeth. Look what he did to my niece."

The first thing about the Malone house that grabbed his attention was the broken windows. From his approach to the house, it looked as though every damn window on both floors was shattered. For a moment he wondered if the house were deserted. He saw no signs of life. But no, the lawn obviously had been recently mowed, and the flowers stood too sturdy and healthy to have been abandoned.

Parking directly in front of the flagstone path to the front door, he could see no glass on the ground around the house. His analytical mind clicked on. An explosion inside would have thrown glass outward. Someone could have already cleaned up the pieces. But then why hadn't anyone bothered to remove the sharp fragments that still hung precariously like daggers from many windows?

Mighty strange.

Walking up the path onto the grass, he saw there were no splinters of glass on the ground. The force that had shattered these windows came from the outside, blowing the glass inward onto the floor. He'd bet on it.

But he'd heard of no gas-main explosion in the area, no unusually strong sonic boom. Besides, only this house had been hit. And it was very close to both neighboring houses. They should have shown some signs of the blast.

What the fuck had happened?

Through the torn screen door he spotted a large, heavy-set man, about in his fifties, working inside. From the sunlight that streamed through the door and paneless windows, he plainly saw that the house was in a shambles.

Shit! That kills the theory of an external blast. It had to originate on the inside.

He did not knock but opened the door and entered the living room.

"Looks like an A-bomb blew off in here," said Bauer.

From the kneeling position in which he had been picking up glass fragments from the windows, the television screen, and various shattered objects, Mike Malone turned with a start. He was relieved to see a policeman. He had been meaning to call the police, was going to as soon as he picked up the glass, took some necessary safety measures to keep the freak out.

His first thought was: they'll get that son of a bitch. Lock him away for good. He knew he'd never feel safe again unless his freak of a son was behind bars.

He hadn't cooperated with that other officer. He'd been too embarrassed to reveal family problems. The police might think the freak inherited it from him. Or his mother. It didn't run in either family. But that had been before the destruction, before the freak had tried to kill him. Now he'd talk to this cop, tell him everything he wanted to know. More.

Painfully he struggled to his feet. Every muscle, every bone in his body throbbed. He had bandaged all the deeper flesh wounds, but the gash in his neck still trickled blood. He viewed the cop through one eye; the other was swollen shut.

"What the hell exploded?" asked Bauer, aghast now at the condition of this battered man. The poor fellow must have been near the center of the blast.

The man was limping slowly toward him, obviously in great pain. Again Bauer asked, "Tell me what exploded. Was it in the kitchen?"

Through puffed lips caked in the corners with blood, Mike Malone managed to say, "My son exploded."

He's shell-shocked, thought Bauer. Probably suffering from a concussion. No kid, no matter how strong he was, could do all this. And Mike Malone was one fuckin' big guy. A monster. No son—*no human*—did this to Mike Malone.

"Sit here, Mr. Malone. I assume you're Mike Malone. Sit down and tell me exactly what happened."

40

From the phone in her office Liz again tried to contact Gerhardt. "He always sees patients from nine to one; why wouldn't he be home?" She was anxious to learn how the meeting had gone with Captain Webb and just how much information Gerhardt had revealed about her work—none, if he'd kept his promise.

She also wanted to tell him about her attempt to contact Rory and what shocking things she had learned.

Worried about the police department's interest in Rory and eager to speak with him about Kathy Bauer's accident, she had phoned his home. From the fusillade of garbled four-letter words Mike Malone had fired at her before slamming down the receiver, she'd caught enough *fuckin' freak*s to know the worst had occurred.

They must have fought, with the final result a poltergeist eruption. What worried her more was Mike Malone's threat: "He'll never come back here. I'll kill him if he does."

Where was Rory now?

Why hadn't he called her?

She still had not figured out why he'd attempted to suffocate her. Had she angered him? There was another possibility: Had she simply walked into his energy field? A warped area of space depleted of oxygen, charged with electricity. After all, Rory was incredibly powerful now, and the energy field he projected must be intense; no one had ever been as close to it as she had been that day. Then why had she been so convinced that he was concentrating on her? That she was his intended target?

"Damn you, Gerhardt!" She hung up and on her way to the Black Room gave instructions to Peggy, the department secretary.

"Peg, try my husband's private number every half-hour. If you get him, I'll be in 629 with the repair crew. And if there are any more calls from Washington, just say we've left town for a few days and you don't have a forwarding number."

She was dodging Cheryl Roland's calls that, according to Peggy, arrived with irritating frequency. She had evaded both Roland and Gray before they'd left the laboratory to return home but Gerhardt had spoken with them. Apparently Gray suspected that the devastation in the Black Room was a set-up pulled off with explosives to impress them. Cheryl had said troublingly little except that she had to speak with Dr. Hartman privately and that she would phone from Washington.

Quite simply, Liz was afraid to hear what Cheryl Roland had experienced in the laboratory, and she didn't fully understand the cause of that fear.

Supervising the cleanup of the Black Room being done by four male graduate students, whom Liz chided for their slowness, was a depressing task. Second only to Rory, the room represented a crowning technical achievement; it would take months to restore it, and thousands of dollars. Assisting the crew with the lighter work, she wondered if Rory had intentionally destroyed the room to terminate the sessions. No, he'd never do that. Not consciously, at least.

With grant money she had hoped to search for subjects who had particularly strong biocurrents and, using feedback, teach them to perform psychokinetic feats. If they could learn to concentrate their psychic energy, to project it, she'd produce other Rory Malones.

And her dreams went beyond this research. The room's exquisite sensitivity to human biocurrents meant it had new medical applications. Where the EKG and EEG measured only heart and brain health, the Black Room detected the entire body's electromagnetic field and could give a whole-body profile of health or disease.

Her thoughts were mercifully interrupted by Peggy's knock at the door.

"Your husband. On 611."

"I'll take it in my office. Thanks for your persistence, Peg."

Peggy had forgotten to phone and wondered if her omission would be discovered. "Actually, Dr. Hartman, your husband called here."

At the kitchen table in their apartment Gerhardt was finishing lunch. He had spent the morning in deep thought, ignoring phone calls, but had reached no conclusions. He would spend all afternoon in the photography lab developing the film of the last session, but first he had to talk with Liz. He didn't know what to make of Susan Stiner's hallucinations of Rory Malone. Perhaps Liz would have an explanation.

41

Rory had put the half-hour wait to good use, poring over dozens of hardcore magazines, viewing three films—all to charge himself for the test of his power on women.

How strange it had felt. In the past he had tried *not* to get excited, fought stoically against it; now he'd forced arousal upon himself. Of course it had worked. He was hornier than he'd ever been before.

It had been easy to accomplish, too. The atmosphere at the Metropole crackled with sex. All around him men passed into private booths, inserted quarters, viewed films of any sexual fantasy they desired, and when they left, the attendant mopped the floor. At this peak hour, though, it was impossible to keep pace with the flow of clients, and he'd entered one booth and skidded on the slippery floor, striking his shoulder against the wall.

Depravity everywhere.

Normaly everywhere, too.

This ceaselessly amazed him. He watched one clean-cut man of about thirty, superbly dressed, deliberate over the purchase of a video cassette: *Black and Blue Broads* or *Little Women Whipped*. He had seen them both; they were sick. The man finally shelled out eighty-five dollars for *Black and Blue Broads*.

Another businessman, about forty, selected from a display case of vibrators, dildos, french ticklers, and cock rings, choosing a pink inflatable vagina. He paid fifty bucks for it.

No one questioned Rory's age, though with his short hair he surely looked younger than seventeen.

He spotted three boys who appeared even younger than he was.

He'd learned that in these places no man ever glanced at another man; there was absolutely zero eye contact—for fear of embarrassment or recognition, he imagined.

One o'clock.

The man at the coin-exchange counter made an announcement over the public-address system. "Showtime. Three lovely young ladies in the flesh. Step to the rear."

Several men meandered nonchalantly toward the back of the Metropole, pausing occasionally as if they were really just surveying the advertisements on the film booths. But they moved a bit too quickly, directly backward, and he knew they were going to the show. He, too, circuitously glided toward the back. No one walked there directly.

The first time he'd gone to the Metropole he'd watched this ritual of pretense and assumed that either it was not polite or mature to appear too sexually greedy, too horny. But once he had started to attend the shows himself, he realized you meandered there neither out of politeness nor maturity but embarrassment—for being so horny.

A circle of contiguous private booths surrounded the central arena in which the girls performed. From experience he selected booth 8, which was directly opposite the door through which the girls entered the arena and for some reason the location where they displayed themselves for the longest time.

Turning the door lock automatically disengaged the overhead light and left him in total darkness. From a pocket full of quarters, he selected two and deposited them in the slot in the box on the wall. Slowly a metal shade retracted upward, creaking, opening a window roughly two feet square into the center arena.

For taller men the opened windows were shoulder high and they had to stoop to peer in. He noticed several men across the arena stooping. He suspected a few other men—and boys— were on tiptoes. For him the window was directly opposite his face. A convenient height.

A series of framed male portraits hanging in a circular museum—that's what the place resembled.

Three girls entered from the door across the arena. One was maybe forty, heavily made up, with a stacked body; the other two were under twenty and foxy. All were naked except for shoes. The eldest woman and one young girl wore spiked high heels; the other, cowgirl boots. As the youngest girl, the one in boots, inched closer to him, he guessed she was about seventeen if not younger.

The floor of the arena was strategically elevated so that when a girl stood at an open window, her crotch was in the customer's face.

The girls danced individually to piped-in music, gliding from window to window, close enough to be only lightly, briefly touched; squatting, bending over, spreading buns with hands, shaking their tits. Teasing customers. Off to the right, one man extended an arm through the window, a dollar bill in his hand.

Immediately the eldest woman danced up to the window, accepted the money, squatted and stuck her breasts into the opening.

Extending his face slightly through the window, Rory

watched the man's mouth encircle the woman's breast. After a few moments the man reached between the woman's legs, but she pulled back, stood, smiled impishly and danced away.

She let the man at another window, who offered five dollars, finger her.

All around the arena men waved bills with one hand. He knew what they were doing with the other hand. He could see their shoulders rocking.

Whom should he choose?

The eldest woman would do—if the two younger girls weren't present, weren't so tempting.

The youngest one, in the cowgirl boots? Black, shoulder-length hair, perfect oval face, pointed chin, blue eyes, milky white skin. Seventeen. For some reason he sensed she was an easy target. Very easy. Why?

The girl in heels, nineteen probably, seemed more of a challenge. Long blond hair, slender body, tits pointing straight out, beautiful legs, incredibly firm ass. What about her filled him with this sense of challenge? That she'd be harder to pleasure? Certainly nothing in her physical appearance. God knows she turned him on. In fact, he preferred blonds. What then?

Never before had he been so analytical in selecting a lover. He had always chosen on impulse, going by the immediate impact a girl had on him. Now he was thinking things through, attempting to learn the truth about himself.

He'd go for the challenge.

Squinting, framing the blond into tight focus, he stood a foot back from the window so the two other women wouldn't approach and obstruct his view.

She danced slowly, languidly, silky hair cascading over her shoulders. She waltzed past pleading hands, turning in small circles, teasing, smiling, herself the offering. So firm were her breasts that they hardly bounced as she dipped, squatted, mooned one window, then the next. Slowly plucking a bill from a hand, she spread her high-heeled feet apart, stiffened her legs, bent over at the waist and let the hand fondle her breasts.

The music pulsed in his ears, its rhythm intensifying his concentration. Unzipping his fly to relieve the aching pressure, he sprang out of his pants, pointing upward towards the window.

Her round buttocks, pearly white, edged at the crotch by a tuft of blond hair, stood directly in his line of sight. Her position reminded him of the Swedish film he had just viewed. The film contained a sexual practice he'd never tried nor dreamed of. So many of his ideas came from pornography.

She squatted.

All the better.

The man's hand reaching from the window was beneath her, rubbing along her crack, front to back.

Drift . . .

Float toward her . . .

His hand reached between her legs. Found her warm hole. The full squat left her stretched open, an easier entry. The five fingers of his right hand drew together into a cone. The fingertips pushed slowly into her. Further. Further in. Up to his knuckles. The palm of his hand. His wrist. In past fantasies he had inserted one or two fingers into women, but never his whole hand. His fist.

Be analytical. Think and fantasize.

Hard to do both. But you can. Must.

She's not reacting.

But I'm going wild.

Closing his hand into a fist pushed out the tense walls of her vagina. The pressure on his fist was crushing. Gently his fist rocked back and forth, increasing in rhythm, in the length of its plunge. The sensation was novel. Exciting. Very exciting.

She's standing up, moving away. Yet my hand's still in her. I still feel her squeezing it.

The hotter he became, the greater the urge to ram her up to his elbow. His shoulder. To be completely inside her. Oh, he wanted to crawl into her. Up, up, all of him way up inside her.

He shot onto the aluminum wall.

Opening his eyes fully, he saw she was merrily dancing, passing other windows, softly singing the lyrics of the song that echoed in his booth.

Inching closer, his face now framed by the window, he stared quizzically at her, and she returned his glance with a smile.

Nothing happened to her. I came. She felt nothing. It was pure fantasy!

There had been no electricity, no bridge, because she had not been aroused, drawing on his power.

Approaching, she knelt on the floor in front of his window.

"Go ahead. Touch," she said, offering her breasts that he had admired. "Don't be afraid. You don't have to pay. You're cute. And very young, I bet."

When he did not reach for her, she leaned her breasts into his window.

"Go ahead—I have to move on soon."

A flesh-and-blood picture of beautiful, perfect breasts hung before him, framed on the wall. Tentatively his lips parted, mouth moving forward, until his tongue touched her firm, pink nipple. He licked her breasts, circled them several times with his tongue.

She was pulling back, standing. Then she smiled, waved, and pranced off to a hand holding a bill.

A first!

The first time he'd ever had a fully naked woman in arm's reach. And damn! His response had been so hesitant, so naive. He laughed, thinking how aggressive he'd been in so many fantasies and how when he had the real thing staring him in the face, he wasn't quite sure what to do with it.

She had recharged him, though. His erection pressed against the cold aluminum wall as his eyes followed her around the arena.

The show would be over soon.

With her it had been a harmless, innocent fantasy. So vivid was the fantasy to him that he'd come, but she'd felt none of his touching. He wanted to leave the Metropole now, convinced that he did not possess the power to pleasure women with his thoughts.

But he couldn't. Somehow he had known that the blond presented a challenge. Did that innate feeling mean that she might not respond? He still felt that the girl in boots was an easy hit. Did this feeling mean she would respond? He had to know if he could trust this strangely instinctive sensation. It might mean his salvation.

Not much time left to test himself.

He focused on the young girl in boots. Squinted.

I won't hurt you. But I have to know. I'll be gentle.

Drift . . .

Float toward her . . .

Be analytical.

Kneeling by a window, she was being pawed by two hairy hands exploring her body from face to crotch.

Suddenly *his* hands caressed her, one slipping under her rear, one encircling a breast, his tongue licking the other small breast.

He moved gently, his touches light as a feather. She was so delicate. So young.

She's pulling back. From my touch? From the other man's hands?

I have to know.

Sliding forward from her buttocks, his fingers ran along her moist crack, spreading the tight black hair, opening a path for his entry, slipping inside, warmed by a silky fluid.

She was squirming, pushing the other man's hands away from her.

I'm sorry, but I have to know for certain.

Quickly, he was kneeling in front of her, forcing her legs apart. He penetrated. So hot. So excited. He'd explode any second.

Think!

Watch her reaction.

Her mouth opened and closed in what appeared to be shouts. But he heard nothing. The sound of the power roared in his ears. But her face! That expression! Terror. Horror. She *was* screaming. Was reacting! She did feel his assault.

Another second, I'll come. Just an instant.

No, I mustn't.

How can I stop now! So close. So hot.

Pull out! I must. I'm raping her. She feels it.

So near. Balls contracting. Aching. Rippling spasms.
It's wrong. She's terrified.

He pulled out.

Suddenly the light in the booth flashed on. He shook his head to quickly, fully recapture reality.

Lights were on in all the booths.

In the center of the arena the young girl in boots cowered, screaming, holding her crotch. She pointed toward a window, not his but the window where she had been kneeling.

Lifting a hand from her crotch, she saw it was bloody and became hysterical.

The other two women attempted to comfort her.

A burly man who guarded the front door of the Metropole ran into the arena. He immediately saw where she pointed and shouted, "Sixteen, Mac. The guy in booth sixteen."

Rory drew back from the window.

The music stopped. Over the PA system a voice boomed: "Okay, open up. Everybody unlock his door. Out!"

Men scurried from the booths, zipping flies, covering crotches with hands, jackets, briefcases. Their faces were red, frightened, confused. Bumping into each other as they squeezed silently, swiftly through the narrow aisle, each pretended the others did not exist.

From booth sixteen two attendants were dragging out a man in a pale blue suit. He seemed stunned.

Hurrying out of the Metropole, Rory heard the man's protests.

"I'm innocent. I didn't do anything to her. Just what the other guys were doing. Nothing else. What's this all about?"

42

On the pavement he moved into the crowd filing out of the Criterion theater, feeling safer, less conspicuous. Then, raising a hand to wipe perspiration from his forehead, he spotted it: Blood. Blood on his fingers. Her blood!

Rory Malone's hand had actually been inside that girl. That meant his cock had, too. It, too, must be stained with her blood. He'd pleasured, no, *raped*, her.

He had the power.

Pushing through the crowd, which now seemed to suffocate him, he attempted to think analytically. One girl reacted, one didn't.

Long ago Dr. Hartman had told him that the poltergeist power somehow depended on his hormone levels. Did a woman's particular response then depend on *her* hormone levels? Did his energy couple with, fall into resonance with, a woman's monthly hormonal cycles? Is that why some women seemed like easier lovers than others? Why some responded while others didn't? That would explain why at certain times each month he'd had to avoid seeing Melissa, even thinking about her; she simply was too easy a lover for his fantasies then. And why some days he'd experienced an almost irresistible attraction toward Dr. Hartman.

Surely that girl hadn't been a virgin. The blood was *menstrual blood*.

He recalled Dr. Hartman's observation that her biocurrents were highest around the time of her period. A woman's electromagnetic field was strongest then, at its peak; his power must couple with that field, feed on it—and this coupling was the electric bridge that he experienced with some women and not others. Evelyn Rhomley didn't respond because she wasn't near her period, at her peak.

A taxi screeched to a halt.

"Watch the fuck where you're goin'."

It took a moment to notice he'd almost been hit. In fact, he hadn't even been aware he was crossing Broadway. Racing around the cab to the opposite pavement, he realized that he still did not understand everything completely. Maybe he never would. But could he trust his feelings about difficult and easy women?

One thing was distressingly clear: He had raped many women, including Kathy Bauer. And Dr. Hartman *had* felt his advances.

Furthermore, he was responsible for Kathy's accident, her amputated leg.

Depression hit.

Turning off Broadway, he walked two blocks east to get away from the filth and sleeze.

What irony! It had all begun so innocently: fantasies of loving women, undressing, then possessing them. Gerhardt had encouraged it, had shown him that fantasizing was normal. The problem was that *he* wasn't normal. His power turned innocent daydreams of sex into nightmares of crime.

Convinced of his power to rape, he felt more alone than ever. Certainly no suspecting woman would ever want him, and he could never trust himself around any unsuspecting woman. For if he'd learned one thing it was that when Rory Malone became horny, he lost all reason. He sought a single objective: orgasm. If it was so easy to possess almost any woman he desired, how could he control himself? Under similar circumstances would any man be able to continually exert self-restraint? No; failure, even if it was infrequent, was a foregone conclusion.

Should he fantasize only about those women who he felt presented a challenge? Who might not respond? But he wasn't always sure of his initial feelings about a woman. It wasn't that cut and dried, black and white.

If only it were.

And it was so difficult to maintain a vivid sexual fantasy while monitoring a woman's response. Sometimes—many times—he might fail. Commit rape. In truth, he really knew for sure about a particular lover only *after* the act.

At Fifty-fourth Street and the Avenue of the Americas he passed a magazine stand. Aware that glossy porn magazines hung on a wire along the top of the stand, he held his glance downward, wanting never again to see a pornographic picture, a naked woman. Then he laughed aloud: You hypocrite! Before the day's through you'll be lusting after the very things you're condemning.

It was then that his eye caught the red headlines in the *Post*.

His knees weakened. His stomach churned. Dizzy, he fell to the pavement. The three words that filled the page in bold letters swirled in his brain: BAUER GIRL DIES!

A man was helping him to his feet, asking questions. The voice was muddled. He heard only Kathy Bauer's screams.

People swarmed around him.

"Hey, kid! What happened?"

"I did it. I'm responsible."

"What's that, boy?"

"Do you think he's drugged?"

"I killed her."

"He's incoherent."

"I raped her, that's why she fell."

"I saw him. He was walking, then he just keeled over. Like he was hit on the head."

"I need help. I'm out of control."

"He must be hurt. He's crying. Young man, are you in pain?"

"I'll hold him. You find a policeman."

Police.

He stumbled forward.

Balance yourself. Straighten up. Police.

He saw only poorly; something clouded his vision. Tears. He was crying.

Run.

He took off quickly: Through the crowd, through traffic, with no idea where he was going.

43

Liz now knew the truth about Rory's power, and it dulled her senses. His Tinkerbell can travel miles and integrate itself into a woman's sexual fantasies; indeed, the energy could plunder a woman's body as physically, as easily, as it could swing a pendulum. Astonishing. And yet how could she have overlooked the possibility that a psychic force real enough to interact with an inanimate object might be even more suited to join energies with another human body, an entity possessing similar currents, fields, and desires?

Tinkerbell was a grossly absurd misnomer; Don Juan, Satyr was closer to the truth.

The truth had compelled her to carefully terminate her phone conversation with Gerhardt. Unaware, he had provided the crucial piece of information that completed the puzzle. Once the elements had fused together, though, she had clammed up and revealed nothing more. Her single thought was to locate Rory before the police did.

Old girl, you've been resisting the truth, deceiving yourself. Now, difficult as it will be, you must face the problem squarely. You contributed to Rory's dilemma; you must save him.

Returning home, she walked the ten blocks from the university to her West End Avenue apartment. The late-afternoon sun turned the dusty windows along West 110th Street into mirrors, reflecting fuzzy images of children at play.

She usually waited for Gerhardt because the walk forced her through a seedy stretch of dilapidated brownstones and apartments in a neighborhood populated mainly by pushers, prostitutes, drunks, and the chronically unemployed. The mixture made the Upper West Side near the university such a dangerous area. But now she had to be alone to collect her thoughts, to decide how to locate Rory and what to do when she found him.

It was strange that she no longer feared him, knowing full well what he could do to her if he wished. Compassion for his plight was her paramount feeling; concern for what must be his own fear, confusion, alienation. No matter how cleverly or circuitously she rationalized the events of the last year, more than anyone else, she was to blame.

Gerhardt had voted to defuse Rory's poltergeist energy, but she had convinced him that he'd be throwing away the research opportunity of a lifetime. A chance for professional fame. Recognition. When Gerhardt failed to establish the requisite rapport with Rory, she'd eagerly joined the project full-time, then taken command. Aware that an overabundance of testosterone was somehow a biochemical factor in Rory's energy, she'd taught him how to concentrate that energy, focus it on a single objective, then physically project it. But testosterone fuels the male sexual drive, is the hormone of aggressive behavior. Knowing all this, she had let ambition blind her to the real dangers.

Turning onto West End Avenue, she wondered just how much Gerhardt had really told Captain Webb.

Could Webb deduce the truth?

No, of course not. Well, not yet. Webb could only assume that Rory had used his power—accidentally or deliberately—to push Kathy Bauer off the subway platform. He'd never dream that Rory was sexually molesting the poor girl.

Gerhardt would. Not yet, but soon. He'd almost hit on the possibility during their conversation, but she had swiftly sidetracked him.

"They probably argued," she'd suggested. "Rory may have wanted to date Kathy Bauer, and she gave him the cold shoulder. In a fit of anger his temper accidentally lashed out at her. You know how strong he is." Let him feel partly responsible.

"Certainly a possibility," he'd answered. "I agree that Rory never would have pushed her intentionally. Still, Captain Webb wants to see you, and I think you should disclose the full extent of the research. Show him the Black Room, the film. After all, what Rory may have done is no crime—not one he could be punished for."

She entered the apartment building without first glancing back as she customarily did. Several tenants had recently been followed into the small lobby and mugged. While she enjoyed living within walking distance of the university, Gerhardt would have preferred a doormanned building in a safer part of town.

In the elevator she pondered just how much to reveal to Captain Webb. Initially she might have told him everything and even shown him the new film. But that was before the weight of the truth had crushed her.

The *full truth!* That's it! Momentarily she brightened.

There were two truths: Rory's psychic power had accidentally knocked Kathy Bauer off the subway platform; truth one. Rory was molesting Kathy Bauer when she lost her footing and fell; truth two. Only she knew of the latter possibility—no, fact.

Of course Captain Webb deduced the first truth simply by knowing of Rory's poltergeist energy. But there was an excellent chance that he might never be able to deduce that Rory possessed the power to . . . what? Rape at a distance? Yes.

What about Gerhardt?

He was a different story. Well, not entirely. Even if he conceived of this possibility, he'd not have the proof of it that she had. How could even Gerhardt—knowing of Rory's testosterone levels and poltergeist power—ever realize that by pumping psychic energy into sexual fantasies, Rory actualized them. No one could—unless she felt the sexual energy in her body.

She had only realized it herself when he'd told her of his patient's hallucinations.

Twice during masturbation Susan Stiner had hallucinated the face of a young boy, another patient of Gerhardt's. She didn't know his name; they only politely smiled and exchanged good mornings, passing each other in the waiting hall. But the hallucinations had been frighteningly vivid, almost real. What was more, she had actually sensed his presence in her bedroom. He'd integrated himself into her sexual fantasies, replacing her boyfriend, Carl.

"Honey, I think Rory's so strongly psychic that his sexual thoughts were telepathically picked up by this patient. Perhaps she's a good telepathic receiver. Is that too farfetched?"

Close. As close as she had let him get before diverting his thoughts, then terminating the conversation.

Entering the apartment, she turned on the air conditioner in the living room, then in the bedroom, and began to prepare dinner, though she had no appetite herself.

Where had Rory spent last night? Did he have money? She hoped he wouldn't have to steal food.

She prepared a cold tuna salad, hard-boiled four eggs, and sliced two cucumbers, covering them with a yogurt and sesame seed dressing.

Then, seated at her desk, she composed a list of names of friends and classmates Rory had mentioned most frequently. She'd call them all; there weren't that many. Maybe he was staying with one of these families. She doubted that, though. He was a loner. Heading the list was the name Melissa Adams.

Amazing how the subconscious can suppress a fact until the right trigger liberates it. Susan Stiner's hallucinations had been that trigger. Instantly facts had cascaded upon her. Rory had been in Susan Stiner's bedroom. He had had sex with Susan Stiner. Just as he'd been in her own bedroom, spying on her and Gerhardt. More than merely spying. For every time she had closed her eyes, Rory, not Gerhardt, had been on top of her. Like Susan Stiner, she, too, had assumed it was all a hallucination, a construct of her own imagination. What else was one to think?

She puzzled: These occurences happened in the middle of the night. Was Rory awake, consciously focusing on her and on

Susan Stiner? Or had he merely *dreamed* of them? Had his sexual dreams been actualized, too! If so, then his power was far stronger and more dangerous than she had suspected.

Of course, that suffocating feeling in the laboratory, the pressure on her chest, the tingling along her body—Rory was not trying to kill her. Plain and simple, he had been feeling her up. Molesting her.

Mother-figure! Apparently not, old girl.

Unnerved, she sank into the kitchen chair under the full weight of these revelations. Rory Malone can have any woman he desires, anytime, anywhere. Probably even in his dreams. He'd stopped with her in the lab—unleashed his energy on the targets—but does he have enough self-control always to stop himself?

She doubted that, imagining how Rory's mind must struggle with one of the most primitive human urges.

> *His id:* I demand immediate sexual gratification. I'll rape the first woman who turns me on.
>
> *His superego:* Rape's taboo. Society punishes such action. And you must live with your own conscience.

It was a strong conflict, a war his ego had to resolve. And what did his ego conclude?

> Society can't punish your rapes. No one even knows what you're doing. Not even your lover is certain. So go right ahead and satisfy yourself. Any other guy would. . . . Remember, though, you must live with your conscience.

That reminder might—just might—be enough to stop him. He was a good boy, after all. Yet in the heat of sexual passion, would the brake provided by conscience grip? Apparently not. There was Susan Stiner. Kathy Bauer. And how many others?

Liz Hartman, almost.

Naturally her mind had suppressed the truth for as long as possible, for personal as well as professional reasons. Of course, acknowledging the truth meant terminating her research, her dreams. But Rory's safety, his future, must be her primary concern. Suppose she found him—could she defuse his power? It had become so terribly strong. Hormone treatment would have to be administered more frequently now and would involve larger doses, which meant greater undesirable side effects.

Then she thought: would Rory permit me to strip him of his power? Would he tolerate being feminized, even for a year or two, until his own hormone production normalizes? Or, in anger, might he destroy us all?

44

After leaving Gerhardt Kiner's office, Webb had planned a surprise visit to Liz Hartman at her Columbia laboratory, but once he was in the car he had changed his mind.

He could guess what studying the physical aspects of Rory Malone's energy involved: electromagnetic permeability, charge coupling, Faraday cages, radiation detectors. Cut-and-dried stuff, things that fascinate a physicist and no one else. Certainly not a psychologist like himself.

Anyway, at that point he felt he didn't need immediate confirmation of what he strongly suspected: that Rory Malone still possessed ample poltergeist energy. Instead, he had delved into the boy's relationship with Kathy Bauer, its interpersonal dynamics. How well had they been acquainted? Did they date often? If so, had she recently thrown him over for another guy? In a nutshell: did Rory Malone have a reason for using his strange power, accidentally or deliberately, on Kathy Bauer? Kiner had stimulated him to pursue his own line of approach: psychology.

Fortunately he'd had the foresight to obtain the names and addresses of Rory Malone's teachers: five in all. And from Nurse Graybar's detailed list of visitors, he had the names of dozens of Kathy Bauer's friends. The entire afternoon had been spent tracking down these people, and by seven-thirty P.M. he had interviewed three of Rory Malone's teachers and nine of Kathy Bauer's friends; all were kids who claimed they'd been her closest, dearest confidants. All the sleuthing, however, led to a single disappointing conclusion: Kathy Bauer probably had never even spoken to Rory Malone. Certainly they had never dated. He was a strange fellow; she was Miss Popularity. He had no friends; everyone claimed to be her intimate.

He was beginning to doubt seriously that a connection existed between Rory Malone's presence on the subway platform and Kathy Bauer's accident. Yet it had to. The false name. His short hair. He was seen running from the station. And now the possibility of poltergeist energy. No, he was certain of it, for he'd bet his pension that Rory Malone still possessed that power; otherwise Liz Hartman just didn't fit into the picture.

Arriving home at eight thirty, he had been surprised to find Carrie's car parked in front of the house. Pulling into the driveway, he had spotted her seated in a lawn chair in the backyard, swatting mosquitoes.

They had not seen each other since yesterday, when she had gone to interview Kiner and he to speak to Mike Malone, and he was glad for her unexpected visit. It had not taken long, though, to realize that something was troubling Carrie. While they were barbecuing hamburgers on the patio, she'd filled him in on the Kiner interview, but, unlike her normally spunky, assertive self, she'd been surprisingly low-keyed, neither cracking jokes nor dropping sexual innuendoes. Adamantly she had refused to reveal or even to admit that something was bothering her—except twice to make the curious remark, "I think I'm going crazy"—but all in all, he preferred this gentler, softer, less aggressive Carrie Wilson. She conformed to his notion of feminine behavior.

Supper had led to drinks on the patio, and when the mosquitoes became unbearable, to more drinks in the house.

Starting off in chairs on opposite sides of the living room, they'd somehow managed through trips to the bar and the bathroom to move to opposite ends of the sofa, and now they sat in the center, side by side, his arm casually resting on the cushion behind Carrie's shoulders. Her unresponsiveness excited him a hundredfold more than if she had as much as leaned toward or touched him.

Throughout the musical-chair maneuvering—and probably as a diversionary tactic—he'd kept conversation flowing, first talking about his "Pornography and Crime" paper, and when that topic had been laboriously exhausted, revealing the details he'd learned from Kiner about the history of Rory Malone's ghostly poltergeist outbursts. At one point, getting the distinct impression that the spooky talk about the boy and his father frightened Carrie, he had changed the subject, but then she'd coaxed him for more information on Rory Malone. Relating all that he knew, he finally cautioned her.

"Luv, breathe not a word of this poltergeist stuff to Bauer. With his niece's death, he'd probably kill the boy himself. In fact, how was our hothead today?"

"I didn't see him. O'Hare said he phoned in and asked for the day off to handle funeral arrangements."

"Good. That'll keep him out of trouble and off my back."

"Chief, do you think this boy's dangerous?"

"Luv, that depends entirely on how strong his energy is. Over a year ago he sent some pretty heavy ashtrays and statues flying around his home. I want to know if he's gotten stronger since then."

"How do you intend to find out?" asked Carrie, reaching for her drink.

"Luv, I don't think you should have any more of that stuff. You already look pie-eyed." Taking the glass from her hand and returning it to the coffee table, his arm fell from the sofa cushion onto Carrie's shoulders and he left it there, delighting in the fact that for the first time in their two-year relationship he was playing the aggressor.

"First thing tomorrow I want to talk with Kiner's wife, a physicist who's been working with the boy, studying his energy. Then I'll speak with Rory Malone." He debated whether to ask why she had duplicated the artist's sketch of the boy, for he didn't want to ruffle her feathers and chance stirring up the old Carrie Wilson temperament.

"Luv, you know I like you this way."

"Crazy."

"No; quiet, vulnerable. Even if it's only temporary."

"It may be permanent if I'm going crazy."

"Call it what you will, but you're more feminine. Anyway, I'd like to think that you can confide in me. Give it a try."

"It's just the grass. I'm still suffering some side effects."

"Nausea? Headaches?"

"No, hallucinations. And wild, bizarre dreams. I got almost no sleep again last night. That's why I've been such stimulating company tonight. I'm sorry."

"Don't be. But I warned you about drugs. The stuff's bad enough in itself. Then your bright young chemist goes soaking it in something that probably gives rats cancer." Treading lightly so as not to rally her defenses, he concluded, "But I won't lecture you. Maybe you've learned your lesson."

"Thanks a lot. . . . It's after midnight. I better be going."

"Going? Now you *are* crazy if you think I'm going to let you drive in your state. No, luv, you spend the night here. You can have the bed. I'll sleep on the sofa."

While Carrie used the bathroom, he stripped the bed and applied fresh sheets. For the first time that evening he realized just how aroused he was and how desperately he hoped something would happen tonight. Finally Carrie Wilson was on his turf, playing the game by his rules, and that made all the difference in the world.

It seemed like an eternity since he had last been so excited at the prospect of making love. Briefly wondering if Carrie would regard him as an absolute heel for making the long-delayed pass when she was depressed and slightly drunk, he concluded that if ever they were going to come together it had to be now, under these circumstances, which might never again be duplicated. He tried not to think of the possibility that tonight of all nights, Carrie might say no.

45

After spotting the devastating headline in the *Post*, Rory had secluded himself in a dollar, all-night movie house in Times Square, certain that the police, Dr. Hartman, and Gerhardt were all searching for him.

Entering the dark, chillingly cool theater—which fortunately featured a rerun that had drawn only a few people—sometime in the late afternoon, he had selected a seat down front, to the far left, and had almost immediately dozed off, not so much from fatigue, though he had no idea how long he'd been running, but to escape the realities that soon would catch up with him.

At seven o'clock he'd awakened, gone to the food concession, and returned to his seat with a giant buttered popcorn, two Nestle's Crunch candy bars, and a root beer. While he was eating, his mind began to function again; his first thoughts were of survival.

If he was caught—or turned himself in—the next step would be hormone therapy, which he dreaded. He dreaded the loss of his sparse facial hair, of the fine few hairs that had recently sprouted between his pectorals, loss of the tight muscle tone all over his body. Instead, fatty tissue would layer itself around his hips and ass and accumulate on his chest to form soft, fleshy breasts. Even his voice might shift to a higher feminine register. What ironic punishment, he thought: The rapist is transformed into a pathetic copy of his victim.

And, of course, he would lose his sex drive entirely; lose his power, too.

But didn't he deserve severe punishment? He was guilty

not only of rape but now of murder, too. Two damnable sins. Even for sins to be pardoned through confession, the penitent must possess a firm resolve to mend his ways; yet would the power, which he now viewed as an external foe, permit him to stifle its demands? It seemed to be growing more formidable each day; the blood he had washed from his fingers was proof of that.

Not willing to surrender to female-hormone therapy, he saw only one alternative: Retreat into hiding, most likely somewhere in Canada, until he naturally lost the power. But the money in his wallet would not get him far; despite the high risk he must get the three hundred dollars hidden in his bedroom—tomorrow, while his father was at work in the shop.

Having resolved the immediate dilemma, he had attempted to concentrate on the movie, watching it through twice. Then around midnight he fell asleep again.

Now his dream of Carrie Wilson was disrupted by the sensation of pressure against his right leg. So vividly real was the dream that he thought the delicious pressure was from Carrie's bare legs clutched tightly around his thighs, and his eyes opened slowly, swimmingly, as a soft, breathy moan escaped his lips. The dream, one of many of Carrie lately, had him aroused; and slouched down in the seat, his legs spread outward, he was aware of the throbbing in his crotch.

Although imagery of the dream lingered tenaciously, robbing his senses of immediate perception, he did feel a faint charge in the air and the incandescent fragments of a sexual bridge between himself and Carrie. Dreams of Carrie had always been erotic, but this was the first to assume a disturbing electrical dimension, forcing him to wonder if even while he was dreaming, the power could function. Instinctively he sensed that Carrie herself was at that moment terribly aroused, and he had coupled with her sexual energy.

Was that possible? He'd been sleeping. Dr. Hartman had always stressed the need for absolute concentration on a single goal, to the exclusion of all extraneous stimuli; well, wasn't dreaming just such a state of mind?

It required several seconds for his senses to zoom into

focus. In the adjacent seat sat a middle-aged man wearing a suit and eyeglasses; the man's leg pressed annoyingly against his own. Glancing around, he quickly realized that the theater was less than a quarter full and that several rows in front and behind him were entirely empty. In fact, the remainder of his own row was vacant. This man had passed over a dozen empty seats to sit beside him.

While the man's eyes never for a second wavered from the screen, the pressure from his leg boldly intensified.

Sitting up, Rory pulled his leg away, forcefully cleared his throat, and stared at the screen, hoping the man would take the hint and move. While he'd been sleeping, his mouth had drooled saliva, wetting his lips and chin, and with the back of his arm he wiped his face dry, sneaking a peak at the man. With almost imperceptible slowness the man's leg was creeping closer and closer, and Rory leaned further to the left, against the wall. He wanted to change seats himself, but the wall blocked his exit; he would have to pass in front of the man.

Leave me alone, mister.

In his peripheral vision Rory saw the man's head pivot slightly, eyes stealing furtive glances at his crotch. It was only then that he realized his erection had not yet subsided.

Covering his crotch with one hand, the other rose up against his cheek, palm opened, to block the man, who was now attempting to make eye contact.

The odor startled him. A pungent, bitterly piquant scent on the fingers of his right hand. But on first entering the theater he had thoroughly scrubbed the blood from the girl at the Metropole from his hand.

Inhaling slowly, deliberately, as though trying to identify the spices in an exotic new dish, he realized the scent was distinctly sexual: musty, heady, provocative; it immediately, spontaneously, conjured an image of Carrie nude in bed and shot fresh hot impulses into his groin.

In the dream he had glided these fingers exploringly into Carrie and been astonished at her profuse wetness. His mouth had explored that same place, licking, sucking, tasting, smelling the same scent he now detected on his fingers. Then he realized that the dribble he had wiped from his lips and chin was not saliva but juices from Carrie. Parting his lips, sweeping his tongue over them, recognizing the erotic taste from the dream, inexorably confirmed his suspicion.

For months he had sensed sexual smells and tastes during a fantasy, but then they had faded with the return of reality. Now smells and tastes remained. No, they did more than that—they manifested their own independent existence. The power had acquired still another heinous, odious dimension, transforming every minute element of a fantasy into flesh-and-blood reality.

The barrier between fantasy and reality had fallen completely. For the power, fantasy *was* reality.

So overwhelming was this new revelation that several seconds elapsed before Rory realized that the man's hand was resting light as a feather on his thigh, only inches from his crotch. How long had it been there? Furious, muttering under his breath "fuckin' fag," he stood, stepped over the man's knees and steamed into the aisle. Noticing that the balcony was virtually empty, he headed upstairs; he'd probably be less conspicuous sleeping the night away in the balcony.

Passing the men's room on the second-floor landing, he went in to relieve himself. Standing at the urinal and peeing, he wondered what was to be gained—except avoiding capture and hormone therapy—by isolating himself in Canada or anywhere else, for that matter, if the power could indeed ravage a woman even as he dreamed of her. Carrie had been the only such incident; at least the only one he knew of, had proof of. Had there been others?

Hearing the door to the men's room open, he glanced sideways and in the wall mirror spotted the man from downstairs entering the room. Automatically Rory's eyes counted: seven empty urinals.

Stay away from me, mister.

Boldly the man positioned himself at the adjacent urinal, unzipped his fly, and began playing with his penis, which was already erect.

Rory stared at the blue and white wall tiles, the lettering

"Royal Flush" on the urinal's steel handle, trying to finish quickly and hightail it out of there.

Before he realized what was happening, the man's hand touched his penis.

"You've got a beautiful cock. How about a blow job? Come on, no one will know. It'll feel good."

"Cut it out!" Rory said, pulling away.

"Kid, you're aroused. Look at yourself."

He wasn't; his erection had mostly subsided.

"Who do you think you're fooling? I saw you turning on downstairs. And it wasn't to that movie."

For the second time the man grabbed his cock, and Rory jerked away. Why did his bladder have to be so full?

"Well, if that's the game you want to play, go ahead, pretend you're straight. So how much do you want? Ten bucks? Twenty?"

This time the man grabbed his cock and squeezed it firmly.

"You'll like it, too. I'm better than any girl that's given you head."

Let go of me, mister. I warn you.

He could not pull free, the man's grip was so strong, squeezing his cock, determined to get it hard.

"So you like resistance. I've met your type before. The more you resist the straighter you think you are."

Stop it, mister. Don't make me hurt you. I can't control the power when I'm angry.

"Twenty bucks for a minute. That's all it'll take, and you'll feel better afterward. Come on. You've got such a sensational cock for a young kid."

The man dropped to his knees, attempting to force Rory's cock into his mouth.

Leave me alone!

Then the man's body was sailing through the air. It smashed against the tiled wall, splattering it with blood, but the body did not fall to the floor. Instead, it bounced off the wall as if it were made of rubber, flying upward, thudding against the dirty white ceiling, depositing more blood, then ricocheting back to the wall, to the floor, and up again. Like a ball repeatedly hit by an invisible racket, always in a new direction, the body volleyed around the room, arms, legs, head flailing like a rag doll's. Each collision scored its own dripping red imprint; each imprint was larger, bloodier than the last.

When the body finally plummeted to the floor, it was unrecognizable as a human form. The room resembled a slaughterhouse.

On the street Rory walked slowly, mindlessly, deprived partially of all awareness, totally ignorant that for the second time his power had killed. In an hour, when perception would return along with memory, he'd admit to himself that he was lethally dangerous and out of control. Though he did not consciously know it, he was heading uptown, for 1026 West End Avenue: Dr. Elizabeth Hartman's address.

Wednesday
Day 6

46

Liz had spent a frustrating night searching for Rory.

After a particularly distasteful visit to the Malone home, where she was verbally abused and physically evicted by Mike Malone, she and Gerhardt had then combed the streets, pinball arcades, and every readily visible teenage hangout in and around Forest Hills. Then they had stopped at the homes of all Rory's classmates whose addresses Liz had been able to find in the Queens telephone directory. All to no avail.

Returning to the city, they had first searched Greenwich Village, then worked their way uptown, trying discos, electronic game arcades, and sundry bars and clubs that impressed them as lax enough to permit a seventeen-year-old boy to enter.

Admittedly the random search was a million-in-one shot, as Gerhardt had irritatingly reminded her every hour or so, but she had felt compelled at least to undertake it, for she couldn't merely sit home hoping Rory would run to her.

Returning home just after three A.M., weary and terribly worried about Rory's mental and physical well-being, Liz had finally fallen asleep at five. Awakening at ten, she had found a note that Gerhardt had gone to the university to finish developing the film of the last session.

Before her bath or breakfast she'd phoned Melissa Adams, and getting the girl's mother, apologized for having dialed the wrong number and hung up. She'd hoped Melissa would answer.

The visit to the Adamses' house the previous night had made perfectly clear the fact that Mr. and Mrs. Adams had forbidden their daughter to date Rory and that Melissa had been lying when she claimed she had not seen Rory for months. The girl's resolute denials and all-too-transparent nervousness had led Liz to suspect that Melissa was perhaps the only person in contact with Rory. She planned to try the Adamses' number until Melissa answered, but her calls would have to be adequately spaced so as not to arouse excessive suspicion and get the girl in trouble.

Now, at one in the afternoon, she arrived at the sixth-floor physics department and went straight to Peggy on the chance that there was a message from Melissa Adams, the police, or even Mike Malone—any word on Rory. Maybe he'd phoned himself.

"Good morning, Peg. Any calls?"

"Good *afternoon*," caroled Peggy innocently. "Two messages, Dr. Hartman. A policeman was here looking for you this morning—a sergeant Bauer. I told him you'd be in late today. And your husband called just a few minutes ago. He asked if you'd go straight to Haller Hall—the photography department. He said it was very important. In fact, urgent."

"Did Dr. Kiner explain what was so urgent?"

"No, he didn't. Would you like me to call him?"

"No, thank you. I'll walk over to Haller."

Descending in the elevator, Liz wondered: Sergeant Bauer? Gerhardt claimed that Captain Webb himself wanted to question her about the Malone experiments. Well, Webb hadn't arrived yesterday, and now he had apparently sent one of his subordinates. Did that mean Captain Webb had down-rated the priority on the Rory Malone case?

Crossing the campus, she attempted to guess the nature of Gerhardt's urgent message. Maybe he had succeeded in developing the film. He'd had considerable difficulty with the negative. In the haste of repeatedly switching from filming Rory in the red light of the Red Room to shots of the rest of the laboratory in ordinary daylight, he'd mixed up filters. Consequently some of footage was underexposed. He had spent yesterday afternoon getting advice from the university photography department on how to compensate in the developing process and had set out early this morning, apparently to begin the job.

What could be so damn urgent about the film?

Passing small groups of students enrolled in summer-session courses, Liz regretted that the campus couldn't always be this relaxed and uncongested. She thought of Rory as a Columbia freshman. She had suggested he apply, offering to write a glowing letter of recommendation and pull strings if necessary to land him at least a partial scholarship. Now his future as a student appeared increasingly remote.

Entering Haller Hall and taking the elevator to the photography department on the fourth floor, she realized that Rory had no friends, no father to speak of, and that she had been his only real confidante. A special bond had always existed between them, and now she was certain Rory was subconsciously reaching out for her help, transmitting a psychic SOS. Twice during the night she'd been awakened from sleep by an image of his face. It had been neither sexual nor frightening but a pleading call for help. Maybe he was embarrassed to confront her directly, but nonetheless, his subconscious was calling to her.

Had Gerhardt received word from Rory?

No, they were not that close; Rory would surely call her before he'd run to Gerhardt. But what if Rory's problem was sexual—which it was? Might he prefer discussing it with a man? God! If so, then Gerhardt already realized the full extent of Rory's power, knew how Rory had sexually molested her.

When she arrived, Gerhardt had finished in the developing room.

"Dr. Kiner's in the projection theater," said a bearded young man, his arms up to the elbows in a tank of vile-smelling fluid. "He had a helluva time with some of the footage. I showed him the best way to process it. Even so, a long stretch of it's ruined."

So what, she thought, heading to the large amphitheater where films were viewed by several classes at a time. The project's dead now, the film useless.

She had to know if Rory had contacted Gerhardt. Yes, damn it! She was jealous.

Entering the darkened theater through a door on the fourth-floor level, she quietly slipped into a seat in the front row. The film was in progress. Glancing behind her up the tiers of empty seats, she assumed Gerhardt must be viewing from the enclosed projection booth.

The photographic quality was astonishingly good; Gerhardt's best effort yet. How ironic, with the project now dead. Superb shots showed Rory concentrating in the Red Room, the ball of light pulsating, expanding, traveling in a gossamer haze across the television screen. There were flattering shots of her, for a change. Of course, she had gone all-out that day with her hair, makeup, and clothes. Again, to no avail now.

At the first sight of the film sequence showing her in the Red Room reattaching Rory's electrodes, Liz became squeamish. Like the deep ache from a remembered pain, her body immediately recalled the strange, suffocating sensations she'd felt: the pressure, the shortness of breath, the tingling across her breasts and along her thighs. The vividness of the recollection was uncomfortably enhanced now, knowing full well that at that very moment Rory had begun to feel her up.

Here, though, was where Gerhardt had forgotten to switch filters to compensate for the room's red light. The footage was a dark purplish, peculiarly underexposed, and grew more mauve each second. Apparently Gerhardt hadn't been able adequately to compensate for his mistake. In fact, his painstaking processing seemed to have made the film worse frame by frame. For as the seconds passed, the images of her, of Rory, of all the objects in the Red Room passed from a charred mauve into almost charcoal blackness.

Everything blacked out except . . .

Those lines. No; waves. Pulsating white-blue waves surrounded her body, rippling along its length, brightening to white-yellow, then to a blistering white-white. A shimmering cocoon enveloped her entire being, massaging her from head to toe.

This halo of light, this force field, also surrounded Rory.

Trembling, instinctively clutching her throat while covering her breasts with her arms, she watched these two blinding halos draw closer, touch, stick together, waves intermingling. Slowly she was being pulled closer to Rory as these two ghostly images were resolutely determined to merge into one throbbing rhythm.

Seeing these two force fields for the first time—their cocoon shapes and the way they expanded and merged—she now understood how Rory hooked up with her or any woman. Her biocurrent laid only the foundation for the linkup, which his energy then latched onto to form a bridge between them. The more aroused he got, the more sexual energy flowed over the bridge to her, carrying with it all his thoughts and actions, which, in a sense, materialized in her body.

Wait! Her biocurrents! They'd been particularly high that day, a few days before her period. Was a high biocurrent in a woman a physical prerequisite for Rory to hook up with her?

It made sense from a physical standpoint. The week before and during menstruation a woman's biocurrents were substantially higher than normal. Women actually radiated electric fields then—ones that could easily be measured. I'll bet he has an easier time hooking up with some women than with others, she thought suddenly. She'd have to ask him. Of course, proof of her theory would come from interviewing the women he'd had sex with. If they had been in a high-energy time of month— Oh! The research implications. Selecting young female subjects, training them in the Black Room only during those critical ten days or so each month—the rapid progress she might achieve. But no, she must stop this selfish thinking of her own plans, her own future. Rory required all her attention.

Being strictly analytical, she scrutinized the film. In the ghostly cocoons surrounding her and Rory, she now clearly saw a bridge, a conduit where rippling current flowed from him to her. It was a subtle effect but easy to locate if you were looking for it. Had Gerhardt spotted the bridge?

Leaning back in the hard theater chair, she thought, So now I know the mechanics involved; I'll be able to explain it all to Rory—*if* I can find him—Dear, when you get sexually excited, your abundant psychic energy rushes to the sex center of the brain, the hypothalamus, the seat of sex drive and copulatory behavior. You must feel like you're going to explode if you don't reach orgasm. Liz understands now.

Abruptly the cocoons vanished. The screen went black. Then . . . Clear footage of the destroyed targets in the Black Room. The camera lingered on each object, documenting the devastation.

Her heart raced.

So this was Gerhardt's urgent message. Would he realize that Rory had zeroed in on her as his target? Forced her closer toward himself?

Certainly Gerhardt would demand to know what she had experienced through it all, and why she'd kept it secret.

And now more than ever she must keep Rory's secret. No other person must have proof that Rory's powers extended beyond lifting objects; that he could sexually possess a woman without physically touching her, make a woman feel his presence over every inch of her body.

The lights came up.

Still stunned by what she'd seen, uncertain of just how to camouflage the truth from Gerhardt, she remained immobile in her seat. Think, old girl! Think.

"Liz!" rang Gerhardt's voice from high up in the back of the theater. "How long have you been there?"

His feet were rapidly descending the steps.

But there were someone else's footsteps, too.

She turned. Gerhardt was not alone. Behind him, stone-faced, ghostly white, hurried a determined Captain Webb.

47

Hell, he had to find the fuckin' kid himself. And fast. No jury'd ever convict the bastard for killing his niece. They'd send him to a loony bin.

"We find the defendant not guilty of the charges. We recommend incarceration in a state mental institution where his unique problem can receive professional treatment."

The bastard would be freed eventually. You couldn't cure a freak like that. You'd never be sure he'd lost his creepy powers. Hadn't the father said the kid was normal for more than a year? Normal! Then look at what the hell he did. Wrecked the house. Almost slaughtered the old man.

Holy fuckin' cow!

He hadn't believed it at first. Poltergeist bullshit! Who the hell would? But the father had convinced him. Given him names of the kid's therapist, of that woman doctor who was supposed to have gotten rid of his powers once and for all.

Fine fuckin' job she did.

It'd been a mistake going to her lab. A pointless delay. What more proof did he need? The witnesses. The sketch of the kid. His short haircut. The false name he'd used. His freaky past. That fuckin' A-bombed house and battered old Mike Malone. Hartman's secretary had bragged that the kid was the doc's star subject. Did that mean there were more freaks like him?

Fuckin' Webb knew all this and was keeping it secret until he had more evidence. Who's to say that in the meantime the kid wouldn't kill them all? He'd just missed killing his father, lifting huge Mike Malone like a feather and tossing him like a softball.

Rory Malone.

The bastard must have known Kathy. Oh God! Poor Kathy, sweet Kathy. He still couldn't believe she was dead. They must have argued on the platform. Maybe she wouldn't go out with the freak. Then he lifts her like a feather, too, and tosses her onto the tracks.

He killed her. No matter how you cut it.

A freak like that had to be destroyed. The boy's dad felt the same way, too.

If Webb brought the kid in, he wouldn't be able to do a damn thing. So he must find him first. Oh, Lou Bauer'd never approach the freak face to face. That would be suicide. He'd have to sneak up on him.

The kid was a freak, but after all, he also was made of flesh and blood. A bullet to the brain would stop him once and for all.

48

Liz stormed out of the amphitheater, hurried down the stairs, and was in the quadrangle before Gerhardt and Captain Webb caught up with her.

But she refused to talk, racing ahead of them, never acknowledging their presence.

Why had Gerhardt shown Webb the film? Behind her back! He had betrayed her. Doomed poor Rory.

"Liz, honey, please be reasonable," said Gerhardt, scurrying beside her. "Captain Webb just came from Mike Malone's house. He's seen the extent of the destruction. Liz, Rory's dangerous."

"Dr. Hartman, I know all about the boy's past and your research. You must help me find Rory Malone."

With not the vaguest idea of where she was headed, suddenly Liz entered the closest building, Scott Hall, letting the door swing in Gerhardt's face.

"Liz, Rory cut his hair the day after that girl's accident. Kathy Bauer's dead now."

Her pace down the hall accelerated.

"At the time of the accident Rory was supposed to be on his way to the lab, but he never arrived. Never called. We both felt that was peculiar behavior for him."

Damn, the hall led to a dead end. Trapped. Almost. To avoid looking like an idiot, she entered the open doors to the faculty cafeteria. Fortunately at this hour of the afternoon it was empty.

Gerhardt persisted. "Honey, a dozen witnesses testified that Rory was on the platform when the girl fell. Only ten feet away. If he could toss those targets like paper planes, demolish his home, he could have accidentally caused Kathy Bauer's fall."

It would look moronic to just plop herself down at a table, so she proceeded first to the coffee machine, filled a styrofoam cup, then headed to a table at the far side of the room.

After a few moments Gerhardt and Webb joined her, each with coffee containers.

You've trapped yourself, old girl.

"Look at this," said Gerhardt, sliding a paper across the table toward her.

From the charcoal sketch she immediately recognized Rory.

"You can help us find the boy, Dr. Hartman," said Webb. "After all, he hasn't committed a crime. He could never be sent to jail for what he may have done accidentally."

She did need help locating Rory; she had no idea how to go about it herself.

"Liz," said Gerhardt in his most compassionate voice, "we both know what we saw in that film: Rory's energy. When I first realized what it was, I worked with the negative to enhance the force field, brightened it. Rory centered his concentration on you. What did it feel like?"

Silence.

"Liz, honey, be reasonable."

"A pressure," she finally answered in a cold voice. "A tight, suffocating pressure. And he wasn't concentrating on me."

"Was the boy angry with you, Dr. Hartman?"

"Not at all. He had been concentrating hard on the targets, generating psychic energy. Suddenly, stupidly, I walked into his force field, so to speak. It was my own dumb fault." She averted her eyes from Gerhardt's questioning stare. Let Webb help her find Rory. But never would she disclose the full extent of his power.

"Were there any other sensations?" asked Gerhardt.

"Just pressure, lack of oxygen. When momentarily I closed my eyes, I saw a clear image of his face. Nothing else."

"That explains it!" said Webb, striking the table with his fist. "I'd been watching the boy in the hospital lobby, his eyes closed. I assumed he was praying. Then I received an emergency page to Kathy Bauer's room. She was screaming hysterically, claiming she saw a face in her room. Of course I assumed it was a hallucination. Perhaps at the time he'd been focusing on her."

"Perhaps," said Liz tersely, coldly.

"Dr. Hartman, I realize this is hard for you, but you've already been an immense help. The pressure you felt clears up another mystery."

Liz sipped her coffee, afraid of what she was about to hear.

"After Kathy Bauer calmed down, I questioned her about her fall. She seemed confused. No one had physically touched her, yet she had felt pressure all over her body. Understandably, she was very perplexed about this; in fact, she broke down in tears when I asked her if she could be more specific. Apparently she felt the same suffocating pressure you did, from the boy's force field, as you call it. Do you know if Rory knew Kathy Bauer? Had he ever mentioned her name?"

"I don't recall. I'd ask her parents."

"I have, as well as her friends. Unfortunately, Kathy Bauer can't tell us any more herself."

Liz was torn between feelings of compassion for the girl and a strong desire to protect Rory for as long as she could. After all, she had "educated" his power. What a joke!

"Dr. Hartman, soon we'll distribute over a thousand sketches of Rory Malone with short hair. His picture will appear in the evening papers and on television. Ten detectives and scores of foot cops will begin searching Central Park, movie theaters, Times Square—all the places runaways feel most anonymous. I assure you, with or without your help, we'll find Rory Malone."

He wondered how far Bauer had gotten in his search. Mike Malone had mentioned that Bauer had stopped by yesterday, the day he was supposed to be handling arrangements for Kathy's funeral. And Bauer had been to Liz Hartman's office that very morning. Fortunately neither Hartman nor Kiner had been there to fuel Bauer's obsession with more incendiary information on Rory Malone's powers.

The facts: Bauer definitely had not seen Kiner's film and most likely did not know the details of Hartman's research. Still, he'd observed Mike Malone and the house—more than sufficient evidence to convince him that Rory Malone possessed a dangerous power, one that he could easily have used on his niece.

"Dr. Hartman, what I'd like to know from you at the moment is if there's anything that can be done to destroy Rory Malone's power once we apprehend him." Maybe even before, he thought.

"Yes," answered Liz. But she wasn't about to be more specific now. First she had to plan her own course of action to keep the full truth from Gerhardt. Then she had to review the hormone-therapy papers; it had been a year since she'd last read them. Rory was stronger, much stronger, now.

Webb sat staring at Liz Hartman. He thought: This

woman's crazy if she thinks I'm going to leave without first hearing all the details on just how this boy can be cured.

49

10:00 P.M. A Greenwich Village Apartment

"Another hit, kid?"
"Man, he's out of it."
Party . . .
Where, West Side?
Drugs, yes . . .
Coke, grass, pills . . .
More, please.
He was beginning to remember.

Sitting up on the sofa, lifting his feet from the coffee table and placing them on the floor, Rory couldn't recall how he had gotten to this party with all its grass, booze, and deafening music, all these weird people.

Was he still on the East Side? No, he'd run from there. Run through the park, heading for . . . Dr. Hartman's apartment.

For help.

The power had controlled him again. She—no, they—had brought it on themselves. Piqued his anger, and in doing so, incensed the power beyond his control.

How fortunate that he had not made it to Dr. Hartman's. That had been a rash decision, a hasty misjudgment made in a moment of self-pity.

The grass had helped him shed that feeling. Relaxed, he

reclined against the faded gray cushions of the huge frayed sofa.

Where had he stopped running? The West Forties? Yes, he'd been thirsty. Stopped at a deli, bought a container of orange juice and chugged it. Then out of the blue appeared this girl. In a dreamy voice, with glazed eyes, she'd invited him to the party. Just like that! A total stranger. And they'd taken a subway to the village. Now he barely remembered her face. It'd be impossible to pick her out of this crowd.

Accepting the red wine offered to him in a plastic cup, he drank it down despite its vinegary taste.

He had smoked grass for the first time. That much he recalled. Wow! How it helped him forget. Wiped out that incident on the East Side. But the details were starting to return. He glanced at the young men around him, who were passing joints. One joint was headed his way.

Hurry with it; I need to forget.

He had to forget that damn prostitute. She had come on to him. Teased him. God, why couldn't she have left him alone?

"A cutie," she had called him. "Real handsome, you are. But I bet you wouldn't know what to do with it. Would you now?"

She had followed him, making sucking noises with her mouth. And her girl friend had laughed because he was embarrassed, because he was hurrying away, not interested in their kind.

He had stopped at the corner for the streetlight and they'd moved up on each side of him. Laughing. Teasing.

"Wait'll this number grows up."

"What a class-A man you're gonna be, baby. Break a lot of hearts, I can tell."

"Dolly, maybe we should help him grow up real fast."

"Like in one night? Business *is* slow."

One black, one white, they'd followed him across Fifty-third Street on Second Avenue. In the doorways along the next block stood several boys his age—male hustlers, standing in shadows of storefronts. Some were posing tough; others, girlish.

"This where you work?" had laughed the black prostitute. "I bet a dude like you really pulls in the dough. Hundred a night?"

Some of the boys had heard and began sniggering.

"Well, Violet, we had him guessed wrong. It's johns he's after."

They had been mocking him. He had tried to control his anger, but they'd teased relentlessly until he'd lost the battle. Provoked, the power had lashed out at the prostitutes like a whirlwind, ripping their clothes, and left them dumbfounded, terrified, and half-naked on Second Avenue. He was becoming increasingly dangerous, he'd realized: First unable to control sexual desire, now unable to contain anger.

Greedily he accepted the joint, pinching the stub between his fingers, inhaling deeply several times, holding in each breath until his lungs ached. He did not pass it on but finished it.

For the first time in memory he didn't feel alone but part of this group of strangers. Few spoke; most just smiled idly at him and at each other. Some danced in the adjoining room. A man his father's age glided with a teenage girl. Girls held girls. Several guys gyrated with guys. That looked the most bizarre, yet it didn't bother him enough that he wanted to leave. He felt more than just safe here: He belonged among these people his father would call freaks. They paraded their freakiness openly; his lay hidden from them.

The wine was passing right through him. He would have to get up again and find the bathroom. Pulling himself to his feet, he ambled unsteadily across the room, around the periphery of the dancers, down the hall.

A line. A guy with a severe crew cut, wearing a black tank top studded with rhinestones. A fat girl with long blond hair, in a midriff and cutoffs, her eyes heavily decorated. They waited ahead of him.

For support he leaned against the wall opposite one of the bedrooms.

At first he thought it was a dream. But no, what he saw was real.

On the bed, on top of a brown and white furry cover, two girls kissed, hands exploring each other's bodies. From beneath one girl's raised T-shirt protruded bare breasts, nipples twisting under her companion's gentle fingers. The open zipper of her jeans revealed a hint of curly black hair.

A bare-chested young man in a black leather vest exited from the bathroom, passing with a look of scorn, as though Rory didn't belong there.

The skinny guy in line took the fat girl's hand and led her into the bathroom, closing the door behind them.

Now naked from the waist up, the girls on the bed writhed in pleasure, each taking turns arousing the other. They did this casually, almost nonchalantly, at times smiling, even laughing in their eye-to-eye stares.

In the movies he'd watched girls getting it on together—it was one of his favorite fantasies—but never did he dream he would one day witness it in the flesh. He, Rory Malone, actually was watching two girls having sex.

The boy-girl couple that appeared so mismatched to him emerged from the bathroom, giggling. As the girl passed, he noticed that her long hair was now in a thick braid, sporting the feather that had been in the guy's belt.

On the bed the curly redheaded girl slipped her hand into her companion's open jeans. Advancing into the door frame, he watched the brunet attempting to shimmy the jeans over her broad hips.

He sighed.

The redhead turned.

She was getting off the bed, approaching him. Her ghost-white breasts, dotted with rosy freckles, bounced in unison. From her friendly smile he thought she might invite him to join them; he'd never known people like the ones at this party.

She said softly, "Sorry; maybe later. But we want some time alone now." Gently closing the door, she forced him into the hall.

"Give you any ideas?" said a tall girl with jet-black hair. Her fine features and slender body contrasted sharply with her full breasts, which were clearly visible through a red fishnet pullover. Very pretty, he thought; in her mid-twenties.

She took his hand and silently escorted him through the kitchen and into a stairwell that led to the roof of the building.

Against the black sky gleamed the lights of uptown Manhattan: the red neon RCA logo, the pink-and-white Empire State Building. He had never seen the city from this perspective, from this height. Below lay a maze of streets dotted with a welter of lamp posts and red taillights of cars.

"This way," she said. "There are lawn chairs by the far wall. My name's Jacqueline; call me Jackie."

She was exotically lovely; she spoke in such a soft, soothing voice. He couldn't believe this was happening to him.

They shared a chaise longue.

After they had been kissing for several minutes, he realized that tonight was the night. No longer would he be a virgin. This was the goal Gerhardt had been steering him toward: real sex with a real girl, without guilt. Frequent real sex, he suddenly thought, might supplant the need for fantasy, slake his horniness, and thus thwart the prodigious power. Suppose the power sprang from a frustrated hunger for real sex with a genuine flesh-and-blood woman? Then the real thing might be a cure. If so, he couldn't wish for a more beautiful and gentle girl than Jackie.

He hoped he had not had too much to drink or smoke, that he'd not disappoint her.

He wouldn't, though. He had never been so aroused. His fingertips crept through the openings in the fishnet, touching her silky breasts—the biggest, firmest ones he'd ever seen.

Jackie's hand held him behind the head, pressing his mouth tighter to hers; the other hand was opening his pants, reaching inside, taking him out.

No woman had ever touched him there. Never had he been so hard.

"Just a minute," she said, pulling his fingers from the fishnet top. "You're going to stretch it out of shape." In one smooth motion she lifted the top over her head, carefully laying it on the arm of the adjacent lounge.

Her breasts shined in the moonlight; so huge, so incredibly firm.

234 . . .

As she pulled his face toward one breast, his mouth automatically opened and soon tasted the sweat and perfume that flavored her skin. It all seemed totally unreal. The night. The view. The moonlight. Magnificent Jackie, loving him, squeezing, stroking that part of him no woman had ever before handled.

She bent to his crotch, taking him in her mouth. He would have come instantly had he not been partly stoned, partly drunk. The wet warmth of her mouth spread throughout his entire body.

Jackie appeared to be such a gentle, refined girl; he wondered if she always was so aggressive with men, always did this. No, probably not. Of course, she too was stoned, liberated by grass and alcohol.

One hand fondled her breast; the other he slid tentatively under her pleated black skirt, inching higher and higher with imperceptible slowness.

After a moment Jackie pushed his hand away. "You just lie back and relax," she said, raising her head, smiling. "Permit *me* to entertain *you*." Her mouth again swallowed him.

Images from all the films played through his mind. He'd seen so many women do this; none, though, as beautiful as Jackie. The men remained passive, accepting the pleasure—for a while. Then they reciprocated, made the women feel good.

Again, more aggressively this time, he reached up Jackie's dress. Her hand gripped his.

"Determined bugger, aren't you," she said, sitting up.

From a pocket in her skirt she pulled a small brown bottle and unscrewed the top, which connected to a tiny spoon. Coke. Scooping up the white powder, Jackie inhaled it deeply; then again up the other nostril. Only once before had he been offered coke—at a party after a St. Vincent's football game—but he had immediately refused. Now he accepted the bottle eagerly, careful to do exactly what Jackie had done.

They each snorted the coke again, then Jackie returned the bottle to her pocket.

Fly open, erection bared, pointing toward the stars; Jackie's mouth devouring his hardness. Impossible, he thought, reclining in the lounge, delighting in her bringing him close to orgasm. Again and again. If it was always this easy, if all girls were like Jackie, he would have no problems; he would never have to fantasize; the power would be pointless, obsolete.

Sounds of traffic rose from the street; music from the party a floor below filtered onto the roof. A breeze ruffled Jackie's skirt. Gently he rested both hands on Jackie's velvety black hair, as black as the night sky, and held her head as it rode up and down on him.

After a while he sat up. He didn't want to come yet. There were so many things he wanted to do to Jackie. This time he reached quickly up her skirt, gripping her crotch, squeezing it firmly. He wanted to arouse her.

For a moment he was confused.

Keeping her mouth on him Jackie pushed his hand away, mumbled words he couldn't understand.

Something was wrong. Terribly wrong.

Quickly he grabbed Jackie's crotch again, exploring her fully, himself more alert this time.

Abruptly his hand withdrew. He jerked back from her, sat up, covered his erection. It hadn't been merely a hallucination, a nightmare.

"Sorry," said Jackie, pulling down her skirt. "I told you that was a no-no."

He stood in horror and disgust, staring at Jackie's huge, naked breasts, yet absolutely, unmistakably aware of what he had gripped. A cock. A rock-hard cock pressing to break out of her silk panties.

Immediately his sexual arousal shifted to anger.

As Jackie reached for her fishnet top, it flew off the arm of the chair, darting over the wall of the roof. Turning in astonishment, she faced him.

The first thing Jackie noticed was the frigid, icy stare in his eyes; not a stoned gaze but a look at once intimidating and horrific. This was not the first time a man had probed too far and discovered her secret; her life had been threatened several times—an occupational hazard. But this boy was clearly enraged.

"Sweetie," she said, attempting to appease him, "you

must admit that you enjoyed it; it felt good." Then cupping her breasts: "And these are beautiful. Now why don't you just forget that you discovered Jackie's little secret?" This punk wanted to beat the shit out of her.

Fuck, she thought, he'll cause a scene at the party.

Experience had taught her that a horny man was far more dangerous to her than one who had reached orgasm. Coming defused a man's contempt for her by making him an accomplice in the act. Now this enraged boy was an innocent victim of a beautiful and devious transvestite; if she could only get him to let her finish the job she'd started, then his own guilt would check him from attacking her or, worse, from precipitating a nasty scene downstairs.

"Look," she said in her most feminine voice, "you're still hard. Why not let Jackie finish you off. One, two, three, pop! And it's all over."

Approaching him, her hand reaching for his erection, she lulled, "Now you just lie back and relax and fondle Jackie's big knockers."

Suddenly invisible hands grabbed her skirt, yanking it off her body. It tore like tissue paper, falling around her black high heels. The black silk panties raced down her legs and over her shoes, knocking Jackie onto her back.

So fast had events occurred that Jackie's erection had not yet subsided. Unknown to Rory, the sight of it provoked the power further.

Screaming, naked except for her heels, Jackie's body rose off the asphalt roof. She spun like a top, faster and faster, into an unrecognizable blur. Then, screaming, she soared over the brick wall, plummeting toward the ground. Her shouts mixed with the party music, with noises ascending from the street.

Climbing down the roof stairs, Rory went straight to the elevator. His senses temporarily dulled, he was operating on instinct alone.

On the street he passed a crowd that had gathered at the far end of the building, then headed up Seventh Avenue, isolated for the cement against the shrill sirens of two racing police cars.

50

Bauer now felt under even greater pressure to find the fuckin' kid on his own. Webb had released that new sketch. The kid's picture was fuckin' everywhere: TV, all the papers. Wanted for questioning. Questioning, hell. Wanted for murder was more like it. Someone was bound to spot the kid and call the station. And soon. He had to move his ass.

For three hours he'd cruised Greenwich Village in an unmarked car, stopping weirdos, asking if they recognized the sketch. He'd bet the kid was hiding there. Many runaways headed straight for the village; it drew all kinds of freaks. He'd read that it had changed during the seventies, becoming less kooky, more middle-class, white-collar. Shit it had! One glance and any level-headed person could see it was kookier than ever. Fuckin' gayer now, too. Fag capital of the East Coast.

He'd struck out, though. A big fuckin' zero.

Now he searched on foot. It gave him more freedom to check the clubs and bars. Gay bars, too. A kid that good-lookin' would easily be snatched up by a fag and offered protection. For a price, of course. His ass.

He felt snug in one certainty: That freak had definitely killed his niece. The fact that Webb had suddenly launched a big search proved that once and for all.

What had Webb discovered? He probably knew what that Hartman chick had been researching with the kid.

Well, Lou Bauer didn't have to have the details to know

that she was up to no good. She sure as hell hadn't helped the kid.

He headed down Christopher Street. Even in this summer heat guys strutted in and out of bars in full black leather. Freaks, too. He'd like to arrest them all. But he had to keep calm, remember his single goal.

He'd be doing society a fuckin' favor by killing the kid. Of course it'd appear to be an accident. He had no doubt he'd concoct the right angle when the time arrived.

If he found the kid in this fag ghetto, he might be able to kill a few freaks with one ballistic stone.

Over his walkie-talkie came a call for a car in the village to proceed immediately to the apartment building at the corner of Christopher Street and Greenwich Avenue. The confused dispatcher's voice said, "A man; no, a woman—make that a transvestite—was pushed or fell from the roof."

One less freak to worry about, thought Bauer as he turned off his radio.

51

11:15 P.M. Liz Hartman's apartment

"Honey," said Gerhardt, easing onto the edge of the bed, calming Liz's trembling hands, "when we find Rory, I'm afraid we have only two choices." Her hands were still feverish. He felt her forehead.

He was worried about Liz's health. Since the discussion that afternoon with Captain Webb on the use of female hormones to destroy Rory's power, Liz had felt listless and feverish, and occasionally her skin erupted in a chilled sweat. She had eaten neither lunch nor dinner—"I just couldn't keep it down"—and for the last few hours had been sitting up in bed nursing a severe headache.

"Oh, Gerhardt, I just can't do it to him—*if* he'll even permit us to. What if Rory says no?"

Throughout the evening, when her headache periodically and briefly subsided, she and Gerhardt reviewed the papers of Columbia University endocrinologist Dr. Howard Landay on the use of synthetic female hormones on imprisoned rapists in Germany. Each case was an individual horror story. Such treatment would never be permitted in America.

"The boy can't refuse," said Gerhardt. "He doesn't have a choice."

"Oh, but he does. You're forgetting just how powerful Rory can be. Do you remember how terrified he was of the therapy when you first suggested it? Well, he's a hundred, a thousand times stronger today."

Over a year ago Liz had explained some of the therapy's milder side effects to Rory, but not the worst of them.

"Oh, Gerhardt, Rory's so young for this kind of therapy. The prisoners in all those studies were three times his age."

"All the more reason to believe the hormones will be doubly effective on Rory."

"Yes, and the side effects more hideous, more disastrous."

She couldn't ruin his life like this. While the feminizing effects on his body would eventually subside once the therapy was terminated—though he might have to undergo a double mastectomy to excise fatty tissue; God forbid!—the potential for permanent sterility and for cancer of the testes and liver later in life was distressingly real.

"I can't! I just can't do it to him."

"Honey, you've already told Captain Webb that female hormones are the only means of destroying Rory's power. Do you think he'll let you back down now?"

"He could be locked up until the power just normally fades."

"Liz," said Gerhardt, taking her hand, touched and not the

least bit jealous at her immense concern for Rory, "you better than anyone realize that Rory's power (they had abandoned calling it a talent) can't be contained by steel bars or even steel walls."

"I almost hope they don't find him."

That afternoon, trapped in the Scott Hall cafeteria, she had reluctantly provided Captain Webb with a sketchy outline of the hormone therapy—as much of it as she remembered at that time. Since their talk she had arrived at the disheartening realization that the task of instituting the therapy would fall to her. Liz Hartman, surrogate mother and confidante, was going to have to persuade Rory to submit to treatment. She felt like a mother forced to feed a son dangerous drugs that would cause him incalculable mental and physical anguish, possibly death.

"What are the choices again?" she asked weakly.

Propping a pillow against the wall, Gerhardt sat close to Liz, surveying the notes he had extracted from Landay's papers.

"Either we implant pellets of ethinyl estradiol under Rory's skin—most likely on the fleshy inside of the upper arm, monthly—or administer weekly injections of Primogyn."

She felt terribly lightheaded; it was hard to concentrate.

"Didn't Landay mention something about a pill? That might be so much easier, less frightening for Rory."

"Well, the antiandrogen steroid Androcur, or cyproterone acetate, is a pill. But, Liz, I think that's the riskiest approach."

"Why?"

"Honey, once Rory starts developing breasts and sees a general feminizing of his body, he'll be greatly tempted either to stop the pills or to pretend to take them. No, we must leave him no way out; he might even refuse injections after a while. I vote for subdermal implants."

Of course Gerhardt was right, thought Liz, but she was horrified by the image of dime-size pellets under Rory's skin, trickling female hormones into his bloodstream hour after hour, day after day.

"Because of their time-released dose," said Gerhardt, "the

pellets are probably the best all-around chemical castrating agent."

Liz shot forward.

"Don't call it that horrible, horrible name. Do you hear! Chemical castrating agent! Oh God!" She clutched Gerhardt's arm. "You must promise me you'll never use that term around Rory. Please! And never, never mention it to Captain Webb."

"Okay, honey, calm down. I agree. Female-hormone therapy—no, just hormone therapy—is how we'll refer to the treatment." He'd never seen her so upset. He was more certain than ever now that whatever she had experienced in the Red Room had been highly traumatic.

Throughout the discussion with Webb and later when they were alone at home, she had insisted that she'd merely walked into Rory's force field, that suffocation, pressure, and hallucinations were all she had experienced. That was frightening enough to be sure, thought Gerhardt, but after fifteen years of marriage he knew when his wife was lying. Something else had occurred in that room, something intensely traumatic, personally shattering for Liz.

Earlier, slipping out of the apartment under the pretense of getting dinner, Gerhardt had spent an hour at the university reviewing the film. When Liz had entered the Red Room, the force field was barely visible and surrounded only Rory's body. Almost immediately it had reached out like a living tentacle to engulf her. The motion seemed deliberate, intentional. Liz claimed the force was passive and that she had actively intruded upon it; the film revealed Liz as the passive one, the force as active.

The tentacle apparently served as a conduit or bridge, for gradually more energy flowed from around Rory's body, through this established connection, to encapsulate Liz's entire being.

Several times Gerhardt had rerun the film, attempting to correlate this increase in glowing energy with Liz's physical actions in the room. Clearly, all the while she was reattaching electrodes to Rory's ear, scalp, and chest, the aura around her intensified. So, too, did the halo around Rory. Gradually the two halos drew closer, as if they were trying to merge into one blazing entity.

In order photographically to enhance the halos, Gerhardt unfortunately had had to sacrifice the images of Liz and Rory, making it impossible to correlate Liz's final actions with the expansion of energy. If memory served him correctly, he believed Liz had stiff-armed Rory; in fact, that she had struggled to pull away from him.

What did that mean?

Jeepy, the cat. Was this a clue?

An autopsy revealed that Jeepy had been crushed to death; the cat's ribs were broken and its internal organs were flattened. All he and Liz had been able to conclude was that in a highly emotional moment Rory had unwittingly released an enormous burst of poltergeist energy—he had physically *hugged* the cat to death.

Well, Liz had felt a terrible suffocating pressure. In a moment of anger Rory may have unwittingly attempted to kill Liz. To crush her to death.

If Liz believed this, no wonder she was so upset. It meant that Rory couldn't always control the power. Rather, that intense emotions were the controlling agents. If so, capturing Rory against his will could prove to be a catastrophe for everyone involved. Apparently this was what Liz had meant when she had implied that no one could force Rory to submit to hormone therapy against his will.

Gerhardt had gone into the bathroom and now returned with a thermometer.

"Open up. Don't argue with me. You feel very warm."

Liz's mouth accepted the thermometer, and listlessly she leaned against the pillow.

So they were going to castrate Rory for his assaults on women, rapes that no one except her knew had occurred. What irony, she thought. The poor boy will be treated like a common, cold-blooded rapist. And I'm responsible for all of this.

"A hundred and three," said Gerhardt. "I realize this order will be hard to follow, but I want you to relax and get some sleep. You've run yourself down. And even if Captain Webb calls tonight, I don't want you patrolling with him. I'll go."

Her arms and legs ached, but only half as badly as her back. Damn! Why did she have to contract a summer cold just now, when there was so much to handle. Of course, she'd been under almost inhuman pressure these last few weeks, and undoubtedly that had taken a toll on her resistance.

Still, if she were healthy she would be out with the police now. She had suggested that it might be wise for her to be present when the police moved in on Rory; and Webb, clearly intimidated by what he'd seen at Mike Malone's house and on film, had immediately accepted her offer. Well, Webb had said he would call as soon as he had a lead.

"Honey, I'm going to shower. You stay under the covers. Tonight we'll keep the air conditioner on a low setting."

Watching Gerhardt undress, she wondered: What man who possessed Rory's ability to have sex with a woman without touching her would not use that power? Oh, there must be a few, but she'd never known any. Scruples, morals, conscience—sure, they would all broadcast a clarion warning: No, don't do it. That's wrong. But the continual temptation to sexually possess any woman—with ease and social impunity—would occasionally, if not frequently, win out. God! If Gerhardt could have every woman he desired, he'd take them two at a time. In fact, every man she had ever dated would probably offer an arm and a leg to possess Rory's power.

Gerhardt piled his clothes on the armchair and, naked, walked to the bed, then kissed Liz.

"You'll probably feel a lot better tomorrow. After all, some of these aches and pains could be from your period. Aren't you due soon?"

"Yes."

When Gerhardt had disappeared into the bathroom, she reached to the bed table for the remote control and turned on the television news. For a while she read Landay's paper on the side effects of hormone therapy. Many of the German prisoners who developed large breasts and rounded, fleshy hips were so lustfully sought after and savagely fought over by their fellow inmates that radical mastectomies provided the only way to avert bloody feuds and riots.

Female hormones in large doses, reported Landay, destroy the male libido, make erection impossible, and, administered for sufficiently long periods of time, cause testicular atrophy. With Rory, they would never go that far. Not testicular atrophy.

God! He's only a boy, with his whole life ahead of him.

The other long-term side effect, cancer, though it was a more remote possibility, caused Liz even greater concern. The risk of cancer, stressed Landay, decreases with a man's advancing age. Thus it was highest for young prisoners, and consequently hormone therapy was not the preferred treatment for rapists in their teens or early twenties.

Of course Landay was referring to whopping doses. They would start Rory off on very small amounts; not enough to totally destroy his power in a single treatment (if that were even possible); just enough to palliate its strength. The literature contained only two cases in which hormones were administered to poltergeist children. Both involved teenage girls, so testosterone was employed; and since neither girl had demonstrated powerful energy eruptions, the doses had been quite small and the injections infrequent.

Considering Rory's prodigious ability, the entire procedure would have to be experimental, trial-and-error all the way, step by painstaking step. Hopefully, with minimal error.

Mention of Rory's name caused her to glance at the television screen, which was filled with a closeup of the police sketch. Tossing off the blankets, she moved to the edge of the bed and spoke softly to the picture.

"You poor boy. Hunted like a criminal. You certainly never intended to harm anyone. And whatever you had been doing to me, you caught yourself in time and stopped. You're a good boy. I know that."

The announcer stated that Rory Malone was wanted for questioning, and a police phone number flashed on the screen across Rory's chest.

If she could only find him, help him. Why haven't you

called? "You probably believe the police know about your sexual assaults. That I betrayed you. Well, they don't know, Rory. And I'll do everything in my power to keep your secret."

She was crying when Gerhardt returned to the bedroom.

52

11:25 P.M. The Malone home

Mike Malone's eyes were riveted to the screen of the portable television set he had rented that afternoon, specifically for watching the details of the capture and arrest of that freak who was no son of his. He wanted Rory behind bars even more than the police did.

The freak's face stared at him across the darkness of the room. Wanted for questioning, hell. He pushed her.

The freak was more dangerous than he'd ever thought possible. He himself was barely living proof of that. It had been a close call. That brush with death had left him with a chill he couldn't shake. If they met again, only one of them would walk away alive.

He had watched every news report that day, read all the papers for additional details. But none of substance appeared. The truth of the matter was that the police still had no leads. That freak was wandering through some neighborhood right this minute. Although the police were searching all five boroughs, Mike felt certain Rory was in Manhattan. The boy had always spent as much time as possible in the city.

He heard a noise and sat up with a start.

Lifting the .38 revolver from the torn sofa cushion, he

rested it on his leg, nervously fingering the trigger. He'd laughed the day Mayor Koch requested that citizens voluntarily surrender unlicensed arms to their local precincts. Hell he would. One day that gun would save his life.

Someone was on the porch.

Lowering the volume of the television, Mike craned his head, listening for another sound. With the living room lamps still broken and the shattered bulbs in the ceiling fixture yet to be replaced, the dim glow from the television was the only light showering the room, illuminating Mike Malone, making him a sitting duck for whoever prowled the porch.

Rory?

The freak wouldn't dare return home. But perhaps he'd come for his clothes or personal belongings, or money. Since the poltergeist outburst Mike had avoided Rory's room like the plague, the only room in the house untouched by the catastrophe. Mike wondered if it possessed some force just waiting to be antagonized. Juxtaposed with the chaos throughout the house, the room's orderliness seemed like a tidy little land mine daring to be trod upon. Prior to retiring last night, Mike had leaned tentatively into the room from the hall and closed the door.

Rising from the sofa, he flicked off the television, then moved silently toward the front door.

Simultaneously the footsteps on the porch skirted around to the side of the house.

Did the fuckin' freak think he could sneak into his bedroom window unheard?

Mike Malone detested the fact that he was sweating profusely down the small of his back, under his arms, above his upper lip, and that his hands quivered, that his heart raced like a fuckin' frightened sissy's.

A face-to-face confrontation must be avoided at all costs. I'll have to kill him first, thought Mike. It's that or be killed by the freak.

Standing with his ear to the door, Mike strained to track the footsteps.

He had taken every measure possible to keep the kid from

the house. If anything could; that was the unsettling reality of it.

All morning he'd worked replacing the windows on the ground floor (the upstairs panes were still out), then hung a new solid-wood front door he had fashioned himself; the strongest he could construct. By the time he'd equipped the door with two Medico locks and a steel crowbar, only an hour of daylight remained and he'd been unable to replace the splintered back door, so he'd nailed it closed and covered it with a sheet of inch-thick plywood. Tomorrow he would construct the back door and purchase additional locks.

Yet, despite all the heavy-duty precautions, if the freak wanted badly enough to enter the house—well, he would probably rip down a wall.

The sudden knock on the door propelled Mike backward.

Gun poised, aimed at the door, Mike waited, holding his breath.

A second knock. Stronger this time.

The audacity of the fuckin' freak to knock, to presume he could come home and be forgiven. Who the hell did he think he was, the prodigal son?

"Mike, you home?"

He opened the door.

"Jesus, Mike, I called all day. Aren't you answering your phone? And what the hell happened to the house? You having it demolished or something? Well, are you gonna invite me in?"

Mike stepped aside, and Lil Rust entered the room.

"How long have you been sitting here in the dark? Well, I don't blame you for being ashamed. I'd be too, if a son of mine was wanted by the police, had his mug on the TV all day. I told you that that boy was peculiar. I'm not at all surprised he's in trouble. And for the subway pushings!"

She felt sorry for Rory but also relieved that now Mike could plainly see that his son was no angel, that Lil Rust had not been paranoid or vicious or bitching in her numerous warnings about the boy's bizarre behavior.

"Well now, Mike, maybe you're sorry you didn't take my advice and send the boy away to school. I told you it'd be—

Jesus! Mike, what the hell hit you?"

He had stepped into the beam of light from the street lamp, and for the first time she'd seen his face. Light also reflected off the gun that hung at his side, and she edged away from him. His face was battered; his expression, empty, dead.

"Oh, Mike, the boy did this to you, didn't he? The bastard! The thankless, no-good bum. I always thought he was dangerous, but I never imagined he'd actually attack his father. His own flesh-and-blood. Well, if the police don't lock him up, he's gotta be sent away, Mike. If you can't live with him, you certainly can't expect me to. Especially knowing the way he hates me."

Lil approached Mike, compassionate, understanding. "What'd you two fight about, Mike? Me? Was it about me? Us?"

Glancing at the gun, she said, "Now, don't go and do anything foolish. He's not worth it. You don't want to ruin your life—our life."

Feeling along the wall, she found the light switch and flicked it, but the room remained black.

"Oh, I knew it would all come to this. I warned you, you can't say I didn't."

"Shut up!"

"Mike! Don't talk to me like that."

"Shut up!"

"I—I'm on your side Mike." He's ashamed, she thought. Ashamed that his boy bloodied him, that he damaged the house—any father would be. Ashamed that his son was wanted by the police in the subway pushings. Irrational in his grief.

Stepping onto the porch, she said, "I'll go now, Mike, give you some time alone to think over what happened, over all that I said. I'll stop around tomorrow." She reached for his face, but he pulled back.

"My Mike'll feel worlds better tomorrow after a good night's sleep."

Mike Malone closed the door and didn't sleep a wink that night.

53

Another attempt; another failure.

Silently they lay in bed, in darkness, Webb wondering: Am I that bad a lover? Finally he mustered the courage to voice it.

"Luv, I admit it's been a long time for me—two years—but am I really that inexperienced? Have I forgotten so much?" Maybe he never was very good. Or perhaps his soft, slightly flabby, aged body actually turn Carrie off.

She had rolled over, draped one arm across his shoulder, and now rested her head on his chest.

"It's not you."

"Luv, you said that the last time, too. But obviously something's wrong when we're in the hay."

Nothing could be plainer. Or more embarrassing.

The first time they had made love—the night he had unexpectedly found her on the lawn chair in his backyard— she'd been detached, almost frigid; not reactions he expected from a woman who had been trying to land him in the sack for two years. Then he'd attributed Carrie's disinterest to her distressed emotional state: her fear that she felt she was going crazy from persistent hallucinations triggered by the chemically treated grass she'd smoked the previous weekend.

Tonight he had invited her over under the ruse of helping with his "Women and Pornography" paper; and after dinner and two hours of only half-hearted research, they had wound up in bed. She'd started off as passionate as any woman he'd ever known. Then, inexplicably, somewhere during the height of sexual frenzy—at least a high point for him, and he'd believed for her, too—she had suddenly stiffened, gone rigid and icy cold. Her body language clearly said I want to stop, yet she had continued—for his sake, he presumed.

Were they tears he felt on his chest?

Cradling her in his arms, nuzzling his nose in her sweet-smelling hair, he eventually lifted her face in his hands.

If he had left the bedroom door a crack opened, he would have been able to see her face in the light from the hall and perhaps read the real problem etched in her expression. Out of innate sexual reticence, though, and anxiety over a second failure with Carrie, he'd made certain to shroud them in total darkness.

Hell! Be frank.

"Luv, if it's not me, then what's the turn-off?" Sure, better to know now if he lay at the root of the problem—which he felt he did—and avoid further embarrassing failures, which could condemn his reborn sexuality to another hiatus in hell.

"Chief, could we have a little light? I like to see the person I'm talking to."

Rousing himself, attempting a jocular tone, he said, "It's that serious, huh!" then raised the window shade half-mast. White-violet light from the lamp post across the street streamed into the room.

"Yes, it is serious. Though at first I didn't think so."

Carrie lifted the sheet, and he slipped back under to join her.

"Chief, you're going to think I'm crazy. In fact, *I* think I'm crazy."

"That again?"

"The hallucinations have never really stopped. In fact, they've been getting worse. They're strongest when I'm sexually aroused."

"Nightmarish things?"

"At first, no." She stared at the ceiling, aware of his nervous breathing. You poor dear, it has nothing to do with you, but you'll probably misconstrue everything I say. "Chief, it's hard to be specific because the visions are extremely sexual."

"By any chance they wouldn't involve me, would they?"

"They might not be as troubling if they did."

"Who then?"

"That boy. The one half the precinct's searching for."

"Rory Malone! You have sexual dreams about a seventeen-year-old punk?"

"God! I don't will them. I don't even want them. They're spontaneous."

"He's better than me, I suppose?"

Carrie reared up on her elbows. "Stop this. Stop right this minute. These visions—hallucinations—have absolutely nothing to do with you—with us."

"Well, luv, for having nothing to do with us, they've certainly screwed up our only two encounters. Two out of two seems statistically significant to these old eyes."

She sat up and yanked the sheet over her breasts. "If you persist in this disgusting self-pity, this great age difference between us, I'll leave right now and not come back. At least hear me out. Maybe I really am going insane."

Conciliatorily he said, "Okay, shoot."

"Last weekend, in the Hamptons, the boy was in most of my dreams. Yes, as a lover. And he was amazingly advanced, actually very knowledgable for a young boy—not that I've actually gone to bed with any. Later, even when I masturbated—which I do more than occasionally—I hallucinated his face and body. Then that first time we had sex, his presence was so vivid, so real—oh, I know you're going to take this personally—well, it was as if *he* were *you*, as if Rory Malone were on top of me."

"Oh, shit, luv! I'm a psychologist. I recognize fantasy substitution when I hear it. Why with a *teenager*? If you're going to replace me, couldn't you have at least used a mature, successful professional?"

"I see we can't discuss this objectively. I'm leaving."

Carrie lurched forward, and he grabbed her hand and pulled her toward him.

"Why did you make copies of his picture?"

"Oh, you don't miss a trick, do you?"

"I'm a detective, aren't I?"

"A detective or a psychologist—which ever conveniently fits the situation."

"Well, why did you copy his picture?"

"To study it, to try to understand why I have this compulsive fascination for a virtual stranger. I've spent hours staring at that picture, trying to fathom the connection. Do you know why I accepted your offer to come over tonight?"

"I thought because you wanted to be with me."

"Well, yes, of course I did. Do. But a crazy lady prefers to be alone. At least until she's healed. I saw Rory Malone on television. The news recapped Kathy Bauer's case and ran a tape where Nancy Parker attempted to interview the boy. Well, he was only on the screen for a few seconds, but I got the creepiest feelings. Almost screamed. I just had to get out of the house. To be with you."

Webb was suddenly pensive. Curiosity was beginning to override his feelings of jealousy and sexual failure.

"Do you think I'm crazy?"

"Probably. Maybe now you'll lay off drugs."

But did the grass really have anything to do with Carrie's hallucinations?

He recalled that Kathy Bauer had hallucinated a face in her hospital room, apparently while Rory Malone had been concentrating on her. Gerhardt Kiner had claimed the boy had concentrated his energy on Liz Hartman in the film, though she denied that Rory Malone's effort was deliberate. Webb himself had seen the effect: Liz Hartman enveloped by a powerful force, one she perceived as constricting pressure. And closing her eyes, she, too, had hallucinated Rory Malone's image.

Had Rory Malone also been concentrating on Carrie?

Webb was beginning to feel that Liz Hartman held the answer.

"Luv, you claim the hallucinations have always been related to sex?"

"With sex, and during dreams."

"Not at any other time?"

"No."

Was Liz Hartman withholding information? Protecting the boy? Grudgingly she had explained that the boy's power could be greatly diminished, and eventually destroyed, with hormone therapy, though not without considerable side effects from the large doses that might be necessary.

"Why wasn't that done initially," he'd asked, "when the boy's power was weaker, and presumably smaller, less risky doses would have sufficed?"

Her terse, "Well, we considered that, but ruled it out," had convinced him to investigate her involvement with Rory Malone. For instance: had she undertaken the experiments with his father's permission? With the kid's full understanding of what he might be letting himself in for? If she had lied to Mike Malone, to Rory Malone, was she now lying to her husband about the events depicted in the film?

Webb attempted to weave a picture from one curious thread: sex. Rory Malone's power, in part, stemmed from *sexual* frustrations. *Sex* hormones could conceivably cure the boy. Kiner had been *sexually* liberating him. Carrie's hallucinations always involved *sex*.

Sex, sex, sex. The theme was too ubiquitous for it to be merely coincidental.

"Luv, what did you mean when you said the hallucinations were getting worse?"

"The last two times they went beyond sex into violence."

"Violent sex?"

"No. Sex with him has always been passionate but gentle."

"Where does the violence fit in?"

"The first time we had sex, the boy sort of became you, took your place. That was bad enough. But then I got horrible flashes of blood spattered over a white-and-blue tiled room. A public locker room, or shower, or bathroom. And I felt the violence as tension throughout my body.

"Tonight the sexual hallucinations were the strongest yet—as if the boy physically were in the room doing to me exactly the things you were doing. And then, all of a sudden, wham! I saw a naked body shoot into the air and fly off the roof of a building. It was horribly real."

Damn! Just when he was onto a promising lead, Carrie pitched a baffling curve. Well, one reassurance was comforting: Apparently she was telling the truth when she claimed he was not the cause of their awkward, thoroughly unsatisfying lovemaking.

So far he had informed Carrie only of Rory Malone's poltergeist background; now he weighed whether to reveal what he had learned from Liz Hartman and Gerhardt Kiner that afternoon.

"Luv, Kiner and his wife have been doing research with Rory Malone—really bizarre stuff."

Yes, that's it; tell Carrie everything you know. Maybe her sharper, more analytical mind will shuffle the random facts into a coherent picture.

Thursday
Day 7

54

Late dusk. Central Park

In the damp darkness of the vine-covered underpass that connected two pedestrian walks on opposite sides of an overhead road, Rory paced frantically, frequently consulting his watch, praying for Melissa's safety.

She was an hour late; the park was already dark.

Many times he had rejected the notion of calling her, of subjecting her to the dangers of entering the park alone, for he knew with certainty she would come. In the end he'd admitted that he had no choice. Without money he was helplessly trapped in the city, a danger to himself and to everyone who crossed his path or temper; with cash he could head for Canada and seclusion, for total isolation from women. Geographically unfamiliar with that country, he harbored an image of cities separated by vast wilderness, a frontier where he could remain conveniently "lost" until he returned to normal. Of course, to have fetched the money himself would have been exceptionally risky—another fiery encounter with his father might be the last. Melissa offered his only rescue.

Traffic buzzed on the road overhead; vibrations echoed eerily in the long, dank tunnel.

Had some catastrophe befallen Melissa?

His brain churned with possibilities. She'd been mugged. After all, she was carrying three hundred dollars. Or maybe his father had caught her in the house. Yet even if she had been unable to secure the money, she would still meet him. Not even her parents could prevent that.

Yes, Melissa definitely was coming.

Then what had detained her?

He struggled to shove the worst and all too real possibility from his mind but couldn't. The greatest threat to men in the park was muggers; for women, rapists. If Melissa had been raped—God, no!—what perverse retribution for his own heinous crimes. The very irony of the notion lead him to suspect it had already occurred or was in progress now.

Shedding the protective shadow of the tunnel, parting the hanging Virginia creepers and ivy, he climbed the stairs to the pedestrians' path that paralleled the lake and boat house.

As long as he remained alert to the presence of passersby and kept his face adequately hidden, he could safely search for Melissa. Returning to an elevated lawn overlooking Bethesda Fountain, well secluded by shrubbery, he thought he spotted her. But it was not Melissa. A young girl and her boyfriend strolled hand in hand. A Puerto Rican boy perched on the rim of the fountain; at his feet a large portable radio blared disco music throughout the area. It filtered to Rory through dense summer foliage.

Could he have missed her?

Unlikely, since he'd left the tunnel periodically and checked the area. He had emphatically instructed her to stay by the fountain, not to search for him. And, above all, to be patient if he didn't appear immediately.

Although he desired a larger view of the entire Bethesda area, he rejected as too risky the possibility of scaling the stairs to street level. Too many cars. Too many joggers. Someone was sure to recognize him. Earlier he had stumbled upon a discarded *Daily News* that contained a half-page picture of him. He'd tossed the paper into a trash basket, tucking it deep beneath the rubbish, as if hiding the picture made him safer, less recognizable. Of course by now every paper and television news show must feature Rory Malone's face.

At least the presence of joggers and cars at street level meant Melissa would be relatively safe along the pavement. He'd warned her against taking a shortcut.

Loitering longer than he felt was safe, he retraced his steps to the tunnel. Ascending the path, he spotted two joggers approaching head-on. Narrow, walled by shrubbery, the path offered no natural exit. They had already seen him, so he couldn't very well scurry like an animal into the bushes. At least if he were on the other side of the path he could turn his head, pretend to be interested in the docked boats. Yet to cross over now might appear peculiar.

They were coming closer, staring directly at him.

Bending his head forward, he looked squarely at his watch, pushed the button to retrieve the time, then shook his wrist as if the watch were malfunctioning and could be disciplined to behave properly.

He felt their penetrating stares.

As soon as the joggers passed, he hurried to the protective security of the tunnel.

55

At Fifth Avenue and Fifty-ninth Street, Melissa disembarked from the N subway train, climbed the stairs, and oriented herself. To the left was the Plaza Hotel; to the right, the General Motors Building. The southeast corner of Central Park lay directly ahead.

Was Rory still waiting?

She was afraid she'd failed him, that he might already have fled the city. But no, he couldn't do that; she held the three hundred dollars.

When he had phoned her that afternoon at the dance studio, he had claimed his life depended on her executing his instructions in precise detail. And she had. Though how could she have anticipated that her father would arrive home from work an hour late, that dinner—and thus her departure for the city—would be delayed?

"Mel, dear, you have the entire night to spend with Linda," her mother had chided, exasperated at her impatience to leave the house. "What difference does it make when you get there?"

Still another lie had been necessary; but Rory desperately needed her assistance. And if she intended to spend the night with him, she needed a cover.

Oh, she would persuade him not to run away. The very fact that he now depended on her, trusted only her to know his whereabouts, proved he did deeply care.

Rory had said she would be safest walking up Fifth Avenue along the park, entering at Seventy-second Street, then following the pedestrians' walk to Bethesda Fountain. "I'll be watching for you. Don't try to find me." In June, after school recessed, they had picnicked by the lake adjacent to the fountain, counting people in rowboats whom they suspected were lovers.

Even if Rory was still waiting, could he spot her in the rapidly descending darkness? Surely the area surrounding the fountain would be black by the time she arrived.

Walking briskly, hurrying to beat the fleeing sun, she was overtaken by fear of a dark, deserted Central Park. All the many warnings she'd heard about the place rushed upon her, chilling her on this warm and windless night. "Entering after dark is taking your life in your hands. "It's asking to be robbed or raped." "Your a sitting duck."

Behind her, footsteps scuffed the pavement, uncomfortably close—they seemed paced with her stride.

Rory's counting on me; I can't fail him. Her pace quickened.

The explicitness of his instructions, down to exact times and train, had been for her safety; now she had gone and fouled everything up.

"Catch the N train at six o'clock at Continental Avenue. The ride's a half-hour; the walk to the fountain is roughly twenty minutes. You'll be there well before dusk."

"Rory, your picture was on the news last night and in the morning paper. I know you had nothing to do with that girl's fall. Why do the police want you?"

He had promised to explain everything when she arrived with the money.

The thought of three hundred dollars in her canvas shoulder bag caused her arm to tighten reflexively against her side.

The footsteps were gaining on her.

You're frightened of the dark, of having to enter the park at night, of carrying so much money. That's all it is.

Yet at Sixty-second Street, under a lamp post, she glanced over her shoulder: A man in a business suit swinging a briefcase; a woman in shorts and a tank top walking a bicycle. Peering further, she discerned only the strolling silhouettes of some half-dozen people in the shadows of trees and under the shade of night. Was that one large man Mr. Malone? she wondered. How would he have known to follow her? If Lillian Rust mentioned her visit, if Mr. Malone discovered Rory's money missing, then he definitely would have been suspicious. But she had gone directly home; hours had elapsed before her departure for the city. She had to admit that she was intensely paranoid and would remain so until she was safely in Rory's embrace.

"I'm leaving town," he had said, "and I may not be back for a long time. That's why I must see you. No, my going away has nothing to do with you. Yes, I do love you."

So profusely, so earnestly he had apologized about having stood her up the previous night, about not calling. His voice had never been that gentle and sorrowful. Though he had resolutely denied it, she had distinctly heard his voice quaver and crack; he was crying. If necessary, she was prepared to run away with him. Three hundred dollars would last them a long time.

Stealing the money had been easier than she had expected. Although Rory had assured her that the house was unlocked when his father worked in the shop, she had found the front door bolted. Sneaking around the side of the house opposite the shop, she had hidden behind a hedge until she was convinced from the absence of sounds that Mr. Malone was not in the shop. With the car gone, she had assumed he was off on a job.

The sight in the backyard had shocked her.

Strewn throughout Rory's vegetable garden were numerous pieces of damaged furniture: chairs spilling stuffing, others missing legs and rungs; table lamps shattered; a floor lamp bent like a pretzel; a cracked coffee table; and a gaping hole in the television set.

Both the kitchen and screen doors were missing; the house was easily accessible to anyone. On the ground lay an unpainted new door, grass poking through a hole awaiting a knob; beside it were a hammer, a screwdriver, and large metal hinges. Concluding that Mr. Malone must have gone to purchase additional parts and that, consequently, time was precious, she'd darted into the house, only to be further astonished by the extensive damage in every room—except Rory's. This impressed her as irrefutable evidence that Rory had fought with his father and in revenge had destroyed the house. Exactly how he had accomplished such extensive destruction did not cross her mind.

In the shoe box beneath the bed she had located the money; and she'd have made a perfectly clean getaway had Lillian Rust not strolled across the lawn. "I was looking for Rory," Melissa had said nervously, "but he's not home."

"Dear, Rory won't be coming home. And you'd be doing yourself a favor if you have nothing to do with him in the future. The boy's dangerous. He's crazy."

Spotting a phone booth at the corner of Seventy-second Street, Melissa again had pangs of guilt about not returning Dr. Hartman's call, indeed, about lying to her in the first place, though she couldn't have confessed to dating Rory in front of her parents.

Dr. Hartman had appeared to be genuinely concerned about Rory; beyond this, Melissa had immediately liked her for one reason in particular: Her voice and expression seemed to say, Dear, I know for a fact you're lying; you and Rory have been dating, yet she had never pressed the issue and bared the lie. In fact, in the subsequent phone calls intercepted by Mrs. Adams, Dr. Hartman claimed only that she was questioning all Rory Malone's past acquaintances, however casual. Even when Melissa herself had answered the final call, Dr. Hartman's questions had been straightforward, concerning Rory's whereabouts, never accusatory or disbelieving, and she'd ended the conversation by soliciting a promise that Melissa report to her the moment she heard from Rory.

She had promised Dr. Hartman.

Crossing Fifth Avenue, she rummaged through her bag for a dime, then the slip of paper containing the phone number.

During the first ring she was tempted to hang up, feeling she was betraying Rory, but Dr. Hartman had immediately answered the phone.

"Who is it?" Silence. "Rory?"

"It's Melissa Adams, Dr. Hartman. Rory called me today. I just wanted to let you know that he's all right. I'm on my way to see him now."

"Where, Melissa?"

"I can't say. I promised Rory I wouldn't."

"Dear, where are you calling from?" Was that traffic in the background? "You're not at home, are you, Melissa?"

"No." If Rory wasn't in the park, she would phone Dr. Hartman again. Only if she couldn't find Rory.

"Melissa, dear, you must tell me where I can find Rory. It's for his own good." And for your safety, too, child. Oh, please don't see him alone. Yes, it was traffic. A public street phone. Most likely she's in Manhattan. "Melissa, please tell me. You'll be doing Rory a favor."

"I only wanted to let you know he's all right. I've got to hurry now. I'm late."

"Wait, please, Melissa. The police are searching for Rory. They might already have picked him up. If they have, he won't be where you're to meet him."

She hadn't thought of that possibility.

"I must hurry. If he's not in the park, I'll call you back."

Crossing the street, she spotted two joggers leaving the

park; they passed her and stopped at the phone booth she'd just abandoned. Maybe there would be joggers in the park. That would make her feel safer.

Entering the park, she felt somewhat relieved to find car traffic heavier than she had expected. A string of taxis sped past, their headlights adding to the dim glow from the lamp posts. Other cars continually turned off Fifth Avenue onto the road that cut through the park to the West side of town. The headlights, hitting from behind, repeatedly threw her shadow along the path in front of her.

She again sensed that she was being followed.

Too frightened to glance back, she stuck close to the curb, in clear view to the passing motorists, determined to rendezvous with Rory.

One of the passing headlights turned out to belong to a police car, and for an instant her heart skipped a beat: They know where he is! Then, realizing that the police must regularly patrol the park, she felt considerably safer.

56

"Luv, that was a dinner fit for a chief," said Webb, rocking back in the wobbly chair at the tiny table in Carrie Wilson's West Side studio apartment. "I'm glad I gave you the afternoon off."

"You're not through yet. There's still dessert."

"Always with the innuendos."

"I meant homemade peach pie, smart-ass."

At the counter area that served as a kitchen, containing a stove, minirefrigerator, and sink, above which hung wooden cabinets, Carrie pried aluminum foil from around the still-warm pie; then, squatting to open the refrigerator's box-size freezer, she shuffled packages of frozen fish, peas, and onion bagels until she freed the pint of vanilla ice cream. "Two scoops or one?"

"You know," said Webb, traversing the two feet that separated the dining area from the kitchen, "I never thought I'd see the inside of this apartment. Not that I'd be missing much." Kissing Carrie's neck, he said, "Two scoops, with keys."

"Keys?"

"To this commodious penthouse, luv. You did offer them."

God! Did he feel better since their heart-to-heart. Abreacting, especially learning that he was not responsible for their sexual failures, had spiked his sex drive and awakened his long-dormant male aggressiveness.

"That was months ago."

"Well, now I'm ready to accept. Guess I've been a bit backward."

"Do you really think so? Perhaps just a wee bit." Carrie placed two dishes of peach pie à la mode on the table and sat down.

"Chief, seriously, do you really think that light was his Tinkerbell?" She had attributed it to the grass.

"I do, as crazy as it sounds."

"First in the Hamptons, then here in the city, and then at your place in Jersey. Boy! That kid gets around." She still found it all so hard to believe: astral travel, psychic energy, psychokinesis. "Sort of a psychic Peeping Tom?"

"Why not? His Tinkerbell sees those targets in the Black Room—even hears music."

"So you think he spied on me when we had sex?"

"It's only a theory. But I'll bet Dr. Hartman could readily confirm it—if she were inclined to. Luv, you outdid yourself with this pie."

"I know your sweet tooth—I doubled the sugar and cinnamon the recipe called for. It really should be tart."

"I like my pies sweet, my women tart."

God! What had gotten into him? Carrie's bold sexual

openness apparently was both catching and liberating; and once infected and freed, there was no holding Tom Webb back. The Tom Webb of twenty years ago had reappeared.

"But, Chief, how would Rory Malone know when I was having sex? With myself or with you?"

"I can only assume that he popped in on you periodically and left when you were, oh, say, baking a pie—"

"Oh! Don't say that. It's creepy. The thought of him in this apartment, spying."

"—and hung around when you were engaged in more stimulating activities."

"And by checking on me at night, he sort of contaminated my dreams."

"As a psychologist I'd say that's highly probable."

"And as a man would you spy on unsuspecting women if you could?"

"Remember, luv, I'm backward."

He had mulled over that possibility, and though he'd never admit it to anyone—not even a male buddy, because, of course, a decent individual respected another person's privacy—he'd decided he would spy, but only under one condition: if the women were not emotionally plagued by hallucinations, as Carrie was.

"Why no leads?" asked Carrie, clearing the table.

He wished he knew. In the last twenty-four hours his men had combed the city; the boy's picture was as ubiquitous as summer air pollution. The *Times* said "Wanted for questioning in the East Side subway pushing"; the *Daily News* headlined "New Suspect in the Subway Pushings"; while the *Post* printed in bold front-page letters above Rory Malone's picture "SUBWAY PUSHER?" And if the kid planned on leaving town, he'd never make it by public transportation: plainclothesmen staked out Grand Central Station, Penn Station, and the Port Authority Bus Terminal.

"Luv, may I use the phone?" He hadn't checked in since arriving at Carrie's apartment.

"Sergeant Cruz," he heard after picking up the phone and dialing. "Seventeenth Precinct."

"It's Webb. I just—"

"Chief! I've been trying to call you at home and in your car."

"I'm at a friend's. What's up?"

"Two joggers spotted the Malone kid. Positive identification."

"Where?"

"Near the boat house in Central Park."

"When?"

"Hell, just five minutes ago."

"Cruz, have you dispatched a car?"

"Sure did. Immediately."

"Pinto and Jefferson?"

"No, sir. Didn't have to. Bauer had just come in. He took the call himself."

"With Mazza?"

"Well, no Chief. Mazza's right here."

"But I said team them up."

"Mazza went to take a crap, and when he finished, Bauer had gone."

"Are Pinto and Jefferson still there?"

"Yes, sir."

"Okay, Cruz. Send them out—with Mazza. Tell them to find Bauer and not to let him out of their sight. Mazza's to ride with Bauer. Get that?"

"Yes, sir."

"Make it clear that I want them searching for the kid in teams—and teams only."

"As good as done, Chief."

Heading for the door, he saw Carrie reach for her handbag. "I don't think you better come, luv."

"Well, think again. I want to see what this kid looks like. In person, this time."

57

Bauer grinned wryly. So the fucker's in Central Park. How convenient. The place would be deserted; it'd be a snap to make the freak's death look like an accident.

"Hell, the bastard attacked me with that power. Hurled a trash basket at me. Nearly struck my head." Etc., etc., etc. He'd embellish it during the search. The final line, though, was evident: "I shot him in self-defense."

Traffic up Third Avenue was a bitch on a Thursday night, with Bloomingdale's and Alexander's open late. Between Fifty-ninth and Sixtieth streets, the Bloomingdale's block, taxis and limousines double-parked, bottlenecking traffic.

Should slap 'em all with tickets, he muttered, but a fifty-buck fine was diddly-shit to them. Anyway, Lou Bauer had an urgent mission to attend to.

Fuckin' Fifty-ninth Street Bridge commuters made the congestion almost impenetrable.

Damn! He should have switched the unmarked car for a regular one; he'd have been able to use the siren to part traffic and run lights.

He hadn't notified the freak's old man about the Central Park lead though he'd been tempted to, merely to boast: "I know where your kid is, and I'll get him for you. I'll do this for you as well as for my niece. He'll never hurt anyone again with that fuckin' power." The old man would thank him for killing the kid.

The trick was to find the kid alone. Even the old man could screw up his plans. Suppose later Mike Malone had regrets or, worse, thought he could make a bundle by suing the department because he'd witnessed Sergeant Lou Bauer cold-blood-edly kill his son. No, this had to be done privately.

Impatient for the light to change at Seventy-second Street and Fifth Avenue, he eyed a jogger emerge from the park and turn uptown. Crazy fuckin' fool. Who in his right mind would jog in Central Park at any time of day? Not Lou Bauer. At least not without a gun.

Patrolling along the park through-road, eyes ever vigilant, he caught an image. His headlights had illuminated a young girl, perhaps no older than his Kathy. Foolish damn kid. In the park at night; and alone, too. Jesus! She was even advertising a giant shoulder bag, half her size. Just askin' to be mugged. Irate at the girl's stupidity—probably a wealthy East Side brat off to fuck with her West Side boyfriend—he'd normally have aban-doned her to fate. But so strong were the rawness of Kathy's death in his mind and the associations with this girl in age, imminent danger, and even possible death, that he guided the car toward the curb, slowed it to a crawl, and shouted out the window.

"Get outta the park. Take a bus if ya have to cross town. Ya hear? It's dangerous."

Having done his duty, he sped on. The witnesses had spotted the kid near the boat house. That was near Bethesda Fountain, the bandshell, the mall. He'd bet the fuckin' freak was still somewhere in that area. He shouldn't be too hard to find.

58

"We'll never locate him," said Gerhardt exasperatedly, driving east on Eighty-first Street, heading for the West Side entrance to Central Park. "The park's immense, Liz. And since he's hiding, the last place he would be is near one of the roads. This is ridiculous. You should have notified Captain Webb."

Wanting to concur in part only—"I know that. I realize the probability of finding him is infinitesimal"—she remained silent, however, thinking; Small but not zero. We must try.

Had Melissa accidentally slipped or had her clue been deliberate when she had confessed to be meeting Rory in the park? Whatever the case, he certainly wasn't hiding in Gramercy Park, Washington Square Park, or any of the others; all were too small to offer protection from the police or too populated with people who might recognize him.

It had to be Central Park.

The light turned green, and Gerhardt crossed Central Park West, entering the park just above the imposing American Museum of Natural History.

"Well, Sherlock," he said, "which way now? You navigate."

They had two choices. Continuing east would too quickly lead out of the park onto Fifth Avenue; not much ground would be covered by that route. However, veering south at the fork in the road would put them on a winding route through the southernmost portion of the park. They would be able to cover considerably more territory.

And the lower park contained many familiar landmarks: the skating rink, the bandshell, the zoo. Obviously Rory had to instruct Melissa to meet him at an easily identifiable location—either a place familiar to her or one he could have straightforwardly directed her to. There must be a dozen such locations.

Maybe they didn't have to search blindly. She had a plan. God, it was worth a try.

"Take a right," she said as they neared the fork.

"How are you feeling?" asked Gerhardt. Her fever had persisted through the night, and twice she'd awakened in a sweat, aching and irritable. "Woman problems," she'd claimed in the morning, but they both knew that was not entirely the truth. She had still been in bed when Melissa phoned.

"I'm fine. Really I am. It's sweet of you to be so concerned, but it's just a summer virus on top of woman problems."

After several minutes' cruising Gerhardt said, "Honey, this is absurd. We're just wasting gas. We should let the police search. They have more resources. Captain Webb promised he would call you when he got a lead, so really, Liz, you should have notified him about Melissa's call."

Never, she thought. Let Webb uncover his own leads.

If it was possible, she wanted to reach Rory first, and alone, to explain that she and only she knew the full extent of his power. That she'd never betray him. And, more important, that he must never reveal his private secret to the police. It was one thing for them to think that in anger his energy lashed out uncontrollably at people; quite another to know that he conjured mental images of women, then had sex with them. The first offense was accidental, forgivable; the second, deliberate, considerably harder to forgive. or forget.

"Well, do I take the road toward the lake or stay on the outer one?" asked Gerhardt. "If I were hiding I'd go as deep into the park as possible."

But would he if he were expecting to meet his sixteen-year-old girl friend? Not if he cared a damn for her safety.

"You know, honey, maybe he's not that far from one of the roads. Probably near a landmark feature. The skating area must be deserted at this time of year."

Approaching the fork, again Gerhardt asked, "Which way, honey? Left or straight? Liz?"

He turned to find her reclined in the seat, head leaning against the head rest, eyes closed.

"Honey, are you sure you're all right? You look terrible."

"Fine," she said in a barely audible voice. "Take a left."

She had to give it a try.

All night she had felt that Rory was broadcasting a psychic SOS, maybe unconsciously, or maybe he really wanted her to find him but was too embarrassed to call. That she could understand. She'd always sensed that a special sympathy existed between them—that was why they'd struck up an instant friendship, why she had made such incredible strides with him in the laboratory.

In fact, she believed that her fitful unrest and anxiety over the last twenty-four hours was not merely personal but resulted from sharing these very emotions communicated by Rory's body.

She imagined his face, concentrating on his eyes. With the image planted firmly in her mind, she permitted her thoughts to drift and instructed her body to relax.

Can I really zero in on him? Actually *see* where he's hiding?

She was attempting to exploit their unique rapport to the fullest, and now she possessed a very special knowledge: Having once experienced the formidable power of Rory's force field, she knew what physiological correlates were involved and could search her body for the slightest hints of pressure, of suffocation, of crackling static current.

I know you're somewhere nearby, Rory, and mentally I'm going to connect with you.

59

Descending the stairs to the fountain, Melissa found that the lower area was more dimly lit than the street, and instinctively her arm clutched the canvas bag.

Her heart still fluttered from the experience on the street. A crazy motorist had sneaked up from behind and shouted something about "take a bus," scaring her ghost-white.

Although she was more than an hour late, she had no choice but to carry out the original plan: specifically, to wait for Rory to spot her. Even if she could muster the nerve to search in this darkness, she would surely be lost as soon as she wandered from the sight of the fountain and the street lights.

Deciding that Rory would not approach her at the foot of

the stairs—there was too much reflection from the street-lights—she crossed the fountain area and positioned herself by the three stone stairs that led down to the lake. Velvety black, mirroring the crescent moon, the water rested motionless on the bottom step.

She had passed a boy rocking on the edge of the fountain and now was aware of his eyes on her back. A chill erupted along her body. He was big, powerfully built, and he'd stared strangely, as if questioning her sanity for being there at that hour.

Turning slightly to observe him with her peripheral vision, she saw he was smiling broadly. If he as much as began to approach her, she would run for the street and hail a passing car.

Taking her bearings, estimating the distance that would have to be traversed swiftly, she noticed a man leaning against the wall at street level, partially hidden by the tall columns that flanked the stairs. Or, wait: was he hiding from her? His face was in shadow. No, she was being paranoid again. That crazy motorist, now the boy, had her nerves raw—the man, if he was alerted by her shouts, could rush toward her, frightening the boy off.

She attempted to switch her thoughts back to Rory, who was somewhere in that blackness just beyond her, alone, desperately in need of her help.

60

Even in the faint light surrounding the fountain, Rory immediately recognized Melissa standing by the lake steps, her head cocked sideways, her arms crisscrossed over the canvas bag against her chest.

Still seated on the lip of the huge fountain, his body swaying rhythmically to the music, was the Puerto Rican boy, now staring defiantly at Melissa.

Rory's plan had called for tossing a stone at Melissa's feet, and when she glanced up, he would step from the cover of the bushes roughly fifty feet away and signal to her to join him. Now even if he stood boldly on the path and waved his arms, darkness would shroud him completely.

At that moment three joggers, pacing themselves on the path, passed a foot from his hiding place, their breathing audible. As they emerged into the light of the fountain square, Rory discerned two women and a man. Melissa seemed to move involuntarily nearer to the joggers, but then they passed the boy and vaulted up the stairs to the street, taking them two at a time.

No sooner had they disappeared than the Puerto Rican boy stood, hiked the radio onto his shoulder, and began strutting—

—struttin' toward that cute chick, who was just waitin' to be picked up. Man, maybe she was stoned or really depressed and lookin' for a shoulder to cry on. Or then maybe she was one of them young hookers. No way was Carlos gonna pay.

Terrified by the boy's approach, Melissa abruptly turned, searching for the man at the head of the stairs, but he'd disappeared. Though she wanted to scream, she was mute, and her legs seemed paralyzed with fright. She would reason with him; do anything; but he mustn't take the money. Hearing footsteps on the path, she turned to see Rory running toward her.

"Hi!" he said, placing an arm around her shoulder, kissing her cheek. "Sorry I'm late." Then he led her in the direction of the path.

"I was worried sick thinking something had happened to you."

"It's here," she whispered, patting the bag. "No, I wouldn't let anything stop me from seeing you." She pressed tight to him, and when they were in the darkness, she handed over the folded bills, which he pocketed.

Stopping on the path, they embraced, kissing more gently and possessively than they ever had before, and Rory escorted Melissa beyond the path, through an arch in the hedges, onto a stretch of grass bordering the lake. Walled in on three sides by shrubbery, they were well hidden. Moonlight showered the bank, shimmering on the water and transforming the colorless rocks, trees, and boats to a lustrous silver-gray.

Now came the part he had been dreading all day— attempting to explain his predicament as gently as possible, attempting to say good-bye without wounding her again. All within the short time they had together. The police were undoubtedly checking long-distance out-of-town buses, so he planned to board a commuter bus to New Jersey, then depart for Canada from Newark. The longer he delayed, the greater the chance of being caught.

61

Carrie's apartment was only five blocks from Central Park. Swiftly they'd covered the distance and now were circling the inner park road that led to Bethesda Fountain, the closest car access to the boat house where Rory Malone had been spotted.

At most Bauer had a ten-minute lead, thought Webb. Not much considering the immensity of Central Park and the fact that the darkness would complicate the search.

"I hope you bring me luck, luv. Because luck will be the major factor in finding the kid."

"Do you really think he's dangerous?" asked Carrie.

"You wouldn't ask that question if you'd seen Mike Malone and his house. Or Kiner's film."

Carrie noticed Webb's fists gripping the wheel.

"You'd feel a lot safer if Dr. Hartman were with us, wouldn't you?"

"At first I thought so. Now I'm not so sure. Her presence might soothe the boy. Then again, it might antagonize him. In that film he seemed intent on harming her."

Once they were outside Carrie's apartment, he had recalled his promise to contact Liz Hartman the moment he received a lead on Rory Malone, and her advice that she be present when the boy was apprehended. "It'd be safer for everyone concerned," she'd said. Using Carrie's phone, he had called Liz Hartman's apartment, then her laboratory, but received no answer at either place.

Rounding the final curve and heading toward the wall at the top of the steps leading to the fountain, he recognized the parked blue Citation: the unmarked car Bauer had checked out that morning.

Carrie glanced at Webb, thinking: I would rather run into Rory Malone in the dark than Lou Bauer.

Parking behind the Citation, Webb turned off the ignition and placed his hand firmly on Carrie's knee.

"No," she said. "I am not staying in the car."

I'm *not* crazy, thought Liz. I *can* see Rory's face—clearly.

It had appeared to her just moments ago, along with vaguer images she still was struggling to identify: clues to Rory's location.

Were those curved, hollowed objects boats?

Was that silvery rippling vastness water? The lake?

Focusing on Rory's face, floating mentally, drifting, Liz was suddenly hit with a rush of chilling clarity. Yes, it was the lake! The boat house! It seemed as if she were actually viewing Rory with her eyes, surveying his location. She had hallucinated before, on experimental drugs, but never with such vivid detail.

Rory must be reaching out to me; that's the only explanation for this strong contact.

Reclining further in the car seat, she breathed slowly,

rhythmically, keeping her mind relaxed and receptive.

"Go to Bethesda Fountain," she said in a whisper. It was the closest they could get the car to the boat house and the lake.

"Liz, don't continue," cautioned Gerhardt. "This is utter foolishness. Rory's not some fledgling psychic you engage in card tricks. He's incredibly powerful. You've trained him, watched him—you know what he's capable of doing. Let the police find him."

He saw that he was not getting through to her. And he knew that if he forced her to return home now, she would never speak to him again.

"Hurry, Gerhardt!"

Something was wrong.

Now she perceived more than Rory and the lake: blurred images of two other people, one sizeably larger than the other. The smaller figure, a hazy silhouette, stood stationary, close to Rory. Was that Melissa? If so, then who was the larger figure, the one in streaked motion?

She tried to focus on the smaller figure, but identification continued to elude her. Intensifying her concentration, she used Rory as a beacon. Viewing him clearly, she instructed her mind to attempt to see the smaller figure through Rory's eyes.

But it was the larger figure, the one quickly approaching Rory, that disturbed her.

Lou Bauer kept his flashlight off, determined to surprise the freak, the fuckin' bastard that killed his Kathy. Then, too, he must keep the light off for his own safety.

Now that he was on foot trudging through the darkened park, he sensed a new emotion: fear. For the first time in his life Lou Bauer experienced intimidation—and by a kid. He didn't like the feeling one bit. Nor did he like thinking of what that demented, demonic freak of nature might do to him—if, of course, his presence was detected first. Since Rory Malone was running from the cops, he might not give a second thought to killing the first cop who approached him.

Though it would be hard to sneak up on the freak, the tactic was absolutely necessary.

He did possess one advantage, though. The kid was unaware that he'd been spotted, so he'd be completely off guard. Right now he was probably staking out a place to bed down for the night—a patch of grass protected by trees, the trestled enclosure behind the bandshell, the seldom-used tunnel by the boat house.

Perhaps out of anxiety, exhaustion, or hunger the freak had already passed out for the night. Wouldn't that make the job easier! Sneak up on him while he's sleeping. Certainly would be the safest course of action.

He heard a sound, paused, stood perfectly still, holding his breath. Lou Bauer was trembling. Fuckin' unbelievable! Nelly nerves. But no way could he shake the image of a battered Mike Malone, of the demolished house.

The sound of dry leaves crunching underfoot.

The crackling of thin, brittle twigs.

Control your fuckin' self. You're no chickenshit. So he's powerful, a freak of nature. But remember: a bullet to the brain will stop him cold.

62

"Why can't you tell me?" Melissa pleaded, draping her arms around Rory's neck. "I want to understand. You said you'd explain everything."

He had promised, but now that it was time to cast his past actions into words, he found that impossible.

"I can't, baby. I just can't."

How could he have imagined for even an instant that he could tell her about his addiction to peep shows and porn films, about the countless fantasies turned real, the murderous acts performed out of anger and frustration in the last few days? The events that culminated in Kathy Bauer's death? About his power? Of course she would never understand.

"I'll write to you. Maybe then I'll begin to explain a few things."

"No!" She pressed closer.

"After a while, when I'm sure they're not tapping your phone, I'll call."

"You won't. You'll forget all about me."

"Baby, I've got to hurry. You don't want me to get caught, do you?"

"But if you're innocent what difference does it make? Why do you have to run away?"

"Not now, Melissa. I just can't explain. You'll have to trust me."

He would escort her safely through the park to the Fifty-ninth Street exit, then he'd head west to Eleventh Avenue and down to Port Authority. Prying her arms from around his neck, taking her hand, he said, "Stick close to me. If we see people or cops, just do what I tell you."

Melissa jerked away. "You just used me to bring the money." Her voice was quavering with anger, disappointment, pain.

"I didn't."

"You needed the money and I was the only one who could get it. I hate you. I—" Tears clouded her eyes and rolled down her cheeks.

"No, baby, that's not true. Sure, I need the money. But I really wanted to see you before I left. To explain—"

"Then tell me," she sobbed, burying her head in his chest. "I can forgive anything you did."

He remained silent, stroking her hair.

But her crying intensified, tears drenching his shirt. He couldn't heartlessly leave her in this state. Lifting her face from his chest, he kissed her eyes; the tears were salty on his tongue. When he squeezed her affectionately, she pressed still tighter against his body, and her mouth sought his and clung firmly, as if by kissing she could physically weld him to her forever.

Arms wrapped around his neck, she was employing her weight to edge him down onto the grass. He resisted, and she countered by forcefully tugging downward. Reluctantly his knees bent as his hand reached for the ground to soften their fall.

The grass was cool, moist. The night air warm and still, pierced by silver-white moonlight.

Melissa lay beneath him, her mouth roving passionately over his lips, her hands under his shirt, her fingers stroking his back.

"No, baby, please."

"Why not?"

She maneuvered him to one side, and when they both were on the grass face to face, she unbuttoned her blouse.

"Melissa, no, let's stop. Please, baby."

She removed her bra, and her small, firm breasts, bathed in moonlight, shone like pearls. She guided his hand up her stomach, over one breast, and he found the nipple spongy-hard. Every instinct shouted to him to pull away, to stop this insanity while he still could, yet he squeezed the nipple, rolled it between his fingers.

To stop now would emotionally devastate Melissa, confirm her suspicion that she'd been used only to get the money. To continue . . .

Unzipping her jeans, she edged his hand under the elastic band of her panties. Only for a moment did she hesitate. Then she encouraged the hand further until his fingers slid over her soft hair, descended into the warm crack that tightened under his touch. Strangely, though he was hard, he was only slightly aroused. It was an unusual combination for Rory Malone.

"Go ahead," she coaxed. "I want you never to forget me."

Curious because of his faint arousal, he was even more puzzled by the absence of the power surging through his body. In the past *any* degree of sexual excitement had rallied the power. Now he experienced no thumping in his head, no din in his ears, no sense of an electric connection between his groin and his brain. Inexplicably missing were all the familiar signs of enslavement.

He seemed free.

Fumbling with the belt of his pants and finally unfastening it, then the waist snap, he lowered his zipper, inched down the band of his jockey shorts, and his erection sprung free. Rolling on top of Melissa, hands sliding into the rear of her pants, he cupped her buttocks.

For the first time in recent memory he was sexually aroused yet apparently in complete control. Where, he wondered, was the power? Maybe he was losing his psychic talent?

When his erection first tingled against the flesh of her abdomen, he realized that he wasn't going to do it, that he couldn't do this to Melissa, not here, under these circumstances, when he was about to run away and might never see her again.

No sooner had his mind reached that conclusion than instantly his head throbbed, his ears rang with a deafening hum, and the enslaving link clicked on. Instinctively he realized he had a choice: either he could, under his own control, have sex with Melissa, or he could refrain, and the power would take its own pleasure in its own way.

He felt helpless. No, worse: he felt he had been tricked—as if the sexual beast within him had for a time deliberately hidden its selfish interests—had calculatedly scaled down his own sense of arousal—until the point of no return had been passed. The power had been gradually assuming its own independence, but now it appeared to possess a conniving intelligence as well.

Rolling off Melissa, hoping to calm himself, he felt the invisible bridge connecting them and knew he must act fast if he hoped to defuse the sexual energy.

To spare Melissa from both himself and the power, he could fantasize about another woman. But no; that, too, was unacceptable, for he'd sworn never again to possess any woman against her will. He would kill himself before permitting the beast to assault another victim. His only real choice seemed to be to unleash the power on his surroundings—if it would permit itself to be spent that way.

Spontaneously, a woman's face flashed to mind, clear,

tenacious, disturbingly familiar. No! Go away! What was happening?

Quickly the image grew stronger, anchoring itself in his mind. Though he had not conjured her face, strangely, inexplicably, it was *drawing* on the power. *Siphoning* his energy.

Why was she doing this to him? To herself? Now she had taken all control out of his hands.

As a painful tug in his groin, he felt the flow of electricity rapidly bridging his body to hers. Fool! Damn fool!

She had encouraged the beast, enticed it, and now it leaped greedily to her like a raging fire leaped to dry brush.

63

The air in the car tightened, cutting Liz's breath short. Reflexively her eyes closed, and immediately she glimpsed Rory's face looming above her, felt a pressure pinning her against the seat; it reached between her legs, bent on prying them apart.

Resisting with all her might, she struggled to conceal the invasion from Gerhardt. He mustn't learn—no one must ever suspect—that Rory possessed this unforgivable power.

Yet the force was so overwhelming, so determinedly unrelenting, that quickly her thighs tired and her legs sprang open.

"Liz!" shouted Gerhardt.

"Hurry," she murmured, her voice strangled, barely audible. Entrenched between her legs, the pressure shot tentacles upward along her chest, circling her breasts, squeezing them. "Beyond the fountain, by the boats. Hurry."

One hand on the wheel, the other reaching to assist Liz,

Gerhardt suddenly was jolted by a painful electric shock and withdrew. Again he grabbed for Liz, and again a fiery spark, materializing out of the air, stung his hand into retreat. He did not have to see the force field to know that it engulfed Liz. He braked the car.

"Don't stop," cried Liz, gasping for air. "There's nothing you can do."

Nothing she could do to terminate this invasion—no, this assault—this unmistakably sexual assault. Above her loomed Rory's contorted face, parted lips moaning with each breath.

Moaning what, though? The words remained indecipherable.

Was he sexually attacking her? It didn't make sense. She was certain that earlier he had broadcast signals for help. Now he was attempting to rape her.

As if assailed by an imperceptible gale, her skirt fluttered, then flapped up onto her chest. Her body slid supine in the seat.

"He *can* do it!" gasped Gerhardt. He'd suspected as much since screening the film. Rory's psychic hug had not been murderous but sexual. "Liz!"

Again he reached for her, only to be stung more painfully this time into submission.

On the dashboard the magnetized dish that held change for tunnel tolls rattled, then ripped free, showering the car with coins, itself smashing against the rear window. The radio clicked on, blaring static. It's like being in a severe electrical storm, thought Gerhardt.

"Liz, shake free of his image!"

Her lips parted, attempting to mouth, I can't. It's impossible, but all her lungs could push out was a faint "Hurry."

Between her legs the pressure had sprouted another tentacle that now was penetrating her. A sharp pain jabbed inside, and her muscles, which had been squeezing to prevent entry, suddenly were stretched and shot into spasms. The pain radiated throughout her abdomen, her body.

This is not Rory, she thought. This can't be his doing.

The thrusts were quick, forceful, desperate. And absolutely real! She felt every sensation. Is this what Kathy Bauer experienced? Sue Stiner? All the others?

Straining to decipher Rory's moans, she deliberately thrust her head against his phantom face and finally caught the airy whisper.

"Run, Melissa. Break away from me."

Freak! Fuckin' sick degenerate. Mauling a girl in the park.

From his position behind a tree Bauer recognized the giant shoulder bag on the grass. Shit! This was the girl he'd seen on the road, the one he'd cautioned against the dangers of the park.

Was the freak raping her?

Quickly he maneuvered into a direct line of fire with the kid's head. They were awfully close; he'd have to be careful not to hit her.

Playing through his mind was a single, paramount theme: You mustn't just wound him. A wounded animal could be wildly dangerous. The freak, wounded, would surely be deadly.

Land a bullet directly in the brain.

A plan flashed to mind. Shout the freak's name, and when he glanced up his head would be a good ten inches above hers—an ample margin for missing her.

Steadying the gun in his outstretched hand, aiming precisely where the freak's head would be in just an instant, Bauer shouted, *"Get off her!"*

64

Liz collapsed in the car seat as Gerhardt rounded the final bend. The terrible pressure that had been steadily mounting, building to a crescendo, had suddenly ceased. Rory's face no longer hung above hers, nor did she possess the slightest mental or physical sensation of his presence.

Had he come, she wondered.

Gerhardt pulled up behind a police car and a blue Citation.

"What happened, honey?" he asked, tentatively touching her arm, although certain the threat of a shock no longer existed.

"I don't know," answered Liz, slightly dizzy. She recalled hearing a bang.

Then realizing he was about to order her to remain in the car, she volunteered, "I'm fine." And to prove it she opened the door, jumped from the car, darted across the pavement, then down the long flight of stairs to the fountain.

Thinking more clearly now, she suspected that Rory had not come—that was not the reason she'd been spared further assault. The police car had meant nothing to her when she'd first seen it. Cops always patrol the park. But now she would bet this car was not here on regular police duty.

Something terrible had happened to Rory.

Instinctively as a bird migrates, she knew exactly where to find him and raced across the dim fountain square, up the darkened path that paralleled the lake, with Gerhardt at her heels.

65

Webb and Carrie ran in the direction of the shot. It had been loud, clear, maybe fifty yards from where they had been searching near the boat house. He had immediately drawn his pistol and ordered Carrie to stay several feet behind him.

Descending the path that paralleled the lake, he spotted two figures racing wildly. At first he assumed they were running from the scene of the gun blast; then he quickly realized they were heading in the direction of the shot.

As the leading figure emerged from the shadows of the trees into moonlight, he immediately recognized Liz Hartman, then Gerhardt Kiner. Abandoning the path, they turned left, toward the lake, and disappeared from view.

He had estimated the location of the shot, but Hartman and Kiner seemed to have unerringly pinpointed the spot. It would not be much of a gamble, he thought, to follow them.

A second later he, too, turned off the path at the same point, Carrie immediately behind him. There was no natural walk, merely a path beaten through the grass and shrubbery. Even with the aid of the moonlight and the light from the few lamp posts on the far side of the lake, he would never have investigated this route—he may not have spotted it at all.

Where, he wondered, had Hartman and Kiner obtained their information?

Hurrying through the arch of bushes, he emerged on the bank of the lake, where the light dimly yet clearly illuminated the scene.

Rory Malone's body lay on the grass. A few feet away, nearer the lake, knelt a young girl, clutching her blouse closed. Her eyes were wide, her body stiff with shock. Blood blotched her face and neck and stained the front of her blouse.

Kneeling beside Rory, Liz lifted his head onto her lap, cradling it in her arms. Blood gushed from a wound in his neck; watery, black, slithering into the grass.

He's breathing, thank God.

With the hem of her skirt she wiped blood from his lips and cheeks. His eyes were closed; he was unconscious.

Who did this to you, Rory?

Gerhardt's arms protectively encircled Melissa, attempting to comfort and, retrospectively, to shield her; yet her rigidity could not be so readily melted. *She's traumatized,* he thought, hugging her.

Glancing away from Gerhardt, Liz spotted Captain Webb and said, "Radio for an ambulance. He's losing blood quickly."

Webb hardly heard Liz Hartman.

Surveying the clearing, his senses keenly alert for the slightest movement or sound, he realized that only a short time had elapsed since the shot, and he'd neither seen nor heard anyone running from the scene. Most likely, whoever fired the shot was still hiding in the bushes, maybe only feet away. Like a radar beacon scanning through fog, his gun simultaneously swept an arc with his head. If it's you, Bauer . . . If it's you . . .

"There, there," said Gerhardt, using a handkerchief to wipe blood from Melissa's face. He noticed no wounds; apparently it was Rory's blood on her. "You're going to be fine. And Rory's alive."

"Shh!" spit Webb, suddenly aware of a rustle of leaves, aiming his gun in the direction of the sound. With one hand he pushed Carrie behind him.

In the blackness the bushes rustled ten feet from where Rory lay. Then the shrubbery parted and into the clearing stepped Lou Bauer, gun drawn.

He's insane, thought Webb. Does he expect to kill us all? No, of course not; he'll claim he shot the boy in self-defense. But he won't get away with it; the girl's a witness. Bauer, you've gone too far this time.

Bauer pointed his gun toward the opening from which he'd just emerged and in a dry, rough voice barked, "Come on," to a figure that now stood in the periphery of the shadowy arch.

To himself Bauer muttered angrily, "You did a fuckin' botched-up job of it. Wounded the goddamn freak. Now it's too late."

From out of the shadow lumbered the hulking figure of Mike Malone.

Mike stared coldly at his son's body, a single thought racing through his mind: He's alive. He's still alive! If the freak lives he'll sure as hell come after me.

Still hanging at his side was the gun that had fired the misdirected bullet. If he only were faster on the trigger, Mike thought, more accurate in his aim, he'd fire another shot at the freak now; kill him this time. Yet his hand never lifted from his side. Both cops' guns were drawn, aimed directly at him. They'd surely kill him before he could finish off the freak.

Taking the gun from Mike Malone's hand, Bauer said flatly, "You wounded him." Then to himself: "You fuckin' lousy shot. How could you have missed at that range?"

"Please! Someone call an ambulance," pleaded Liz.

For the first time she was uncomfortably aware of Mike Malone's piercingly cold stare. Like a laser it seemed to cleave the darkness, to shower her alone in a single spotlight. She glanced back at Rory.

Suddenly Mike Malone's voice raged through the clearing. "*You* did this to him. *You* turned him into a freak. He was fine till he met you. Normal. A normal boy. You taught him how to do that freaky stuff. Witch! Fuckin' witch! That's what you are. It's *you* I should have killed."

He lurched at Liz and was grabbed by Bauer, handcuffed by Webb.

"I'll call for an ambulance from the car," said Webb. Liz did not look up as Webb and Bauer marched Mike Malone out of the clearing.

Carrie inched closer to glimpse Rory Malone.

Eyes closed, face expressionless, he appeared so young, so fawnlike and innocent. She thought, this boy is dangerous? This is the boy who spied on me?

Images of the blood-spattered tiles, of the body twirling and flying off the roof, flashed through her mind, and once again she wondered what these violent pictures had to do with Rory Malone.

She advanced no closer because Liz Hartman in her grief had bent over the boy and was whispering to him.

"Of course, your father's wrong, Rory. You weren't normal when you came to me. The poltergeist power had already infected your body." Then Liz thought: And through training, I strengthened it. There is some truth in your father's accusations. More than he, Webb, any of them, realize.

The shrill siren of an ambulance shattered the silence.

Turning to Melissa, Liz said, "Rory's going to be all right.

Whatever you've been through with him, it's over now." Then more to herself: "It's *all* over now." The experiments, the grant, her dreams.

Although Rory probably couldn't hear her voice, she leaned closer to his ear and whispered. "I'll keep your secret. Our secret. And I swear, I'll be the one to help you through this. We'll do it together."

66

It had been mounting steadily, rolling to what would have been its most shattering crescendo yet. And then, just seconds before it would have leaped in relief, erupted in climax, something or someone had interfered, meddled, forced it into retreat, to linger in hibernation.

But not to linger passively. For anger at having been thwarted midstream, frustration over the interminable delay, had served as fuel, trundling its energy to new heights. While the boy lay unaware of events around him, it resided at a level of mind that never rested, never slept, remained ever vigilant. But it needed the boy's body as a vehicle.

Churning impatiently, furiously aggravated by this untimely interruption, it lay seething and helpless, waiting for Rory Malone to regain consciousness.

67

A face appeared as if filtered through dark gauze: familiar features, vaguely identifiable. The face was suspended just a few feet above his own. From his perspective on the ground a halo of light surrounded the woman's head and suffused the periphery of her hair, which was blacker than the night.

Dr. Hartman? What was she doing here? How could she have known where . . .

His neck throbbed painfully, and the pulses of blood seemed intensely magnified, perniciously hot; yet one side of his neck felt distinctly wet and cold, as if a chilling spring rain trickled over the flesh.

Dr. Hartman seemed to be moving her lips, talking to him, but he discerned only the faintest humming and remained uncertain of its source.

Why were his senses impaired?

Melissa!

Craning his neck, surveying the moonlit clearing, he spotted her at the water's edge. She was being assisted to her feet by . . . yes, by Gerhardt . . . being escorted across the clearing, closer to him. Gerhardt's words to Melissa commingled with the monotonous, irritating hum.

Shadows of Dr. Hartman, Melissa, Gerhardt, swayed over him, alternately obstructing the moonlight, which otherwise shined straight into his eyes. Most prominent in his field of view was the moon, pearly white, which hung directly over-head.

Suddenly a fourth shadow, opposite Dr. Hartman's, crept across him. The figure was standing, advancing slowly, timidly

. . . a woman. For an instant the image stirred warm feelings in him. Then he placed her . . . No, it couldn't be . . . Carrie Wilson?

The entire experience—its ephemeral quality, the many familiar faces—all seemed to be a dream.

Reconstruct what occurred; that might help. Yes, he had rendezvoused with Melissa. The power had been building . . . then suddenly Dr. Hartman's face had flashed, tugging on his energy. He had fought to divert the power, but once enticed by her, it would settle for nothing less than her. Then a voice had shouted his name . . . he'd been shot.

How foreign his wounded body felt. Feverish, melting from internal heat, it seemed girded to explode.

From what, though?

Accumulated energy?

No, it couldn't be. The power had been released; he'd come . . . But no, he had not come! . . . the shot had thwarted the power.

Was all that energy still stored in his body?

Alert now to this possibility, he recognized the febrile sensations in his body, the infernal humming. Yes, the power churned, percolated, still sought release.

Dr. Hartman, Melissa, Carrie Wilson . . . they stood so close . . . too close! He closed his eyes and their images flashed to mind, more vivid than in real life.

"Get away from me!" he shouted. But even his deaf ears knew that his voice was mute.

68

A breeze rippled through the clearing, fluttering leaves,

faintly rustling branches. The tall blades of uncut grass tilted in unison, first to the left, then to the right, then in a circular motion as the breeze mounted to a gusty wind.

Carrie's skirt whipped around her legs, and Melissa's shirttail, not yet tucked into her jeans, flapped against her back.

The sudden wind did not particularly rouse anyone's suspicions; in fact, it felt exactly like the atmospheric change that heralds a summer flash storm, accompanied even by a crispness to the air.

The increase in static electricity between her skirt and stockings, and the air's freshness that derived from dull oxygen being electrically converted to brisker ozone, convinced Carrie that a storm was rapidly approaching.

For a while the shrill siren of the ambulance racing toward Bethesda Fountain completely masked the static crackling in the air. But as the atmospheric electricity grew the crackling became audible, as did its visual manifestation: sparks.

Like a jungle swamp teeming with the flickerings of fireflies, the air above the lake glistened bejeweled. Carrie first heard the mysterious crackling, while Melissa first observed the lovely sparks, which reminded her of the fallout from a fireworks display.

Kneeling, attending to Rory's wound, anxiously monitoring his rate of pulse and breathing, Liz remained oblivious to the atmospheric changes. The blessed sound of the ambulance rang paramount in her ears.

While Carrie and Melissa found the phenomena baffling, Gerhardt, puzzling at the cloudless sky and the sheet of sparks expanding across the lake, sensed danger. Clearly no ordinary storm was brewing.

Unfamiliar as the crackling and sparks were to him, he recognized them as electrical events; there could be no denying that the air had suddenly become highly charged with energy. To his eyes the only dynamo that could have produced such tremendous energy lay on the ground, gradually regaining consciousness.

Moving to the water's edge, he raised his arm until the advancing wall of diamonds touched his hand; the resulting pain was the same as he had experienced in the car.

"Liz! Get away from him!" God! She was still cradling Rory in her arms.

Glancing up, Liz saw the sparks fanning into the clearing like a trundling fog, heard the crackling, and immediately knew.

But he's barely conscious.

Gently laying Rory's head on the grass, she said, "I know you're not responsible for this, Rory. I'm certain of it." All the more reason, she thought, to be cautious, to back away.

She placed her arms protectively around Melissa, whose legs were surrounded by a galaxy of stars, and motioned to Captain Webb's companion, who stood in the center of a glittering supernova, to accompany her out of the clearing, following Gerhardt. But on reaching the opening in the bushes, Gerhardt was shocked by a wall of current as impassable as an electric fence.

He glanced at Liz, who turned to Rory on the ground and pleaded, "Don't let this happen, Rory. Fight the power that's possessed you."

Melissa screamed as a bridge of fiery stars leaped from Rory's body to hers, burning her arms, turning her blouse into a torturously charged garment she wanted to rip off her back.

Within seconds the bridge left her and leaped to Carrie, sending her hair flying wildly on end. Carrie raced toward the opening in the bushes. Seeing it was still walled off, she darted to the water's edge. But the bridge stretched and twisted and resolutely followed her movements.

"Direct it at me!" shouted Liz. "These girls did nothing to harm you. They're innocent, Rory."

As if it were a living demon being offered sacrifice, the bridge of current instantly accepted Liz's challenge, pummeling her body with voltages that bruised and seared her flesh and ultimately knocked her to the ground. The insides of her thighs burned as if they'd been blasted with a torch, and the pressure between her legs felt as though it would soon split her in two.

Gerhardt rushed toward Liz but was repeatedly repelled by excruciating shocks.

Then, mysteriously, the bridge abandoned Liz and dashed wildly around the clearing. For several seconds it whipped like a severed live wire, lashing from Melissa to Carrie to the trees to the docked boats, even to a lamp post across the lake; once returning to Liz, again jolting her to the ground.

There appeared to be no pattern to the whip's random thrashing. Then Liz realized that even in Rory's weakened state, he was battling with the power. As he had spared her in the laboratory by destroying the Black Room, she thought, he's now fighting to release the energy on the surroundings.

Racing to his side, suddenly unafraid, she shouted, "You can do it, Rory! Concentrate! Focus on the single goal. Dissipate the power."

A searing current shot through her body, ravaging her breasts, thighs, as though ten thousand blistering hands mauled every inch of her being, as if she were the victim of some depraved collective consciousness.

"You must beat the force, Rory!" she cried. It's primitive, gluttonous, insatiable. Then it dawned on her that this was his id, that irrational, pleasure-hungry instinct, a monstrous amoral urge that had accidentally found form and freedom—traits it was never meant to possess, responsibilities it could never cope with. Now it was bent on instant gratification, at the expense of any woman present.

The bridge of current beamed on a cluster of trees, setting them ablaze, then charred the boats at the water's edge. He's battling it, thought Liz. But its energy is too vast, its appetite too fiercely sexual, to be satisfied with leaves, trees, or dry wooden boats.

Suddenly Carrie was thrown to the ground; the fiery spike shot between her legs, lapping. Her piercing screams soared through the clearing, joining the chorus of male voices on the opposite side of the bushes. Two paramedics, the ambulance driver, and Tom Webb shouted, cursed, and gasped in disbelief at the shocks delivered by some invisible, impenetrable electric screen that held them off.

Liz gripped Rory's shoulders. "You can overpower it, Rory."

He was fighting the beast in man, that recognized neither laws nor logic. She could only imagine that his potent psychic energy had somehow coupled with his sexual drive to spring the beast—a creature that resided in the deep darkness of every human psyche.

Carrie writhed on the ground, her hands shielding her crotch as the beast fought to gain entry.

"You can beat it, Rory," shouted Liz, "like you did in the lab. Please Rory, do it for me!"

Suddenly Carrie was released. The fiery bridge leaped out of the clearing and hovered over the lake, glowing and crackling. Beneath the spot the water swirled into a dark vortex, and then, like a diver, the white-hot spike plunged into the whirlpool.

White steam billowed into the air, rolling onto the banks of the lake, masking the human figures in the clearing from each other and from Webb, who was the first to rush through the bushes.

Rory felt himself being lifted onto a stretcher. The release of energy had all but obliterated his already-dulled senses, and though he neither saw nor heard events around him, he was certain that the person tightly gripping his hand was Liz Hartman.

He wanted to tell her that he had won the biggest battle of his life, and that he could do it again if he had to.

But then, soon, he would never again have to do battle. He would willingly submit to whatever therapy they thought best for him, regardless of the consequences. He felt that way now and was certain he would be just as resolute when he regained his senses, even in the face of enticing temptations.

This was one promise that was not going to be forgotten in the frenzy of sexual arousal. No, not this one. Absolutely not! Swear it! So help me God!